A COLORADO
CHRISTMAS

WILLIAM W. JOHNSTONE

with J. A. Johnstone

A COLORADO CHRISTMAS

PINNACLE BOOKS
Kensington Publishing Corp.
www.kensingtonbooks.com

PINNACLE BOOKS are published by

Kensington Publishing Corp.
119 West 40th Street
New York, NY 10018

All Kensington titles, imprints, and distributed lines are available at special quantity discounts for bulk purchases for sales
promotions, premiums, fund-raising, educational, or institu-
tional use. Special book excerpts or customized printings can
also be created to fit specific needs. For details, write or phone
the office of the Kensington sales manager: Kensington Publishing Corp., 119 West 40th Street, New York, NY 10018, attn:
Sales Department; phone 1-800-221-2647.

ISBN-13: 978-0-7860-3591-5
ISBN-10: 0-7860-3591-9

First Kensington hardcover printing: July 2016
First Pinnacle mass market paperback printing: November
2016

10 9 8 7 6 5 4 3

Printed in the United States of America

First Pinnacle electronic edition: November 2016

ISBN-13: 978-0-7860-3592-2
ISBN-10: 0-7860-3592-7

PROLOGUE

Colorado
December 1926

Even though Christmas wasn't far away and people were still shopping for presents, not many of them were out and about. During the day, a storm had dumped quite a bit of snow on the town, and although the main streets had been plowed, the air was so cold most folks were content to stay inside, enjoying the warmth of home and hearth.

Not everybody, though. A heavy black roadster crawled along the still-snowy street toward an oasis of light in the mostly darkened downtown area. Many of the businesses were already closed for the evening, but not Al's Diner. The warm yellow glow of lights spilled through the plate glass of the big front window.

A man with something tucked under his arm walked toward the diner. He moved briskly, like a young man, but when he opened the door and stepped inside, the light revealed silver hair and weathered features of an older man, probably in his seventies. He wore no hat, but he had on a sheepskin jacket that he opened to reveal a flannel shirt, as well as thick denim trousers and high-topped boots.

"Evening, Al," he greeted the proprietor, who was the only one working. The diner wouldn't do enough business on a snowy evening to justify having anyone else on duty.

Al was a burly, barrel-chested man who wore a white apron to protect his clothes from grease splatters while he was working at the grill. He took a china cup from a shelf, filled it from a coffee pot, and set it on the counter. The newcomer moved toward the metal stools topped with red leather in front of the counter, giving a friendly nod to the diner's only other customer, an older man who sat in one of the booths reading a newspaper. He returned the nod, then went back to his paper.

"Figured you'd be in," Al said to the man who slid onto a stool and reached for the cup. "Rain or shine, snow or sleet, you always stop by for coffee."

"Well, you know us old-timers. We're creatures of habit." The man took a sip of the coffee and then nodded. "Excellent, as always."

"Thanks. My dad taught me how to make it. He was a cowboy for a long time, then when he got too stove up to stay in the saddle all day, he became a ranch cook. He said the hands always wanted their coffee strong enough it could get up and walk away by itself if you didn't keep an eye on it."

The customer chuckled. "You've mentioned that before."

"Well, a good story never really gets old, does it?"

"No," the man agreed, "it doesn't."

While Al picked up the pot again and went over to top off the cup in front of the man sitting in the booth, the man at the counter opened the magazine he had carried in under his arm.

Printed on rough wood pulp paper, it had a colorful cover showing a Mexican bandito, sombrero laying on the ground at his feet, blazing away with a couple six-guns. Big letters announced the title of the magazine, *WESTERN STORY*, and emblazoned across the top of the cover in red letters were the words *Big Clean Stories of Outdoor Life.*

"That the new issue?" Al asked as he came back behind the counter.

"Yes, I just picked it up at the cigar store. It has a Max Brand yarn in it."

"You sure like them Western stories."

"They remind me of the old days around here," the customer said with a grin. "Before everything got so civilized. There are times I wonder if that's such a good thing."

The bell over the door dinged and cold air swirled into the diner as three more men came in. They all wore dark, Eastern-style derby hats and long black overcoats. Visible through the front window, the big roadster that had brought them was parked at the curb.

One man was slightly ahead of the other two, taking the lead as if he were accustomed to doing so. His face was flushed from the cold, or maybe it was just beefy to start with. He rubbed gloved hands together, smiled, and said in a voice that confirmed he wasn't from those parts, "Boy, it's cold as a witch's titty out there, ain't it?"

"Pretty chilly night," Al agreed with the affability

he would use to greet any potential customer. "Come on in and warm up for a spell, gents."

The three men walked over to the counter but didn't sit down. The leader said, "They really roll up the sidewalks around here after dark, don't they? I was starting to think the whole town was closed down for the night until I saw your lights."

"Yeah, I stay open later than most places. I got some customers who like to come by in the evenings." Al nodded to the two older men.

The one at the counter had started reading his magazine. He had the pages curled back as he read and sipped his coffee.

"Back where we come from, the joints haven't even started jumpin' good by this time of night. And the real action comes later, in the speakeasies."

Al said, "I wouldn't know anything about that. You fellas want some coffee? I've got some mighty good apple pie, too, or I could grill you up a sandwich."

The red-faced man shook his head. "Nah, we're not hungry." Apparently he didn't mind speaking for his two companions. "The coffee sounds good. Might take some of the chill off. What we're really looking for, though, is information."

"Oh? What sort of information?"

The red-faced man was tugging off his gloves, revealing hands with thick, strong-looking fingers. He dropped the gloves on the counter and waved a hand to indicate their surroundings. "This town used to be called Big Rock, didn't it?"

"That's what I've heard. I think they changed the name right around the turn of the century."

The man on the red leather stool looked up from

the pages of *WESTERN STORY*. "Couldn't help over-hearing, fellas. Yes, this used to be Big Rock. That was the name of the place when I came here. Of course, it's changed an awful lot since then, not just the name. It's a regular city now."

"Is that right?" said the red-faced man. "So you've been around here for a long time?"

"I have. What's your interest in Big Rock?"

"We're working on a, uh, family history, I guess you could call it." The red-faced man looked at the other two. "Ain't that right, boys?"

"A family history," repeated a thin man with a dour expression. "Yeah."

"Oh, you've got relatives here."

"Not exactly," the red-faced man said. "But I did. My grandfather spent some time here."

"What's the name? Maybe I knew him."

"I doubt that. He wasn't here for very long, and he wasn't really the friendly sort, if I do say so myself. But I'd still be interested in learning more about the town and the time he spent here."

"When was that? Chances are, I can tell you anything you want to know about Big Rock."

"Forty years ago," the red-faced man said. "Almost exactly forty years, since it was Christmas time when Granddad came through here."

The old man's silvery eyebrows rose. "Forty years ago, you say? I remember it well. I've got good reason to."

"Yeah? How come?"

The old man slid the magazine aside. "Well, that particular Christmas was a pretty eventful one in Big Rock. Yes, sir, a lot of things happened that year, some good, some bad."

"I'd love to hear about it," the red-faced stranger said.

"Why don't we go sit down at one of the tables and I'll tell you," the old-timer suggested. "Al, pour some of that java for my friends here. On me."

"That's kind of you," the stranger said.

"Oh, that's just Western hospitality. We like for folks to feel welcome out here."

Al filled three more cups.

The silver-haired man left his magazine on the counter and went over to a round table with a red-checked cloth to sit down with the three men from back East. "Where do you want me to start?"

"I want to hear everything about that time," the red-faced man replied. "As much as you know."

The old-timer smiled and clasped his hands together in front of him on the table. "Well, I wasn't around for all of it, you understand, but I heard a lot about it later from the people who were involved, so I reckon I can give you a pretty good idea of what went on."

The man with the dour expression said, "Jeeze, this is gonna take all night. I never heard anybody who talks as slow as you cowboys."

"Take it easy, Freddy," scolded the man with the red face. "Our new pal is helping us out here." He went on to the old-timer. "You go right ahead, friend, and take your time. Tell us about that Christmas in Big Rock."

"Well, all the trouble actually started *before* Christmas, you know, and not all of it started right here *in* Big Rock, as it was known then." The old-timer took a sip of coffee. "In fact, you might say it started on a ranch about seven miles west of town, a week or so before Christmas. . . ."

CHAPTER 1

Sugarloaf Ranch, Colorado
December 1886

"What do you think, Smoke?" Sally Jensen turned slowly in front of the fireplace, holding out her arms to give her husband a good view of the new dress she wore.

"I think you're asking the wrong fella," Smoke Jensen replied with a grin as he sat back in the armchair, stretched his legs out in front of him, and crossed them at the ankles. "You're so beautiful you look good in everything you wear, Sally. I even think you look good when you're not wearing anything at all."

The dark-haired young woman blushed, which if anything just made her more lovely. "I was asking for your honest opinion, not flattery. Somebody might come in. Besides, you shouldn't be talking like that at this time of year. It'll be Christmas soon."

"Seems to me there's nothing wrong with a man loving his wife no matter what time of year it is."

"Well, no, there's not," Sally agreed.

Smoke leaned forward as if to stand up. "So, maybe you could take that dress off—"

"And put my apron on and get back to baking," Sally interrupted him. "That's a really good idea. Since we're spending Christmas at home for a change, and since we'll be going to the big Christmas Eve celebration in Big Rock, we'll need lots of cakes and pies—"

"And bear sign," Smoke put in. "Don't forget the bear sign."

"I wouldn't dare," Sally said with a laugh. "Pearlie and Cal would never forgive me if I did."

"I'm not sure I would, either."

"Seriously, though, Smoke"—she ran her hands down over her belly and onto her thighs, smoothing the blue fabric of the dress—"you think this will be all right for the Christmas Eve party?"

"I think it'll be fine," Smoke assured her. He stood up, moved over to her, put his arms around her waist, and kissed her on the forehead.

Folks said they made a handsome couple, and that was certainly the truth. Smoke was tall and muscular, with extremely broad shoulders, and his face was ruggedly attractive under close-cropped ash blond hair. Like Sally, he had the vigor of youth about him.

Only his eyes seemed older than his years. They had seen so much death, starting two decades earlier with his mother on the hardscrabble farm in the Ozarks and the death of his father after the war, when the two of them had gone west because there was nothing to hold them in Missouri anymore. The battle with Indians had prompted the old mountain man called Preacher to dub young Kirby Jensen "Smoke" because of his speed with a gun, and countless evil men had fallen to Smoke's guns since then, including those responsible for the murders of his first wife and their child.

Yes, Smoke Jensen had seen enough death for a dozen men his age, but he had never let it destroy his soul like it did some men. He could be hard, with a heart like iron when he needed to be, but decency and humor and love lived within him, as well. He figured that was because he had met Sally at just the right time in his life. She'd been there to help him find the right path after he had avenged the brutal deaths of his first wife Nicole and son little Arthur.

Smoke stood in the parlor of the comfortable home he and Sally shared on their ranch, the Sugarloaf, and thought about what a truly lucky man he was.

Boots clomped loudly on the porch and Sally smiled up at him for a second. "It sounds like we're about to have company."

"I'll bet I know who, too. I think I can hear them squabbling already."

A knock sounded on the door. Smoke let go of Sally, turned toward it, and told the visitors to come in. Two cowboys stepped into the room, the older one in a sheepskin coat, the younger—little more than a boy, really—wearing a short denim jacket.

"See, I told you he'd be here." A former hired gun and outlaw, Pearlie had reformed thanks to Smoke's influence and had been the foreman on the Sugarloaf for several years.

"I never said he wouldn't be." Calvin Woods was a

top hand in spite of his youth and also Pearlie's best friend. If there was any trouble around, the two of them could be counted on to find it, but they also watched each other's backs and had helped pull Smoke out of more than one dangerous scrape. "I just thought he might be busy."

"In the middle of the day like this? Busy doin' what?"

Cal looked a little uncomfortable as he said, "Well . . ."

Sally cleared her throat. "I think I should beat a hasty retreat right about now."

"Aw, dadgum it!" Pearlie exclaimed. "I'm sorry, Miss Sally. I never meant to embarrass you none—"

"It's all right, Pearlie," Smoke told him. "Actually, we were just talking about bear sign, weren't we, honey?"

"As a matter of fact, we were."

Pearlie's face lit up at the mere mention of the delicacy. "Were you fixin' to cook up a batch up of 'em, ma'am?"

"Well, not right now. But I'm going to make some to take to Big Rock for the Christmas Eve party, along with some pies and cakes."

Pearlie licked his lips. "I can't hardly wait. It's a-gonna be the best Christmas ever, I reckon."

"Well, we'll have to wait and see about that," Smoke cautioned. "Why were you boys looking for me?"

"Oh, yeah." The expression on Pearlie's craggy face grew more solemn as he forced thoughts of baked goods out of his mind. "That panther's back, Smoke. One of the hands found what was left of a cow it drug off last night, over by Melville Peak."

The Sugarloaf filled up most of a long, broad valley bordered by mountains. Melville Peak was about a mile to the north of the ranch headquarters. Smoke frowned as he thought that the big cat was getting a little too close to home.

All fall, the hands had been catching glimpses of an abnormally large panther that came down out of the mountains to raid the herds two or three times a month. A few of them had taken shots at it but missed, and others had tried to track the predator back to its lair. The big cat was elusive, though. He showed up out of nowhere and seemed to vanish the same way.

Not surprisingly, the panther's success had emboldened it, made it more daring. It had been coming closer and closer to headquarters. It had struck again, only a mile away. That bothered Smoke. He didn't want Sally to step outside some morning on her way to the chicken house to gather eggs, only to be confronted by several hundred pounds of snarling, killer beast.

"I reckon we're going to have to do something about this," he said.

"That's just what I was thinkin'," Pearlie agreed. "The three of us'll go up into the mountains, take enough supplies for a few days, and not come back until we've done found that varmint."

"He's got to have a den up there somewhere," Cal added.

Smoke nodded in agreement with that. "The only thing wrong with what you said, Pearlie, is that there'll just be two of us going—me and Cal."

Pearlie looked surprised as he said, "You're gonna leave me here?"

"Somebody's got to keep the ranch running."

"Shoot, at this time of year, there ain't much to that. The place'd be fine for a few days without me."

"I'd like to think so, but you never know when trouble will crop up. I'll just feel better if I know you're here to keep an eye on things."

Sally said, "I don't like the idea of you leaving right before Christmas, Smoke."

"It's still a while until the big doings in Big Rock," he said. "We'll be back well before then. In fact, I promise that if we don't find that cat in a couple days, we'll turn around and come back and pick up the hunt again after the holiday."

"Well . . . in that case, I suppose I can't complain too much."

"Anyway"—Smoke grinned—"I wouldn't take a chance on depriving Cal of Christmas."

"That's right," Pearlie jumped in. "He's still a growin' boy. I'll bet he plans on hangin' up a stockin' for Santy Claus to fill with goodies."

"Aw, you two," Cal complained. "I'm a full-growed man. I don't believe in Santa Claus no more."

"Question is, does Santy Claus believe in you?" Pearlie asked.

"Huh?"

"Just go get your gear ready and saddle a horse," Smoke said. "We'll ride out today. There's still plenty of light left. Who knows, maybe we'll get lucky and be back tomorrow with that panther's pelt."

A little shudder went through Sally. "You be careful, Smoke. If that beast is big enough to drag off cows the way it's been doing, it could do the same to you and Cal."

"No, ma'am." Cal shook his head. "No critter is gonna keep me away from that bear sign of yours, come Christmas Eve."

A short time later, Smoke walked out of the house carrying his Winchester and a bag of grub and supplies that Sally had put together quickly, still wearing the dress she intended to wear to the Christmas Eve party in the settlement. It was a beautiful day, crisp and cool enough for his breath to fog in front of his face as he walked toward the barn where Pearlie and Cal were waiting for him with two saddled horses.

Smoke glanced at the blue sky, dotted here and there with white clouds. There was nothing threatening about it, but some instinct stirred inside him. Like a lot of Westerners, he had a feel for the weather, maybe a better one than most, and it wouldn't surprise him if snow fell sometime in the next few days. Maybe he could smell it in the air.

"You still plan on me stayin' here?" Pearlie asked as Smoke walked up.

"Yep."

"Well, then, I reckon that's what I'll do. I'd rather be goin' with you boys, though."

Cal said, "Of course you would. A few days of huntin' beats stayin' here and working, doesn't it, Smoke?"

"This isn't an excursion," Smoke pointed out. "That cat is dangerous. If we don't put a stop to its prowling, it's liable to come right up to the house before long."

Pearlie nodded. "I kind of figured that's why you wanted to find it. Reckon I'll wish you good huntin'."

Smoke tied the supplies to his saddle, which already had his bedroll lashed behind it. Then he and Cal swung up onto the mounts and headed out.

As they rode away from the ranch headquarters, Smoke frowned slightly and looked around, not seeing anything out of the ordinary, but he had felt something, a slight prickling on the back of his neck. That usually meant he was being watched.

He wondered suddenly if on this trip into the mountains, he was going to be the hunter—or the hunted.

CHAPTER 2

Pearlie had passed along to Smoke what the puncher had told him about finding the mangled carcass of a cow near the base of Melville Peak, so he had no trouble locating the grisly remains. He knew every foot of the valley and the surrounding mountains, having explored the area thoroughly in his younger days.

Those days really weren't all that long ago, to be honest, but most of the time it seemed like he and Sally had always been together, had always been in the rugged paradise making a life for themselves.

"Dang," Cal exclaimed as he and Smoke rode up to what was left of the cow. "Looks like that panther had himself a feast."

"Yeah," Smoke said, nodding gravely, "his belly ought to be full, that's for sure. That means he'll head back to his den and sleep for a while. Maybe we can find him before he wakes up."

"You reckon you can follow the sign?" Cal asked,

then laughed. "Shoot, that was a dumb question, wasn't it? Of course you can follow the sign. You're Smoke Jensen, the canniest tracker, the boldest fighter, and the fastest gun west of the Mississippi or anywhere else."

Smoke frowned. "You haven't been reading those dime novels again, have you, Cal? I told you, those are all just stories that some scribbler makes up. Wouldn't surprise me if he is drunk while he's doing it, either. I might not be able to stop them from writing about me, but I don't have to read them and neither do you."

"Well, no offense, but I sort of like the ones about Frank Morgan better, anyway," Cal said as he thumbed back his hat. "He's this gunfighter, folks call him the Drifter—"

"I know who Frank Morgan is," Smoke broke in. He couldn't stop a chilly edge from entering his voice. Morgan had a notorious reputation as a gun for hire.

"Oh, yeah, sure, I reckon you would. Have you ever met him?"

"No, I haven't, and I swear, Cal, if you ask me which one of us I figure is faster on the draw—"

"Heck, there's no doubt in my mind about that," Cal said. "Nobody's faster than Smoke Jensen."

Smoke just grunted and turned his horse to ride around the bloody carcass. "Come on. We've got us a panther to tree."

"You really think he'll be up a tree?" Cal asked as he moved his mount alongside Smoke's.

"That's just an expression. More than likely he'll be in a cave." Smoke sure didn't believe all the dime novel nonsense that had been written about him, but it was a fact that he was a pretty good tracker. Of course, he'd had the best teacher anybody could ever have in the person of the old mountain man Preacher.

He was still kicking, still quite active despite his advanced age, and if he had been there, he could have followed the panther's trail as easily as if there had been signs posted showing the way.

As it was, Smoke had to search some for the paw prints, the broken branches, the overturned rocks, the occasional tuft of hair stuck on a tree trunk or a bush. The panther didn't leave many such signs, but there were enough for Smoke to follow the trail. He just couldn't hurry it, so the progress they made was on the slow side.

The trail led up the pine-covered slope toward the upper reaches of the mountain. The higher they went, the more the vegetation thinned out. The peak itself was above the tree line, gray and forbidding even on a sunny day, and topped with a white cap of snow.

Smoke wondered just how far up the panther's lair was. Cats liked high places, so there was no telling.

They had been making their way up the mountainside for a couple hours when he said, "We'll lose the light in another hour or so, Cal. We'd better start looking for a good place to make camp."

"We won't be gettin' back to headquarters today, will we?" the young man asked.

"Nope. I didn't really figure we would. That would've been just blind luck, if we'd found the varmint that fast. I'll always take good luck when it comes along, but it doesn't pay to *expect* it."

Before the sun went down, they found a fairly level, open spot among some trees to make their camp. Smoke tended to the horses while Cal hunted up some firewood along with the rocks they would arrange in a circle to contain the blaze. Smoke had spent many a night under the stars, so it wasn't anything new to him. Back in the days when he'd been riding the hoot owl trail with false murder charges hanging over his head, he'd made camp in a lot lonelier places.

They didn't have to cook their supper as Sally had made sandwiches, placing thick slices of roast beef between slabs of sourdough bread. Smoke brewed coffee in the pot he had brought along, and they washed down the bread and meat with tin cups of Arbuckle's. She had put several airtights in the bag of supplies as well, so he used his knife to open a can of peaches and split it with Cal for dessert, letting the young man drink the thick, sweet syrup left in the can.

After they had eaten, they sat next to the fire, enjoying the warmth cast by the merrily dancing flames. Neither looked directly into the fire. They knew doing so would make a man lose his night vision temporarily. With a killer cat loose on the mountainside, neither of them wanted that.

"It'll be good to have you and Miss Sally home for Christmas this year, Smoke," Cal said as he nursed a second cup of coffee. "Are either of your brothers gonna be here?"

"Not that I know of. The last letter I got from Matt, he was out in California and didn't say anything about heading this way. I haven't heard from Luke in a long time." Smoke smiled faintly. "He was never much of one for staying in touch."

That was putting it mildly. For many years, Smoke had believed his older brother was dead, killed in the last days of the Civil War. Luke had been betrayed by men who were supposed to be his friends and comrades—the same men ultimately responsible for the deaths of Smoke's father Emmett, Nicole, and Arthur. Luke had survived that treachery and made a new life for himself, under a new name, as a bounty hunter during the violent days following the great conflict.

Finally, fate had brought the brothers back together. Not surprisingly, that reunion had seen a lot of hot lead flying around, and somehow, gunplay continued to be quite common whenever Smoke and Luke got together. Smoke would have been happy for his older brother to give up his wandering ways and settle down on the Sugarloaf, but he had a hunch that would never happen. Luke was just too fiddle-footed for that.

The same was true of Matt Jensen, their adopted younger brother. Even though he wasn't a Jensen by birth, he had taken the name and had the same adventurous streak, the same natural ability with gun and knife and fists that a Jensen had to have in order to survive on the frontier. The same sense of honor and courage, too, Smoke was proud to say since he'd helped raise the youngster. The day might come when Matt decided to put down roots, but Smoke suspected it was still a long time in the future.

Those thoughts went through his head as he sipped the strong black brew in his cup, but they were jolted away suddenly by a harsh scream that ripped through the night.

Cal was so startled that he dropped his cup, causing what was left of the coffee to splash and sizzle in the campfire. He came halfway to his feet and exclaimed, "Lord have mercy! Was that—"

"Sounded like our panther, all right," Smoke said, apparently not the least bit shaken.

"I thought you said he'd probably sleep in his den for a while."

"Maybe he was hungrier than I thought, and he's already out looking for another meal." Smoke drained the last of his coffee and flung the grounds into the flames. He set the empty cup aside and stood up.

A few yards away, the two horses he had picketed earlier were skittish, thoroughly spooked by the big cat's cry. Smoke moved over to the animals and quickly calmed them with a light touch and low-voiced words of reassurance. The horses responded to him, but if the panther let out another scream, they would be frightened again. It was pure instinct.

"That sounded like he was close, Smoke." The young puncher was on his feet, holding his rifle.

"Maybe he thinks he's hunting us, instead of the other way around." Smoke's thoughts went back to the feeling he'd had earlier when they were riding away from the ranch headquarters. That sensation of being watched had stayed with him, off and on, the rest of the day, but he had never spotted anyone spying on them. He didn't think he could blame it on the panther, though. The creature had been far away the first time he had experienced that uneasiness.

"I'd better build up the fire," Cal said as he reached

for the pile of broken branches he had brought in earlier and dumped on the ground.

"Hold on," Smoke told him. "That cat's probably scented our horses. He might make a try for them, if he's hungry enough, and if we let the fire burn down a little more."

Cal frowned. "You mean to use 'em as bait?"

"I don't like the idea," Smoke admitted, "but I like even less, the idea of that killer prowling around the ranch. Here's what we'll do. Let's fade back into the woods on both sides of the camp and keep an eye out for a while. If the panther makes a try for the horses, we should be able to pick him off." Smoke lifted his head, tested what little breeze there was, and pointed. "You go in the trees over there."

Cal agreed without hesitation. He always did whatever Smoke told him and would have even if he didn't ride for the Sugarloaf. He had that much respect for the older man.

Carrying his Winchester, Smoke drifted like a phantom into the trees on the other side of the camp. He hoped the wind wouldn't carry their scents to the panther. He leaned his shoulder against the trunk of a tree growing in front of a boulder that rose several feet above his head and settled down to wait. He had a good view of the fire and the horses from there.

The panther hadn't screamed again, and the horses had gone back to cropping on the grass where they were picketed. Smoke had considered tying them to some trees, but he wanted them to be able to pull loose and at least have a chance to get away if the big cat reached them.

He didn't intend to let that happen, however. He

had the rifle ready with a bullet in the chamber and could bring it to his shoulder and fire in less than the blink of an eye. Even in poor light, his aim would be deadly accurate, too.

He heard a faint whisper of sound behind him and realized he had been outsmarted—or had outsmarted himself.

Either way, as he turned and looked up, he saw a sleek shape launch itself from the top of the boulder, fangs and claws poised to rip the life from him.

CHAPTER 3

Smoke's lightning-swift reflexes might have been enough to save him, but before he could even bring the rifle up, a shot blasted. The big cat twisted in mid-air as a bullet tore through it. The panther's momentum made it crash into Smoke anyway, but at least it was no longer trying to claw at him or rip his throat out with its fangs. As Smoke fell, driven off his feet by the impact, he shoved hard on the panther and sent it falling to the side.

The cat thudded to the ground and didn't move again. Smoke knew it was dead. The shot must have been a perfect one through the heart to kill the beast that quickly.

Smoke leaped to his feet and was about to call his congratulations to Cal for making such a shot, when he realized the sound of the blast hadn't come from the other side of the camp. Whoever had fired was on *his* side. Once again, he remembered the odd sensations he had experienced since leaving the ranch headquarters earlier in the day.

The other rifleman might well have saved his life by killing the panther with that phenomenal shot— but that didn't mean the hombre wasn't a threat.

"Smoke!" That was Cal, from the far side of the fire. "Smoke, are you all right? Did you get him?"

Smoke didn't say anything. He didn't want to give away his position. He ghosted backwards into deeper shadows and waited for his rescuer—if that's what the man was—to show himself.

Somebody close by chuckled, and then a voice raspy with age said, "You might as well come on outta there, youngster. I can see you, and if I'd wanted to shoot you, I'd have done it already. Or else just let that big ol' varmint have you."

"Preacher!" Smoke exclaimed.

A lean shape stalked out of the darkness into the faint light coming from the dying campfire. The man might have been mistaken for a panther himself, the way he moved with such dangerous, fluid grace.

The ease with which he carried himself belied his years, as did his erect stance. He was well into his eighties, but he could have been mistaken for a man much younger. He seemed to have stopped aging when he was around sixty years old. Smoke sometimes wondered if the old mountain man would still be around when he and everybody else he knew were gone.

"Smoke!" Cal shouted again. The young puncher was really starting to sound worried.

"It's all right, Cal," Smoke called back to him. "The panther's dead."

"I knew you'd get him!"

Preacher cleared his throat, and Smoke said, "It wasn't me who fired that shot. We've got company. Come on back to the fire, Cal."

They all walked into camp.

Cal looked surprised but pleased to see the mountain man. "Howdy, Preacher! You're the one who killed that panther?"

"I dang sure did." Preacher was lean almost to the point of scrawniness and had a rather angular face with a predatory look to it, reminiscent of a hawk. Silver bristles covered his jaw. His skin was the color of old saddle leather and seemed to be about the same thickness. He'd been known to boast that he had a hide like an alligator.

He wore denim trousers, a fringed buckskin shirt, and a battered old brown hat with a high crown. Twin Colt revolvers were holstered on his hips, and he carried a Henry rifle that was in perfect working condition and gleamed like new. He was old enough to have participated in the Battle of New Orleans during the War of 1812 and had experienced the fur trapping era at its height. He had also lived through the Civil War, had seen the coming of the railroads and the telegraph, had witnessed the near-eradication of the great buffalo herds, and fought countless battles against bad men of all sorts. The term *mountain man* could have been coined to describe him.

"I didn't know you were anywhere in these parts," Smoke said. "Have you come to join us for Christmas?"

"Well, it's kinda worked out that way, I reckon. But I had another reason for wanderin' this direction."

"What's that?" Smoke asked.

Preacher ignored the question and pointed to the coffee pot. "Anything still in that?"

"Might be a cup or so," Smoke allowed.

"I could use it."

Smoke had brought an extra tin cup with him—just as a matter of Western hospitality. You never knew when you might have a guest at the campfire, so it was a good idea to be prepared. He fetched the cup, filled it, and handed it to his old friend, who smacked his lips in anticipation before he took a drink.

Knowing that Preacher would get around to explaining himself when he was good and ready, and trying to prompt him before then would likely be a waste of time, Smoke asked, "Were you down close to the ranch headquarters earlier today, keeping an eye on the place?"

"Matter of fact, I was," Preacher replied. "You know I don't like to just waltz into a place without havin' a look-see first, so I sat in the trees and watched for a while. When I seen you and the boy ride out with rifles and supplies for a few days, I figured you must be goin' on a hunt o' some kind so I decided to foller along and see what sort o' game you was after."

"You might've told us you were around."

Preacher grinned. "Shoot, that woulda taken the fun out of it."

"I had a hunch somebody was following us, you know," Smoke said.

"You did?" Cal put in. "You didn't say anything about it, Smoke."

"Didn't see any reason to." Smoke shrugged. "I figured whoever it was would show himself sooner or later, and if he meant us any harm, we'd deal with it then."

Preacher sipped some more coffee and said, "When I seen you boys headin' up the mountain, I had a hunch you was after a big cat. Either that or a grizzle bear gone bad. I ever tell you about that griz that stalked me most o' the way from Kansas to New Mexico Territory when I was leadin' a wagon train over the Santa Fe Trail?"

"You've mentioned it before," Smoke said dryly. "Along with every other outlandish adventure you had back in those days. Some of them were so loco I wondered if you were making them up."

Preacher shook his head solemnly. "Nope, it was all the gospel truth. And I ain't but scratched the surface. There's all kinds o' wild ruckuses I got myself mixed up in that I ain't never told you about."

"I'm sure you'll get around to it," Smoke said.

"Anyway," Preacher went on as if the younger man hadn't said anything, "when you fellers made camp, I circled around to get ahead of you. Figured I'd keep an eye on you, like a guardian angel, you know."

"Anybody ever accuse you of being an angel, Preacher?" Cal asked.

"Well, not to speak of. But as I was sayin' . . . even before that big ol' cat let out that yowl, Dog and Horse had scented him, so I knowed he was hereabouts."

"Where *are* Dog and Horse?" Smoke asked. "I was wondering about that."

Preacher jerked a thumb over his shoulder. "They're back in the trees a ways. I'll fetch 'em in a bit. Thought we'd visit a spell first."

Cal said, "So you knew the panther was around and were just waiting for him to show up?"

"Yep," Preacher replied, nodding gravely. "I seen him climb up on top o' that boulder and was linin' my sights on him whilst he was fixin' to jump on Smoke."

"Cut it a little close before you fired, didn't you?" Smoke asked.

"Varmint's dead, ain't it? And it appears you don't have a scratch on you."

Smoke had to laugh. Preacher was right. Anyway, even when he wasn't, it didn't do any good to argue with him. With so many years behind him, the old mountain man was pretty set in his ways.

"I'm much obliged to you for what you did, Preacher. And you know we're always glad to see you around here, especially at this time of year. Sally will be happy to find out that you've come to spend Christmas with us." Smoke paused. "You *are* staying for Christmas, aren't you?"

"Figured I would," Preacher said, then a frown creased his forehead. "I ain't so sure that pretty little wife o' yours will be happy to see me, though."

"Why in the world wouldn't she be?"

"Because I got trouble on my trail, Smoke. Somebody's out to kill me."

Cal stared at Preacher in surprise, but Smoke's face remained calm and almost expressionless. He had known that sooner or later Preacher would get around to explaining the real reason he was there, and it seemed like the old mountain man was about to do so.

"You'd better tell us about it," Smoke said. "This isn't the first time somebody's been gunning for you."

"Not hardly," Preacher agreed, "but it's one of the few times that the feller who wants my hide is an old friend of mine. You recollect me tellin' you about Eagle-Eye Callahan?"

"The name's vaguely familiar."

"Him and me done some fur trappin' together about forty years ago. Good man, but he never really took to the life. He wound up buildin' a tradin' post up Montany way and ran it for years and years. Folks always liked him, so he did a good business. He acquired hisself a wife, too, gal name of Louisa who came from St. Louis. Fine woman. Never afraid of hard work, and easy on the eyes, too."

"Sounds like you admired her," Smoke commented.

"I did," Preacher admitted, "but not in any sort o' improper way, you understand. Eagle-Eye is my friend. I'd never go to messin' with his woman. I always stopped by and visited with 'em when I was in that neck o' the woods. Turns out that mighta been a mistake."

"How's that?"

Preacher grimaced. "Louisa passed away nigh on to six months ago, and Eagle-Eye found a cache o' letters she'd writ over the years. Letters, uh, to me." The old mountain man held up a gnarled hand to forestall anything Smoke or Cal might say. "She never mailed 'em. I never laid eyes on 'em and didn't know nothin' about 'em until Eagle-Eye told me about findin' 'em. It seems like Louisa, uh, had . . . feelin's . . . for me, and she poured 'em all into those letters. Reckon that helped her get it all out, even if she never sent 'em. I still ain't read 'em and hope I never do. From the way ol' Eagle-Eye was actin', they was a mite on the, uh, bold side, I reckon you could say."

"We get the idea," Smoke said. "But if nothing ever happened between you and this woman—"

"It didn't, I swear up one way and down the other. Nothin' ever happened 'cept inside her head."

"Then it's not your fault she wrote a bunch of love letters to you. Surely her husband realized that."

"I tried to get him to see that when he come to see me," Preacher said glumly, "but he's got it in *his* head that I musta done *somethin'* to encourage Louisa to feel that way. He figures that casts a shadow on his marriage and besmirches his honor, so there's only one thing he can do about it."

"He wants to kill you."

"That's right, and ol' Eagle-Eye is so blamed stubborn he ain't gonna stop comin' after me until he's done it—or forced me to kill him to stop him." Preacher sighed. "To tell you the truth, I don't think he cares much which way it turns out, as long as one of us dies."

CHAPTER 4

Texas State Penitentiary, Huntsville

Uniformed guards surrounded the big man as he walked along the corridor toward the warden's office. They seemed nervous, as well they might have. The man they were escorting gave off an energy like that of a caged animal. He looked a little like an animal, in fact—a mountain lion, big and muscular, with tawny hair. His face was round, and his eyes were set a little too close together, making him look like he wasn't very smart.

People had thought that about him before, and they had underestimated Jim Bleeker much to their regret. Actually, there was a very cunning brain behind those close-set, pale blue eyes.

He shrugged his brawny shoulders, stretching the fabric of the suit coat he wore. He would have preferred wearing what he'd had on when he was arrested in San Antonio eight long years earlier, but those duds were long gone, replaced by the Bexar County jail uniform he had worn until he was convicted and sent to prison, where he'd been issued penitentiary garb. Upon release, the state gave a man a new suit when he was released from prison, although it was the cheapest possible outfit they could manage.

Doesn't matter, Bleeker told himself. *Once I'm out from behind these gray walls, I won't be wearing it for long.*

The group arrived at the warden's office and one of the guards knocked.

The warden's pasty-faced secretary opened the door. He tried not to look directly at Bleeker, but he kept cutting wary glances in the convict's direction.

"Here he is," the guard said, "just like Warden Cartmill wanted."

The secretary nodded. "Come on in. He's waiting."

Bleeker didn't wait for the guards to prod him into motion. He strode through the door and into the outer office with the bold, easy gait of a free man—which was exactly what he would be, very soon.

The secretary hustled over to open the door to the inner office, the warden's private sanctum.

A good-sized man with thinning dark hair and a jutting beard, Warden John Cartmill stood to his feet and extended his hand across the big desk. "Jim," he greeted Bleeker as the two men shook. "I suppose you felt like this day would never come."

"It took its own sweet time getting here," Bleeker agreed. "The past six months seemed more like six years."

"It took that long to work on the governor and get him to see that your sentence should be commuted. You were sentenced to twenty years for that bank robbery in San Antonio, you know, and you've served less than half of that."

"Figured saving a warden's life ought to be worth something."

"It is, it is," Cartmill assured him, waving him into the black leather chair in front of the desk. "And there's no denying that you've been a model prisoner as well, even before the day of that riot."

Bleeker settled himself into the chair, enjoying the comfortable feel of its upholstery. After eight years of never sitting anywhere except his bunk with its thin mattress or the hard benches in the prison mess hall, it was amazing how good it felt just to sit in a nice chair.

Cartmill cleared his throat and went on. "Of course, if they had been able to convict you of any of those murders you were suspected of . . ."

Bleeker just smiled and let that pass. They both knew that if the law had caught up to him for everything he had done, he would have swung from the gallows.

But that wasn't what had happened, and now he was a changed man. He had proven that by being on his best behavior inside the walls, and then by stepping in to save the warden's life when Cartmill was cornered in the yard by several angry convicts during a riot. Bleeker had taken a hell of a beating that day, but he had dished out plenty of punishment, too, and he'd held the would-be killers at bay until a group of guards showed up to rescue Cartmill.

One of the guards hadn't realized exactly what was going on, had taken Bleeker for one of the rioters, and slammed a club into his kidneys with enough force that he pissed blood for a week afterwards. He still did from time to time.

But he didn't hold any grudge about that, no, sir. Just a misunderstanding, that was all it was.

Once again Cartmill cleared his throat. He picked up a piece of paper from his desk and said, "This is the order from the governor commuting your sentence, Jim. You're a free man. You didn't have to come here to my office. You could have walked out of those gates and never looked back. But I'm glad you were willing to stop by on your way out. That gives me the chance to thank you once more for what you did for me . . . and to apologize for what happened afterwards."

Bleeker waved a hand. "Don't worry about that, Warden. Wasn't your fault. Doolittle just made a mistake, that's all."

"Yes, well, I appreciate your attitude."

"Was there anything else, Warden?" Bleeker was starting to get a little restless. He was ready to be out.

"No, no, that's all." Cartmill stood up and held out his hand again.

Bleeker got to his feet and shook with the warden a second time, and then the guards escorted him out.

A few minutes later, after they had passed through the various gates and checkpoints, Bleeker and two of the guards stood at the main gates of the prison. As the gates opened slowly, Bleeker spotted Ray Morley standing in the shade of some trees across the road from the prison entrance, holding the reins of two horses.

"Don't come back here, Bleeker," said one of the guards standing behind him.

"I reckon you can count on that." Bleeker walked briskly past the gates and across the road. He heard the gates closing behind him but didn't look back to watch them.

It was enough just to be free again.

Morley grinned as Bleeker came up to him. "Damn, it's good to see you again, boss."

"You brought the clothes with you?" Now that Bleeker was outside, there was no time for sentiment. He had things to do, and the first one was getting rid of the lousy prison suit.

"I sure did." Morley took a package wrapped in brown paper from the back of one of the horses, where it had been tied behind the saddle.

Bleeker took the package and walked into the trees. When he emerged a few minutes later, he was dressed in black from head to foot—boots, trousers, shirt, hat and gun belt strapped around his hips. The bone handle of the heavy revolver riding in the holster stood out in stark contrast to the rest of the outfit.

Bleeker took the reins of one of the mounts from Morley and swung up into the saddle.

"We gettin' out of here, Jim?" Morley asked.

"Pretty soon," Bleeker replied. "I've got one stop to make first."

The house was out in the country, about five miles from Huntsville. The man who lived there had tried his hand at farming, but he wasn't very good at it so his wife and three kids tended the crops while he supplemented their income by working as a guard at the prison.

Bleeker and Morley sat on their horses in the shadow of some oak trees about twenty yards from the house. Night had fallen, and nobody would see the two men unless they knew where to look.

"You sure you want to do this, boss?" Morley asked. "We could've put some miles behind us while we were waitin' for it to get dark."

"You're not questioning me, are you, Ray?" Bleeker asked in a deceptively mild voice.

"Oh, hell, no," the other man replied hastily. "I'd never do that, Jim. You know that. You never steered us wrong."

"Except for that day in San Antonio. And it wouldn't have happened then if we hadn't been betrayed."

"That's right. It sure wasn't your fault."

Bleeker knew the outlaw was just trying to curry favor with him by agreeing, but it didn't matter. Morley was a pretty sorry example, but he could be counted on to do what he was told, and he had never run out on his partners and caused his leader to be arrested and thrown into prison for eight long—*very long*—years.

Bleeker lifted his reins and nudged his horse into motion, riding toward the house slowly. Morley was beside him and just a little behind him.

"You know what to do," Bleeker said over his shoulder as they neared the house.

"Yeah, sure." Morley turned his horse and angled away in the darkness.

Bleeker rode openly up to the porch. Warm yellow light came from the front windows. He dismounted, looped his reins around the railing next to the steps, and climbed to the porch. In the dark clothes, he was barely visible.

His knuckles rapped sharply on the door. There was no response, but the silence on the other side of the panel had an unusual quality to it, a sense of something about to happen. It wasn't the silence of an empty house.

It was the silence of a house where everyone inside was afraid.

Bleeker knocked again, more insistently.

After a moment, he heard a little shuffling on the other side of the door, and a nervous voice called, "Who's out there? I've got a shotgun."

"No need for that, Harry," Bleeker replied in a jovial tone.

"Bleeker!" Harry Doolittle exclaimed. "You . . . you get away from here! Warden Cartmill told me I didn't have to work today, so I wouldn't have to see you—"

"Take it easy. You're getting all worked up for nothing. I just wanted to say so long. I mean, hell, you apologized for the mistake you made, and I accepted it, so there's no reason for you to worry about me doing anything to you."

"You . . . you swear to that, Bleeker?"

"I'm a man of my word."

"Then you can just ride on," Doolittle told him. "I'm sorry, and now it's all square between you and me, right?"

"Sure. But our business isn't *quite* done."

As if events had been waiting for that cue, a crash sounded at the back of the house, followed by a scream. Doolittle yelled.

Hearing the guard's feet pound on the floor, Bleeker lifted his right leg, pulled it back, and kicked the door open. He drew his gun as he went through the doorway.

He leveled the revolver at Doolittle's back and snapped, "Stop right there, Harry!"

Doolittle stopped. Wide-eyed, he looked over his shoulder and stammered, "Y-you said you weren't gonna do nothin'."

"I said I wouldn't hurt *you*," Bleeker told him with a smile. "I never said anything about your wife and those brats of yours."

Morley came through an open door leading to the rest of the house. He had his left arm around the neck of Doolittle's wife, a plain-faced woman in her thirties. He pressed the barrel of the gun in his right hand to her head. Herded along in front of them were the couple's three children, a boy about eight and girls of twelve and fourteen.

"Now then, here's the deal, Harry," Bleeker went on. "You can stand there and watch while we kill your boy and have our fun with your wife and daughters before we kill them, too . . . or you can put the barrels of that shotgun in your mouth and pull the triggers." Bleeker shrugged. "It's entirely up to you. But either way, I'm not gonna lay a hand on you, just like I promised."

"P-Please," Doolittle forced out. "Don't hurt them. Let 'em go—"

"Maybe I will . . . if you do what I suggested."

The prison guard's eyes looked like they were about to pop out of their sockets, but he was able to turn the shotgun around and lift the barrels toward his own face. His hands shook so badly that the barrels wavered back and forth several inches.

"P-Promise you won't hurt them?"

"Harry!" his wife screamed. "No! Oh, God, no!"

"Just do it, Harry," Bleeker said quietly. "It's for the best. You don't want them to suffer."

Doolittle steadied the shotgun and closed his lips around the twin barrels, then stretched out his right arm, trying to reach the triggers. His wife and all three of the children screamed and cried. The woman struggled against Morley's grip, but she was no match for the outlaw's strength.

Morley was starting to look a little green around the gills, Bleeker thought. He knew the man wouldn't lose his nerve, but he hoped Doolittle wouldn't take too much longer. . . .

The boom of the shotgun was like the loudest thunderclap anybody ever heard. It momentarily deafened everybody in the room, so they didn't hear what was left of Harry Doolittle thud to the floor. The roar of shots from two revolvers followed instantly and added to the din.

Bleeker's ears were still ringing a few minutes later when he and Morley stepped out onto the porch. Behind them, flames had begun to crackle. Morley had brought some kerosene with him, and they had put it to good use.

He muttered something under his breath.

Bleeker asked, "You all right, Ray?"

"Sure," Morley replied. "It's just . . . that was pretty raw, Jim, even for us."

"Well, they didn't suffer, just like I promised Doolittle. I keep my word, Ray."

Morley wiped the back of his hand across his mouth. "I know that."

"Just like I swore to get even with that damn gunny who left us high and dry in San Antonio." Bleeker went down the steps with Morley following him. The flames inside the house were brighter, casting a garish orange light through the windows. "What I've got planned for him will make this look pretty tame."

"You know where to find him?" Morley asked as they mounted up.

"Damn right I do." Bleeker turned his horse away from the burning house. "A few years after he double-crossed us, he pinned on a lawman's badge, believe it or not. Monte Carson's the sheriff of some place in Colorado called Big Rock."

CHAPTER 5

New York City, New York

The buildings of the city formed canyons through which a cold wind whistled. Mercy Halliday ducked her head against it and felt it tug at the black bonnet she wore. The wind whipped the skirts of her drab black dress around her legs, as well. She was chilled to the bone. Luckily, she had almost reached her destination.

Another block and she was standing in front of the entrance to the headquarters of the Children's Aid Society. She opened the door and went in quickly so as little icy air as possible entered with her.

Once the door was closed behind her, she untied the bonnet and took it off, revealing a thick mass of auburn curls. She knew that vanity was a sin, but she couldn't help being a little proud of her hair. It was her best feature, she thought, although she had been told by suitors that her green eyes were rather compelling, too. The bolder ones had said that her figure was quite striking.

Despite their flattery, none of those suitors had ever won her heart. It was devoted to the great and noble work in which she was engaged.

"Cold out there today," Peter Gallagher commented from the desk where he was working with a welter of papers spread out before him.

"Indeed it is," Mercy agreed as she started toward her own desk. She was aware that he was watching her. She could feel his eyes following her movements. If she were to glance at him, though, she knew he would look away quickly and pretend he hadn't been regarding her with such intensity.

Mercy wasn't offended. She knew he was devoted to his wife and fellow missionary Grace . . . but it was in the nature of men to look at women. What was important was that they didn't allow those baser urges to rule them.

"I've been to the train station and made the final arrangements," she went on. "We'll be able to depart tomorrow as planned."

Peter put his pen back in its inkwell, leaned back in his chair, and smiled. He was a slender man with dark hair parted in the middle, pince-nez perched on his nose, and a mustache that drooped over his mouth. "I don't know what the Society would do without you, Miss Halliday. You're perhaps the most efficient person among our ranks."

"I wouldn't go so far as to say that. You and Grace do a great deal of the work yourselves."

"Yes, but you're the one who keeps things functioning smoothly, no doubt about that."

"Well, I try." There was no false modesty in Mercy's

tone or in the way she looked down at her desk. That was just the way she was.

"The representatives of the railroad understand that we'll have twenty children traveling with us?"

"Yes, of course. I turned the draft for payment of our passage over to the general manager of the line."

"And he gave you a receipt for it?" Peter held up a hand to forestall her answer. "What am I saying? Of course he did. You wouldn't have left without one. You'd never overlook such a vital detail."

"Yes, I have it," Mercy said with a smile, "showing that our passage to California is paid in full, as well as return fare to New York for you and your wife and myself."

"Excellent. Soon those poor children will be well on their way to new homes."

"I'm a bit concerned," Mercy admitted. "This will be the farthest we've ever taken one of the orphan trains."

The members of the Society had adopted the term used in the newspapers for the effort to place orphaned children in new homes. Unfortunate children with no one to care for them had been rescued from the squalor and desperation in the slums of New York and housed in a dormitory owned by the Society until they could be taken west by train. In St. Louis, Kansas City, Wichita, Denver, and other western cities, announcements were placed letting people know that children were available for adoption.

Mercy knew that some people wanted to adopt simply so they could have more workers for their farms or businesses, but the Society did its best to weed out those applicants and place the children with families that truly wanted them and had love to give them. That was perhaps the most important job she and Peter and Grace had as they accompanied the youngsters on their westward journey.

The group they would be leaving with the next day was bound for Sacramento, in California. It would be a long trip, but Mercy thought it was important to open up as many new possibilities for adoptions as they could.

One thing was certain. There would always be orphans in need of a good home. Sometimes the city seemed to be a great beast, grinding up people between its teeth and spitting them out, leaving their children to fend for themselves. She had experienced something similar when she was young, losing both of her parents in a tragic carriage accident. Luckily, she'd had relatives to take her in. The children the Society helped didn't have that luxury.

She sat down at her desk and began going through the stack of papers in front of her. Each sheet listed one of the orphans and gave the details of how the child came to have no family, if that information was known. In all too many cases, that background simply wasn't available. The children were too young to tell where they had come from or what had happened to their parents. Some had been captured by the police while they were engaged in criminal behavior and refused to talk. Most of those were like feral animals at first, until they realized they no longer had to fight merely to survive. Some of the orphans seemed simply not to know their origins.

Mercy paused with one of the sheets in her hand.

A boy who appeared to be around six years old had been found huddled on the back steps of the dormitory one morning. He had refused to talk and hadn't said a word since the Society had taken him in. Perhaps he *couldn't* talk, although the doctor who examined the children seemed to think there was nothing physically wrong with him. His clothes were rags, and the thick layer of grime that covered his hands and face testified that he had been living on the streets and in the alleys for quite some time. Obviously, he had no home or family.

The workers at the dormitory had named him Caleb. He seemed to respond to it, and so the name had stuck.

If they could find a good home for him . . . if they could place him with a family that would love him and bring him out of whatever malaise gripped him . . . all the hard work would have been worthwhile, Mercy thought as she added the paper to the stack.

"Oh, the little boy who doesn't talk," Peter said from beside her.

She tried not to jump in surprise. She had been caught up in her thoughts and hadn't heard him come over. "That's right."

Peter leaned over and tapped the paper. "We'll find a good home for him." The movement took him closer to Mercy.

Close enough, in fact, that she could smell the bay rum from when he'd shaved that morning.

"Of course we will." She felt a bit uncomfortable with him hovering so close to her. She wasn't attracted to him in the least, but she knew that he admired her. She told herself that his admiration stemmed solely from her devotion to their shared cause, but she wasn't sure.

Another door opened, and Grace Gallagher came into the office. Peter straightened quickly and turned toward her. She was a pale, blond woman in the same sort of sober black dress that Mercy wore. Somehow it didn't quite look the same on her.

"Miss Halliday and I were just going over the list of children who'll be leaving with us tomorrow, dear," Peter said to his wife. "Our passage is paid for, and everything is ready for us to go."

"Splendid," Grace said. "We can always count on Miss Halliday, can't we?"

Coming from her, that sentiment didn't sound quite as admiring, Mercy thought. *Yes, this trip to California might turn out to be quite a long one . . . but it will be worth it if we find good homes for all those children,* she told herself again. *Especially the enigmatic Caleb.*

Elsewhere in the city on that chilly December day, a man in a dark overcoat and a brown fedora strolled apparently aimlessly along a sidewalk, although as cold as it was, the odds of a man being out for a casual walk were small.

Ed Rinehart knew that, and the knowledge bothered him. He ought to be moving briskly, but instead he had to wait until the man he was going to follow came out of the bank across the street.

Rinehart had his head turned away so that he wasn't watching the bank directly. Neither was he using the window in front of him as a mirror. Behavior like that was a dead giveaway to someone trying to spot a tail.

He had excellent peripheral vision, a valuable quality for a private operative to possess, and he could see the bank's front doors from the corner of his eye.

One of the bank's heavy doors swung open. A man came out carrying a satchel and strode along the sidewalk toward the east. Rinehart followed on the other side of the street, half a block behind.

The detective was a tall man around thirty years old, with thick sandy hair under the fedora. He walked with his hands in the overcoat pockets, but not just because the weather was cold. The pocket on the right contained a shot-filled leather sap, and Rinehart curled his gloved fingers around its grip.

He didn't like guns, although he could handle a pistol fairly well and was an excellent shot with a rifle. The sap was usually the only weapon he needed, since most of the altercations in which he was involved happened at close range. He preferred not to fight at all, unless he didn't have a choice.

The man he was following sported muttonchop whiskers and a red nose that indicated he drank too much. His drinking had gotten him in trouble, since he'd been inebriated when he succumbed to the charms of a woman named Seraphine DuMille. That was what she called herself, anyway. Rinehart had a pretty strong hunch she hadn't been born with that name.

The man with the satchel, E. G. Halliwell, was a vice-president of the bank from which he had emerged. He was married to a stern-faced woman named Edna, whose father was the president of the bank, and had three stern-faced children. E.G. was active in church and civic affairs and couldn't afford to have it known that he'd been dallying with a French hussy. The only way he could keep Seraphine from paying a visit to Mrs. Halliwell was to fill a satchel full of negotiable securities taken from the vault and turn them over to a confederate of hers, a man named Binder.

It was the same sort of sordid arrangement Ed Rinehart had seen numerous times in his career. Halliwell's father-in-law had grown suspicious of the man's increasingly erratic behavior and had hired the agency that employed Rinehart. As an experienced detective, it hadn't taken him long to get to the bottom of things.

It was a matter of extricating Halliwell from the mess he had gotten himself into and keeping him from ruining his life. If that wasn't possible, Rinehart would retrieve the securities, at the very least. Protecting the bank was the most important objective as far as the agency was concerned.

Up ahead, Halliwell turned and started down an alley. Rinehart paused across the street from the opening between buildings. He pretended to be lighting a cigarette and struggling with it in the wind. That peripheral vision of his allowed him to see a man step out from an alcove and confront Halliwell.

Recognizing Binder, who was large and brawny and none too bright, Rinehart turned and walked quickly across the street as the man stretched out a paw and motioned for Halliwell to give him the satchel.

"Don't do it, Halliwell," Rinehart called, startling both men into turning sharply toward him. "If you do, next month they'll just ask for something else."

"Get outta here, mister," Binder rasped. "This ain't any o' your business."

"Actually, it is." Rinehart poked his hands forward in both overcoat pockets as if he were aiming pistols from them. "You've got a choice, Binder. You can go back to Seraphine empty-handed and tell her it would be wise to forget about Mr. Halliwell here, or you can both be behind bars before the sun goes down. It's up to you."

Halliwell was gaping at him, opening and closing his mouth like a fish out of water.

Binder just glared. "I don't know what you're talkin' about, bub, but if you don't turn around and leave—*right now*—you're gonna wish you had."

Rinehart shook his head. "I don't think so."

The threatening words and the implied threat of non-existent guns had kept Binder distracted until Rinehart was fairly close. The big tough grimaced. He was thinking, and he didn't like doing that. Rinehart could see him make up his mind. Binder had decided to use his muscles . . . as he always did.

He lunged at the detective, swinging a massive, rock-hard fist.

Rinehart ducked under the blow, pulled the sap from his pocket, and snapped it against Binder's right shoulder. The man yelped in pain and that arm flopped loosely, gone numb from the impact. In a smooth, backhand move, Rinehart slapped the shot-filled leather against the side of Binder's head. Not hard enough to crush bone, but with plenty of force to drop the man, out cold.

Halliwell was still staring at Rinehart.

The detective told him, "Take those securities back to the bank, put them back in the vault, and don't say anything about this to anyone. Not ever."

Halliwell found his voice and stammered, "B-but that woman . . . that terrible woman . . ."

"Don't worry about her. I'll have a chat with her . . . after I've tipped off the coppers where to find her friend Binder. He's wanted on a number of charges. So is she, for that matter. Once she finds out she's lost her helper and that I know where to find her, she'll almost certainly decide the climate in New York is too cold for her this winter and leave for somewhere more pleasant."

"But she said she'd tell—"

"She won't say anything if there's no profit in it for her. She's smart enough to realize that a plan hasn't panned out and move on."

"Who *are* you?"

"Just a friend," Rinehart said with a smile as he replaced the sap in his pocket. "I'll give you some friendly advice, E.G. Stop drinking so much. Spend more time at home with your wife and children. Do your job at the bank and enjoy the breaks you've had in life."

"I-I suppose you're right. . . ."

"I know I am."

"I don't know why you're helping me"—Halliwell swallowed hard—"but I appreciate it." He turned and scurried away, leaving Rinehart alone in the alley with the unconscious Binder.

Rinehart figured he would give the banker a chance to get several blocks away, then he'd go find a police officer and turn Binder over to him. Then he'd pay a visit to the hotel where Seraphine DuMille was staying . . .

He heard a faint scuff of shoe leather on cobblestones and turned to see a woman lunging at him, her face contorted with hatred and the knife in her hand raised high, poised to strike and drive deep into his chest.

CHAPTER 6

Despite his relative youth, Ed Rinehart had come close to losing his life many times during his career as a detective, so he didn't panic when he found himself under attack. He darted to the side, avoiding the swiftly struck blow, and reached out to grab the woman's arm as she stumbled slightly, thrown off balance by missing him.

He had learned early on that chivalry had no place in his work if he wanted to stay alive. He hung on to the woman's arm with both hands, pivoted sharply, and threw her into the brick wall beside them. She crashed into the building with enough force to jolt the knife out of her hand.

Moving with speed of his own, he lashed out with his leg to kick the knife away from them. The weapon clattered on the dirty cobblestones as it bounced and slid along the alley until it was well out of reach.

She recovered before Rinehart could do anything else and came at him, arms outstretched, fingers curled into harpy-like talons. He suspected she filed her long fingernails to a sharpness that would shred his skin if he allowed her to claw his face. She would go for his eyes, too, and attempt to blind him.

His hands flashed up, caught her wrists before she could carry out her attack, and thrust her arms up to keep those fingernails away from his face. Her momentum carried her forward and she rammed into him with enough force to knock him back half a step. The collision didn't loosen his grip. He still maintained a firm hold on her wrists.

Her face was only inches from his. If she hadn't been snarling so savagely, she would have been beautiful. Tumbled masses of ebony curls framed a lovely face. Her dark, sultry good looks allowed her to deceive plenty of men into believing that she cared for them. In truth, she cared only for the money they had—or had access to, in the case of marks like E. G. Halliwell.

"You might as well stop fighting, Seraphine," Rinehart told her. "It's over."

A torrent of French words spilled from her mouth. Rinehart understood enough of the language to know she was cursing him bitterly for interfering with her plans. Whether it was her native tongue or not, she was fluent in the profanity part of it.

"I'll kill you!" she finally said, spewing the threat through tightly clenched teeth.

"I don't think so. Your friend Binder is still unconscious, and you're unarmed. All I have to do is shout for the coppers, and you'll both wind up behind bars."

"If I'm locked up, I'll ruin that fool Halliwell!"

Rinehart shook his head confidently. "You can tell

whatever story you want, but it'll be your word against his. Actually, it would be your word against his and mine and my agency's. I'll make sure the authorities understand you attempted to ensnare my good friend E.G. in your schemes, but he resisted and came to me for help."

She stared at him for a second and then burst out, "But that's not true!"

Rinehart couldn't resist the urge to laugh, which just angered her more. It was ludicrous that a thief, confidence artist, and woman who was no better than she had to be was acting so outraged at the prospect of someone telling a lie.

"When I tell my boss and everyone else that Halliwell was working with me to set a trap for you and Binder, they'll believe me," Rinehart assured her. "So you have a choice, Seraphine or whatever your name really is. You're losing Binder's services either way. You have to decide whether you want to go to jail, too, or whether I let you *escape* with your promise to leave New York and never bother E. G. Halliwell or his family again."

She glared at him and asked sullenly, "You give me your word that you won't turn me in to the law?"

"I realize I should have you arrested, too, but some of Halliwell's problems came about as the result of his own stupidity. So, against my better judgment, I'll give you a break. You can get out of town. You have my word on that." Rinehart shook his head. "Not Binder, though. He's hurt too many people in the past. He needs to pay for his crimes."

"Very well. I accept your proposal." Hatred still burned in her eyes, though.

Rinehart let go of her wrists and stepped back. He didn't trust her—she had agreed a little too quickly—so he watched her closely, ready to snatch the sap from his pocket and lay her out, too, if it proved necessary.

Seraphine just backed away, glaring at him. She raised a finger and pointed it at him for a second, and Rinehart felt a chill go through him that had nothing to do with the weather. Then she turned and broke into a run, her shoes tapping swiftly on the cobblestones as she fled.

Maybe he shouldn't have let her go, he thought. That last gesture of hers had held a definite threat.

If I worried about every threat that had been made against me over the years, I wouldn't have time for anything else, he told himself.

He turned back to the still senseless Binder, took a whistle from his pocket, and blew a shrill blast from it, knowing the summons would soon bring the nearest copper.

An hour later, Binder was locked up, awaiting charges of attempted murder, assault, and criminal conspiracy that would have him behind bars for a good long time. With the criminal record he already had, a judge might just put him away for good.

The story Rinehart told the police didn't include anything about E. G. Halliwell or Seraphine DuMille. Acquainted with the detective, the coppers knew he was an operative for a private detective agency, so they believed him when he told them he had received a tip from an informant concerning the where-abouts of a dangerous fugitive.

"Ye should've told us about it, instead of goin' to capture him yerself," a burly sergeant pointed out.

"This way I get the reward," Rinehart responded with a smile.

"Aye, for what it's worth. It's not like this fellow is Jesse James come back from the grave! If ye want rewards, Rinehart, ye'd do better to go after some o' them Western desperadoes."

Rinehart just shook his head. "Anywhere west of New Jersey is too far west for me."

He left the police station and walked a number of blocks before trotting up the steps of a brownstone where the front door had the North American continent painted onto the glass of its upper half, along with the agency's name in gilt letters.

As he walked into the outer office, a man at a desk on the other side of a dividing railing looked up and said, "Cap Shaw wants to see you, Ed."

"What, you mean he's already heard about what happened this afternoon?"

"I wouldn't know about that," the other operative replied with a shake of his head. "He has clients with him. I suppose he thinks you're the man for whatever job it is they have." There was a slight note of jealousy in the man's voice. He knew their boss, Captain Albert Shaw considered Rinehart the top investigator in the New York office.

Rinehart took off his overcoat and fedora and hung them on a rack. He briefly considered transferring the sap from his overcoat to one of his trousers pockets, then decided he wouldn't need it in the agency's office.

He knocked on the door of Shaw's office and heard the captain's harsh tones tell him to come in. When Rinehart walked in, he found Shaw standing behind the desk, thumbs hooked in his vest. A man and a woman sat in front of the desk in the leather chairs, and Rinehart's experienced eye told him their clothes probably cost more money than he made in a year.

Captain Shaw was a mostly bald, florid-faced man with an impressive girth. He was not soft, however, despite his fleshiness. He fixed the newcomer with a steely gaze. "I expected you back before now, Mr. Rinehart."

"The matter took somewhat longer to wrap up than I thought it would, but it came to a successful conclusion, Captain."

Shaw nodded curtly. When he read Rinehart's report later, he probably wouldn't be happy that Seraphine DuMille had gotten away, but Binder had been arrested, E. G. Halliwell's reputation was safe, and most important, the bank's securities were back in the vault where they were supposed to be. The captain would be satisfied with that outcome, at least.

"Mr. and Mrs. Litchfield have been waiting for you," Shaw said with a nod at the couple seated in front of his desk. "Or rather, for my top operative, which I've assured them you are, Mr. Rinehart."

"Thank you for that vote of confidence, sir." Rinehart nodded to the Litchfields. "It's a pleasure to meet you."

"I wish the circumstances were better," snapped the man. "I'm William Litchfield. This is my wife."

Rinehart had already gathered that, but he nodded politely to the woman and murmured, "Ma'am."

Mrs. Litchfield had a thin, pale face under the stylish hat on her upswept dark hair, but she possessed a fragile beauty that would catch the eye of most men. Her husband, on the other hand, was thick of waist and neck and had a jaw like a stone slab.

His name was vaguely familiar. The detective thought he had something to do with railroads or shipping or maybe even both. He was rich, no doubt about that.

Suddenly, the name tripped another trigger in Rinehart's brain, and he couldn't stop himself from exclaiming, "The Litchfield murder case!"

"That's right," William Litchfield said, nodding.

Beside him, his wife bit her lip.

Sensing that she was disturbed, he reached over and clasped her hand. To Rinehart, he went on. "You've heard of it, of course."

"Certainly." Rinehart started to make some comment about how could he not have heard of it, since the story had been plastered all over the newspapers for weeks, but then he thought better of it. "My condolences on the loss of your brother and his wife, sir."

"It was months ago," Litchfield said impatiently. "We're past mourning now and want to do something about it."

Financier Grant Litchfield, who if anything was even richer than his older brother, had been murdered in his Riverside Drive mansion, along with his wife Claire, one of the darlings of the society pages.

The police had devoted every possible effort to finding the killers but had come up empty-handed.

"You want the agency to attempt to locate the murderers?" Rinehart asked.

Litchfield shook his head. "This is about my nephew."

Once again, Rinehart thought back over the newspaper stories he had read. Grant and Claire Litchfield had had a young son named . . . Donald, that was it. Donald Litchfield. The detective frowned. "You took the boy in, didn't you, Mr. Litchfield? That was what the newspapers reported."

"That was a lie," Litchfield said harshly. "The police suggested it. They believed the murderers were supposed to kill Donald, too, but he escaped them somehow. The police found footprints outside the mansion the next morning after the . . . murders . . . and were convinced that Donald made them as he fled the house. The detectives thought it best—and I agreed with them—to fabricate the notion that Donald was safely with my wife and me so the killers wouldn't try to find him. At the same time, the police were searching for him, in the hope that he can tell them what he saw that night and lead them to the killers. But they've failed . . . failed utterly! And I'm tired of it. My nephew must be found, and I'm willing to pay this agency whatever it takes to find him!"

CHAPTER 7

Northern Colorado

Gray clouds scudded through the sky above the mountain trail, a darker gray than the peaks themselves, although the appearance of the clouds was just as jagged as that of the snow-capped crags. The two young men riding along the trail paused to rest their horses.

As they reined in, one of them looked up, squinted at the sky, and commented, "Looks like rain." He was medium-size and a bit of a dandy in a brown tweed suit, brown Stetson, boiled white shirt, and string tie. When he took off his hat, he revealed close-cropped sandy brown hair.

His companion shook his head. "Nope. Those are snow clouds, I reckon." He was bigger and more obviously muscular than the first rider. A thatch of dark hair curled around his ears and stuck out from under his thumbed-back hat. He wore denim trousers and a buckskin shirt.

Both young men wore holstered revolvers, and something else was the same about them. Despite their differences, the resemblance between their facial features was so strong it was immediately apparent they were brothers. Most people wouldn't have taken them for twins, but that was, in fact, what they were.

"If it's going to snow, we'd better be moving on," Chance Jensen said. "We don't want to be caught up here in a storm. You know how fast these mountain passes can get blocked during a blizzard."

Ace nodded "Well, it's December, after all. You have to expect some bad weather in these parts at this time of year."

Chance raised a finger in the air. "Exactly! That's why I told you six weeks ago we needed to start heading south. Texas, I told you. Or even Mexico. It never gets cold in Mexico."

"Some places it does," Ace argued. "There are mountains down there, too, you know. I've read about 'em."

Ace was the more studious of the pair, seldom without a book or two in his saddlebags. Chance tended toward less solitary pleasures—like the shuffle of cards on a felt-topped table, the gurgle of whiskey being poured in a glass, and the smiling laughter of a pretty girl.

"Yeah, I know you warned me about the weather," Ace said as he rested his hands on his saddle horn and leaned forward to ease tired muscles. "But we couldn't just ride off and leave those folks up in Montana in the lurch, could we?"

"No, I suppose not, the way hell was popping all around." Chance shrugged. "But now we'll be racing winter all the way to the border country."

Ace leaned forward to pat his horse on the shoulder as he said, "We'd better get moving, then—" He stopped short as a shot blasted somewhere not far away, setting off a series of echoes that bounced back and forth between the rocky slopes around them.

They stiffened in their saddles. A single shot could mean just about anything. It didn't have to signify the beginning of trouble—even though the Jensen boys seemed to find themselves up to their necks in it on an alarmingly regular basis.

The trail they were following ran through a gorge twenty yards wide that sloped down at a fairly gentle angle for several hundred yards before it made a sharp bend to the right. Cliffs at least two hundred feet high rose on either side of it. Once inside the gorge, they would have to follow it to its end or turn around and go back. There wouldn't be any climbing out of it.

The few stunted pines growing here and there beside the trail would furnish some cover if they needed it, but overall, vegetation was sparse because the cliffs prevented light from penetrating down there.

A moment after the first shot more gunfire sounded, along with the pounding hoofbeats of several riders in a hurry.

"That's a running fight," Chance said tensely. "Somebody's in trouble."

Ace pulled his horse toward the nearest clump of trees and called over his shoulder to his brother, "Come on!"

Chance followed Ace's lead and galloped toward the pines.

Reaching the trees, they swung down from their saddles with the lithe grace of born horsemen. The brothers yanked Winchesters from saddle boots and split up, each taking cover behind a different tree. The trunks weren't thick enough to shelter them completely, but they were better than nothing.

"Are we gonna take a hand in this?" Chance called over to Ace.

"Don't know. Reckon we'll have to wait and see."

"How are we going to tell who's in the right?"

That was a good question. Ace didn't know the answer.

A lone rider suddenly exploded into view around the bend. He was pushing his horse up the trail for all it was worth. The animal struggled valiantly. Ace could tell the horse was giving everything it had, but it might not be enough, especially going uphill.

He couldn't tell much about the rider. The man wore a hat with a big, floppy brim that had blown back against the crown because he was moving so fast. Ace caught a flash of white that he thought might be a mustache.

Other details would have to wait. At that moment, five more riders came into sight, boiling around the bend and starting up the trail after the lone man. Flame from the guns in their hands spouted from the weapons as they fired at their quarry.

The odds of hitting anything by firing from the back of a galloping horse were pretty small, but by throwing enough lead around, anything was possible. They were directing a veritable storm of lead at the lone man, who leaned forward in the saddle as far as he could to make himself a smaller target. The echoes from all the shots set up a tremendous racket.

Ace looked over at Chance and called, "Five to one odds!" He wasn't sure if his brother understood him or not, but Chance nodded grimly so Ace assumed he did.

"That's enough for me!" Chance yelled. He lifted the Winchester to his shoulder and lined the sights.

Ace did the same but didn't want to kill anybody when he wasn't sure what the situation was. He aimed past the fleeing man and in front of the pursuers, and fired three rapid shots, working the rifle's lever between rounds. Chance did likewise. The bullets struck the ground several yards in front of the five men and kicked up a spray of dirt and rocks into the faces of their horses.

It was enough to make the mounts shy. Suddenly, the pursuers had their hands full keeping their horses under control. They had to stop shooting at the man in front of them, giving him a chance to pull away from them.

The five men didn't discourage easily, though. As they began to bring their mounts under control, one of them yelled, "Up yonder in those trees!"

Ace wasn't worried about the odds. Five to two didn't seem that bad to him, especially when the two were him and his brother. But there was no point in a fight to the death when it wasn't necessary, especially when the reason behind the whole thing was still a mystery.

He opened fire again—not shooting to kill but putting his bullets a lot closer to the five riders—

sending the slugs zipping around their heads. One bullet even knocked a man's hat off, prompting a shrill yelp of alarm and a lot of cussing.

Chance peppered them the same way. After a few seconds of that barrage, the men's nerves broke. The one whose hat Ace had shot off yelled, "Let's get the hell out of here!" He wheeled his horse around and raked the animal's flanks with his spurs.

The others threw a few last shots up the gorge toward Ace, Chance, and the man they had been chasing, then they pounded back down the trail after their companion. Ace and Chance stopped shooting as the men vanished around the bend.

"You think they'll double back?" Chance asked as he lowered his Winchester.

"If they do, we'll see them coming." His eyes wary, Ace was watching the man whose aid they had come to. The brothers still didn't know who he was or why the other five men had been trying to kill him.

The lone rider slowed his horse as he approached the trees. He looked back over his shoulder as if to make sure the danger was over, then reined his mount to a halt. "I don't know who you fellas are," he called, inadvertently echoing the thought that had just gone through Ace's brain, "but I sure am obliged to you for your help! Those varmints would've ventilated me for sure."

He was an older man, as that glimpse of a white mustache had hinted. His hair was snow-white, too, as he revealed when he pulled off the big hat, took a bandanna from his pocket, and used it to mop his face.

Chilly day or not, being chased by men out to kill you was enough to make a man sweat.

He was burly and barrel-chested, clearly powerful despite his age. Like Ace, he wore a buckskin shirt, but his trousers were fringed buckskin as well, and instead of boots he had high moccasins on his feet. An old flintlock rifle was slung alongside his saddle, and he had a brace of flintlock pistols thrust behind his broad leather belt. What appeared to be a hunting knife with a long, heavy blade rode in a fringed sheath at his hip.

The man looked like a throwback to the fur trapping days, thought Ace as he eased out from behind the tree. His Winchester was pointed toward the ground, but he was ready to bring it up and use it in a hurry if he needed to. He didn't think that was going to be necessary. "Who were those fellas? Why were they after you?"

The old-timer shook his head. "Danged if I know who they were. I'm pretty sure they were after my poke, though. I could've been a mite too careless about showin' it in the last settlement I passed through where I bought some supplies. Trail trash like that, they think a man's got money, they'll come after him and try to rob and kill him."

That sounded reasonable enough. Although Ace had no way of being sure if the old man was telling the truth, the words had the ring of sincerity to them.

Chance emerged from the trees. "It's a good thing we happened to be here when you came along. They would have run you to ground pretty soon."

"Yeah, I know." The old man patted his mount's

shoulder. "This is a mighty good horse, but he's come a long way from Montana."

"Montana?" Chance repeated. "That's where we're coming from."

"Really? Whereabouts?"

"A town called Rimfire," Ace said. "That doesn't really matter right now, though. If those men were aiming to rob you, they're liable to come after you again."

"Yeah, they sure might," the old man said as he nodded slowly. "And next time I won't have you fellas around to give me a hand and run 'em off . . . unless, of course, we were to ride together for a spell."

"We're going in different directions," Ace pointed out. "My brother and I are headed south."

"Well, so am I. Didn't you hear me just say that I've come down to these parts from Montana? I was about a mile on down the trail when I ran into the ambush those varmints set up. Didn't have no choice but to turn around and head back this way."

"That makes sense," Chance said.

Ace supposed it did, although he still sensed there was more to the affair than was readily apparent. There was no getting around the fact that the five hellions they had run off were somewhere ahead of them, and if there was going to be more trouble, three men stood a better chance of getting through it than two.

"All right," he said, reaching a decision. "I suppose we can ride together for a while and see how it works out. I reckon if we're going to do that, we ought to know each other's names. I'm Ace Jensen and this is my brother Chance."

"Ace and Chance, eh?" The old-timer grinned. "I like it. I can tell you boys are the genuine article. As for me, my name's Callahan." He paused. "They call me Eagle-Eye . . . 'cause I can shoot the wings off a gnat at a hundred yards."

CHAPTER 8

"I say we bushwhack 'em!" Curly Weaver declared.

"And I say they already came within an inch or two of blowing my brains out," Mitch Clark snapped back at Weaver. "Sure, I was willing to make a try for the old man's money, but it didn't work out. Just bad luck, that's all. I don't want to take another chance on getting killed before we meet up with Bleeker. That'll be a lot bigger payoff."

"Yeah," mused Jed Darby. "All the loot of a whole town, there for the takin'!"

The three men, along with Blind Jimmy Pugh and Hector Gomez, sat on their horses a couple miles from the spot where they had tried to ambush Eagle-Eye Callahan. After the failed robbery, they had ridden at a fast pace before reining in to let the horses blow.

Even more than most men—law-abiding men—an owlhoot couldn't afford to have his horse go down and be set afoot. He never knew when he might encounter a posse and have to make a run for it.

The five men weren't really a gang. They'd just been riding together for a while so they didn't have an official leader. But over time, the others had come to look to Clark to make the important decisions.

He didn't appear particularly dangerous. With his hat shot off, revealing his thinning brown hair, he might have been a store clerk or a traveling salesman. Weaver was the handsome one, with curly black hair that gave him his nickname and made the ladies like him, but he was reckless and none too bright. Jed Darby was thin, sallow, and mean. Gomez was a typical bandito who had wandered into the States from south of the border. And Blind Jimmy wasn't really blind, although his eyes were very weak. He could see well enough through spectacles as thick as the bottom of a whiskey bottle to survive in a fight, though.

Altogether, they weren't an impressive bunch, but they were greedy and unpredictable and therefore dangerous.

A couple days earlier, while they were up in Wyoming at a road ranch where men on the dodge tended to congregate, they had heard the gossip that Jim Bleeker was looking for men to throw in with him on a deal that offered a big payoff.

Clark and his friends had heard of him, even though Bleeker had been locked up in Texas for several years. He'd been released from prison recently and then dropped out of sight. That same day, a guard and his entire family had been killed in an act of wanton slaughter. Everyone assumed Bleeker was responsible for that atrocity, although there was no proof of it, and nobody knew where he had gone.

Word of what had happened traveled swiftly along the owlhoot trails, along with rumors about Bleeker having something else in mind. He wanted to settle a score with an old enemy, and that involved treeing a whole town and looting it. Clark and the others didn't know where exactly that town was, but they wanted to find out.

Supposedly, a man in Denver could put interested parties in touch with Bleeker. Clark and his friends had been heading there when they'd gotten side-tracked by the old man being a little too careless about revealing how much money he was carrying.

As far as Clark was concerned, it was time to get back to business. He reached over and plucked the bowler hat from Blind Jimmy's head.

"Hey!" the nearsighted young outlaw objected. "That's my hat."

"You can get a new one," Clark told him. "My head gets cold, and you've got a lot more hair than I do."

"Well, yeah, that's true, I reckon." Blind Jimmy's head sported a thick mop of yellow curls.

Clark lifted his reins and heeled his horse into motion. "Let's go. We can reach Denver in another couple days. We don't want to get there and find out we're too late to get in on whatever Bleeker's planning."

"I worry a little about this Señor Bleeker," Gomez said as the others fell in with Clark. "It is said that sometimes he acts like a mad man."

"I don't care if he's as crazy as a cow full of loco weed," Clark said. "As long as this job he's going to pull pays enough, that's all that matters to me."

Mutters of agreement came from the others.

Crazy was one thing. Money was another.

Wyoming

The building with the sod roof was low and sprawling, with a shed and a pole corral out back. Four horses were in the corral at the moment. The man who rode up to the fence under an angry, overcast sky studied the horses but didn't recognize any of them. He had a good eye for horseflesh and a good memory for the animals, as well.

He rode around to the front of the place. Two more horses were tied to a hitch rack there. He didn't recognize either of those mounts, so the men he was looking for weren't there . . . unless they had changed horses. That was always a possibility.

He swung down from his saddle, a tall, well-built man in dark clothes. His craggy face was set in grim lines, relieved slightly by a wide mouth that was quick to grin and laugh. A narrow, neatly trimmed mustache adorned his upper lip.

As he tied his horse at the rack with the other two, he looked around. The windowless building sat by itself on a trail that ran roughly north and south. A range of low mountains lay to the west. Northward, flat-topped buttes were scattered across the landscape. Windswept plains stretched to the east and south, although a dark line on the southern horizon marked the location of more mountains.

It was lonely, desolate country, which made the isolated saloon and trading post a perfect stopping spot for men who didn't want to be noticed. They could replenish their supplies, guzzle down some rotgut, and maybe spend a few minutes with one of the three Indian squaws who worked for Jeremiah Beebe, the proprietor. Beebe claimed to be a Mormon and called them his wives, but nobody knew or cared if that had any basis in fact.

The newcomer certainly didn't care, although he'd heard the stories about Beebe and the squaws. One was a Crow, another a Blackfoot, the third a Shoshone, and they all hated each other. Each would have gladly killed the other two if given the chance, so Beebe had to keep an eye on them and make sure nothing of the sort happened.

Seemed like an awful lot of trouble.

The man went inside, a swirl of cold wind following him.

Three men were sitting at a table, playing cards. One of them glanced up and snapped, "Hey, shut that damn door!"

The newcomer swung the door closed on its leather hinges, and the gloom inside became even thicker. Candles were set here and there on the rough-hewn tables, and an oil lamp burned over the crude bar, but the weak, flickering glow they provided didn't do much to penetrate the shadows.

Despite that, the newcomer's gaze moved quickly around the low-ceilinged room as he took stock of its occupants. Besides the three card players, two men stood in front of the bar, apparently nursing drinks in dirty glasses. The man in a dingy apron behind the bar was shaped like a watermelon. He had a walrus mustache and wore a flat-topped hat with an eagle feather stuck behind the band. An Indian woman stood at the far end of the bar, apparently doing nothing, while a second woman sat in a corner near the pot-bellied stove, mending some clothes.

That left one woman unaccounted for, so the newcomer was fairly confident they were together.

A moment later, he heard animalistic grunts coming from a room behind a threadbare curtain and was certain of it. How disappointing someone could take such a beautiful act and make it sound like a couple hogs wallowing in mud, he thought.

The important thing was that he didn't immediately recognize any of the men in the place, although there was a good chance they all had prices on their heads. A couple of them looked familiar, and he had a hunch that if he tried hard enough, he could dredge up their names from his memories of the WANTED posters he had studied, but he didn't care enough to go to that much effort. As long as they didn't bother him, he wouldn't bother them.

When his eyes had adjusted to the dim interior and he was sure he had taken note of everyone, he walked over to the bar. He nodded to the two grizzled drinkers, who just looked at him with blank expressions.

To Jeremiah Beebe behind the bar, he said, "I don't suppose you have any wine, do you?"

"Wine," Beebe repeated. "Mister, I got beer— which I brew my own self—and whiskey—which I also brew my own self—and that's what you got to choose from."

"Which one has fewer rattlesnake heads in it?"

Beebe drew himself up and glared. "I don't put rattlesnake heads in my liquor. What do you take me for, a Mexican?"

"Mexicans put worms in their liquor, not snakes."

"Well, either way, I sell only the highest quality stuff here. Now, you want a drink or not?"

"I suppose I'll try the beer," the stranger said mildly.

"Hmmph." Beebe dipped a tin mug in an open barrel and set it in front of the man. "Four bits."

The man picked up the mug and angled it so that he could look into it by the light of the oil lamp. He saw things wiggling in it, then said, "The price is a bit steep, but I suppose since the beer comes with bonus ingredients, that justifies the cost." He set the mug back on the plank bar and pushed it away slightly.

"I dipped it, you pay for it," Beebe said, tapping the end of a sausage-like finger on the bar.

"Of course." The stranger reached into a coat pocket with his left hand, took out a half-dollar, and slid it across the planks.

Beebe made the coin disappear. "If you just come in here to make sport of my place, I'll thank you to leave."

"Actually, I'm looking for someone. Mitch Clark. You know him?"

"I don't know nobody," Beebe answered with a scowl.

"How about Curly Weaver? He rides with Clark. Jimmy Pugh? Hector Gomez? Jed Darby?" The stranger paused. "If you've seen them, I can make it worth your while."

Beebe frowned. "I don't like strangers who come in here askin' a bunch of—"

"I know you. You're Luke Smith," interrupted one of the men at the bar, pointing a finger at the man.

"Actually," said the stranger, "I go by Luke Jensen now."

"You're a damn bounty hunter!"

All around the room, hands flashed toward guns.

CHAPTER 9

Luke wasn't surprised by the reaction of the men in the road ranch, even though he wasn't after any of them in particular. He had taken up the profession of bounty hunting not long after the end of the Civil War, when he had healed enough from the injuries inflicted on him by men who were supposed to be on the same side he was.

A lot of years had passed since then. A lot of men had fallen to his guns, and even more had wound up behind bars or dancing at the end of a hangman's rope because of him. Word got around among the men on the other side of the law. They had heard of Luke Smith, as he had called himself then, and many of them now knew he was really Luke Jensen, older brother to the famous gunfighter Smoke Jensen.

And most of them hated him. He represented a force for law and order who wasn't afraid to use the same sort of violent tactics the outlaws did.

Because of his natural wariness, Luke had no

trouble letting his instincts take over as soon as he realized he was in the middle of a hornet's nest. He
swept his coat back and his hands moved with blind-
ing speed to the butts of the twin Remington revolvers
he carried in cross-draw rigs. He half-turned as he
drew the guns, putting his left side toward the bar.
The gun in his left hand roared and spouted flame as
he fired at the man closest to him in that direction,
who happened to be the one who had first recognized him.

The slug punched into the man's chest and knocked
him back a step into his companion, interfering with
the second man's draw. Luke was aiming from the
corner of his eye as he continued to turn. The left-
hand gun blasted again, and the bullet went through
the second man's mouth as he started to yell a curse.
The hot lead smashed through the lower part of his
brain and exploded out the back of his skull, leaving
him dead as could be even though he was still on his
feet.

Before either of those men had a chance to fall,
Luke had opened fire with the right-hand Remington on the poker players, all three of whom had
flung their cards away as they bolted up out of their
chairs and clawed at their guns. The first man hadn't
cleared leather when he died, Luke's bullet ripping
through his throat and knocking him backwards as
blood fountained from the grisly wound.

The second card player got his gun out, but it was
still pointed at the table when a slug from the Remington drove deep into his gut and folded him double. He
pitched forward onto the table, leaking blood onto
the scattered pasteboards and the money in the pot.

Only the third man who'd been in the game got a shot off. It went considerably wide and smashed a bottle on a shelf behind the bar. Glass and homemade whiskey sprayed over the back of Jeremiah Beebe, who was fumbling underneath the bar for something. He flinched automatically from the shower, which slowed him down long enough for Luke to kill the third card player with a bullet to the chest and then finish his spinning move.

The gun in Luke's right hand smacked against the side of Beebe's head just as the man came up with a shotgun. The blow sent his hat flying and made him drop the shotgun. He sagged over the bar, moaning as he put both hands to his head and the bloody gash that Luke's gun had opened up.

Even with all the shots echoing in the place, Luke heard the curtain over the doorway being ripped aside. He twisted in that direction in time to see the final man emerge from the room where he'd been occupied with one of the squaws. Even a little tangled in the curtain, he managed to have a gun in his hand, and orange flame spouted from the muzzle as he fired.

That shot went wild, too, but Luke's didn't. He used the left-hand Remington to drill the man between the eyes. The bullet's impact jerked his head back, but his momentum made him fall forward to land heavily on his face. Already dead, he didn't feel any pain. He wore a set of long underwear with the back flap hanging open, and Luke wondered briefly just what the hell he'd been doing in there.

"Yaaaaahhhhh!"

The furious scream made Luke turn toward the

Indian woman standing at the far end of the bar. A long-bladed knife was in her hand raised over her head, ready to strike as she charged at him.

Luke leveled the right-hand Remington at her and eared back the hammer. The woman stopped as short as she could, her face still contorted in anger.

"Go ahead and shoot her," said the woman in the other corner who had been mending clothes. She still held one of the garments in her hands. "She is a filthy Crow and deserves to die."

Luke grunted. "You must be the Blackfoot one."

The woman shrugged and turned her attention back to her mending.

Keeping the woman at the bar covered with the Remington, he said, "I'm sure you understand English. Drop the knife."

"You hurt Jeremiah," she accused.

Luke glanced at Beebe, who was still slumped over the bar holding his head in his hands and whimpering.

"Hell, he hasn't even passed out. In case you haven't noticed, he's still alive, which is more than any of those other men can say."

That was true. The other six men were dead, gunned down by Luke in about as many seconds. It had been an incredible display of deadly gun handling, but he didn't take any pride in it. The grim, ugly business was just something he had to be extremely good at in order to stay alive.

Beebe finally looked up. "Damn it, woman, put that knife down. You think this man won't kill you just because you're a squaw?"

"You'd be wise to do as he says," Luke added.

The woman blew her breath out disgustedly, set the knife on the bar, and gave it a shove so that it slid along the planks out of her reach.

Luke let the hammer down carefully on the gun he had pointed at her. "Sorry about busting your head like that, Beebe. It could have been worse, though."

"Yeah, I reckon. I suppose you'll want all the money they've got in their pockets?"

"I'm not a common thief. Where's the nearest town with a lawman, a telegraph office, and a bank?"

"That'd be Selby. Two-day ride from here."

"South?"

"Yeah."

Luke considered and nodded. That was the direction he'd been going anyway. He could cover some of the ground today and make it to Selby by the day after tomorrow, leading the dead men's horses. The bodies would be pretty ripe by the time he got there, although the cold weather certainly would help on that score.

If it had been just one man, he might have said forget it and told Beebe to plant the carcass out back somewhere. But after going to the trouble to kill all six of them, Luke wanted to get something out of that much work.

Besides, even if the individual rewards weren't that big, they might add up to a substantial chunk of change.

"You can have what's in their pockets," he told Beebe. "That might pay for the damages, although I'm not sure. After all, that *was* a bottle of your finest high quality liquor that got broken."

"I do the best I can here to scrape by," Beebe said sullenly. "You don't have to make fun o' me."

"No, I suppose not. You're right, Mr. Beebe. My apologies. The smell of gun smoke and freshly spilled blood sometimes puts me in a disagreeable mood."

Beebe said, "Unnnhhhh . . ." and waved off the apology with a hand smeared with blood from the cut on his head.

Some business remained unfinished.

Luke said, "We were talking about some other gentlemen before all that unpleasantness broke out."

"You mean before you started gunnin' down ever'-body in the place?"

"Self-defense, Mr. Beebe, self-defense. Now, about Mitch Clark and the men who usually ride with him . . ."

"After all this"—Beebe stared at him and waved at the carnage—"you expect me to help you?"

"I expect you to be grateful I didn't kill you, too," Luke said bluntly. "Not to mention, I *did* agree to let you keep whatever is in their pockets without even checking them first."

"Yeah, yeah." Beebe took a deep breath and sighed. "Clark and some o' his friends were here a couple days ago. Curly Weaver was with him . . . and Jed Darby. There were two more, some greaser I didn't know and a kid wearin' these real thick spectacles. I didn't catch either o' their names."

"Hector Gomez and Blind Jimmy," Luke murmured.

"Could be, but you couldn't prove it by me."

"Which way were they going when they headed out?"

"South," Beebe replied with a nod in that direction, then winced, the movement making his head hurt.

"Did you happen to hear them say anything about where they were going or what their plans were?"

"No, I—" Beebe stopped short and frowned in what appeared to be genuine thought. "Wait a minute. I think I overhead one of 'em mention a name . . . Beaver? Was that it?" He answered his own question, saying, "No, no, hang on. There's no owlhoot named Beaver, for God's sake. Bleeker! That was it. One of 'em said somethin' about a fella named Bleeker."

Luke frowned. "Jim Bleeker?"

"I dunno, mister. I've already remembered more 'n I thought I was likely to. I don't pay much attention to what these damn owlhoots go on about. Hell, it'd drive me loco if I did!"

Luke nodded slowly. The name *Bleeker* was familiar to him, of course. There had been a time, several years earlier, when Jim Bleeker had a big bounty on his head. Luke had never had a chance to collect it. He had never crossed Bleeker's trail before the man wound up in prison down in . . .

Texas, Luke thought it was. *Yes, San Antonio was where he'd been caught.*

Luke hadn't heard anything about Jim Bleeker since then. Was it possible the man was out of prison and putting together a new gang? Luke supposed it was, although it didn't seem to him like enough time had gone by for that. Bleeker should have been behind bars for a long time yet.

"There's nothing else you can tell me?" Luke prodded Beebe.

"My hand to God, mister," the man said, "there sure ain't."

"All right." Luke stepped over to one of the tables, set one of the Remingtons on it within easy reach, and started reloading the other gun. He picked up the one on the table and did the same then pouched both irons. "I'll saddle the horses in the corral, then load up these men and get them out of here. You can go through their pockets while I'm tending to the horses. I'm afraid you'll have to clean up the blood-stains yourself."

"Oh, hell," Beebe said, "I'll get one of the squaws to do that."

Luke was turning away when a woman's voice said softly, "Mister."

He stopped and looked over at the doorway to the room where the Indian women carried out their business. The third woman, the one he hadn't seen until then, stood there halfway behind the jamb, ner-vous like a deer about to bolt. She had a blanket wrapped around her with one smooth brown shoul-der showing. She was younger and more attractive than the other two.

The Shoshone, he thought. "Yes, miss?"

"The men you asked about . . . when they were here . . . the one with the"—she gestured vaguely at her eyes—"the one who cannot see well."

"Blind Jimmy Pugh," Luke said.

"When he was . . . with me . . . he said something about them going to Denver. He said they were going there to see a man named Morley about a job . . . and when they were finished with it, they would all be rich. He said he would come back here . . . and get me and take me away."

Beebe snorted. "The hell he will. Men always get carried away and say things like that to women like you. They don't mean it."

Luke ignored the man and said to the young woman, "You're sure he mentioned Denver and Morley?"

She nodded, tentatively at first, then with more certainty. "I knew not to believe him . . . but I think he meant it when he said it."

"I'm sure he did," Luke told her gently. He reached up and pinched the brim of his black hat. "I'm very much obliged to you for your help, miss." He reached in his pocket, took out another half-dollar, and moved over to the doorway with the coin held out to her. He had to step around the dead man with his bare rear end hanging out of the longhandles. The woman pulled back at first, clearly frightened, then snatched the coin from his fingers.

"Do you need to get away from this place?" Luke asked her quietly.

He could tell that she considered the idea, but only for a second. "Where else would one like me go?"

She had a point there, he supposed, and besides, he wasn't in the business of saving souls.

He was in the business of bringing outlaws to justice, by any means necessary.

At the moment, that meant hauling those carcasses to the nearest star packer, collecting whatever rewards were offered for them, and then heading for Denver to see what he could find out about a man named Morley who was looking to hire gunmen and killers.

And maybe, just maybe, how all that was connected to the infamous Jim Bleeker.

CHAPTER 10

New York City

The overcast of the day before had broken up without any snow or sleet falling, so Mercy Halliday was prepared to take that as a good omen. There were still clouds, but a brilliant blue sky showed through the gaps. Dressed in a dark green traveling outfit, she was perched on the seat of a wagon being driven through the streets toward the railroad station. A large black man named Nicodemus—handyman at the orphanage—handled the reins.

"You children quiet down back there," he said over his shoulder in his deep, powerful voice. "You don't want to spook these horses with all your chatterin'."

Ten children, ranging in ages from six to fourteen, sat in the back of the wagon clutching bundles that contained their few meager belongings. Naturally, they were excited. They were setting out on a journey that would end with them being adopted into loving homes. That was what they all hoped for, anyway, and so they were laughing and talking among themselves with great anticipation.

Mercy glanced at them. Well, nine out of the ten are excited, she thought.

Caleb, his paper-wrapped bundle in his hands, was just sitting there, looking straight ahead and saying nothing.

Another wagon followed with Peter Gallagher handling the team. Like the first one, it carried ten orphans destined for new homes somewhere in the West. He wasn't nearly as adept with the reins as the black handyman, but he managed to keep the wagon moving. His wife Grace sat beside him, bundled in a thick coat. Despite the sunshine, it was a chilly day, and she had often mentioned how cold weather didn't agree with her thin blood.

The wagons pulled up in front of the massive train station. Mercy, Peter, and Grace supervised the unloading of the children and ushered them inside the cavernous building. Nicodemus would return one of the empty wagons to the orphanage, then walk back to get the other one.

When Mercy came back outside to bid him a quick farewell, he told her, "You be careful out there, Miss Mercy. It's wild country."

"I've been West before, Nicodemus," she reminded him. "This isn't my first trip."

"No, ma'am. But you ain't ever been as far west as you're goin' this time, and from what I hear, the farther west you goes, the more dangerous that frontier gets."

"You mean from what you read in the dime novels

and the *Police Gazette*," she said, but her warm smile took any sting out of the words.

"You know I was born a slave down in Georgia, miss."

"Yes, of course," Mercy said solemnly.

"They wouldn't allow us to learn how to read. That's been one o' the best things about bein' freed and comin' up here. I purely do love to read."

"I'm glad you learned," she told him. "Don't worry about me. I'll be fine. Mr. and Mrs. Gallagher will be with me all the time, and from what I hear, California is actually quite civilized."

Nicodemus looked skeptical. "Beggin' your pardon, Miss Mercy, but the idea o' Mr. Gallagher bein' around don't exactly fill me with confidence."

"Peter does the best he can—"

"You best keep an eye on *him*, too," Nicodemus said.

Mercy knew he was right, so there was no point in arguing with him. "I do hope this trip works out well for Caleb. Of all the children we're taking with us this time, he seems to be the most in need of a good home."

Nicodemus nodded gravely. "That little fella's carryin' around a mighty big weight o' some kind, that's for sure. It's so heavy he can't even bring himself to talk. Maybe a new family could lighten that load for him."

"I certainly hope and pray that's how it turns out." She came up on her toes and brushed a quick kiss across the handyman's silver-stubbled cheek. "Goodbye, Nicodemus. I'll see you when we get back."

"So long, miss. Godspeed to you."

She went back into the station, joining the stream of humanity that thronged the place. It was even busier than usual. With Christmas coming up soon, a lot of people were traveling to see family.

If all went as planned, she would still be in California for Christmas, far from her own remaining relatives. In recent years, she hadn't been as close to them. Her work . . . and the children . . . had become her family.

Someone jostled her, and she felt a brief flash of anger. It faded quickly because of her forgiving nature.

When the man who had bumped into her said, "Sorry, ma'am," she responded with a smile.

"That's quite all right," she told him. "No harm done."

"Well, I'd like to make it up to you anyway. If you've got a bag, I'd be glad to carry it for you."

"My bags have already been loaded, but thank you anyway. There's really no need for you to worry."

"If you say so." He smiled, which made his stern face appear not so forbidding. He was tall and on the lean side, with brown hair under the fedora he wore. He stuck his hands in the pockets of his overcoat and went on. "Where are you bound?"

"Sacramento." She couldn't stop herself from adding, "Not that it's any of your business, sir."

He chuckled. "Then I beg your pardon again. I'm just naturally inquisitive, I guess. Sacramento's nearly all the way at the other end of the country. That's a long trip."

"Yes, it is. And I have to be going now. . . ."

"Of course." He touched a finger to the brim of his hat. "Can you say *bon voyage* to someone who's leaving on a train instead of a ship?"

"I don't see why not."

"Then, bon voyage, Miss—" He stopped a little awkwardly.

Mercy thought for a second he'd been about to call her by name, but that was impossible, of course, since she had never been introduced to him or even seen him before their inconsequential collision a few moments earlier.

"Good-bye." She turned and made her way toward the platform where the train bound for Sacramento was waiting.

Peter, Grace, and the children were all aboard, and soon they would be on their way to the destiny that waited for them.

Well, that was almost an extremely stupid mistake, Ed Rinehart told himself as he watched Miss Mercy Halliday weaving through the crowd toward the platforms. He had almost called the young woman by name when she was supposed to be just as much a stranger to him as he was to her. He wasn't sure why he had almost made such an uncharacteristic slip-up.

Surely it couldn't be because of that auburn hair or those devastatingly green eyes. . . .

William Litchfield hadn't said anything about the woman's hair or eyes the day before when he was telling Rinehart and Cap Shaw about the Children's Aid Society and the people who worked there. The detective thought back to the conversation.

* * *

"They're devoted to finding homes for orphaned children," Litchfield said as he sat in front of Shaw's desk holding his wife's hand. "I've made donations to them myself, and it's a cause my late brother supported wholeheartedly. They take the children on trains and transport them to locations in the western part of the country where there are people looking to adopt."

"That sounds like a very worthy effort, Mr. Litchfield," Shaw said, "but with all due respect, what does it have to do with the murders of your brother and his wife, and your missing nephew?"

Rinehart was glad the captain asked the question, because he'd been wondering the same thing.

Litchfield drew in a deep breath. "I believe that Donald may have wound up amongst those orphans. In fact, I think there's a good chance he's one of a group being taken to California tomorrow."

Litchfield's declaration made Rinehart want to stare. A glance at Shaw told him the captain felt the same way, but both men managed to control their reaction.

Shaw merely pursed his lips and asked, "What makes you think that?"

"I told you, the police believe Donald escaped from the mansion on the night of the murders. He had to go somewhere. The detectives checked all the hospitals and the . . . morgue."

His wife made a slightly choked sound and tightened her hand on his.

"No bodies matching my nephew's description were found that night or the next several days," Litchfield went on. "In fact, I've seen to it that the detectives keep checking those *places, and ever since that terrible night, no bodies resembling Donald have ever turned up."*

That could just mean that the murderers had caught up to the boy after all and concealed the body so well that it hadn't been found, but Rinehart knew the Litchfields didn't want to hear that. He glanced at Shaw again, and saw that same thought in the captain's gaze.

"Donald has to be somewhere," Litchfield said. "What better place for a child to hide than among other children? He had been there at the orphanage before, you see, when Grant and Claire visited the place. He would have known that he'd be able to blend in there."

Rinehart couldn't help but say, "You're giving a six-year-old a lot of credit, Mr. Litchfield. If he was as scared as you say, he probably wouldn't be thinking straight enough to realize he could hide out at an orphanage."

"Well, perhaps it was all instinctive on his part, without any real, coherent thought."

"Maybe," Rinehart said with a shrug, although he didn't really believe it.

"Mr. Litchfield," Captain Shaw said, "it's been six months. Did this business about the Children's Aid Society just occur to you?"

"That's right. And it might not have even now if I hadn't come across some papers of my brother's dealing with his support of the institution."

"I'm not trying to beat the agency out of a fee, but why don't you go to the police, have them visit the orphanage and see if Donald is there?"

"Because"—Litchfield looked down at the floor, cleared his throat, and glared—"because I'm afraid. You see, someone wanted my brother dead."

Rinehart asked, "Do you mean you're afraid for yourself? Surely it was just a botched robbery or something of that sort. That wouldn't represent any threat to you."

Litchfield shook his head stubbornly and snapped, "I never said I was afraid for my own safety. It's Donald I'm concerned about. And I don't believe the killings were any sort of botched robbery. The men who killed Grant and Claire were sent there to murder them that night, pure and simple. I'm convinced that they intended to kill Donald as well. But they missed him somehow, and whoever was behind the crime may still desire to have him killed."

Shaw said slowly, "I think I understand. You didn't want to tip off the killers by involving the police."

"To put it bluntly, I no longer trust the police," Litchfield declared. "Grant had many enemies, one of whom must have hated him enough to set those killers on him. I have no way of knowing whether that man, whoever he is, may have paid off some of the detectives on the case to help him find Donald."

Rinehart rubbed his chin and frowned in thought for a moment. "You might be right about that, sir. There are plenty of coppers on the force who aren't exactly honest. No more than they have to be, anyway."

"I know that, and that's why I've come to you gentlemen with my theory," Litchfield said. "Your agency has a reputation for the utmost honesty and discretion."

"That's the only way we can stay in business," Shaw pointed out.

"I made inquiries at the Society—in the guise of being one of their benefactors, you know—and discovered that a group of children is leaving tomorrow, as I mentioned. Among them are several boys of Donald's approximate age."

Rinehart said, "It would be easy enough to go down there and have a look at them for yourself. You'd know your nephew if you saw him, I take it?"

"Of course," Litchfield replied, sounding irritated by the question.

Reasonably so, Rinehart supposed.

"But you see, I don't want him found just yet."

Shaw frowned and shook his head. "I'm afraid I don't follow you."

"I'm hiring your agency for a two-pronged assignment," Litchfield said. "I want a man to go with those orphans and keep a watch over them, noting where all the boys who might be Donald wind up. At the same time, I want the rest of the available resources of this office devoted to the task of finding evidence that will prove which of my brother's business rivals was behind his murder."

"The police have already investigated the case. If they made no progress—"

"As we've already discussed, I'm not convinced that the police have given the matter their best effort."

That's convoluted and more than a little paranoid, but there might be something to it, Rinehart mused. Anybody rich enough to want Grant Litchfield out of the way could probably afford to pay off the coppers. All that would be necessary to steer the case down all the wrong blind alleys were a few detectives on the take.

"If you want to find out who's behind this," Rinehart said, "then I'm your man. I can get started right away—"

"No, Mr. Rinehart, I want you to go with the Orphan Train," Litchfield broke in. "Captain Shaw says you're his best man, and I'm relying on you to keep my nephew safe while the agency's other operatives break the case here in New York."

Rinehart stared in surprise for a moment before he said, "You want me to . . . go West? Out to the frontier?"

Litchfield nodded solemnly. "I think that would be best, yes."

Detective Rinehart shook his head and grumbled, "Of course, what the client wants, the client gets, as long as it's within reason." His boss was the one who determined what was reasonable, and he'd agreed with William Litchfield.

That was how Ed Rinehart found himself on the station platform, about to climb onto a train bound for Chicago and points west, all the way to California. All the way across vast stretches of the continent where, it seemed to him, civilization had barely taken hold. He had no idea what to expect, other than the fact that it would be savage and primitive.

When the conductor shouted the all-aboard, Rinehart took a deep breath and went up the steps of the nearest car. It was his job, after all.

CHAPTER 11

The Litchfield mansion,
Riverside Drive, New York City,
the previous evening

William Litchfield paced back and forth in front of the crackling blaze in the fireplace. The heat felt good, but it didn't seem to reach quite all the way to the cold core at the center of his being. He had been chilled for months, and it seemed that the malady would never go away.

He had a snifter of the finest brandy in his hand, but he had forgotten it momentarily as his thoughts wandered. He paused in his pacing and looked around the opulently furnished study where he stood.

Everything bespoke wealth, from the paneled walls to the overstuffed furniture to the valuable paintings on the walls. A large bookcase filled with beautiful leather-bound volumes took up most of one side of the room. The brass fittings of the gas lamps gleamed in the warm light.

It had been his brother's room, and Litchfield

seemed to feel him there, despite the passage of time. In fact, the presence of Grant and Claire still permeated the entire mansion. Litchfield had been opposed to moving in after the murders—he and his wife had a perfectly good house of their own out on Long Island, after all—but Deirdre had insisted, and as happened most of the time, she got what she wanted.

Litchfield looked down at the drink in his hand as if he were surprised to find that he was holding it, then lifted the snifter to his lips and drained the rest of the brandy. Like the blaze in the fireplace, it warmed him . . . but not enough to get rid of that infernal persistent chill.

A light tapping sounded on the study door. He set the empty snifter on a sideboard and turned in that direction. "Yes?"

An elderly man in butler's livery opened the door. He had a round, florid face and a mostly bald head. In a British accent—the best butlers were British, Deirdre had decided—he said, "There's a *gentleman* here to see you, sir." It was clear from the servant's tone that he didn't think the visitor was a gentleman at all.

Litchfield had been expecting it. He had sent word to the visitor earlier in the day that he needed to see him. He told the butler, "Send him in, Hennings."

"Of course, sir," Hennings murmured, still vaguely disapproving of the whole matter.

The stuffy old goat didn't dislike the situation any more than he did, thought Litchfield. Things were as they were, and nothing could be done except try to make the best of everything.

The butler withdrew, leaving the study door slightly ajar. Litchfield thought about pouring himself another drink but decided not to. If he had a drink in his hand when the man came in, he would feel like he had to offer him one as well.

And Litchfield didn't want to have a drink with Laird Kingsley as if the two of them were friends. It was bad enough he had to do business with the man.

The door opened and Kingsley walked in. The suit he wore was well-cut and cost quite a bit, though nowhere near as much as Litchfield's suit, of course. The man's thick dark hair was combed sleekly across his head. He was clean-shaven, although he was the sort where dark stubble began to appear within an hour of him taking a razor to his face.

He smiled. He fancied himself suave and liked to put on airs, liked to act as if he were just as good as the people in the circles he aspired to, but of course he wasn't. Under that smooth façade was a hooligan, a common criminal just like his father and grandfather. Litchfield had looked into the man's background. His grandfather had been Bloody Tom Kingsley, leader of the gang that had ruled a good portion of New York's underworld forty years earlier.

Laird Kingsley might dress himself up, but the blood of murderers and brutes still ran in his veins.

"You wanted to see me, Mr. Litchfield?" he asked.

"That's right. There's been a new development in the case."

For just a second, Kingsley's eyes opened a little wider, and a look appeared in them like one that might have been seen in the eyes of a wild animal caught in a trap. Then he regained control of himself and asked, "Oh? What sort of development?"

"I believe I know where my nephew is hiding."

That atavistic gleam appeared in Kingsley's eyes again, but he banished it even more quickly and murmured, "Is that right?"

"Have you heard of the Children's Aid Society?"

Kingsley seemed to think about that question, then shook his head. "I can't say as I have."

"They're the ones who put together those so-called Orphan Trains the newspapers talk about. They take children who have lost their homes and families and place them with families in the West."

"Well," mused Kingsley, "Donald *is* an orphan."

For a second, Litchfield felt a wave of red rage go through him. He wanted to grab one of the several fireplace pokers leaning in a stand close beside him, sweep it up, and smash the man's evil brains out.

But of course that was impossible. If he attacked Kingsley, in all likelihood the man would take the poker away and use it against him until all the life had been pounded from him. It wouldn't be the first time Kingsley had beaten a man to death. Litchfield was certain of that.

"Tell me where the place is," Kingsley went on. "I'll take some men and go down there later tonight—"

"No," Litchfield interrupted. "Good Lord, no. There's been enough notoriety here in New York. If some orphan is mysteriously killed, the press will come clamoring around and might discover the truth."

Kingsley shook his head and waved a hand dismissively. "I think you're worrying too much, Mr. Litchfield. The press doesn't give a damn what happens to orphans. Nobody cares about them except a few do-gooders like this . . . what did you call it? The Children's Aid Society?"

"I want things done properly this time," Litchfield snapped.

Kingsley's handsome face hardened as he said, "Listen, what happened before wasn't my fault. We've been over that a dozen times. None of us knew the kid had discovered that old smuggler's tunnel leading out to the carriage house. I had all the doors and windows covered so nobody could get out. If he'd tried to escape that way, one of my men would've nabbed him."

"There's no need to rehash all that now," Litchfield said coldly. "It's enough for me to tell you how I want things done. You work for me, after all."

"Well, there's that," Kingsley admitted with a shrug. "How do you want me to handle it?"

"I believe that Donald will be among the group of children heading West on a train tomorrow. The train is bound for California. You and as many of your men as you deem necessary will follow on the next train."

"Why not just go on the same train?"

Litchfield shook his head. "No, I don't want anything that could possibly ever lead back to me. That's why I deal only with you, and your men have no idea who your employer is. Correct?"

"Sure. I've kept 'em in the dark. They don't care who they're working for as long as they get paid."

"And paid well, I might add." Litchfield took a deep breath and clasped his hands together behind his back. "You'll be close enough behind the lad that

once you're in California, you can find him and . . .
take care of the matter . . . before there's been enough
time for him to be adopted. Make it appear to be an
accident if you can . . . run over by a carriage or a
wagon in the street, something like that. But if you
can't, just use your best judgment. It'll be a tragedy . . .
a young boy going all the way to California to find a
new home, only to be killed before that can happen . . .
but it'll be on the other side of the continent and no
one will ever think to connect it with anything that happened here."

"And you'll be safe." Kingsley looked around.
"Safe in your brother's house, with your brother's
money."

Litchfield stiffened and burst out, "Damn you!"

"I'm not judging you, Mr. Litchfield. It's none of
my business. Just saying that once this is taken care
of, you'll be in the clear."

With an effort, Litchfield brought his anger under
control. "There's one more thing."

"What's that?"

"I've engaged a detective agency to investigate the
case here in New York and send an operative west
with the orphans to keep an eye on them."

Kingsley's eyes widened again, with surprise instead of fear. "Why in the hell would you do that?" he
demanded.

"For appearance sake, of course. It has to look like
I'm still devastated by my brother's murder. As far as
everyone else is concerned, I must be the benevolent
uncle, still searching for my poor nephew. If by some
chance the boy in California is ever identified as

Donald, no one will suspect me because, after all, I was trying to protect the child, wasn't I?"

For a long moment, Kingsley stared at him, then said, "No offense, Mr. Litchfield, but you think too much. You didn't need to do all this. But I suppose it's too late to stop what you've set in motion—"

"It is."

"So we'll just make sure this detective you've hired doesn't get in the way. If he does, too bad for him." Kingsley rubbed his chin and frowned. "Or maybe once he's served his purpose, it would be better for him to die in an accident, too. Lots of people do, you know." His tone became brisk. "What about the agency's operatives here? What if they poke around enough to uncover the truth?"

Litchfield shook his head. "That won't happen because they'll be following clues that I provide, clues that will implicate Grant's business enemies and send them along one false trail after another. They'll stay busy carrying out a very earnest investigation, but in the end it will come to nothing and I'll dismiss them, as anyone in my situation would do."

"If it all works, you'll wind up behind a wall of respectability that no one will ever penetrate," Kingsley admitted.

"None of this would have been necessary if the job had been completed as planned six months ago."

"Back to that, are we?" Kingsley smiled humorlessly and shook his head. "All right, we'll leave it. Anything else?"

"No. You understand?"

"Sure. It might help if I knew more about those

people from the Society, so I'll know who we may be dealing with."

Litchfield turned to his desk, picked up an envelope, and held it out to his visitor. "I took the liberty of preparing such information."

"Good. Who's this detective who's going with the kids? You know his name?"

"Rinehart, I believe it is. He seemed like a competent man."

"Competent or not, if we have to take care of him, he'll never see it coming." Kingsley said good night and left the study.

Once the man was gone, the iron grip that Litchfield had maintained on his emotions slipped somewhat. He went to the desk, leaned over and rested his fists on its polished top, and took several deep, shuddery breaths.

He was still standing like that when the door opened again. He straightened and started to turn, saying, "There won't be anything else tonight, Hennings—" He stopped short when he saw that it wasn't the butler who had come into the room. His wife stood there in a silk dressing gown, her long dark hair brushed out so that it hung around her shoulders, as beautiful as ever.

"Mr. Kingsley was here?" asked Deirdre.

"Yes, he was."

"And everything will soon be as it should be?"

"Of course." Litchfield forced a smile onto his face. "I promised you that all would be as you wanted it, didn't I, my darling?"

"You did," Deirdre said, smiling back at him. "And I appreciate you so much for that, my dearest." She lifted her arms. The loose sleeves of the robe fell back slightly on her smooth, pale skin. "Come here."

He went to her—he could never resist any invitation she issued—and embraced her trim waist as she put her arms around him. One hand patted him lightly on the back.

"Everything will be all right," she murmured. "You'll see. You'll see."

He wanted to believe her, but he wished that cold spot buried deep inside him would warm up.

CHAPTER 12

Sugarloaf Ranch

As Smoke had predicted, Sally was very happy to see Preacher. When the three men rode up to the ranch house the next day after the encounter with the panther, she came out onto the porch and smiled broadly at the old mountain man. "Preacher!" she exclaimed. "I didn't expect to see you here this year."

He glanced over at Smoke, then said, "Well, you know how I am, Miss Sally. I'm like that ol' bad penny folks talk about. You never know when I'm a-gonna show up."

"I don't think you're a bad penny at all. I've got fried chicken just about ready for lunch. You *are* staying for a while, aren't you?"

"I don't think you could run me off with a stick," Preacher told her with a big grin on his whiskery face.

As they'd approached the Sugarloaf, he had asked Smoke not to say anything to her about Eagle-Eye Callahan's unjustified vendetta. "I know she'd prob'ly understand, but it's a leetle embarrassin', findin' out at my age that some other hombre's wife was pinin' away for me all those years. I'da been just fine never knowin' about the way she felt, and I'm sure ol' Eagle-Eye woulda been, too."

"I won't say anything," Smoke had promised.

"I'll keep my mouth shut, too," Cal had added.

"If Eagle-Eye shows up, Sally will have to be told what's going on. It might not be safe for her not to know."

Preacher had nodded glumly at Smoke's warning. "Yeah, the last thing I want to do is put you folks in any danger. Reckon you're as close to family as anybody I got left. I don't think you got anything to worry about, though. Eagle-Eye's plumb peaceable when it comes to ever'body 'cept me."

As Sally came down the porch steps to greet the men, Dog, Preacher's big wolf-like cur, moved up to her and sniffed her hand, then nuzzled against it. Most folks were scared of the vicious-looking creature, and if they meant Preacher any harm they were right to feel that way since Dog could tear out a bad man's throat practically in the blink of an eye.

Sally and Dog were well-acquainted, though. His tongue lolled out of his mouth and he grinned happily as she scratched his ears and said, "Who's a good dog?"

Smoke, Preacher, and Cal had swung down from their saddles, and Smoke was ready to embrace his wife when she went into his arms. Even though they hadn't been separated for that long—this time—their hug was passionate and heartfelt. Sally tilted her face up, and Smoke kissed her. Their lips clung together only briefly, but the kiss packed a lot of punch.

She hugged Preacher, too, patting the old mountain man on the back.

Cal said, "You know, Miss Sally, Preacher's the one who bagged that panther. That big cat was just about to jump on Smoke when Preacher drilled it, clean as a whistle. And that was in the dark!"

"Really?" Sally said, arching an eyebrow at Smoke. "You nearly let yourself get eaten up by a panther?"

"Well, I don't know that it would have turned out that way," Smoke said, "but I was obliged to Preacher for being such a good shot, that's for sure."

Since Sally still had her arms around Preacher, she hugged him again and brushed a kiss across his leathery cheek. "Then I'm obliged to you, too, for not letting that panther get Smoke."

"Some o' that fried chicken you mentioned would go a long way toward settlin' the score," Preacher told her. "And maybe some pie if you got any."

"Of course!"

"Fried chicken and pie," Smoke drawled as they went inside. "Nice to know what my life's worth around here."

After they had eaten lunch, Sally said to Smoke, "I need to go into Big Rock this afternoon. Now that you're back, you can come along with me."

"Why are you going to Big Rock?"

"Some of the ladies from the churches are getting together to finish organizing the Christmas Eve celebration and the midnight service."

Every year, Smoke knew, all the churches in the settlement got together in spite of their denominational differences and threw a party to celebrate the Lord's birth. If the weather wasn't too bad, they would build a bonfire and have the gathering outside, setting up tables loaded with food until they practically groaned. After the meal there would be games for the children and everyone would sing Christmas carols before one of the town's ministers conducted a traditional Christmas Eve service. When conditions didn't permit that, everyone crowded into one of the churches or the town hall and the party went on as planned. It was one of the highlights of the year, especially for the children and the ladies. And the men didn't mind all that much and actually enjoyed it, although some of them wouldn't have admitted it.

That didn't mean Smoke wanted to take part in the planning for the event, so he began, "You don't really need my help for that—"

"Of course we don't," Sally said with a smile. "But I thought that maybe if you and Preacher came along, you could go down to Louis's and have a nice visit with him while I'm meeting with the ladies."

The thought of spending some time at Louis Longmont's saloon was a lot more appealing. Smoke grinned. "Now you're talking."

A short time later, while some of the hands hitched up the buggy horse for Sally, Smoke and Preacher saddled mounts from the ranch's stock for themselves. Preacher was going to leave his big gray stallion—which he called Horse, of course—at the ranch, since the animal had put a lot of miles behind him over the past few weeks and could use some rest.

Sally came out of the house wearing a dark blue dress and a gray wool jacket. She had a blue bonnet tied over her lustrous dark hair. Smoke helped her into the buggy, then mounted up. She wouldn't need a driver. Sally could handle anything from a buggy horse to a twenty-mule team if she had to. For a girl born and raised in the East, she had adapted quickly to life out on the frontier, thanks to Smoke's influence.

A short-barreled Winchester carbine was behind the seat in the buggy, and Sally could handle that quite well, too, if the need arose. Smoke didn't expect that to happen, but his adventurous life had taught him never to take peace for granted.

As they rode the seven or so miles to Big Rock, Preacher squinted at the thick gray clouds overhead, sniffed the air, and announced, "Gonna snow."

"Today?" Smoke asked.

"Naw, I don't reckon. But tonight, maybe."

"Are we talking about a blizzard or just a little dusting?"

"What do I look like to you, one o' them dang Gypsy fortune-tellers? You see me carryin' around a crystal ball?"

Smoke grinned. "I figured you knew just about everything there is to know, that's all."

That seemed to mollify Preacher. "You mean on account of how I'm so wise."

"No, I mean on account of how you're so old."

"Dadblast it, boy, if it weren't so much durned trouble, I'd take off this ol' hat o' mine and lambaste you with it for a while. I know for a fact your pa taught you to respect your elders."

"I just said I figured you knew everything. I didn't actually mention Methuselah . . ."

"There you go again—"

From the buggy, Sally laughed. "I swear, you two squabble just as much as Pearlie and Cal, and they're at it all the time. Do you really think it's going to snow, Preacher?"

"Yes'm, I do," the old mountain man replied. "I've seen a heap o' clouds with snow in 'em in my time, and I've smelled it in the air. I reckon we'll get a right smart amount. But that part of it's just a hunch, you understand."

"As long as it doesn't snow enough to interfere with the Christmas celebration, that will be fine. Actually, snow seems appropriate to the holiday season. There's nothing like singing Christmas carols on a brisk, snowy evening. What do you think, Smoke?"

"Sounds good to me. One thing I'm sure of . . . whatever the weather's going to do, there's not a thing in the world we can do to stop it, one way or the other."

That was true. A lot of things in this world were beyond the control of mortal men, and the weather was one of them.

"We'll just have to trust to the Lord, then," Sally said, and Smoke couldn't argue with that, either.

Big Rock, Colorado

They reached town, and Sally drove on down the street toward St. Paul's Episcopal Church, where the meeting she planned to attend was being held, while Smoke and Preacher reined their mounts to a halt in front of Louis Longmont's saloon.

Smoke had known Louis for several years. He was a gambler and gunman, known widely as a fast draw although his speed wasn't a match for Smoke's. But then, it was entirely possible no one's was. Louis had drifted in and out of Big Rock for a while before finally settling down and opening the saloon that bore his name.

The place was more than just a drinking establishment and gambling den. With Louis's French ancestry, he had a taste for fine food, so the saloon was also one of the finest restaurants in Big Rock, even though he didn't push that part of the business. Certain of his good friends could always count on getting a good meal if they happened to be in town at dinner time, and among them were Smoke and Sally Jensen.

Smoke and Preacher had already filled up on Sally's fried chicken, so they weren't looking for food. Or drink, for that matter. Preacher enjoyed a good shot of whiskey and Smoke usually had a mug of beer when he went into Longmont's, but neither of them drank to excess. It was companionship they were after.

As Smoke walked in, he spotted his old friend standing in front of the bar, talking to the bartender Johnny McVey, who in addition to being a drink juggler also played a fine classical piano. Johnny had performed a few times at the local theater.

Louis saw Smoke and Preacher come into the saloon, of course. As a man who had spent a long time living by his wits and his gun, Louis was in the habit of noticing everything that went on around him, all the time. A sleekly handsome man with dark hair and a narrow mustache, he smiled and lifted a hand in greeting. "Smoke, always good to see you. And Preacher! I didn't realize you were in the vicinity."

"I, uh, just drifted into these parts again," Preacher said without offering any other explanation.

Louis didn't find that suspicious. As Smoke's oldest friend, Preacher could show up any time and always be welcome.

"What brings you to town today?" Louis asked Smoke.

He jerked a thumb in the direction of the church. "Sally came in for a meeting with the other ladies about the big Christmas fandango. Preacher and I just came along for the ride."

"And to pay a visit to this fine establishment, obviously. Johnny, a beer for Smoke. And Preacher, I have a bottle of some very fine brandy you might like to sample . . ." Louis's voice trailed off as the old mountain man shook his head.

"Fine brandy would be wasted on me, son," Preacher told him. "I'd never appreciate it. A shot o' plain ol' rotgut will do me just fine, thankee."

Louis chuckled and said to Johnny, "You heard the man. But *I'll* have the brandy. I've been wanting to try it."

When the men had their drinks, Louis raised his glass of amber liquor. "To your health, gentleman, and to Christmas, soon to be upon us."

"I'll drink to that," Smoke said. "Here's to Christmas."

"The holiest, most peaceful time of the year," Louis added.

Smoke didn't say anything to that. Whether Christmas was actually the holiest time of the year was something for the theologians and Bible scholars to debate. In his experience, Christmas hadn't been exactly peaceful a lot of years. Trouble could break out during the holiday season just as it could any other time of year, and it seemed to be fond of plaguing not only him but any other Jensens who happened to be in the vicinity, too.

Maybe this year will be different, he told himself as he sipped the beer. *Maybe this Christmas all will be calm, like in that song "Silent Night."*

Those thoughts had just gone through his head when the door of the saloon opened, a heavy footstep sounded, and a man's voice said, "There you are, Smoke. I've been looking for you."

CHAPTER 13

A lot of times in the past, when somebody came into a saloon where Smoke was and said something like that, it was a prelude to violence. Way too many hombres fancied themselves fast on the shoot and wanted to build their reputation by outdrawing the famous Smoke Jensen.

However, the men who wanted to challenge him to a gunfight usually just called him *Jensen*, not the nickname Preacher had hung on him years earlier. Often there were phrases like "You dirty polecat!" involved. Obscenity and profanity were common.

None of that happened. Smoke recognized the man's voice, so he moved leisurely as he turned away from the bar and lifted a hand in greeting to the newcomer. "Hello, Monte." He frowned slightly as he saw the worried expression on Sheriff Monte Carson's face.

Something had put a burr under Monte's saddle.

The lawman was a solidly built hombre a number of years Smoke's senior. Before pinning on a badge, he had made his living as a hired gun, first, working for Tilden Franklin when that ruthless cattle baron had set out to become the biggest rancher in Colorado, even if it meant killing anyone who got in his way, including Smoke Jensen.

When Franklin put out a call for professional gunmen, Monte Carson had turned up in Fontana, the town controlled by the cattle baron, but he had soon realized that he was too decent at his core to be doing Franklin's dirty work. He had switched sides during that bloody range war and had been a staunch friend to Smoke Jensen ever since.

Tilden Franklin was dead and Fontana was gone. Abandoned, fallen into ruins, it had slowly faded away as if it had never been. Big Rock had replaced it and had grown by the proverbial leaps and bounds in the relatively short span of its existence. Already it was one of the leading towns in that part of Colorado. Monte Carson deserved a sizable amount of the credit for that. He maintained law and order in the settlement with a firm but fair hand and had enough of a reputation as a gunhand to prompt many troublemakers to steer clear of the place.

"What's wrong?" Smoke asked as the sheriff came across the room toward him.

"Bart Pascoe and some of those muleskinners of his are over at the Brown Dirt Cowboy getting a snootful."

"Nothing unusual about that, is there?" Smoke said with a shrug. "That's what they do every time they come into town to pick up those loads of goods."

The railroad had come to Big Rock, but the smaller communities in Eagle County and the surrounding counties didn't have that luxury. The businesses in those settlements had to have their merchandise and supplies brought in by wagon. Bart Pascoe owned the freight line that served many of them. He was a veteran muleskinner and bullwhacker and went along on most of the freight runs himself, instead of trusting the operation to his employees.

He was also a big, hard-fisted man who was quick to anger and always on the lookout to take offense. The men he hired tended to be on the proddy side as well.

"That's right," Monte Carson said in response to Smoke's comment about Pascoe and his freighters being fond of their liquor. "Usually when they start getting rambunctious, I herd them down to the jail, let them cool off for a spell, and then turn them loose. Pascoe's not a bad hombre, he's just too quick-tempered." The lawman made a face. "Today's different, though."

"How's that?" Smoke asked.

"Gil Green and some of his bunch are in town."

Louis Longmont said, "That doesn't bode well."

Smoke agreed with that. Gil Green owned the only other freight outfit in Eagle County, and naturally a rivalry existed between him and Pascoe. Pascoe's line had been operating longer and as such was sort of entrenched in the county, but Green had been making inroads into Pascoe's business in recent months by undercutting his prices and Pascoe resented it. More than once, he had threatened loudly to run Green out of that part of the country.

Louis went on. "I thought you'd ordered Pascoe and Green to stay out of town at the same time."

"I did," Monte said, "but as long as they're not breaking any laws I don't have any legal basis for enforcing that order. It's more of a . . . suggestion, I guess you'd call it."

"Where's Green now?" asked Smoke.

"Picking up a couple wagonloads of goods at the depot. But the stationmaster overheard him telling his men that they'd stop at the Brown Dirt Cowboy for a drink before they started out of town. The stationmaster knew Pascoe was down there, so he figured he'd better warn me."

"Need me to be an unofficial deputy and help you head off any trouble?"

"That's what I was hoping," Monte admitted. "I don't mind saying so, either."

"And I don't mind backing your play," Smoke said with a smile. They had known each other long enough and were good enough friends that neither of them ever hesitated about calling on the other for help in times of trouble.

Preacher downed the last bit of whiskey in his glass and said, "I'll come along with you boys. Might be entertainin'."

"No offense, Preacher," Monte said, "but I hope not. I happen to know you consider a big ruckus entertaining."

"Well, it keeps things from gettin' monotonous, anyway," the old mountain man said with a chuckle.

The three of them left Longmont's Saloon and turned toward the Brown Dirt Cowboy, which was Big Rock's second most-successful saloon. By any criteria, it was far down on the scale when compared to Louis's place. A man named Emmett Brown owned and operated it. He tried to keep order there, but brawls frequently broke out among the customers.

Another one might well be in the offing if Bart Pascoe and Gil Green got together before Smoke, Preacher, and Monte Carson arrived.

That was exactly what had happened, Smoke saw as he entered the saloon behind the sheriff. Two groups of men faced each other, one at each end of the bar, and a tense feeling of impending violence hung in the air. The other customers had drawn back, giving the rival freighters plenty of room.

Emmett Brown stood behind the bar, looking worried. An expression of relief appeared on his face when he saw Monte Carson, followed by Smoke and Preacher. "Sheriff!" he called loudly in a clear attempt to get the attention of the men standing in front of the bar. "I'm glad to see you."

"I ain't," growled Bart Pascoe. He was a burly bear of a man in a buffalo coat. A long black beard bristled from his jutting jaw. A floppy-brimmed black hat drooped above his rugged face. "You ain't needed here, Sheriff. Won't be no trouble. My boys and me are just gonna get rid of some trash is all."

Gil Green said, "I'm lookin' at the only trash in here." He was taller and leaner than Pascoe, with a clean-shaven, lantern-jawed face and fists like mallets at the end of long, wiry arms. Pascoe probably outweighed him by fifty or sixty pounds, but in a fight Green would have a considerably greater reach.

Green's bunch was outnumbered. He had three men at his back. Pascoe had five. Still, six to four odds weren't that bad. Most men on the prod wouldn't back down from them—especially if any booze was involved, as it obviously had been.

"All right. Listen to me, all of you," Monte Carson began. "There's not going to be any ruckus today. Pascoe, you and your men have been here for a while. You've had your drinks. You file on out and go about your business. Green, you and your men stay right where you are and don't move until Pascoe's wagons are out of town. Is that understood?"

Green sneered "What I understand, Sheriff, is that you're mighty quick to strut in here and start givin' orders when you've got your pet gunfighter with you. You might not act so damn high and mighty if you couldn't sic Jensen on anybody you want gunned down."

Anger welled up inside Smoke. He had a bit of a temper himself, and didn't like what Green had said. He started to step around Monte when the lawman held out an arm to stop him.

Monte strode forward and said in a tight voice, "You just bought yourself and your boys a ticket out of town. You're going to be the first to leave after all."

One of Green's muleskinners protested. "That ain't fair. We just got here. Ain't even had a drink yet, let alone a chance to dally with one o' Brown's saloon gals!"

"That's too bad. Take it up with your boss. He's the one with the big mouth."

Green's hands clenched into bony fists as he moved closer to Monte. "I'm not gonna stand for this, Carson."

"That's *Sheriff* Carson," Monte reminded him.

"You take a swing at me, you'll be assaulting an officer of the law. That'll be thirty days behind bars, if not more."

"Might be worth it, you high and mighty son of a—"

Smoke stepped in, knowing that—badge or no badge—Monte wouldn't take being called a name like that. As he crowded between the two men, he told Green, "I don't see any guns on you or any of your men, mister."

"You gonna threaten us with those smokepoles of yours now?" Green asked with another sneer.

"Nope." Smoke's hands went to the buckle of the gun belt around his waist. "I'm going to take them off and ask you to step outside with me. No sense in us laying waste to Mr. Brown's saloon."

"Smoke, you're out of line," Monte snapped. "We came down here to stop a fight, not start one."

"Sometimes things can't be stopped, only played out to their natural conclusion."

"I'm not afraid to fight you, Jensen," Green blustered. "Not man-to-man."

"Let's get at it, then," Smoke said as he handed his gun belt and holstered Colts to Preacher.

The old mountain man had a big grin on his grizzled face. He was going to get some entertainment after all, it looked like.

"Hold on, hold on," rumbled Bart Pascoe. "I got a grudge o' my own against Green. If you beat the tar out of him, I can't wallop him my own self."

Green said, "Any tar beatin', I'll be the one doin' it."

Smoke rubbed his chin and frowned in thought for a moment, then said, "We've got a problem here, all right. If I whip Green for what he said, then you're going to be mad at me, Pascoe. Have I got that right?"

"You damn sure do!"

Smoke spread his hands. "Then I guess the only solution is for me to whip Green, then fight you," he said to the burly man in the buffalo coat.

"Wait just a minute," Monte Carson said. "This is going from bad to worse. There's not gonna be any fights, between anybody!"

As Smoke turned his head to talk to his old friend, Green suddenly yelled, "The hell there ain't!" and lunged at Smoke, bringing his right fist around in a looping, devastating punch.

CHAPTER 14

The blow that Green aimed at Smoke's head was a real blockbuster, the sort of punch that might kill a man, as well as break a few knuckles on the hand that landed it, but it had to connect solidly with its target to do that.

Smoke twisted aside just in time to avoid the full force of the punch. Green's knobby knuckles glanced off the side of his head with enough power to knock him against the bar, but he didn't go down. In fact, he recovered so quickly that he was able to ram a punch of his own into the middle of Green's face while the man was still close to him. The blow rocked Green's head back.

The freight line owner might have a rangy, wiry look about him, but a lifetime of hard work had left him whang-leather tough. He shook off the effects of Smoke's punch and bored in, hooking a left and a right to the belly while he had Smoke pinned against the bar.

Smoke lifted both arms and brought his fists crashing down on Green's shoulders at the point where they met the man's neck. The precisely aimed blows made Green's arms go numb momentarily. As his arms sagged, his eyes widened in anticipation of what was about to happen.

Smoke finished him off with a right hook that smashed into the jaw and sent him flying backwards. Green landed in a skidding sprawl across the sawdust-littered floor and wound up lying stunned at the feet of Bart Pascoe.

Smoke's hat had fallen off during the brief altercation, but Preacher had picked it up. Smoke took it and brushed sawdust off of it.

Pascoe stared down at Gil Green then lifted his head, and let out a raucous, "Haw-haw!"

Smoke put his hat on and said, "I seem to recall something about you and me tangling now, Bart."

"No, sir!" Pascoe replied with an emphatic shake of his head. "Sure, I would've liked to bounce my fists off that hard skull o' Green's a few times, but seein' the addled look on his face right now is worth a mite of disappointment." He grunted. "Besides, I ain't a tarnal idiot. Green got in the first lick, but you still handled him without even breakin' a sweat. I figure if you and me was to go head-to-head, I could take you sooner or later—maybe we'll find out one o' these days—but the boys and me got a long haul with those goods and supplies, and I don't hanker to spend the whole trip achin' in ever' bone and muscle."

Monte Carson pointed a thumb toward the door. "Go ahead and get out of town, then. It'll take Green a while to regain his senses, and by the time he does, I expect you and your wagons to be long gone."

"All right, Sheriff." Pascoe jerked his bushy head in a signal for his men to follow him. They all trooped out of the Brown Dirt Cowboy.

Monte spoke to Green's men. "Pick up your boss and lay him on a table until he comes around. No more trouble."

"No trouble, Sheriff," one of the freighters promised.

With a disgusted shake of his head, Monte Carson left the saloon. Smoke and Preacher followed him, Smoke buckling the gun belt back around his lean hips.

Monte stopped on the boardwalk outside the Brown Dirt Cowboy, fingered his chin for a moment, then wiped the back of his hand across his mouth. He looked like he had a bitter taste under his tongue.

"Something wrong, Monte?" Smoke asked.

"Yeah. Damn right there's something wrong."

"I don't see what it is. We headed off a brawl that likely would've done considerable damage to Brown's saloon."

"*You* headed it off," Monte said sharply. "It's gotten to where folks around here don't always listen to what I tell them . . . unless you're with me. Maybe you really have become my pet gunfighter, Smoke."

"I'm nobody's pet, and you know that," Smoke replied with a sharp edge in his voice.

Monte waved a hand. "I didn't mean it like that. Sorry for the way it sounded. But things have got me to thinking . . . who's the real law around here, Smoke, you or me?"

Smoke frowned. He could tell that his friend was

genuinely upset. He suggested, "Why don't we go back to Louis's, have a cup of coffee, and talk about this?"

Preacher said, "Talk, talk, talk. That fight didn't hardly last no time at all, and now you want to go *talk.*" He snorted. "Maybe I'll just mosey along to the church and see if Sally and the other ladies need any help plannin' their party. Sounds like it might be more excitin' than listen' to you two jaw at each other."

"Preacher's right," Monte said. "Forget it, Smoke. I'm going to walk down to the depot and make sure Pascoe and his bunch get out of town with their wagons. Green'll be waking up before too much longer, if he hasn't come around already."

"All right," Smoke agreed. He started to add that if Monte needed him for anything, he'd be at Longmont's, but decided that given the sheriff's mood, that might not be a good idea.

As Monte strode off toward the railroad station, Preacher said to Smoke, "Come on, let's get back to that French fella's place. Maybe I'll try some o' that fancy brandy o' his, after all. At my age, I need somethin' to get my blood pumpin' again, and that little scuffle sure didn't do it!"

Sugarloaf Ranch

Sally seemed quite pleased with the way the plans for the Christmas celebration were going. Before they left the ranch, she had put a roast on the stove to cook slowly for supper, and she was humming Christmas carols to herself as she sliced potatoes and wild onions to add to the pot.

Smoke was glad to see her so happy. In the years they had been together, they had experienced many adventures and endured more than their share of danger. She deserved some peace and quiet and contentment.

In the back of his mind, though, was a little nagging voice warning him that trouble always seemed to be right around the corner.

It might show up in the person of Eagle-Eye Callahan. Smoke cornered Preacher on the front porch where the old mountain man was stoking a foul-smelling briar pipe.

"Figured it'd be best not to pollute the air inside the house with this ol' pipe o' mine," Preacher commented.

"You figured right," Smoke told him as he casually leaned a shoulder against one of the porch posts. "Preacher, I've been wondering . . . what are the chances that this fella Callahan is going to trail you here to the Sugarloaf?"

Preacher looked uncomfortable, which was unusual for him. He was always sure of himself, and too old to be embarrassed, he claimed. "I don't know. I wasn't exactly hidin' out when I got word that ol' Eagle-Eye was lookin' for me. Like I done told you, he run a tradin' post for a lot o' years, so it's been a while since he had to do any real trailin', but he was always pretty good at it, back in our younger days."

"How did you find out about it in the first place?"

Preacher had the pipe going. He puffed on it until a cloud of gray smoke wreathed his face then said, "He sent me a letter. It caught up to me in Laramie."

"He told you about his wife and her, uh, feelings for you?"

"Yeah." Preacher sighed. "Gals always did seem to find me dang near irresistible, for some reason."

"It's a mystery, all right," Smoke commented dryly.

"Anyway, Eagle-Eye went on to say in his letter that he was comin' after me. He stated flat-out that his honor had been insulted, and one of us had to die. Now, you know me, Smoke, I ain't a-feared of dyin'. Lord knows, I've lived a long time and seen more 'n my share of life, good and bad. Sure, I wouldn't mind stayin' around for a spell longer, but if my string has played out, then so be it."

"That doesn't give Callahan any right to kill you for something that's not even your fault!"

"No, it don't," Preacher agreed, "and I worried that if there was a showdown betwixt the two of us, I might not be able to stop myself from . . ." Preacher's voice trailed off.

After a moment Smoke finished the thought for him. "You're worried that you might kill Callahan, not that he might kill you."

"Well, let's just look at it reasonable-like. I been fussin' and fightin' and scrapin' for my life for nigh on to seventy years now! Eagle-Eye's been sittin' in a tradin' post, sellin' goods and countin' his money, for forty years. Who do you figure's likely to be the more dangerous o' the two?"

"So you plan on laying low here until he forgets about this vengeance quest of his?"

Preacher nodded solemnly. "That's what I'm hopin' will happen."

"Preacher . . . did it occur to you that a lot of folks know that you and I are friends?"

"Well, I s'pose they's some." Preacher's weathered forehead creased even more than it already was as he frowned. "You reckon he'll know to come here to look for me?"

"He well might," Smoke said. "What are you going to do if he shows up?"

Preacher heaved a sigh. "Try to talk some sense into his fool head, I reckon."

"You think that'll do any good?"

"'Tain't likely," admitted the old mountain man.

"If Callahan comes here, you can stay out of sight and we'll tell him you haven't been here."

"You mean lie?" Preacher shook his head. "I know that wouldn't sit good with you, son. Your pa raised you to be honest and always tell the truth. Anyway, if you was to do that, you'd have to let Miss Sally in on what's goin' on, and I'd just as soon she didn't know."

"If Callahan's trying to kill you, she's going to figure out that something's wrong."

"Well, hell. You're right about that." Preacher heaved another sigh. "I've got myself in a plumb mess there ain't no good way out of, haven't I?"

"It might not be any of your doing . . . but yeah, you're sort of between a rock and a hard place."

"Kinda like you and that star packer from Big Rock?"

"Monte?" Smoke straightened from his casual stance against the porch post. "What are you talking about, Preacher?"

"I mean he feels like you sorta stepped on his toes today, by handlin' that trouble in the saloon the way you did."

"Hell, he asked me for my help!" Smoke exclaimed.

"Yeah, he sure did, but I reckon he figured he'd take the lead in puttin' down any ruckus, not you."

"Then he shouldn't have dragged me into the mess to start with."

"Maybe he didn't think about that. Or maybe after it was over he just realized how many times you done pulled his fat outta the fire. Been a heap of them, ain't there?"

Smoke shrugged. Trouble had come rampaging into Big Rock on plenty of occasions, and he and Monte Carson had faced it together. The idea that Monte might sometimes wind up resenting his help had never crossed Smoke's mind.

"You might have a point," he told Preacher. "Monte's a plenty tough hombre in his own right. Maybe next time there's a problem when I'm in town, I'll just back off so he can handle it himself."

"Might be a good idea," Preacher said. "Providin' that the trouble ain't *too* bad . . ."

Both men were deep in their thoughts that they didn't notice a few snowflakes drifting down from the overcast sky. The snow fell for only a moment and then stopped, unseen as if it had never been there.

CHAPTER 15

Denver, Colorado

The saloon was a good one, with chandeliers and a gleaming mirror behind the bar and a large, gilt-framed painting of an amply endowed woman who was nude except for a filmy scarf drifting around her. The brass foot rail shone, and the top of the mahogany bar was polished to a high gleam. Mitch Clark could see himself in it as he stood there waiting for the bartender to come over.

He was alone. Curly, Jed, Hector, and Blind Jimmy had stayed behind at the cheap hotel where they had gotten rooms with some of their rapidly dwindling funds. Clark hoped that not only would Jim Bleeker take them into his gang, but that he might provide them with a little walking around money, as well.

Clark thought he looked pretty good. He had shaken out the brown tweed suit from his bedroll, and he still wore Jimmy's bowler hat. Not exactly a swell, but not bad. Of course, that might not be enough to impress a man like Jim Bleeker.

The bartender, a red-faced man with long, drooping sideburn whiskers, finally walked along the hardwood to him. "What'll it be, mister?"

"Beer." Clark wanted a shot of whiskey, but money was tight. As the bartender filled a mug from a tap and set it in front of him, Clark went on. "I'm looking for a fella named Morley. Ray Morley."

For a second the bartender looked like he was going to deny knowing the man, but then he shrugged and nodded toward the far side of the room. "He's at that table back in the corner."

"Much obliged," Clark said as he slid a coin across the hardwood. "For the beer and the information."

The man grunted, scooped the coin from the bar's polished top, and moved on.

Clark picked up the mug of beer and took a sip. It was good. He had to stop himself from downing a larger swallow. He wanted to keep his wits about him so he carried the mug with him as he approached the table where Ray Morley sat alone, nursing a drink and dealing poker hands to himself.

A thin, dark-faced man in a black hat, pants, and coat over a white shirt, the outlaw also wore a string tie . . . appropriate to his surroundings. When he leaned forward to add a card to the ones laid out on the table in front of him, Clark caught a glimpse of a gun butt in a holster under Morley's left arm.

Some men liked a shoulder holster like that.

Clark never had. He preferred to have his Colt out in the open when he wore one, which he wasn't at the moment. He paused at the table. "Mr. Morley?" He kept his hat on. He wasn't about to go up to the man hat in hand, like a damn beggar.

Morley glanced up. "That's right. What can I do for you?"

"I was up in Wyoming a while back. Talked to a fella named Clyde Saunders. He said you were looking for good men and that you were working with Jim Bleeker."

"Clyde runs off at the mouth, doesn't he? What's your name?"

"Mitch Clark."

Morley looked him over for a second, then nodded. "Sit down for a spell and finish your drink."

Clark felt like he had passed a hurdle. He lowered himself into the empty chair across from Morley.

"Who do you know besides Clyde Saunders?" asked Morley. "And do you ride alone?"

Clark answered the second question first. "I've been riding with some other fellas for a spell. Curly Weaver, Jed Darby, Jimmy Pugh, and Hector Gomez. I expect you've heard of them."

Morley pursed his lips. "No, can't say as I have. Wait a minute. Pugh . . . is he the one they call Blind Jimmy?"

"That's right," Clark said, surprised that of the five of them, the youngster was the only one whose name Morley recognized. Of course, he might just be claiming not to have heard of them for reasons of his own, although Clark couldn't think of what those might be.

"What have the five of you been up to lately?"

Clark knew Morley was asking about the jobs they had pulled. He leaned forward and said in a confidential tone, "We made some withdrawals from a few banks in Idaho and Wyoming. Stopped a stagecoach here and there." He didn't say anything about that last fiasco, when they had attempted to hold up an old man who was too careless about flashing his money, only to be chased off by a couple unseen riflemen. He pretended that hadn't happened.

When Morley just sat there in silence, Clark went on. "I hear tell Bleeker's got a mighty big job planned. Word is that he's going to tree a whole town and take everything that's not nailed down. Well, I'm here to tell you, Mr. Morley, my pards and I will make good additions to your outfit. We're a tough bunch, make no mistake about that."

"People like to gossip," Morley said. "I don't know you, Clark. You expect me to just tell you all our plans. Hell, you could be a lawman working undercover for all I know!"

"A lawman?" Clark pressed a hand to his chest. "Me? Look at this." He slid a hand inside his coat.

Instantly, Morley sat up a little straighter and dropped the deck of cards. His hand was poised to grab that revolver in the holster under his arm.

Clark brought out a folded piece of paper. He unfolded it and smoothed it onto the table. The paper had a crude but recognizable drawing of him on it, plus words in big letters that read WANTED FOR MURDER $500 REWARD.

"That's me," Clark said as he tapped a finger on the WANTED poster. "You can see for yourself. I killed three people in Texas. The Rangers are after me, so I steer clear of the place. This town Jim Bleeker's gonna tree, it's not in Texas, is it?"

Morley studied the reward dodger for a moment, then smiled thinly. "No, as a matter of fact it's right here in Colorado. Jim makes the final decisions, but

I've got a hunch he'll want to take you and your friends along when we ride to Big Rock."

Eagle County, Colorado

A signpost hammered into the hard ground at the side of the road pointed like an arrow to the south. Burned into it in slightly wavery letters was the legend BIG ROCK 40 MILLES.

Chance Jensen grinned and said to his brother, "You want to fix it, don't you?"

"If you're going to make a road sign, you ought to know how to spell *miles*," Ace replied.

Eagle-Eye Callahan frowned at the words burned into the wood. "Big Rock. Seems like I oughtta recognize the name of the place, for some reason."

"I know I've heard of it," Ace said, "but I can't remember why. Let me think about it for a minute."

The three of them had been riding together for a couple days after the holdup attempt Ace and Chance had thwarted. The Jensen boys had found old Eagle-Eye quite likable as he spun yarn after yarn about his years spent running a trading post in Montana. His time spanned from the height of the fur trapping era to the current days of the cattle empire.

"We could ride on in that direction while you're thinking about it," Chance suggested in response to his brother's comment. "I don't know about you fellas, but I believe I saw a few snowflakes floating down a little while ago. We don't want to get caught out in a blizzard."

"Big Rock's too far away for us to reach it before dark," Ace pointed out.

"Maybe, but we might come upon another settlement between here and there where we can spend the night. Even if we don't, we'll need to find a better place to make camp than out here on this open trail."

It was a little unusual for Chance to be the practical one of the two brothers, but Ace had to admit he had a point. Ace heeled his horse into motion again. "Yeah, let's head that direction."

The three men rode for a few minutes in silence, then Ace snapped his fingers. "I've got it. I remember Smoke Jensen saying that his ranch isn't far from a town called Big Rock."

"Smoke Jensen!" Eagle-Eye exclaimed. "When you boys told me your names, it didn't occur to me that you might be related to that goldang shootist!"

"As far as we know, we're not," Ace said. "But as a matter of fact, we've met him a couple times. It's been about a year since we saw him last, him and his brothers Luke and Matt."

"Is he as much of a ring-tailed, rip-roarin', hell-raiser as they say he is?"

"He just seemed like a nice friendly fella to me," Chance said.

"That's right," Ace agreed. "The sort of hombre you'd like to have for an uncle, maybe."

"But I wouldn't ever want to get crosswise with him," added Chance. "All those stories about how good he is with his guns . . . well, if anything, they just don't say enough about how gun handy he is."

"Smoke Jensen," Eagle-Eye said again, with a musing quality to his voice. "I know that name."

"Well, of course you do," Chance said. "We were just saying—"

"No, I've heard of him, of course, like most folks out here have by now. After what he did up in Idaho, facin' off against all those killers at once . . ." Eagle-Eye shook his head in admiration. "I mean, there's another connection. Him and me have a mutual friend. An old mountain man called Preacher."

Ace said, "Sure, I remember hearing him mention Preacher last year. He's sort of like a mentor to Smoke, I guess you could say."

"You ever met him?" Eagle-Eye asked.

Ace shook his head. "Nope, just heard Smoke talk about him. You say he's a friend of yours?"

"We did some trappin' together a heap o' years ago. And we've visited with each other a few times since. Been a long time since I've seen him, though." Eagle-Eye rasped his fingers over his white-stubbled chin. "Wonder if he might be spendin' the holiday at Jensen's ranch, since the two of 'em are old friends."

"I suppose it's possible," Ace said.

"What say we find out?"

The brothers looked at the old-timer in surprise.

Chance said, "You mean go to Smoke's ranch?"

"Just show up there?" added Ace.

"Well, why not?" Eagle-Eye wanted to know. "You boys said you were friends o' his. I don't reckon he'd turn you away, especially at this time of year."

"Probably not," Ace admitted. "But there's no guarantee Preacher will be there."

"No guarantee he won't be." Eagle-Eye looked like his mind was made up. "Anyway, if Preacher ain't there, maybe Smoke'll know where I can find him. I'd sure like to see that old codger again. The way both of us are gettin' on up in years, this might be our last chance to get together. What do you say, boys? We head for the Jensen ranch?"

Ace and Chance looked at each other again.

Chance shrugged.

We're headed in that direction anyway, Ace supposed. "All right, Mr. Callahan, we can do that." He remembered something else from their conversations with Smoke the year before. "The Sugarloaf, that's what the ranch is called. I'm sure somebody in Big Rock can tell us exactly where to find it."

CHAPTER 16

Aboard the Orphan Train

Mercy thought that it was a remarkable achievement, the way railroad lines had spanned the entire continent from the Atlantic to the Pacific, making it possible to go from one side of the nation to the other in less than a week, rather than a journey of months like it had been in the days of the wagon trains. She had read about those arduous expeditions and doubted that she could have survived one of them.

Of course, just because traveling on the railroad was a vast improvement didn't mean that it was perfect. In fact, the compartment she shared with Grace Gallagher had a cold draft blowing through it, and they hadn't been able to find the source of the chill.

She pulled her coat collar tighter around her throat as she stood up. "I think I'll go check on the children"

Grace looked even colder as she sat on the compartment's other bench shivering under a lap robe.

"Peter's keeping an eye on them." She had been reading from the Bible she held in her gloved hands.

"I know, but they can get too rambunctious for one man to watch over them."

"Peter can handle it," Grace said with a sullen note in her voice.

Mercy realized that the other woman didn't want her to be alone with Peter.

They wouldn't actually be alone, of course. The children would be there. The Society had engaged the entire car, and the children had strict orders never to leave it without one of the adults. Not only did Peter, Grace, and Mercy enforce that rule, but they also had help from the two oldest girls, Connie and Roberta, both of whom were twelve. Back in the orphanage, the two girls had been like second mothers to the younger children.

Having a gaggle of youngsters around all the time was like having a constant chaperone, and if Mercy was being honest with herself, she didn't really mind. Although she knew Peter Gallagher admired her, she didn't believe he would ever make any improper advances. She felt just uncomfortable at times when he looked at her that she was grateful for the children's company.

"I won't be gone long," she said, reaching for the compartment door.

Grace just sniffed behind her.

Probably from the cold, Mercy told herself . . . although she knew her attitude might be a little generous.

She stepped out and was nearly plowed over by one of the boys racing along the corridor between the compartments. Another youngster was giving chase, but he stopped short at the sight of her.

"Sorry, Miss Halliday," he muttered as he looked down at the floor of the slightly swaying train car.

"You know you're not supposed to be running up and down in here, Trevor," she told him. She glanced over her shoulder at the other boy, who had also stopped and scuffed his feet guiltily. "You, too, Allan. You must practice proper decorum and behave like gentlemen."

"But Miss Halliday, deck . . . deco . . . decorum's mighty hard to come by when you're ten years old!" Trevor protested.

Mercy managed not to laugh, but it wasn't easy. She struggled to keep her face and voice solemn as she said, "I know it's difficult, but you must try. You need to get in the habit of presenting the best impression you possibly can."

"Yes'm," agreed Allan. "So's folks will like us and we can get new families!"

"That's right." Mercy looked up and down the corridor without seeing Peter and frowned slightly. "Where's Mr. Gallagher?"

"He said he was goin' out on the platform for a breath o' fresh air."

"I think he was goin' to smoke a see-gar!" added Allan.

"Oh, I doubt that," Mercy said, although she thought there was at least a chance the boy was right. Regardless of Peter's motivation, he was supposed to be keeping an eye on the corridor and the children's compartments. She wasn't very happy about him stepping out onto the platform. "The front of the car, or the back?"

"The back."

She would have liked to give Peter a piece of her mind, but technically he was her superior in the Society, so she couldn't really do that. She could speak to him, though, and find out if he planned to come back in any time soon.

"The two of you run along," she told the boys, then held up a hand to stop them in case they took off at top speed. "I don't mean that literally."

"What does lit'rally mean?"

"It means don't run." She started toward the vestibule at the rear of the car, where a door opened onto the platform at that end.

As soon as she stepped out onto the windswept platform, she immediately caught a pungent whiff of tobacco smoke and knew that the little boy had been right. Peter had left the railroad car so he could indulge in one of the foul-smelling cigars he liked. Grace had forbidden him to smoke around the children, claiming that it might be bad for the youngsters' health, but Mercy suspected her objections came mainly from the fact that she didn't care for the way the cigars smelled.

Peter was standing at the wrought-iron railing puffing on the cylinder of tobacco. He started guiltily as the door swung open, then relaxed a little as he recognized Mercy.

"Don't worry," she told him with a smile. "It's just me."

"Thank goodness for small favors," he muttered. "Not that you're— Never mind. If I continue, I'm certain to say the wrong thing."

"I'm annoyed with you, you know."

Peter arched an eyebrow. "You are? What for?"

"You left the children alone in there."

"Not really. You and Grace were right there in your compartment, and I knew that if there was too much commotion, you'd hear."

"Trouble doesn't have to have a commotion with it. Sometimes it strikes quietly."

Peter shrugged. "I suppose. I just felt . . . what is it they say out West? I felt a hankering for a cigar." He paused, then went on. "Don't you ever feel a hankering for anything, Mercy?"

That struck her as a little too personal a question, so she didn't answer it. She rested her gloved hands on the railing and gazed out at the passing countryside. "It's not much to look at it, is it?"

She wasn't sure where they were. Somewhere west of Chicago, passing through farmland that was flat and empty under a gray, overcast sky. In the spring, there would be plowing and planting, and in the summer the fields would be a verdant green with their crops, but in December the landscape was rather stark. It had rained recently, leaving puddles of muddy water standing here and there.

"I don't know," Peter said as he leaned on the railing beside her. "From where I'm standing, the view is quite nice. Beautiful, in fact."

The air was cold on Mercy's cheeks, but she felt her face warming anyway. Peter had been looking directly at her when he made that comment. He had never been quite so bold in the past.

She frowned. "We had better go back inside—"

He tossed the half-smoked cigar and it was whipped

away by the wind of the train's passage. Reaching out, he lightly touched her arm. "Not just yet."

"But it's really not pleasant weather out here at all, and the children—"

"Will be fine," he broke in. "Grace is in there if they need anything. You and I haven't had a moment alone since we left New York, Mercy."

"We're not *supposed* to have a moment alone."

"Why not? Don't we all deserve something for all the good work we do?"

"Helping the children is its own reward." She knew that sounded a little sanctimonious, but she genuinely felt that way.

"I'm not sure that's enough anymore." His fingers curled around her upper arm, gently at first but then tightening. "A man can't devote his entire life to good works. He needs a moment of appreciation now and then."

"I-I know the children appreciate everything that you do."

"I'm not talking about the children."

"Well, *I* appreciate that you're a good man, Mr. Gallagher, with a fine wife and—"

"Don't talk about her," he snapped, moving closer to Mercy. He was between her and the door and had her trapped against the platform railing. True, he was only crowding her, not pressing her against the railing, and his grip on her arm was just insistent, not so tight as to be painful.

She was about to pull away from him when a man's voice said, "Might be a good idea for you to step away from the lady, friend." A hand with long, strong-looking fingers closed over Peter's shoulder.

He winced a little, further proof that the new-comer's grip had some strength behind it. Peter let go of her arm and tried to turn around, but he couldn't move very fast while the stranger had hold of him. He demanded, "What are you doing? Let go of me!"

"Step away from the lady," the stranger repeated.

He wasn't completely a stranger, Mercy realized. She didn't know his name, but she had seen him before. He was the tall, sandy-haired man who had bumped into her in the train station back in New York, just before they'd boarded to head west.

How had he gotten out there on the platform with them? She hadn't seen him open the door and cross from that platform to where she and Peter were.

He must have come from the next car back, she thought, frowning. He must be good at moving smoothly and quietly.

Peter stepped back, giving Mercy plenty of room. His face was flushed with anger as well as cold. "I don't know what you think gives you the right—"

The stranger finally let go of his shoulder. Ignoring him, he said to Mercy, "Are you all right, miss?"

That annoyed Peter even more.

"I'm fine," she told the man. "Did you think I was in some sort of distress?"

A slight smile curved his lips as he replied, "Well, to be honest, it looked like you were about to lose your temper with this fellow, and I figured I'd better step in before he got hurt."

Peter's eyes widened. He exclaimed, "Now see here—!"

The stranger went on. "A lady like you, who seems

like you know how to take care of yourself, I thought you might plant a hat pin or something like that in him. He wouldn't have liked that at all."

"Don't talk about me like I'm not here!" Peter fumed.

The stranger did exactly that. "You might have even kicked him where it would hurt the most. So, in the interest of keeping the peace, I thought I ought to take a hand. I hope I didn't overstep my bounds."

"Well, I didn't really need your help," Mercy said, "but I appreciate the sentiment."

"Mercy, don't even talk to this man," Peter blustered.

"That's your name?" the stranger asked coolly. "Mercy?"

"You can call me Miss Halliday," she told him.

"I'm Ed Rinehart," he said as he reached up to take off the brown fedora he wore. "It's an honor and a pleasure to meet you, Miss Halliday."

"And this is Mr. Gallagher," Mercy added as she nodded toward Peter.

Ed Rinehart just grunted and gave Peter the most perfunctory nod possible as he put his hat back on.

"We should get back to our charges," Mercy went on.

Rinehart's eyes narrowed. "Are the two of you traveling together?"

"Mr. Gallagher and his wife and I are escorting a group of orphaned children to California, where new homes will be found for them and they'll be adopted."

"Noble work." His scorn evident, Rinehart glanced at Peter. "You're married, eh?"

Peter turned, jerked open the door, and stepped

back into the car. He held the door and asked, "Are you coming, Miss Halliday?"

Mercy took a step toward the door, then paused to ask, "Where are you bound for, Mr. Rinehart?"

"San Francisco," he replied.

"Oh. You're going all the way west, then?"

"Yes, ma'am. I'll be on this train just as long as you are."

Chapter 17

Denver

Mitch Clark offered to return to the hotel where the others with him were staying, but Ray Morley said that wasn't necessary. "I'll take you to talk to Jim. If he likes you, and if you vouch for the rest of your bunch, that'll be enough."

"What if he doesn't like me?" Clark asked without thinking.

A thin, cold smile appeared on Morley's face, but he didn't say anything.

Clark liked to think his nerves were pretty good, but something about Morley's smile bothered him. Realizing that Bleeker might think he already knew too much about the plan, especially if Morley told him he'd mentioned the name of the place they had in mind, Clark's mind raced. If Bleeker didn't take him into the gang, he might decide it would be better just to get rid of him so he couldn't talk to anybody else about the job.

He had come too far to back out, though. Agreeing to meet the boss outlaw, he left the saloon with Morley.

They strolled along the streets of Denver, Morley smoking a thin black cigarillo. It was the first time Clark had been to the city, so he wasn't sure where they were going.

Morley led him to a large house on a tree-lined side street. Even bare, the spread of tree branches was impressive. The house sat behind a well-tended lawn bordered by flowerbeds, also empty. The place was fronted by an elegant, columned gallery that made it look vaguely like a Southern plantation house.

"Looks like a fancy cathouse," Clark commented with a chuckle as the two men went along a flagstone walk toward the gallery.

"Not hardly, and don't call it that when you're inside," snapped Morley. "The lady who runs the place wouldn't like it."

"Sorry. I didn't mean any offense. If it's not a brothel, what is it?"

"I didn't say you couldn't find any female companionship inside. Lady Arabella's main business is gambling, though."

"Lady Arabella," Clark repeated. "The woman who runs the place?"

"That's right."

The heavy front door opened before they reached it. An extremely large man with a shock of rust-colored hair and a handlebar mustache the same shade stood there wearing a suit that looked out of place on his brawny frame. He nodded curtly "Ray."

"Evening, Dorgan," Morley greeted him. "Jim's upstairs?"

"No, he's sitting in on a private game right now, along with Herself, a couple cattlemen, and a member of the board of the Union Pacific."

Morley laughed. "I wouldn't want to interrupt that. Once Her Ladyship has cleaned out the cattle barons and the railroad man, let Jim know I'm here and need to talk to him, all right?"

"Sure. There's somebody else he plans to talk to first, though."

"Who's that?"

"Frank Morgan's here tonight."

The man who stood at the bar in the quiet salon at the side of the main gambling room was big and muscular, but his frame was so perfectly proportioned that it didn't appear overly large. He wore a brown suit instead of the range clothes he usually sported, but his wide-brimmed brown hat was the only one he owned. He had brushed it until it was halfway respectable. The same was true of his boots. He wasn't the sort of man who went in for anything fancy.

The gun holstered on his right hip fell into the same category. It was just a plain, dull gray Colt .45 with walnut grips that were starting to show some signs of use. Nothing distinguished it from thousands of other guns carried by men out on the frontier.

You'd never know by looking at the gun—or the man—how many men they had killed.

Frank Morgan lifted a brandy to his lips and sipped it. He wasn't that much of a drinking man—a phosphate or a cup of coffee would have been more to his taste—but the bartender had promised him the cognac was excellent and so it was. Frank intended to nurse his one drink for as long as he was there.

He didn't feel comfortable in such a place. Raised on a ranch down in Texas in the days before the Civil War, he had gone off to fight in that great conflict and endured years of hardship, misery, and danger.

Returning home hadn't been much better. He had clashed with the father of the girl he loved, the girl he'd left behind when the war started. All that had ended badly. Had ended with Frank Morgan discovering just how fast and deadly with a gun he was.

Unfortunately, plenty of other people had found out about it, too, and in all the years since, he had never been able to settle down. Wherever he went, somebody always wanted to prove he was faster on the draw, so Frank had drifted, hoping to someday find a place where he wouldn't be forced to kill.

So far that hadn't happened.

It was natural, given his unique skills, that eventually he had put them to work. He was a hired gun, some said the fastest of them all. He didn't sign on with just anybody, though. Before he took up arms in a range war or a railroad dispute or any other conflict where men used violence to settle their differences, he needed some sense that he was fighting on the right side.

He wasn't sure what this next job involved. He had gotten a wire down in Santa Fe asking him to come to Denver and promising him five hundred dollars for making the trip.

For that amount of money, Frank was willing to make the ride, even though it hadn't been overly pleasant in December.

The telegram had also instructed him to come to Lady Arabella's place, let the man at the door know who he was, and wait to be contacted. Frank had done that, but he was getting a little impatient.

Maybe if he could have done his waiting with Lady Arabella, it would have been different.

He had heard of Her Ladyship, of course, although they had never met. The famous Lady Arabella had operated saloons in various places, from raucous trail towns to big cities. Mostly, however, she made her living as a gambler. She was supposed to be one of the best poker players west of the Mississippi.

She was just as renowned for her beauty.

Frank hoped that before the night was over, he would get to find out for himself. He had been serious with only two women in his life, but the dim trails got lonely, so he took his companionship and comfort where he could.

He used his left thumb to poke his hat back on his graying brown hair and caught the bartender's eye. When the man came over to him, Frank said, "I was supposed to meet someone here tonight—"

"I know that, Mr. Morgan."

"I'm getting a little tired of waiting."

"Sorry, sir." The bartender shrugged. "There's really nothing I can do about—" He stopped short and looked over Frank's shoulder.

Frank didn't turn immediately—he'd had enemies try to fool him into taking his eyes off of them just like that—but then he heard the sound of a soft footstep in the salon's hushed atmosphere and knew someone actually was there.

"Mr. Morgan?" The woman's voice was quiet, but it packed a sultry heat similar to that of the cognac he had sipped a moment earlier.

Frank turned and saw her standing there with a slight smile on her face. Her warm brown eyes were what he noticed first, then the cameo-like features made even more lovely by the imperfection of a tiny scar on the right side of her upper lip.

Her raven hair was piled high on her head in an elaborate arrangement of curls. One or two of them had escaped and dangled enticingly beside her face. She wore a black skirt and a black jacket over a daringly low-cut red silk blouse. Rings sparkled on several of her fingers and jewels glittered on the black velvet choker she wore around her neck. She looked sinful and decadent but thoroughly beautiful.

"I'm Lady Arabella Winthrop." Her voice, still an intimate murmur, held just a trace of an accent to testify to her British heritage, but she had been in the States for a long time and had lost most of it.

Frank reached up and took off his hat. He didn't talk to a lady like that with his head covered. "It's an honor to meet you, ma'am. I mean, Your Ladyship."

Her laughter was like music. "Please, call me Lady Arabella. Or just Arabella. I don't stand on formality with certain gentlemen, and I can see that you're one of them."

Indeed, she looked him up and down with a boldness unusual to find in a woman. Frank had studied her with the same interest, so he supposed that was fair enough.

"I understand that you're here to discuss a business proposition," she went on.

"That's right," he said as a possibility occurred to him. "If that business is with you, I can tell you right now, I'm inclined to say yes to the deal."

She laughed again and shook her head.

"No, I'm afraid not, although I must admit, the idea is intriguing. The gentleman who sent for you asked me to have you step into one of the private sitting rooms. If you'll follow me . . ." She held out a slim, elegantly manicured hand.

Frank had been led into more than one trap by a beautiful woman, but his instincts told him that wasn't the case. He put his hat on, linked his left arm with Lady Arabella's right, and told her, "Lead the way."

He was considerably taller than her, but he figured they made a good-looking couple anyway as they strolled through the gambling hall. She took him to a door and opened it. On the other side was a room furnished with four comfortable leather armchairs, a roll-top desk, and a small table with a granite inlaid top that had been polished to a high gleam. A tray with a bottle of whiskey and two glasses sat on the table.

The room had no windows, but one wall was taken up mostly by a fireplace in which flames crackled. A man stood in front of the fireplace, obviously waiting for Frank. He was a couple inches shorter but probably thirty pounds heavier than the gunfighter. His thinning blond hair topped a face that at first glance didn't seem very intelligent. A second look at the man's pale blue eyes told Frank his first impression wasn't correct. The man had plenty of cunning.

"Frank Morgan, my name is Jim Bleeker."

CHAPTER 18

The name didn't mean anything to Frank, although he sensed that Bleeker expected him to recognize it. He gripped the man's outstretched hand and nodded. "Pleased to meet you, Mr. Bleeker."

"Since I hope we're going to be working together, you should call me Jim."

Frank was blunt in his response. "I reckon that depends on what the job is."

From the doorway, Lady Arabella murmured, "I'll leave you gentlemen to discuss your business."

Bleeker turned to smile at her. "You're welcome to stay if you'd like."

She shook her head. "I never intrude on my guests. Whenever anyone comes through my door, I want them to treat the place as if it's their own home. That's why everyone is welcome and I don't turn anyone away."

Frank thought he detected a faint edge in her voice, like maybe she didn't care for Bleeker all that much but tolerated him being there because part of her business was not passing judgment on people.

Or maybe I'm reading too much into it, he told himself, *because already I don't like Jim Bleeker very much.*

"Do you need anything else?" Lady Arabella asked.

Bleeker shook his head. "How about you, Frank?"

"I'm fine."

"Very well. You can pull that bell cord if there's any way I can help you." She left the room, closing the door quietly behind her.

Bleeker turned toward the table with the tray on it. "How about a drink?"

"Maybe later. After we've talked business."

"A man who gets right down to brass tacks, eh?" Bleeker said with a chuckle. "I like that. I'm the same way. I think I may have you at a disadvantage here, though. I know who Frank Morgan is, of course. Do you know who I am?"

Frank shook his head. "No offense, but I can't say as I do."

"None taken. Our trails never crossed, and for the past eight years you wouldn't have heard much about me."

"Is that a fact?" Frank could make a guess as to why Bleeker said that.

"Yeah. I've been in the Texas state pen, down in Huntsville."

A vague memory stirred in Frank's brain. Now that he knew how far back to cast his thoughts, he dredged through them and came up with the recollection he was searching for. "You held up some banks."

"Among other things," Bleeker responded with a

shrug. "That's what I was in the process of doing when I got caught."

"Bad luck," Frank said, although he didn't really think so. He had no use for owlhoots. Just because he was a hired gun, lawmen tended to lump him in with all sorts of desperadoes, but in truth Frank Morgan was a law-abiding man and always had been. He wasn't a back shooter, and he had never killed a man who hadn't been trying to kill him. He didn't prod them into gunfights, either. He'd never had to.

Trouble always came to him.

He had a hunch it was doing the same thing tonight.

Bleeker shrugged. "Luck didn't have anything to do with it. A fella I depended on ran out on me. He'd only been riding with my bunch for a short time, but I trusted him to watch my back. The job was already planned when he decided he didn't want to go through with it. Said he wasn't cut out for robbing banks." Bleeker snorted in evident disgust. "Don't know what would make a man get all high and mighty like that. It's not like he was some backsliding deacon! He'd been a hired gun before he threw in with us. Probably did plenty of things he could've wound up behind bars for."

"You were in prison in Texas," Frank said. "Did they let you out?"

"Or did I escape, you mean? Might as well ask the rest of it." Bleeker laughed and shook his head. "The governor commuted the rest of my sentence. You see, Frank, I was what they call a model prisoner. Hell, I even saved the warden's life during a riot down there. They were grateful to me, so they let me go."

"Are you trying to say you reformed while you were behind bars?"

"Reformed?" Bleeker shook his head. "I didn't cause any trouble because I knew they'd let me out sooner if I kept my nose clean. And the sooner I got out of there, the sooner I could settle the score with that gunfighter who ran out on me." His face was flushed with anger at the memory of what he considered a betrayal. He snagged the bottle of whiskey, pulled the cork from its neck, and splashed liquor into one of the glasses. "Sure I can't pour you one?"

"Not just yet," Frank said.

Bleeker grunted, picked up the glass, and downed the shot.

"That hombre you were talking about, you said he left the gang before you tried to pull that job. I don't see how it's his fault things went wrong."

"Playing devil's advocate, eh?" Bleeker said. "That's all right. You want to understand what you're getting into."

The longer he talked to Bleeker, the more Frank thought he wasn't getting into anything. All his instincts told him not to get involved with whatever the outlaw had in mind.

"The law was waiting for us that day in San Antonio," Bleeker went on as he poured himself another drink. "Now, I don't know for sure what happened. Could be that one of my men slipped up somewhere and said something he shouldn't have to some saloon girl or bartender, but I'm convinced that what really happened is Monte tipped them off. Even if he didn't, things would have been different if he'd been there. He would've been one more gun on our side.

A damn good gun, too. Like I said, he made his living with it . . . like you do, Frank."

"I never robbed banks," Frank said, allowing a harsh note to come into his voice. He was starting to like Bleeker less and less.

"First time for everything, right?" Bleeker waved off any answer Frank might have made. "Anyway, I've waited eight years to settle the score. I can wait a little while longer, but time's getting short. I'm recruiting men to ride with me to the town where he lives now. He's pinned on a badge, can you believe that? Calls himself a sheriff!"

"You're going to kill him?"

"Eventually." Bleeker took a sip of the whiskey instead of throwing back the whole shot. "But not until I've taken over his town, looted the whole damn place, and burned it to the ground in front of him. If any of the folks there get hurt—and I'm sure they will—it's just too damn bad. They shouldn't have hired a lobo wolf like Monte Carson to keep the peace."

Monte Carson . . . Frank stiffened and drew in a deep breath.

Bleeker noticed the reaction. "You know the name? The two of you have met?"

Frank nodded. "We've met."

A cabin in the Rockies
Ten years earlier

A thick haze of gray powder smoke hung in the air inside the old log cabin, stinging the eyes and noses of the two men who were forted up there as they knelt at loopholes and fired through them. A prospector had built the cabin and abandoned it when his search for gold had proven fruitless. Since then, cattlemen had moved into the area, and the cabin was used as a line shack by hands from one of the spreads.

It was the last line of defense for the two men who had been pursued by a much larger force of gunwolves working for a rival rancher.

Frank Morgan levered a fresh round into the chamber of his Henry rifle and peered over the sights, watching for a target. When he saw a flicker of movement, he pressed the trigger. The Henry cracked, and he was rewarded by the sight of a man flopping out from behind a rock. From the way the hombre thrashed around on the ground, Frank knew he was hit hard.

A moment later, the man went still. Death had claimed him.

"Chalk up another one, Frank," Monte Carson said from a loophole on the other side of the door.

"No point in keeping track of it now. We won't be getting out of here."

"You don't know that."

"I know that was my last round for this rifle." Frank withdrew the Henry's barrel from the loophole and leaned the weapon against the log wall.

"I'm about out, too," Monte said. "But we've got plenty of ammunition left for our Colts."

"Which won't do us a hell of a lot of good as long as Flagg's men stay out as far as they are. They can sit there and starve us out."

There weren't many provisions in the cabin, only a couple cans of peaches sitting on a crude shelf.

Water was even more of a concern, since Frank and Monte didn't have any. They could hold out for a day, maybe a day and a half, but no longer than that.

Monte took his rifle out of its loophole and turned to sit on the hard-packed dirt floor with his back leaned against the wall. He pushed his hat back on his head and grinned across the cabin's dim interior at his companion. "What do you think, Frank? Go out there and meet 'em head on?"

"They'll shoot us to pieces."

"Yeah, but if we wait until we're half dead from thirst, we won't be able to put up much of a fight. Right now, we're still so full of piss and vinegar, we can probably stay on our feet long enough to take some of 'em with us."

Monte had a point there, thought Frank. Ever since he had taken up the way of the gun, he'd expected to die a violent death. That was just the way things were. Everything that lived, died. That meant life was nothing but a grim, pointless joke. The only thing a man could really do was try to make sure he took as many of his enemies with him as possible.

So why the hell should they stay in there and wait for the end? Better to go out and charge right into it, dealing out as much hot lead as they could.

Frank stood up and drew his Colt. He took a cartridge from one of the loops on his shell belt and slid it into the cylinder's empty sixth chamber. Grinning, Monte Carson got to his feet and did likewise.

"I just wish Flagg was out there," Frank said. "I'd like to put a bullet in him."

Jefferson Flagg was the rancher trying to take over the spread that belonged to Frank and Monte's employer, Ben Kelton. The conflict between them had started as a boundary and water rights dispute, then quickly escalated into a full-scale range war. Frank had seen similar situations many times and had drawn fighting wages in a lot of them. It appeared that it would be the last for him.

Rifles still blasted outside as Flagg's hired killers peppered the cabin with slugs.

Knowing that the gunmen might target the empty loopholes, Frank moved to one side to glance through the hole he had been shooting through. Movement caught his eye and made him peer more intently through the opening. "Riders coming up the valley," he reported.

"What? More of Flagg's men?" Monte laughed. "It's already bad enough. No need for it to get worse."

"No, I think it's some of Kelton's bunch."

Monte sprang to his side and bent over to look through the loophole. He let out a whoop. "Yeah, that's Schaefer and Billings in front!" he exclaimed. "They must've heard the shooting when Flagg's bunch jumped us."

"Yeah, but they're hidden in those rocks on both sides of the gap. They'll have our men in a crossfire. The way Shaefer, Billings, and the rest are headed this way so fast, they won't have time to realize how much trouble they're in before Flagg's men blast them to hell."

Monte looked over at Frank with a grim frown creasing his forehead. "You're right. Listen."

Frank listened and realized that the shooting from outside had stopped. "They spotted our bunch and are holding their fire so they'll gallop right into that trap."

"Yeah . . . unless we warn them."

Most folks thought of hired guns as cold-blooded killers, men who had no morals or code who would do anything if the money was right. In some cases, that assessment was correct. But even the most hardened gun-wolf had a sense of loyalty toward the men he rode with. If you trusted a man to watch your back during a fight, you couldn't stand by and do nothing while he rode into a deathtrap.

"We were going out there anyway . . ." Frank said.

"Yeah," Monte agreed as a reckless grin spread over his face. "Now we've got an even better reason."

Frank went to the door they had barred when they'd holed up earlier. He set the bar aside, then looked at Monte and nodded. Monte returned the nod.

Frank flung the door open and they charged out into the open. For the first few lunging steps, Frank held his fire because he couldn't see any of the gunmen hidden in the rocks. Then shots blasted and he saw muzzle flashes and spurts of gun smoke. Bullets whined past his ears. A hundred yards away, Schaefer, Billings, and the other men who worked for Kelton reined up as gun thunder rolled through the valley.

Then they charged again, guns blazing as they raked the rocky sides of the gap with slugs.

One of the men in the rocks raised up and turned to have a better shot at the onrushing riders. Frank was close enough to drill him with a .44 round from the Colt. The man arched his back in agony, then dropped his rifle and pitched forward over the rock that had protected him.

A pair of shots slammed to Frank's left. He looked in that direction and saw another of Flagg's men tumbling down the slope with a rifle sliding ahead of him.

Monte Carson, smoke curling from the barrel of his gun, called, "He had a bead on your head, Frank!"

"Much obliged!" Frank shouted over the continuing uproar as he twisted back toward the rocks on his side of the gap. He saw another rifleman aiming at him and quickly dropped to a knee. As the man's bullet whined over his head, Frank fired twice and sent the hombre spinning off his feet.

Dust and powder smoke swirled around them. Hoofbeats, gunshots, and shouted curses all blended into a brain-numbing roar. Like most gun battles, it was noise and chaos and heart-stopping fear.

And in the midst of it, there was no denying that Frank Morgan felt truly alive.

Denver, December 1886

"You look like you're a million miles away, Frank," Jim Bleeker said.

Frank shook the memories of that day out of his head. "Not a million miles, just a couple hundred. And quite a few years. The years usually mean more than the miles."

"Ain't that the truth!" Bleeker said with a laugh. "I've had eight of 'em to think about what I'm going to do. How about it, Frank? Can I count you in? It'll be a hell of a payoff. Big Rock's got a bank and a lot of successful ranches around it. Probably be more loot there for the taking than either of us have ever seen before."

"Forget it," Frank said.

Bleeker drew back a little in obvious surprise. He frowned and asked, "What do you mean?"

"I mean I'm not throwing in with you," Frank said in a flat, hard voice. "You've got me wrong, Bleeker. I hire out my gun, but I'm not an outlaw."

Bleeker looked angry. "Sounds like you think you're better than me."

"I didn't say that. I just said I don't want any part of your plan, no matter how much money you figure to rake in."

"They call you the Drifter, don't they?"

"That's right."

"Badge-toters look for an excuse to lock you up as soon as you ride into a town. Women grab their kids and hustle across the street with them rather than meet you on a boardwalk. Their menfolks are just as scared. They just try not to show it."

"What you say is true," Frank admitted. "That still doesn't mean I want to be part of what you have in mind."

"Why the hell not? What do you owe those people?"

The people of Big Rock . . . that was the name of the town Bleeker had mentioned, Frank thought. He might not owe the people of Big Rock anything, but he owed his life to Monte Carson and his quick gun hand. One of Flagg's killers had come within a hair of blowing Frank's brains out.

"Just let it go, Bleeker," Frank said. "I'm not throwing in with you, that's all."

Bleeker stepped closer and grated, "Damn it, I'm not used to people saying no to me."

"You'd better get used to it where I'm concerned." Frank didn't flinch, didn't back off even a fraction of an inch. If Bleeker wanted to push, no matter how far, Frank was ready.

A tense few seconds ticked past, then Bleeker abruptly grinned and laughed again. "Ah, hell! There's no need for you and me to get crosswise, Frank. I made a suggestion, you said no thanks, that's all. No hard feelings either way."

Frank shrugged noncommittally. He had some hard feelings, all right, but he preferred to get out of there without shooting up Lady Arabella's place. She probably wouldn't like that.

"We can still have that drink together," Bleeker went on.

"I've got to be going," Frank didn't want to have a drink with that mad dog.

"All right. I reckon I can count on you to keep this little discussion between us?"

"Sure," Frank lied. He knew Bleeker's sort. The man had sat behind those gray prison walls for eight long years, stewing and stoking his hatred and planning his revenge. No matter what Frank said, Bleeker wasn't going to give up his goal.

It might be best just to go ahead and kill him, but Bleeker didn't appear to be armed and if Frank gunned him down, it would be murder. He had never killed a man in cold blood, and he didn't intend to start. But somebody had to warn Monte Carson that trouble was on the way, bad trouble.

Frank knew that job had fallen to him. As soon as possible, he needed to find out where Big Rock was and head in that direction. With that in mind, he gave Bleeker a curt nod, turned, and walked out of the room.

As he left, he felt Bleeker's eyes boring holes into his back.

CHAPTER 19

When Frank stepped out of the sitting room, the first person he saw was Lady Arabella Winthrop. She was standing next to a roulette table, but didn't appear to be paying any attention to the spinning wheel and the bouncing ball. She was watching the doorway of the sitting room and smiled when Frank came out.

He started toward her, and she moved forward to meet him.

"How did your business deal go?" she asked.

"It didn't," he replied bluntly. "What Bleeker's got in mind isn't for me."

"You know, I'm glad to hear that. I could tell just by looking at the two of you that you weren't the same sort of man."

Frank grunted. "That's the truth."

She linked her right arm with his left and suggested, "Come have a drink with me."

He didn't know if she was deliberately leaving his

gun hand free, as he had done earlier, or if it was just instinctive on her part. Either way, it added to his impression of her. "That sounds good. Especially if I can get a cup of coffee instead of a drink."

"Of course. The finest coffee you'll find in Denver, in fact."

"Then lead on, Your Ladyship."

"I told you, call me Arabella."

"Sure . . . Arabella."

She led him across the room, and after a moment he realized they weren't going toward the salon where he had waited earlier but rather toward a curving staircase with an elaborately carved banister.

"Where are we headed?"

"I thought we'd have our coffee in the sitting room of my suite . . . if that's all right with you?"

"I reckon it is."

Morley ushered Mitch Clark into the private sitting room a short time later. Clark had never seen Jim Bleeker before, but he felt certain that the big man sitting in an armchair near the fireplace was the boss outlaw.

Bleeker had his legs stretched out in front of him and crossed at the ankles. Despite that casual pose, Clark sensed an aura of ruthlessness and command about him. He held a glass of whiskey but wasn't drinking it. He appeared to be brooding about something.

"Who's this?" Bleeker asked as he looked up at Morley.

"Fella name of Mitch Clark." Morley's voice held a

faint mocking tone that Clark didn't like, but he kept his mouth shut. It wouldn't do to seem too proddy.

Morley went on. "He's been riding with some other fellas, and he figures they'd all make good additions to our ranks."

"He does, does he?" Bleeker threw back his drink, stood up, and set the empty glass on a granite-inlaid table. A long-legged stride brought him over to face Clark. Bleeker hooked his thumbs in the vest he wore and asked, "What was that name again?"

"Mitch Clark," he introduced himself. "It's a pleasure to meet you, Mr. Bleeker. I've heard a lot about you."

Bleeker grunted and looked at Morley, who shrugged and said, "You're the one who put the word out, Jim. You can't expect it not to get around."

"I wanted to get in touch with certain men," Bleeker said, "not every ambitious piece of trail trash out there."

Clark stiffened. He couldn't help it. "You've got it wrong, Bleeker. My friends and I are top hands when it comes to this game."

"It's not a damn game." Bleeker nodded over Clark's shoulder to Ray Morley.

Clark's breath hissed between his teeth as he felt the hard ring of a gun barrel prodding his back. He cursed silently to himself. He never should have allowed Morley to get behind him. He should have known better.

"For a top hand, you let Ray get the drop on you mighty easy," Bleeker said with a sneer.

"I thought I was among friends," Clark replied coldly.

"Well, see, that was your mistake. Never assume somebody's your friend. Nobody's truly got any friends in this world—just people who think it'll be to their advantage to use you."

"You can use us however you want," said Clark, "as long as we get a share of the loot you're gonna take out of Big Rock." There was no point in denying that he knew something about Bleeker's plans. All it would take was a word from Morley to make that clear to his boss. Admitting it before Morley said anything might help his case, thought Clark.

Bleeker stared hard at him for a long moment.

Clark wouldn't have been surprised if the man ordered Morley to put a bullet in his back. The instant that was about to happen, he would make a move of his own, spinning around and knocking the gun aside before Morley could pull the trigger. More than likely, the effort would fail, but Clark wasn't going to just stand there and let them kill him.

Bleeker chuckled abruptly. "You've got some bark on you, don't you?"

"I don't reckon life's been easy for any of us," Clark said.

"You're not full of big talk. I like that." Bleeker stepped back and gestured to Morley.

The gun barrel went away from Clark's spine.

Bleeker inclined his head toward the table, which held a tray with a bottle and a clean glass. "Want a drink?"

"That'd be pretty good right now," Clark admitted.

Bleeker picked up the clean glass, splashed whiskey in it, and held it out to Clark. Then he refilled his own glass. "So you know I'm putting together some men to hit Big Rock," he mused.

Clark shrugged.

"Do you know why?"

"Don't figure that's any of my business. I'm only interested in the payoff."

"That's a pretty smart way to be. How many men do you having riding with you?"

"Four. Jed Darby, Curly Weaver, Hector Gomez, and Blind Jimmy Pugh."

Morley put in, "I've heard of Pugh. He's not really blind, just nearsighted. Supposed to be pretty good with a gun anyway."

"We all are," Clark said. "You won't be disappointed if you take us on, Mr. Bleeker."

"So it's *Mister* again now, is it?" Bleeker drawled.

Clark drank some of his whiskey. "I'm more polite without a gun in my back."

Bleeker laughed again. "I think I like you . . . Mitch, was it? But I don't really know you or your friends, and you've got to admit, you don't have a big reputation."

"We're getting there," Clark said tightly.

"How about this? I need some men to handle a job for me. Not the Big Rock job. This other deal comes first, but it's related to it. Think you and your bunch can take care of it for me?"

"If it means you'll let us throw in with you for the big payoff, then damn right we can take care of it," Clark replied with easy confidence. "What's the job?"

Bleeker looked at him over the whiskey glass and said, "I want you to kill a man named Frank Morgan."

* * *

A maid brought the pot of coffee from downstairs and poured cups of it for Frank and Arabella. The brew was as good as Arabella claimed it would be.

As they sipped from the fine china cups, they sat on a well-upholstered divan with sturdy wooden claw feet. The sitting room had a thick woven rug on the floor and dark blue curtains over the windows. It reminded Frank of Milady deWinter in Dumas's novel about those Musketeers over in France, a book he had read a while back. Milady was a beautiful, ruthless, evil schemer.

Lady Arabella was every bit as lovely as that character was supposed to be, and honestly, he didn't know if she really had any noble blood or just pretended to the title of lady. He figured she could be ruthless across a poker table, but she wasn't evil. He could sense that and trusted his instincts.

Even though he hated for ugly reality to intrude on the pleasant moment, worry nagged at him. "How well acquainted are you with Jim Bleeker?"

The question didn't appear to bother Arabella. "I never met the man or even heard of him until tonight. A man who works for him—Morley is his name, I believe—came to the house earlier today and asked if it would be possible to arrange for Mr. Bleeker to have a private room at his disposal this evening. For his meeting with you, as we know now."

"He's an outlaw," Frank said bluntly.

Arabella's shoulders rose and fell slightly. "I can't say that I'm surprised. In my business, you learn how to be a good judge of character. I knew right away that Bleeker and Morley were bad men."

"But you did business with them."

Her words were crisp as she said, "Don't judge me, Frank. I run clean games and I don't allow any trouble in my house. What goes on outside of the house is none of my concern." She paused, then added, "Some people would no doubt disapprove of me bringing a notorious gunfighter up here to my sitting room for a cup of coffee."

"So you know who I am."

"The Drifter is known far and wide on the frontier."

Frank couldn't argue with that, although plenty of times he wished it wasn't so. He sipped his coffee and said, "We're getting off on the wrong foot here. I didn't mean to imply that you're in any sort of cahoots with Bleeker. I just wanted to know if you were aware of what he's planning."

"I have no idea," Arabella said. "And I don't want to know, so I'd appreciate it if you didn't tell me."

"All right. Let's just say that he's up to something that'll hurt an old friend of mine."

"Then you're going to stop him, of course," Arabella said without hesitation.

"How do you know that?"

"Because that's the sort of man you are." She smiled at him over the rim of her cup. "I told you, I'm a good judge of character."

Frank nodded slowly. "I'm going to stop him, all right. Tomorrow morning, I'm heading for the town where my friend lives. I'm going to warn him and then back his play, whatever it is."

"You're not worried that I'll tell Bleeker what you're planning to do?"

"Nope. I can tell a little about a person, too. Not only that, you said that whatever happens outside this house is none of your concern, and I believe you."

"You and I have some things in common, don't we? We keep to ourselves for the most part, and we have a code that governs our actions."

"I don't put it in fancy terms like that," Frank said. "I just do what seems right."

"So do I." She set her coffee cup on the table in front of the divan, moved closer to Frank—she didn't have to go far—and slid her arms around his neck.

He had already set his cup aside, too, so it was no problem for him to put his arms around her.

"And right now, this definitely seems right," Arabella murmured as she tilted her face up, ready for the kiss he brought down on her lips.

It was late when Frank left Lady Arabella's suite and went downstairs. Despite the hour, some of the games were still going on, of course. He wasn't sure if the place ever shut down completely, as long as there were gamblers eager to lose their money.

The big, rawboned, redheaded man called Dorgan was still on duty at the front door.

Frank smiled slightly and asked, "Do you ever sleep, amigo?"

"Every now and then. Will we be seein' you again, Mr. Morgan?"

"*¿Quién sabe?* But not for a while, I reckon. There are some things I have to do."

"I'll be biddin' you good night, then," said Dorgan as he held the door open.

Frank nodded and stepped out. A few buggies were still parked in the circular drive in front of the house, and several horses were tied at a hitch rack, Frank's big gray stallion among them. As he started toward the horses, his eyes scanned the shadows under the trees. Only one lamp burned on the columned gallery, and even though the branches were bare, they grew thickly enough to create large areas of impenetrable gloom.

Caution was ingrained in him, and his mind and body were always ready for action. He reacted instantly when he heard a very faint clicking sound from the shadows and recognized it as the sound of a gun's hammer being eared back. He dived to the ground as a shot suddenly roared and Colt flame bloomed in the darkness.

CHAPTER 20

Frank's Colt was in his hand by the time he hit the paved drive. The big revolver roared and bucked against his palm as he snapped a shot at the muzzle flash he had seen.

A bullet coming from a different direction plowed into the ground just inches from his head, and he rolled quickly to his left, toward the horses. The gunfire made the other animals spook, although Frank's stallion was used to that sound. As they danced around skittishly, he came up on hands and knees and scrambled among them, using them for cover.

More guns were blasting. From the sound of them, he knew several bushwhackers were lurking in the shadows, trying to kill him.

From the direction of the house, someone bellowed, "Hey, you!"

Frank glanced in that direction and saw Dorgan galloping toward the gunfight with a sawed-off shotgun in his hands.

The big man stumbled suddenly. He extended the shotgun toward the trees with one hand and fired both barrels. Foot-long tongues of flame erupted from the weapon, and for a split-second the garish orange flare lit up the night. Frank caught a glimpse of another man flying backwards with his face and chest shredded by the double load of buckshot.

Then it was dark again, except for the light from the gallery. Dorgan doubled over and collapsed, obviously wounded.

Frank worked his way through the horses. The gun thunder faded for a second, and he heard distant shouts. The sounds of battle in the quiet neighborhood was drawing a lot of attention. The blue-uniformed Denver police would show up fairly quickly. The would-be killers couldn't afford to linger, so if they wanted to ventilate Frank, they had to do it in a hurry.

As he reached the edge of the drive, a foot scraped behind him. Frank whirled and crouched at the same time, just as a gun went off so close the flame from its muzzle almost singed his eyebrows. He triggered his Colt twice, and in the glare of the shots, he saw a squat Mexican drop his gun and reel backwards with his hands pressed to his belly. Blood welled blackly between his splayed fingers.

Frank knew the gut shot man shouldn't pose any more problems. He wheeled and ran along the edge of the drive, away from the house. He didn't know how badly Dorgan was hurt, but he didn't want to draw any more fire toward the man.

Several more shots slammed through the darkness. A pair of slugs whistled past Frank's head, close enough that he felt the wind-rip of their passage. He plunged into some shrubs. Their branches crackled around him, giving away his position and making him bite back a curse.

He dropped to one knee and stopped moving. Again, during a lull, he heard confused, frightened shouts from nearby houses. Time was running out for the killers.

While he knelt among the bushes, he took advantage of the opportunity to replace the shells he had fired. Working by feel—he didn't need to see in order to carry out a task he had performed thousands of times—he thumbed fresh cartridges into the Colt's cylinder.

When the ambushers attacked again, they came at him from three directions at once. They had a pretty good idea of where he was hiding, and they were almost right. A storm of bullets tore into the shrubs, sending broken branches flying into the air.

Unfortunately for the bushwhackers, their fire was concentrated on a spot about five feet in front of him.

He rose to his full height, thrust the gun out, and aimed just above one of the muzzle flashes. His first shot was rewarded by a strangled scream.

Hearing that, he was already pivoting toward muzzle flashes that were moving as the killer charged forward, firing. Frank bracketed them and squeezed off two shots. Again he heard a pained yelp.

That left just one man—although Frank couldn't be sure the other two were actually out of the fight—but as he swung in that direction a hammer blow against his side knocked him back a step. He felt a hot gush of blood as he caught his balance.

The fifth man was almost on top of him. He fired again at the same time Frank fired, and the guns were so close the spouting flames seemed to reach out and cross each other. Frank didn't feel the impact of another slug, so he knew the man's shot had missed.

A second later, a stumbling form ran into him, carried forward by its momentum with enough force that the collision knocked Frank off his feet.

They sprawled to the ground together. Frank's head spun crazily, and he knew he was on the verge of passing out from losing the blood that pumped from the hole in his side. The light from the gallery reflected off something metallic, causing him to realize that his enemy was still trying to bring a gun to bear on him. He lashed out with his own revolver and cracked its barrel across the man's wrist. The man let out a shrill cry of pain as he dropped the gun.

Then he stopped fighting. He lay there struggling to breathe, the high-pitched wheeze evidence that he was shot through the lungs. He gasped, "You . . . you can't have killed . . . all five of us!"

"I didn't," Frank said, feeling pretty much on his last legs himself. "That fella who works for . . . Lady Arabella . . . did one of you." He could see the man's face.

Thoroughly undistinguished and topped by thinning brown hair, the man looked like a storekeeper or a traveling salesman. He gasped out, "I know you're . . . a famous gunfighter . . . but it seemed like five of us . . . would be enough. . . ." Another sharp wheeze was followed by a grotesque rattle. The man was dead.

Frank had no doubt that Jim Bleeker had set those assassins on him. Bleeker didn't want to take a chance on him warning Monte Carson or otherwise interfering with his plan.

And even though all the bushwhackers seemed to be dead or badly wounded—none of them were shooting at him anymore, at least—Frank knew that they might have accomplished what Bleeker wanted. Badly wounded, Frank had already lost a lot of blood, and there was no telling if he would survive the attack or not.

But he had to, otherwise Monte Carson might not know about the trouble coming his way until it was too late.

With that thought burning in his mind, Frank took his bloody left hand away from his side where it had been pressed to the bullet hole. He braced himself with it and pushed his body upward until he was able to struggle to his feet. Still holding the Colt in his right hand, he staggered a few steps toward the house, then had to stop and steady himself.

He heard the rapid patter of footsteps coming toward him and raised the Colt, ready to fire. His finger relaxed on the trigger at the last second as light from a bull's-eye lantern spilled over him and Arabella's voice cried, "Frank!"

He let his arm sag again. His strength had deserted him, and he couldn't stop the revolver from slipping out of his fingers and thudding to the ground at his feet. The world tilted and then began to turn in the wrong direction around him.

He heard Arabella call his name again, but that was the last thing he was aware of as he plummeted into black oblivion.

Frank floated on a dark sea for what felt like an eternity, but after so long a time, light began to seep into the blackness. It grew brighter and brighter until it seemed to fill his entire consciousness. He recoiled against it.

In actuality, he barely moved, but it was enough to set off a clamoring pain in his side. A voice said hollowly as if from a great distance, "Frank, you're awake."

Slowly, he became aware of more than just the pain. He realized he was lying in a soft, warm bed with covers draped over him. When he tried to take a deep breath he couldn't do it, and after a moment he understood why. Bandages were wrapped tightly around the middle of his torso.

Clearly, he wasn't dead after all.

But he might be dying. It was too soon to tell.

Something cool touched his face, soothing it with deft strokes, and he forced his eyes open. The bright light that had almost blinded him was, in reality, a small lamp on a bedside table with its flame turned down low so that much of the room was in shadow. However, it gave off enough illumination for him to make out Lady Arabella Winthrop's smiling but worried face as she leaned over him, wiping his face with a wet cloth.

"You're going to be all right," she told him. "Can you understand me, Frank?"

"Yeah," he husked. "I . . . understand."

"You lost quite a bit of blood and you have some bruised ribs, but Dr. Fletcher said that no bones were broken. You were lucky in one respect that the bullet glanced off your ribs without fracturing any of them, but it tore an even uglier wound coming out. Still, the doctor says you're going to be fine in a few weeks."

Something about that bothered Frank, but his brain was so addled at the moment he couldn't figure out what it was. The fogginess came from more than just pain and blood loss. He thought the doctor must have given him some laudanum.

Something else occurred to him, and he asked in a ragged voice, "What about . . . Dorgan?"

"He's alive, although his injuries are worse than yours. Dr. Fletcher believes he'll pull through. He'll receive the best possible care. I'll see to that." Arabella smiled again. "Angus Fletcher is one of the best doctors in Denver. He also loves playing blackjack, so he's here quite often and was more than happy to tend to the wounded in exchange for me tearing up some of his markers."

"Cost you . . . some money," Frank said.

"Worth every penny."

He was so weak he had to muster up his strength to ask another question. "Those men . . . who jumped me . . ."

"Five of them." Arabella's tone was brisk and more than a little angry. "All dead. According to the authorities, they were all wanted outlaws. I suppose they must have thought you had a pocketful of winnings and intended to rob you."

"No . . . Bleeker . . . sent them after me."

"Bleeker! Are you sure?"

"Pretty . . . sure. He's not . . . still here?"

Arabella shook her head. "No, he left a long time ago, shortly after you talked to him, according to several of my employees. While we were . . . up here having coffee."

Talking about Bleeker had made some other things come into focus in Frank's brain. Instinctively, he tried to raise himself into a sitting position as he said, "I've got to . . . go. . . ."

Arabella set the wet cloth aside and pressed both hands to his shoulders to hold him down. "You can't go anywhere. The doctor said you shouldn't even be up and around for a week."

"Can't . . . wait. Got to warn . . ."A wave of dizziness washed over him. The little bit of strength that had returned deserted him again, leaving him too weak to do anything except sag back against the mattress and pillows. He heard Arabella cry out in alarm.

"You're bleeding again! Oh, my God . . . Frank!"

The flickering light in the room was fading. Blackness closed in from the corners. He couldn't see Arabella anymore, but he heard her say, "I think the doctor is still here—"

Then a door banged and someone was shouting and feet rushed here and there, but all that went away and took Frank's consciousness with it.

His last thought was that death was coming for Monte Carson in Big Rock, and no one was there to warn him or help him. . . .

Outside the big house in Denver, snow had begun to fall.

CHAPTER 21

North of Big Rock

The storm that swept down from the Canadian Rockies was a potent one to start with, and it only gathered force as it slowly followed the great line of peaks that formed the backbone of the continent. It sent brief snow squalls out ahead of it, but in the main body, a bone-chilling wind howled and blew so hard that the thick snow seemed to fall sideways. Visibility was reduced to a matter of feet.

A man caught in a blizzard like that wouldn't stand a chance.

Fortunately for the three men riding south, they were well ahead of the worst of the storm. The snow swirled prettily rather than blew. The ground was turning white around them, but it didn't present any barrier to their horses.

Ace, Chance, and Eagle-Eye Callahan had found themselves a nice overhang the night before. Considering it the next best thing to a cave, they had made camp there, building a warm fire and having a good supper before they'd rolled up in their soogans. With the weather the way it was, it had seemed unlikely that anyone would bother them.

The snow had started to fall during the night, and it hadn't stopped since.

As they followed the trail the next morning, Eagle-Eye said, "Gonna come a pretty bad blow, I reckon. That's what my bones tell me, anyway. After all those winters up in the Montana territory, I expect they know what they're talkin' about."

"We ought to reach Big Rock by the middle of the day," Ace said. "We can find somebody to tell us where to find Smoke's ranch. With any luck, we'll get there by nightfall."

Chance shivered in his saddle. Unlike Ace's sheepskin jacket, his suit coat didn't provide much protection from the wind. "Can't be soon enough to suit me. We're damn fools for being out traveling at this time of year to start with."

"You don't always have much choice about when you go," Ace said.

"The world don't give you much choice about most things," commented Eagle-Eye. "It sort of just does what it wants, and you get knocked this way and that, and there ain't a whole hell of a lot you can do about it."

"You don't believe that a man is master of his own fate?" asked Ace.

"Well, he can try to be, I suppose, but in the end, the odds are again' him. If that wasn't true, folks' lives would be a heap different."

Chance nodded. "Maybe you're right, Mr. Callahan. With a name like mine, I know how big a part pure luck plays in most people's lives."

"Call me Eagle-Eye," the old-timer told him. "We've shared a campfire, so I consider you boys to be friends o' mine now."

"Sounds good to me, Eagle-Eye," Chance said.

The snow gradually fell thicker and faster during the morning.

Big Rock

There was an inch or two of snow on the ground as they approached the town at midday. The roofs of some of the buildings and a couple church steeples were still visible despite the flakes filling the air.

It appeared to be a good-sized settlement with several streets lined by businesses and a number of cross streets with residences on them. An impressive brick building on one side of town served as the railroad depot. Tracks came in from the northeast.

Although Big Rock had a sleepy, half-deserted look on the cold December day not long before Christmas, Ace imagined it was quite bustling at other times. "I figure the local lawman will be the best person to ask about Smoke's ranch," he said as they walked their horses slowly along the main street. "I'm sure he can tell us where to find the Sugarloaf."

"Why don't you fellas do that?" Eagle-Eye suggested. He nodded toward a café they were passing. "I'm gonna go in there and warm up a mite. I'll order coffee for the three of us and whatever their special is. The food's on me."

"Nice of you," Chance said.

"We're obliged to you," Ace added.

Eagle-Eye shook his head. "No, sir, it's me who's obliged to you boys for lendin' me a hand a few days ago when those hombres jumped me. I ain't forgot that, and I ain't likely to." The old-timer reined his mount toward the hitch rail in front of the café, which bore a sign identifying it as the CITY PIG.

Ace and Chance continued on down the street, looking for the sheriff's office.

They found it a minute later and headed toward the sturdy stone building. No horses were tied up in front, but that didn't mean anything. Likely the sheriff kept his mount in one of the local stables when he wasn't using it.

The brothers swung down from their saddles and looped their reins around the rail. Ace brushed at a couple snowflakes that clung to his eyelashes as he and Chance stepped up onto the boardwalk in front of the sheriff's office and jail.

Chance clutched his coat tighter around him. "I'll be glad to get out of this weather."

"You have to expect it to be cold and snowy around Christmas time," Ace pointed out. "Most folks like it that way."

"Most folks don't have to ride for miles in it."

"We'd be in it on horseback all day if we were cowboying."

Chance snorted. "That's one reason we don't take riding jobs unless we absolutely have to."

Ace let that comment go and opened the door. They stepped into the welcome warmth coming from a pot-bellied stove in the corner of the office.

A man stood beside that stove pouring coffee from

a battered pot into an equally battered tin cup. He replaced the pot on the stove, set the piece of leather he'd been using to handle it on a nearby shelf, and turned to face the newcomers as he blew on the coffee, which had tendrils of steam rising from it. A badge was pinned to the brown leather vest he wore over a white shirt. "Help you boys?"

"You're the sheriff?" Ace asked.

"That's right. Name's Monte Carson. What can I do for you?"

"We're looking for a ranch that's supposed to be somewhere around here," Chance said. "We thought you could probably tell us where to find it."

Sheriff Carson took a sip of the coffee and nodded. "I reckon I know all the spreads in these parts. I've got to warn you, though, I doubt if any of them will be hiring at this time of year."

"We're not looking for jobs," Ace said.

"All right," Carson said. "Which ranch is it you're interested in?"

"The Sugarloaf," Chance said.

"Smoke Jensen's spread," Ace added.

Carson stiffened. His affable face took on a harder, more suspicious cast. He stepped over to the desk and set the tin cup down. "You'd better just move along. It's going to be Christmas in a few days, so I'm going to do you a favor and not lock you up. But I want you out of Big Rock before the afternoon's over."

The Jensen boys stared at him in surprise. Neither found his voice for a couple heartbeats then Ace said, "Sheriff, I don't know what you think we're doing here, but obviously you've got us all wrong."

"I don't think so," snapped Carson. "A couple young

gunhands who figure to make a reputation for yourselves by killing Smoke Jensen, right? I've seen a dozen just like you over the years I've known Smoke. Know where most of them are now?" He didn't wait for them to answer. "In the cemetery. Some of them in unmarked graves because we never had a chance to find out their names before Smoke killed them."

Ace shook his head. "Sheriff, you're making a—"

"Don't you idiots see that I'm trying to save your lives?" Carson broke in. "If I tell you where to find the Sugarloaf, you'll ride out there and Smoke will blow holes in both of you. Now move on like I told you."

"Damn it, Sheriff!" Chance burst out. "We're not gunfighters. We're looking for Smoke's ranch because he's a friend of ours." He inclined his head toward his brother. "Ace here thinks he might even be a long-lost relative, because our last name is Jensen, too."

Carson frowned. "Wait a minute. Did you say Ace?"

"That's my name, Sheriff," Ace said. "And this is my brother Chance. We've met Smoke a couple times, most recently down in Texas last year."

"You're those Jensen boys he talked about," Carson said with a nod. His eyes narrowed in suspicion again. "But how do I know you're really who you say you are?"

"How would we know those names if we weren't?" asked Chance.

"And how would we know that Smoke was involved

in a big dust-up down in Texas during all those bad floods last year?" added Ace.

"Yeah, he told me about that," Carson admitted. "And he told me about the two of you." The lawman extended his hand, obviously accepting their identities. "It's a pleasure to meet any friend of Smoke Jensen's."

"We feel the same way, Sheriff," Ace said as he shook Carson's hand. "Have the two of you known each other for long?"

"Several years. As long as Big Rock's been here, in fact. If it weren't for Smoke, I wouldn't be the sheriff, either." Carson grunted. "More than likely, I'd be lying in one of those unmarked graves I was talking about. I owe the man a lot, which is why I wasn't going to sic a couple crazy young gun-throwers on him. That would just be an annoyance for him."

"You don't have to worry about us, Sheriff," Ace said. "We're not looking to cause a bit of trouble for him."

"What brings you to Big Rock, then?" Carson picked up the cup again and took another sip of coffee. "Can't blame me for being curious. Finding out why strangers are in town is sort of my job."

"Well, we're not really looking for Smoke's ranch for our own sake." Ace didn't see anything wrong with telling Sheriff Carson the truth. "We ran into an old-timer the other day who's been riding with us ever since. He's looking for a mountain man called Preacher, and we're hoping Smoke can tell us where to find him. I remember Smoke talking about

Preacher. It sounded like the two of them are pretty close."

"Close as father and son, almost," Carson agreed, "although there's no blood relation between them. And you're in luck, coming to Big Rock right now."

"How's that?"

"Unless he's ridden out in the past day or two, Preacher should be out at the Sugarloaf right now."

CHAPTER 22

A buxom, middle-aged waitress was just setting three steaming bowls of stew on the table in front of Eagle-Eye Callahan when Ace and Chance walked into the City Pig. A full cup of coffee sat beside each place at the table.

The burly, white-haired old man grinned at the brothers as they walked across the room toward him. "And here I was thinkin' I might just have to eat all three bowls o' this Irish stew myself. It smells good enough I might coulda done it."

Ace pulled out a ladder-back chair at one of the places and hung his hat on it. Chance did likewise, grinning at the waitress.

She giggled. "You stop looking at me like that, young fella. I'm old enough to be your mama."

"Not hardly," Chance protested. "My aunt, maybe. My mother's much, much younger sister."

"Go on with you!" She put her hands on her ample

hips and looked around at the three of them. "Do you gentlemen need anything else right now?"

"Well—" Chance began.

She held up a hand to stop him. "I meant anything else to eat?"

Eagle-Eye pointed at the chalkboard on the wall. "That says you got pie. What kind?"

"Peach cobbler."

"Well," he said heartily as if it were the most obvious thing in the world, "we're all gonna need some of that once we polish off this fine stew. And more coffee."

"I'll take good care of you," the waitress promised, then wagged a scolding finger at Chance as he started to say something else.

Once the woman was gone, Ace said to his brother, "Do you have to flirt with everything in a skirt?"

"Nope. I saw a picture once of a fella from Scotland, and he was wearing a skirt. If one of those Scottish hombres was to walk in here right now, I wouldn't flirt with *him*. Not one bit." Chance laughed quietly. "Besides, she enjoyed it, didn't she?"

"Seemed to," Ace admitted with a shrug.

Eagle-Eye stopped shoveling stew into his mouth and pointed his spoon at the brothers. "Dig in, before it gets cold."

Ace and Chance started eating, and the food tasted as good as it smelled. They tore hunks off the fresh loaf of bread on the table and used them to sop up some of the gravy from the stew. Washed down with strong, hot coffee, it made an excellent meal.

After they had eaten for a few minutes, Ace said,

"Stew, pie, and coffee has to cost some, Eagle-Eye. You don't have to pay for me and Chance."

"Hush that up. I told you boys this was my treat, and I'm stickin' to it. Besides, I got plenty o' dinero. Like I told you when we met, I sold my tradin' post when I left Montana, and I got a nice price for it. No, I ain't worried about money."

"Must be nice," Chance said.

"Well, you can't expect to spend your life just roamin' around, ridin' from place to place, only workin' when you feel like it or when you're outta money, and figure you're gonna get rich. No, sir, to do that, you've got to settle down, find somethin' you like to do that's worth the doin', and work hard at it."

"But what if we like roaming around?" Chance wanted to know.

"Then you got to get used to havin' a hungry belly ever' now and then."

"Yeah," Ace said dryly, "I think we're already starting to learn that."

Chance swallowed the bite of stew he had spooned into his mouth. "Next thing you know, Eagle-Eye, you're going to be telling us that we've got to have the love of a good woman to succeed, that we should be looking for wives as well as good jobs."

A frown caused the old-timer's shaggy eyebrows to draw down. He rumbled, "No, I ain't gonna tell you that. Wish I could, but I just plumb can't."

Ace wondered what that meant. He could tell some sort of story went with the old man's statement but sensed that Eagle-Eye wouldn't want to tell it, and anyway, it was none of his business.

Chance said, "You were the one who was telling us a little while ago that the world is cold-hearted and a man can't escape his fate, and now you're telling us to settle down and work hard and make something of ourselves. Which is it?"

"Well, you can at least *try* to accomplish somethin' with your life. Odds are, it won't work out, but at least you'll know in your heart that you put some effort into it. And speakin' of puttin' some effort into it . . . Did you boys find the sheriff's office or didn't you?"

They were finally getting down to the reason they had come to Big Rock in the first place, thought Ace. "Not only did we find the office, but we talked to the sheriff. And he told us that he thinks Preacher is spending the holidays at the Sugarloaf with Smoke Jensen and his wife Sally."

Eagle-Eye slapped a palm against the table excitedly, and the noise was loud enough to make some of the other customers in the café jump a little in their chairs and look around.

"I knew it!" he declared. "I could feel it in my bones. I knew I was gettin' close to that old son of— that old rapscallion."

Ace noticed that Eagle-Eye had come close to referring to Preacher in a bad way, not like somebody might use that term jokingly when talking about an old friend. He also noticed what might have been anger had flared in the old-timer's eyes when he said it.

Ace frowned, wondering if Eagle-Eye was carrying some sort of grudge against Preacher. Was that the real reason he was looking for the legendary mountain man?

Ace supposed it was possible. Even the best of

friends sometimes had hard feelings between them. It was also a possibility that Eagle-Eye wanted to lay to rest some old dispute.

Whatever the situation, Ace wasn't really worried about it. He still thought they should ride on out to the Sugarloaf that afternoon. Sheriff Carson had told him and Chance how to find the ranch, and Ace was confident they could reach it before nightfall.

No matter what Eagle-Eye's real objective was, Ace and Chance would be with him, and Smoke would be on hand, too.

In a situation like that, how much trouble could one old man get into?

Sugarloaf Ranch

Sally had made good on her promise to fry up a mess of bear sign. It was for the planning meeting she had with the ladies in town. She had to protect them from not only Pearlie and Cal but also Preacher. She had her hands full with those three scroungers, much to Smoke's amusement.

Much as the whole house was filled with the delicious smells of baking, he'd felt a little sorry for her, so he'd gotten the old mountain man and the two ranch hands out of the house. The four of them had ridden out to some of the winter pastures to check on the stock that had been moved down for the season.

"Told you there was gonna be a blizzard," Preacher said as they rode back toward the ranch house. It really wasn't that late in the day yet, but it looked like it was coming on toward night anyway because of the thick overcast and the heavily falling snow. It was wet snow, too, packing down densely as several inches built up on the ground. The horses' hooves kicked it up in a white spray as they moved along the trail.

"It's snowing pretty good," Smoke said, "but I wouldn't call this a blizzard."

"Just wait," Preacher said as he nodded sagely.

Pearlie said, "I recollect one time up in the Dakota Territory when a storm came through overnight and the next mornin' I couldn't get out of the line shack where I was spendin' the winter. Snow had drifted up so high the dang door wouldn't budge."

"How'd you get out?" Cal asked.

"Oh, I didn't," Pearlie said with a deadpan expression. "I done starved to death, and my bones may still be a-layin' in that cabin right now for all I know."

Cal blew out an exasperated breath and shook his head. "I should've known I couldn't get a straight answer out of you."

"Naw, really, what I done was open the shutter on the window and dug a tunnel out through the snow. Once I done that, I was able to dig a big ol' ditch to the door so I could get in and out and take care o' the stock like I was supposed to." Pearlie nodded solemnly. "When a man's got a job of work to do, he finds a way to do it."

"Well, I hope the snow doesn't get that high this time."

Preacher said, "It prob'ly won't, down here in the valley. I figure all those passes up in the mountains will be closed, though."

"What about the one the railroad goes through?" asked Smoke.

"I wouldn't count on it stayin' open for long."

If Preacher was right, it wouldn't be the first time such a thing had happened. Smoke recalled other times when the railroad had been forced to suspend operations until the snow in the pass melted. The locomotives could force their way through if the snow wasn't too deep, but sometimes it was better just to be patient and wait.

Anyway, he didn't plan to go anywhere on the train, so he didn't figure it really mattered to him.

They were getting close to the ranch headquarters. In fact, as they started down a long hill, Smoke spotted the yellow glow of lamplight in the gathering dusk. In a few more minutes, he could see the house itself, as well as the trail leading to it from the road to Big Rock. The sight put a warm feeling inside him, knowing that the woman he loved was safe and secure inside that house.

He sat up straighter in the saddle as he spotted movement on the trail. With the snow and the fading light, it wasn't easy to make out details, but his eyes were sharp and he was pretty sure he saw three riders approaching the house along the trail.

"Riders comin' in," Preacher said at the same time. The old mountain man had noticed the men and horses, too.

Pearlie asked, "You didn't send anybody to town today, did you, Smoke?"

"I sure didn't," Smoke replied. "With this bad weather coming in, I figured it was best to keep everybody close to home. I don't recognize those hombres."

"Well, then, let's go see who they are," Cal said.

"Good idea." Smoke heeled his horse into a trot. His three companions did likewise.

Smoke wasn't expecting any trouble, and for some reason, the snowy day just seemed peaceful. He had made a lot of enemies during his adventurous life, but to be honest, most of those enemies were dead . . . just not all of them.

Sally was down there, baking and looking forward to Christmas.

Smoke pulled out a little ahead of the others as he felt a growing urgency. They quickly closed the gap, and the four men were riding abreast as they reached the bottom of the slope and crossed an open stretch of snowy ground to reach the trail. The three strangers had seen them coming and had reined in about a hundred yards away from the house.

That was good, thought Smoke. He could find out what was going on while Sally was still out of the line of fire.

As he slowed his mount, something about a couple of the visitors struck him. One of them lifted a hand in greeting.

Smoke suddenly exclaimed, "Son of a gun. That's Ace Jensen. Must be his brother Chance with him."

"Those young fellers you met down in Texas last year?" asked Preacher. "The ones with the same last name?"

"That's right." With only about twenty yards separating the two groups of riders, Smoke recognized the grinning faces of Ace and Chance and wondered what the boys were doing on the Sugarloaf.

The man with them, who had had his head down,

lifted it and bellowed, "Preacher! I'm gonna kill you, you old geezer!" He jabbed his heels into his horse's flanks and sent the animal leaping forward. At the same time he put the reins between his teeth and pulled a pair of old-fashioned flintlock pistols from behind his belt.

"Oh, hell!" Preacher said. "Eagle-Eye!"

CHAPTER 23

The sudden attack didn't take Ace completely by surprise. He had seen the look in the old-timer's eyes back in Big Rock, as well as heard the tone in Eagle-Eye's voice when he talked about Preacher. Obviously, there actually was a grudge between the two old mountain men.

Not far behind Eagle-Eye when he yanked out his pistols and charged, Ace galloped hard to catch up before the old man got himself into more trouble than he could handle. Chance didn't react quite as quickly, so he brought up the rear, a few yards behind his brother.

Ace recognized Smoke and figured the scrawny figure in a buckskin shirt beside him had to be Preacher. Who the other two men were, Ace didn't know. Probably some of Smoke's ranch hands.

All had instinctively yanked out guns, and in another second Eagle-Eye was liable to ride right into a storm of hot lead if he continued his attack. He had the pistol in his right hand leveled at the four men on horseback.

Ace brought his horse even with Eagle-Eye's, reached over, and knocked his arm up just as Eagle-Eye pulled the trigger. The flintlock boomed, but the heavy lead ball arched harmlessly into the sky.

"Damn it, Eagle-Eye, stop that!" Ace shouted at the old man. He didn't like treating one of his elders so disrespectfully, but he wasn't going to let Eagle-Eye provoke a possibly fatal shootout. He yelled, "Hold your fire!" at Smoke and the others.

Chance pulled up on Eagle-Eye's left side and grabbed the gun in that hand, closing his hand around the lock so Eagle-Eye couldn't fire. He wrenched the weapon out of the old-timer's grasp.

Smoke wheeled his horse around so that he was between them and the other men and added his own command. "Hold your fire!"

Ace grabbed the headstall on Eagle-Eye's mount and hauled back on it, slowing the animal.

Eagle-Eye struck at him with the empty pistol he still held and bellowed, "Let me go, damn it! I got to kill that old geezer!"

"Stop it!" Ace responded as he dragged Eagle-Eye's horse to a halt and reined in his own mount. "Have you gone loco? I thought you said you and Preacher are friends!"

"There was a time we once were!" Eagle-Eye cried. "Until the treacherous old goat tried to steal my woman away from me!"

Preacher leaned over in his saddle to yell around Smoke. "You dang crazy old coot! I never done any such a thing! Your wife Louisa was one o' the finest women on the face o' the earth. There was never a blasted thing between us. Nothin'!"

"You didn't read her letters—"

"Because she never sent 'em to me!"

"She couldn't have made all those things up," Eagle-Eye forged ahead stubbornly. "The things she talked about wishin' that . . . that you and her had done!"

"Maybe she wished for 'em, but I never knew nothin' about it!" Preacher insisted. "Stop and think about it for a minute, you tarnal idjit! If we'd really *done* anything, she wouldn'ta been *wishin'* that we had, now would she?"

Bushy white eyebrows bristling, Eagle-Eye glared at Preacher. After a second, he snapped, "Stop tryin' to confuse me!"

"I ain't tryin' to confuse you. I'm tryin' to make you see straight for once in your goldang life!"

Smoke lifted a hand. "Both of you just hush up for a minute. Ace, Chance, what are you boys doing here?"

Since the gun Eagle-Eye still held was empty and couldn't be reloaded without the rest of them seeing what he was doing, Ace figured it was safe to answer Smoke's question. "We ran into Mr. Callahan a few days ago, a ways north of here. Some owlhoots had jumped him and were trying to rob and probably murder him, so we figured we ought to take a hand."

"We chased those fellas off," Chance added, "then the three of us decided to ride together for a while."

"Mr. Callahan was headed this way to look for Preacher, so we thought we might as well ride along with him." Ace looked over at the old-timer. "He never said anything about wanting to kill anybody, though!"

Chance said, "I'm still not sure I know what this is all about."

"It's about betrayal." Eagle-Eye leveled a finger at Preacher. "It's about that varmint goin' behind my back and doin' things no man should ever do to a friend!"

Preacher let out a disgusted snort. "I give up. I can't say it no plainer 'n I already did. There was never anything goin' on betwixt your wife an' me! Never! And I ain't to blame for whatever was inside her own head."

"That seems reasonable enough," Smoke said. "Why don't we all go inside, out of this snow, and warm up some? A cup of coffee might make everything seem a lot clearer." He paused, then added with a smile, "I might even be able to talk Sally into letting us have a few of those bear sign she's been making."

"Now you're talkin'!" Cal said.

Eagle-Eye stuck behind his belt the empty pistol he was still holding, then crossed his arms, glared haughtily at Preacher, and declared, "I ain't sittin' down at no table with that man."

"I ain't over-fond o' the idea my own self," said Preacher. "I don't gen'rally sit around and chew the fat with somebody who just took a shot at me!"

"I would've hit you, too, if it hadn't been for this young whippersnapper interferin'!" Eagle-Eye glowered at Ace.

"You wouldn'ta hit me," Preacher said confidently. "Eagle eye, my hind foot. Hell, you're so old you're prob'ly half blind by now and couldn't hit the side of a barn if you was a-standin' next to it!"

"Old! Why, I'm not as old as you, you . . . you relic!"

"You got a mighty bad habit o' callin' folks names," Preacher cautioned. "I don't cotton to it."

"I don't care what you cotton to—"

Smoke lifted his voice. "Blast it, that's enough. Both of you!"

Preacher pointed at Eagle-Eye. "Why're you yellin' at me? *He's* the crazy one."

Ace said, "I think Mr. Jensen is right. We should all go inside, sit down, and hash this out peacefully."

"Peaceful?" Preacher frowned. "Are you sure your last name's really Jensen, boy? Things ain't never been peaceful for very long around any o' them Jensens!"

Chance said, "We don't know that we're part of the same bunch. Ace thinks so, but I'm not convinced."

Smoke lifted his reins. "Come on. Let's do our jawing out of the weather."

Eagle-Eye looked over at Chance and asked, "How about givin' me back that gun o' mine?"

"I don't think so. Not just yet, anyway."

"You ain't got no right to do that!"

Ace told him, "Let's just say we're trying to keep you alive for a while longer."

Eagle-Eye muttered unhappily, but he went along with the decision. The men all turned their horses toward the ranch house.

Sally had heard the shot and stood on the porch wearing a heavy coat over her dress and apron. A Winchester was in her hands, but she relaxed as she recognized everyone except Eagle-Eye. "Ace! Chance!" she called with a smile of welcome. "Is that really you?"

"Yes, ma'am, it is," Ace replied as he reached up and tugged on the brim of his hat. "Sorry if we're intruding on you—"

"Nonsense. You boys are our friends and could never intrude, especially at this time of year when guests are always welcome. Come on inside. I think I can spare a few fresh bear sign."

Pearlie groused to Cal, "She offers bear sign to those young fellas, but if the likes o' you or me reaches for any, we get our hands slapped with a big ol' wooden spoon."

"You'll have plenty of bear sign at the Christmas Eve party," Sally told the foreman with a smile. Her sharp ears had overheard what Pearlie said. "Anyway, you're included in the invitation now."

"Yes'm," Pearlie said quickly. "And Cal an' me, we're much obliged to you, too."

A couple other hands had emerged from the bunkhouse to see what was going on. Smoke, Ace, Chance, and the others swung down from their saddles and turned their mounts over to the punchers, who took them into the barn and unsaddled them.

As the men climbed the steps to the porch, Ace watched Eagle-Eye to make sure the old-timer didn't try anything else. Chance was equally alert.

They all made it inside without any further incidents, although Eagle-Eye kept his distance from Preacher and continued to send hostile glares toward him.

Sally put the rifle back on the rack where she had gotten it and turned to Eagle-Eye, still wearing a smile on her beautiful face as she said, "I don't believe we've been introduced."

Even as upset as he was, his frontiersman's chivalry made him reach up and snatch his battered old hat from his head. "Beggin' your pardon, ma'am. My name's Callahan. Eagle-Eye, they call me."

"Well, Mr. Callahan, it's a pleasure to meet you. I'm Mrs. Smoke Jensen." There was a twinkle in her eyes as she added, "They call me Sally."

Eagle-Eye held his hat over his heart. "It's an honor, ma'am."

"Are you one of Preacher's old friends?" she asked.

Ace waited for Eagle-Eye to blow up in anger at Sally's question, but other than a tightening of the grizzled jaw, the old man didn't show any reaction. He managed to nod and say noncommittally, "We've knowed each other a heap of years, we sure have."

Even if Sally failed to note how evasive that answer was, Preacher's disgusted snort made her aware that something was wrong. Ace could feel the tension in the air himself, so he was sure she could, too.

But her gracious smile never wavered as she said, "Why don't all of you gentlemen go on into the dining room and sit down? I'll bring coffee and something to eat. Just enough to tide you over until supper," she added with a warning glance at Pearlie and Cal, who were known far and wide as chow-hounds. "You're all staying for supper and spending the night. In weather like this, I won't take no for an answer."

Chance grinned. "We weren't figuring on saying no, Miss Sally. Isn't that right, Ace?"

"It sure is."

Preacher and Eagle-Eye still kept their distance from each other as the men took off their coats and hung them on hooks near the door, then filed into the dining room and took places around the long table. The two old-timers were as wary as a couple animals who might tear into each other with fang and claw at any second.

When they were all seated, with Smoke at the head of the table as he ought to be, he said, "All right, you two. Do you want to talk about this now or wait until Sally gets back? Might be a good idea to get a woman's perspective on this argument."

Preacher and Eagle-Eye looked at him as if he had gone insane.

Preacher said, "This ain't the sort o' thing that ought to be talked about in front of no woman."

"She wouldn't know nothin' about it, anyway," added Eagle-Eye. "A lady couldn't understand a matter of a man's honor."

"I think you're underestimating the fairer sex, Mr. Callahan," Smoke said.

Eagle-Eye looked down at the table. "I ain't talkin' about it."

"Neither am I." Preacher snorted again. "Ain't nothin' to talk about, anyway, 'cept the crazed rantin's of an old fool."

Eagle-Eye started to scrape his chair back, but Smoke said sharply, "That's enough. You two aren't going to try to kill each other in my house."

The two old mountain men settled for glaring darkly at each other.

Smoke turned to the brothers. "What have you

boys been up to since we all saw each other down in Texas?"

"Just drifting," Ace replied with a shrug. "Same as always."

"You haven't run into any trouble?" Smoke said with a knowing smile.

"Well, we didn't say that," answered Chance. "There was a ruckus or two along the way."

"There always is," Smoke said. "They do seem to go with the name, like Preacher said."

"Speaking of that," Ace said, "how's Matt doing?"

"Just fine, the last I heard. I think he's out in California."

"What about your older brother? Luke, right?"

Smoke shook his head. "Luke's out there in the wind somewhere. I don't hear from him very often. He's a man who goes his own way, and we don't usually know where he is or what he's doing." Smoke paused. "You know, in that respect, he sort of reminds me of you fellows. Like being fiddle-footed is just in his nature."

"Yeah, that's us, all right," Chance agreed. "Never stay in one place for too long."

Carrying a tray full of bear sign, Sally came into the room in time to hear that last statement. "I trust you'll stay around long enough to finish these off."

"If they don't, Miss Sally, I will!" Cal said.

CHAPTER 24

Like a monster crawling out of its cave, the storm continued making its way down the mountains from the north, drawing ever nearer to the Colorado valley that was home to the Sugarloaf Ranch and the town of Big Rock. As darkness settled over the landscape, the snow began falling a little heavier and the wind picked up. The temperature slid down a few more degrees. It was already below freezing, and skin didn't have to be exposed for very long for frostbite to be a danger.

The people inside the ranch house didn't have to worry about that. Between the fireplace in the main room and the big stove in the kitchen, the place was toasty warm and comfortable.

The same was true out in the bunkhouse, where Pearlie and Cal had retreated with the other hands after supper in the house, which had been the usual boisterous meal around the long table. Not even the continuing animosity between Preacher and Eagle-Eye had spoiled the mood of the Sugarloaf cowboys, who were in high spirits because Christmas was fast approaching. Smoke kept only a skeleton crew on hand during the winter, trusted men who had worked for him for quite a while. All of them got along well, so the jokes and the laughter flew back and forth rapidly.

Pearlie and Cal were conspicuously quiet about a certain subject—bear sign—since they didn't want the other hands to know they had enjoyed a treat that afternoon. The other hands would be jealous if they found out. Sally's bear sign provoked a passionate response in anybody who ever tried them.

After supper, as the others lingered over second cups of coffee, Ace said, "I reckon Chance and I ought to head out to the bunkhouse with the rest of the fellas—"

"Nonsense," Sally said crisply. "We have plenty of room. Smoke and I built this house intending to have a big family someday, and until we do, guests are more than welcome. Besides, your name is Jensen. You should think of this as your home, whether you're related by blood or not."

"That's mighty kind of you, Miss Sally," Chance said. "We'll try not to be in your hair for long."

She shook her head. "You're more than welcome. Anyway, with that storm blowing in—listen to the wind howl!—the weather may not be fit for traveling for several days. And it's almost Christmas. No one wants to be alone for Christmas."

"We're really obliged to you, Miss Sally," Ace told her. "You and Smoke make us feel like we're home, that's for sure. We never had much of one when we were little, you know. The man who raised us, Doc Monday, he moved around a lot and took us with him."

"He was a gambler, you said?" asked Smoke.

"That's right."

"But he wasn't your father?"

"No, sir. According to what Doc told us, our real pa was killed in the war."

There was no need for Ace to specify which war he was talking about. The Late Unpleasantness was years in the past, but memories of it still cast a large shadow over the nation.

Smoke nodded solemnly. "That fate befell a lot of good men on both sides. Too many. My pa survived, and so did my brother Luke, although for a lot of years I believed he hadn't. They were a couple of the lucky ones."

Everyone was silent for a moment then Sally stood up and said, "I'll finish clearing the table. Why don't you men go into Smoke's study and talk? Preacher, you and Mr. Callahan need to settle whatever this trouble is between the two of you."

Preacher started guiltily. "Why, uh, I reckon I don't know what you're a-talkin' about, Miss Sally."

"Nonsense. I have eyes in my head, don't I? I can see that you're angry at each other, and old friends shouldn't let things like that fester between them. You should work it out now while you have the chance."

"Before one or both of you cross the divide,"

Smoke added bluntly. "Sally's too tactful to say that, but given how old you both are . . ."

"All right, dagnab it," Preacher snapped. "You don't have to remind me I'm old as dirt. I ain't likely to forget it."

"Neither am I," said Eagle-Eye. "My bones remind me ever' mornin', especially the cold ones, like it's sure gonna be tomorrow. Ten below zero, I figure."

Preacher snorted. "Won't even get down to zero, I'll wager."

"Well, you're just wrong."

"You see. You should be arguing about the weather, not whatever else it is that's bothering you." Sally made shooing motions with her hands. "Go on now. Hash it out, as Smoke would say."

"Ain't nothin' to hash out," Eagle-Eye said in a surly tone. "Won't but one thing settle this, and Preacher knows what it is."

"Don't make me have to oblige you on that, Eagle-Eye," Preacher warned.

Smoke stood up. "Come on, or I'll grab you both by the ears and drag you in there."

"I'd like to see you try it!" Preacher and Eagle-Eye responded in perfect unison.

A few minutes later, Smoke was sitting behind his desk in the comfortable room that functioned as his study, office, and library. Sally loved to read, and he found it an enjoyable pastime himself, so he had filled the shelves with scores of leather-bound volumes, mostly histories and novels, along with a set of

Shakespeare's plays that Preacher's old friend Audie had given to him.

Preacher sat in a leather armchair in front of the desk. Eagle-Eye had refused Smoke's offer of a seat and paced back and forth. Ace and Chance stood over by the bookshelves. Since they had befriended Eagle-Eye, Smoke thought it was all right for them to be there for the discussion, and the old-timer hadn't raised any objections.

"Preacher told me the whole story, Eagle-Eye," Smoke began. "As much as he knows of it, anyway. This whole thing has taken him completely by surprise."

"I never saw the day when Preacher could be surprised by much of anything," said Eagle-Eye. "He knowed about it, all right."

"See," Preacher said, "you got your mind all made up already, and it'd take a whole case full o' dynamite to blast any sense into that thick skull o' yours!"

Chance said, "Ace and I don't know the whole story. We thought Eagle-Eye and Preacher were old friends."

"We might not have thrown in with him and ridden down here if we'd known the truth," added Ace.

"*Might* not have?" Preacher asked.

"Well, as it turns out, it's a good thing we were here," Ace pointed out. "We were able to stop that gunfight before it ever got started."

"That's true," Smoke agreed. "I guess that earns you boys the right to know what's going on. Preacher, would you like to tell them?"

Eagle-Eye flung out a hand "He'll just lie about it, like he's lied about ever'thing else! I'll tell it."

Preacher twisted around in the chair and started to get up angrily. Smoke motioned him back down.

Eagle-Eye turned to Ace and Chance. "I was married for nigh on to forty years to a woman named Louisa. She helped me run that tradin' post up in Montana, and I always figured she was fine, just fine."

"She was," Preacher growled.

Eagle-Eye glared at him for a second, then went on. "She passed away awhile back, and after she did, I found a bunch o' letters she'd wrote to that worthless skunk over there, tellin' him how much she loved him and how she"—he seemed to choke for a moment—"how she longed for the two of 'em to be together. She got, uh, pretty plain-spoken about it, too. There was talk about . . . hand-holdin' and porch-sittin' and things like that. It was clear to me from what she wrote that Preacher had been wooin' her behind my back for a long time. Ain't no telling what-all he done to put the lie to what I figured was a good marriage."

"I'll tell you what I done," Preacher said. "Nothin'! I never saw Louisa but ever' three or four years when I'd swing by the tradin' post to visit a mite. She was a good cook, may she rest in peace, and I sure did admire to sit down at the table for a meal she cooked, but that's all. All that . . . courtin' stuff . . . in her letters . . . that was in her head, Eagle-Eye. That's all. I swear it."

Eagle-Eye stared at him and said in a half-whisper, "You're askin' me to believe that my wife never really loved me."

Preacher couldn't contain himself any longer. He

sprang up out of the chair and exclaimed, "O' course she loved you, you durned ol' ignoramus! She stayed married to you for all them years, didn't she? She worked hard ever' day of her life to keep you happy and to make that business o' yours a success. Just 'cause she liked to amuse herself in an idle moment now an' then by thinkin' about what things might've been like if she'd done got hitched up with me, that don't mean she loved you any less!"

Chance leaned over to Ace and said quietly, "I think he's got a point."

Ace inclined his head in agreement.

Eagle-Eye stared intently at Preacher while several seconds ticked past. Then he lifted his right hand and scrubbed it over his face as his shoulders slumped wearily. "You're tellin' me the truth?" he asked in a hollow voice.

"Damn right I am. About me, and about Louisa, too. Blast it, Eagle-Eye, I don't cotton to you actin' like this. You oughta be happy you had all those years with her. That's a whole heap more 'n I ever had with any gal I had feelin's for. The only dishonorin' bein' done here is by you . . . dishonorin' her memory."

Eagle-Eye's hands clenched into fists, and he took a step toward Preacher. Across the room, Ace and Chance stiffened, but Smoke lifted a hand and gestured discreetly for them to stay out of it. This was between Preacher and Eagle-Eye, and it needed to be settled at last, short of a fight to the death. Smoke was confident that his old mentor wasn't in any danger, and if necessary, he could step in to keep Preacher from seriously injuring his old friend.

Eagle-Eye's hands dropped and relaxed before he could throw a punch. A long sigh came from him. "You're right. I know you're right, damn it. I reckon in my heart I've known it all along. It was just . . . so hard to accept."

"Well, hell, I can see how it would be," said Preacher. "But you can see now that there ain't no reason we shouldn't still be old friends." He stuck out his hand.

Eagle-Eye hesitated, but only for a couple heart-beats. He grasped Preacher's hand, pumped it twice, and pulled Preacher into a rough hug. The two old mountain men pounded each other on the back.

"Damn it," Eagle-Eye said. "I sure am glad I didn't blow a hole through you."

"Yeah, you and me both," Preacher responded dryly. "Although there ain't much chance that would've ever happened."

"The hell it wouldn't! I'm as sharp-eyed as ever."

"Maybe we'll just have to have us a little shootin' contest."

While the two old-timers were talking—peacefully, thank goodness—Ace and Chance went over to the desk.

Ace asked quietly, "So it's all over now?"

"Just like that?" Chance asked.

Smoke nodded "Appears to be. Those old mountain men were hot-tempered, but they got over it pretty fast unless there was a real reason to hold a grudge. I don't think we have to worry much about Eagle-Eye anymore."

"So everything turned out peaceful after all," Ace said.

"Well . . . *this* did," Smoke said. "You never know what else might be waiting around the next bend in the trail."

The window pane rattled a little as a gust of wind hit it. If the men in the study had looked out then, they would have seen that the snow was so thick, visibility was down to just a few feet and closing in fast.

CHAPTER 25

Outside Big Rock

The men on horseback formed a long line as they rode along, leaning forward in their saddles. They hunched their shoulders inside their coats against the bone-chilling cold of the hard wind that blew in their faces. They had pulled their hats down and wrapped scarves or bandannas around the bottom part of their faces, so that only the area around their eyes was exposed to the wind.

That was still enough to cause a problem. If they didn't find some shelter soon, they were going to be in serious trouble. Frostbite wasn't even the worst thing they had to worry about. There was a distinct possibility that they might freeze to death.

The group was fifty strong, with another four men bringing up the rear on two wagons loaded with supplies. Their leader intended for most of them to lie low for a while, so they would need food. There might be supplies wherever they holed up, but Jim Bleeker wanted to be prepared for any contingency.

He was in the lead. Ray Morley moved his horse up next to Bleeker's and called over the keening wind, "We got to find somewhere to get out of this weather, Jim! The men can't go on much longer, and neither can the horses!"

"You're not telling me anything I don't already know, damn it," growled Bleeker. "I know it's December, but I wasn't expecting to run into a storm like this!"

Morley didn't say anything in response. Sometimes silence was the best option.

Bleeker wasn't sure what time it was, and he didn't want to fish around under his coat for his turnip watch so he could look and see. It didn't matter, anyway. Night had closed down early because of the storm. It was black as pitch around them, and the thick, blowing snow made it even more impossible to see. They were riding blind, and he didn't like it.

He had never expected that everything about his plan would go perfectly. There were always hitches.

Damn Frank Morgan, he thought.

Recruiting Morgan had seemed like a good idea at the time. Deep down, Bleeker believed in being honest with himself, even if he wasn't with anybody else. He knew that Monte Carson was fast . . . faster than him.

But Carson wasn't faster than Frank Morgan. It was possible nobody was. If Bleeker had been able to get Morgan on his side, he was confident that Monte Carson could be taken care of when the time came. It had never occurred to him that Morgan might turn down the lucrative payday he was being offered. The man was a hired gun, after all.

Well, Morgan was dead, so that option was gone, Bleeker thought.

That bumbling bunch of owlhoots, Clark and the others, had gone and gotten themselves killed, but at least they had pumped enough lead into the notorious gunfighter that Morgan had died, too, although he'd been stubborn enough to hang on until the next day before crossing the divide. Bleeker had read about it in the *Rocky Mountain News* before he'd gathered up the rest of his small army and headed for Big Rock.

Instead of relying on Morgan's speed, they would just have to make do with their numbers. Bleeker didn't know how many people lived in the settlement, but he was sure that more than fifty hardened killers would be sufficient to handle them.

He sat up straighter in his saddle as the wind suddenly parted the curtains of snow and shadow for a moment and he caught a glimpse of light up ahead.

Morley spotted it, too, and exclaimed, "Hey, Jim, did you see that?"

"Yeah, I did," Bleeker replied. "Tell the men to stop."

"They might not like that."

"I'm not riding into something without knowing what it is," snapped Bleeker. "You and I will go check it out. Now pass the word to halt."

"Sure, Jim." Morley turned his horse, moved it back to the next man in line, and passed along Bleeker's command. Then he returned to the leader's side.

The light had disappeared as the snow closed in again, but Bleeker had fixed its location in his mind during the brief moment he had glimpsed it. He was confident that he was headed in the right direction as he rode forward with Morley beside him.

If they *weren't* going the right way, he thought, they ran the risk of getting lost in the storm and not being able to find the rest of the men again. The end result of that would probably be freezing to death.

Bleeker shoved that idea out of his head. Nothing was going to interfere with his revenge on Monte Carson. Certainly nothing like pure luck.

"There it is again!" Morley called, pointing.

Bleeker saw the light and a few minutes later, they reined to a stop in front of a log house. A barn loomed darkly off to one side, with an attached corral.

The horses would be crowded in that barn, thought Bleeker, but at least they would be out of the weather. Some of the men would have to stay in the hayloft, too, since they couldn't all fit into the house.

"Looks like some greasy sack ranch," Morley commented over the wind. "I don't see a bunkhouse. Whoever owns the place must work it by himself, or maybe with a few of his kids."

"Doesn't matter," Bleeker said. "There's a roof and a fire." He could smell the wood smoke from the stone chimney.

They swung down from the saddle and tied their horses to the hitching post near the door. They could put the animals in the barn later, after they had found out what the situation in the house was—and dealt with it.

Bleeker stepped up and knocked heavily on the door. There was no response for a moment, then a man called cautiously, "Who's out there?"

"A couple cold, weary travelers, friend," Bleeker replied, leaning close to the door as he tried to make his voice sound amiable and non-threatening. "We figured on making it to Big Rock, but the storm caught us before we could get there!"

Silence again, then, "How many of you are there?"

"Just the two of us." It was possible someone inside the house was looking out through a window or loophole, so Bleeker didn't want to lie about that. As far as the folks who lived there were concerned, only two half-frozen pilgrims stood on their doorstep.

Bleeker pressed his head to the door, thought he heard a woman's voice speaking quickly, then a man replying to her. A few more seconds went by, then came the scrape of a bar being removed from the door.

It swung open, and the man inside said gruffly, "Come on in. Hurry up so not too much cold air comes in with you."

Bleeker and Morley stepped through the doorway. It was warm inside, and the snow clinging to their clothes, hats, and faces began to melt right away.

Bleeker smiled and wiped some of the snow from his cheeks. "We're much obliged to you folks. Don't think we could have made it much farther."

Despite his friendly pose, his brain was working quickly as he glanced around the room. The man who had let them in then hastily closed the door behind them stood there with a shotgun tucked under his left arm. He had the lean, leathery, perpetually hungry look of a none-too-successful rancher about him.

A few feet away, next to a rough-hewn table, stood

a woman about the same age as the man who had the same worn-down-by-life appearance. Four youngsters were in the room as well, two boys in their middle teens holding single-shot rifles, a girl slightly older than the boys, and one a little younger. All of them stared warily at the newcomers.

"I'm Jim Johnson, and this is Ray Wilson," Bleeker lied as he jerked a thumb at Morley.

"Ab Crockett," the man introduced himself.

"Like old Davy, eh?" said Bleeker with a friendly grin. He started pulling off his gloves.

"That's right. No relation that I know of, though." Crockett didn't offer to introduce his wife and children. "You can shake the snow off your coats and hats and hang them up to dry over by the fire, if you'd like."

"It's mighty kind of you to take us in like this."

"Couldn't do otherwise," the woman said. "Not on a night like this. 'Twouldn't be the Christian thing to do."

"No, ma'am, it wouldn't be," agreed Bleeker, thinking how ironic it was that in trying to be Christian about it, these people had invited the Devil right into their house.

"Bound for Big Rock, you said?" asked Crockett.

"That's right. How far did we miss it by?"

"It's about twelve miles west of here. You can make it tomorrow, if the snow's not too deep. If it is, you're welcome to wait until it melts off some. Plenty of room out in the hayloft for you fellas. We're a mite cramped here in the house."

"The hayloft is just fine with us," Bleeker said. "Isn't that right, Ray?"

"Sure, Jim." Morley was waiting for Bleeker to make the first move, as usual.

But they couldn't afford to wait too long, Bleeker knew. Not with the rest of the men still out in the storm, in danger of being overcome by the cold.

"I've got some roast beef and bread left from supper," Mrs. Crockett said. "And there's coffee in the pot."

"That sounds mighty good," Bleeker told her as he hung up his hat and overcoat like the rancher had said.

Morley did likewise.

Crockett decided that the visitors didn't represent any threat. He stepped over to the wall and hung his shotgun on a couple pegs. His boys followed his example, leaning their rifles in a corner. The girls had gone with their mother over to the stove to see about getting the food ready.

Still smiling, Bleeker turned away from the hook where he had hung up his things, pulled his Colt from its holster, lifted the gun, and shot Ab Crockett in the side of the head. The boom was deafeningly loud in the house. The bullet went all the way through Crockett's brain and exploded out the other side of his skull in a grisly pink spray of blood and bone. The rancher was dead before he knew what had happened, and certainly dead by the time his corpse thudded to the floor.

Morley had his gun out a hair's-breadth after Bleeker's weapon roared. He shot the oldest boy in the chest, then Bleeker drilled the other lad. The youngsters crumpled as blood began to well from their wounds. Neither of them had had time to even make a move toward their rifles.

The outlaws swung their guns toward the females, all three of whom had whirled around in shock at the shots and started screaming.

"Shut up!" bellowed Bleeker. "We're not going to hurt you!"

That was a lie, of course, but it would be easier if they cooperated for a while.

The woman and the girls kept screaming. Bleeker strode toward them, causing them to cringe backwards. They couldn't go very far. The hot stove was right behind them. He thought about shoving the woman's face against it to make an example of her and terrify the girls into doing whatever they were told, but from the looks of their shocked faces, they were already scared enough.

He settled for backhanding the woman and knocking her to her knees. He put the Colt's muzzle to her head and snapped at the girls, "I said to pipe down!"

Their mouths hung open, but no more sound came out. The woman had stopped screaming, too, although she sobbed in pain as she held a hand to her cheek.

"I'm sorry about having to kill your menfolks," Bleeker went on. That was a lie, too. He didn't care one way or the other about Crockett and the boys. "Couldn't take a chance on them causing trouble for us."

Mrs. Crockett looked up at him with eyes that were horrified and hate-filled. "We would've done anything you wanted. You could've taken anything we have."

"What we need is this place," Bleeker told her. "The house, the barn, whatever else we can use. I've got some friends waiting out in the storm, and we're all going to be staying here for a while."

"You could have stayed! You didn't have to kill—"

"Couldn't take a chance. Your husband or one of your boys might've decided to make a run for Big Rock and tell the sheriff about us before we had a chance to conduct our business there."

She stared at him. "What's so special about Big Rock?"

"That's where my revenge is waiting," Bleeker said, "and when I'm done with that, we'll all ride away and everything will be fine."

That was true in a way, he thought—because they would leave the tranquility of death and utter destruction behind them.

CHAPTER 26

Aboard the Orphan Train

Now that he had introduced himself to Miss Mercy Halliday, Ed Rinehart spent as much time as possible around her. Not because he was attracted to her—although he had to admit that her green eyes were beguiling and her thick, curly auburn hair made a man want to bury his hands in it and lift her face to his—but because being around her meant being around the children.

It annoyed him that Donald's uncle had kept the agency as much in the dark as he had. William Litchfield could have gone down to that orphanage, demanded to take a look at the children, and picked out his nephew, if Donald truly was there. Only his worry about mysterious killers still being after the boy had prevented him from doing that.

But he could have at least provided a photograph of Donald so Rinehart would have recognized him. Surely, parents as wealthy as Grant and Claire Litchfield had had pictures of their only child. William

Litchfield had given Captain Shaw some feeble excuse about that, too.

Rinehart was stuck with the job of protecting the boy when he wasn't certain which of the orphans was Donald Litchfield. The detective had his eye on one of the four little boys the approximate age of the missing child, a little boy Mercy called Caleb. He fit the bill the best—the right age, and according to Mercy, he hadn't spoken a single word since he had turned up at the orphanage six months earlier. All that fit in with the idea that a child, stunned by witnessing the murder of his own parents, might flee to somewhere familiar and then withdraw into himself, seeking safety in solitude.

As the train moved across the Great Plains, steadily drawing closer to the Rockies, Rinehart found whatever excuse he could to spend time around the children. He could tell that Peter Gallagher didn't like that. The man was still angry and embarrassed about the confrontation on the platform.

If he could carry out his assignment and annoy Gallagher at the same time, then so much the better, thought Rinehart.

As they left the plains behind and moved into the foothills of the towering mountains, he was in the second car housing the orphans, the one where Caleb was. He wanted to get a chance to talk to the boy.

At the moment, the detective was talking with Mercy, and he couldn't complain about that. He had brought her a breakfast roll and a cup of coffee from the dining car.

As she took the roll, looking surprised and pleased, she said, "What a thoughtful gesture, Mr. Rinehart.

You didn't have to do that. You've already been so kind and attentive the past couple days."

"Happy to do it. I thought we agreed you'd call me Ed and I'll call you Mercy."

"Of course," she said, blushing slightly.

He couldn't help but notice that it made her even prettier.

Just doing my job, he told himself. *Doesn't matter one whit how lovely Mercy Halliday is.*

If he kept repeating that thought, he might eventually convince himself that it was true.

"Why don't you go ahead and enjoy that," he suggested. "I'll keep an eye on the children." He had noticed that neither of the Gallaghers seemed to be in the car at the moment. They were probably having breakfast together in the other car.

"That's not your job."

"I'm volunteering for it," Rinehart told her with a smile.

"Well . . . all right. But if you need any help, just shout."

"I will," Rinehart assured her.

Mercy sighed and sat back against the bench seat in her compartment. A few moments of relative peace and quiet was well appreciated when a person was responsible for the safety and well-being of ten children under the age of twelve.

Most of the youngsters were gathered in one of the other compartments, playing some sort of game. It had been a long time since Rinehart had had the opportunity to play kids' games, so he wasn't really sure of what they were doing other than having a good time.

Caleb wasn't there, though.

When Rinehart asked about him, one of the other boys said scornfully, "He's off hidin' like the baby he is. He never plays with us or even talks to us."

"He gets in the closet, or in a wardrobe, and shuts the door after him," a little girl said. "I don't like him. He's odd."

So Caleb likes to hide, mused Rinehart. That was one more point in favor of him being Donald Litchfield.

The detective's orders were to accompany the children to California and determine where all the boys around six years old wound up. Then, once the operatives back in New York had cracked the case and arrested the murderer, or murderers, of the Litchfields, Donald's uncle could show up, claim him, and take him home. The people who had adopted Donald might be heartbroken, especially if he had been with them long enough for them to grow attached to him, but that was a shame. William Litchfield would have a right to the boy.

In the meantime, Rinehart didn't see anything wrong with trying to determine, at least for his own peace of mind, which of the youngsters was really Donald Litchfield.

Keeping an eye on the door of the compartment where the children had gathered, Rinehart moved along the aisle in the middle of the car, checking the other compartments. He stopped in front of one of them and looked through the open door at a small boy sitting on the seat with his legs drawn up and his head tucked onto his knees.

"Hello, Caleb," Rinehart said.

The youngster didn't respond. His head was down,

so Rinehart couldn't see if there had been a flicker of recognition in his eyes or not.

"You know me. I'm Ed Rinehart, Miss Mercy's friend." Hearing the words he spoke, Rinehart was a little surprised to discover that he hoped they were really true. "Is it all right if I sit with you for a while?"

Caleb didn't look up or say anything.

However, Rinehart sensed that the boy was paying attention. His instincts had been honed by years of investigative work. He sat down on the bench, being careful not to crowd Caleb. He didn't want to spook the lad.

"Some of the other children tell me you like to find good places to hide. Is that because it's a good game or are you scared of something, Caleb? You don't have to be scared, you know. Miss Mercy will always look out for you, and since I'm her friend, so will I." He didn't expect the boy to suddenly start talking, words spilling out of his mouth as he admitted that he was really Donald Litchfield and told exactly who had murdered his parents and why. A break like that would be nice, of course, but Rinehart knew how rare they were.

He wasn't disappointed when Caleb just sat there silently, chin on knees, not looking at him or at anything else.

Once Rinehart had set his sights on the boy, he had asked enough subtle questions of Mercy to know that Caleb had a good appetite and never turned down food, and he caused no trouble with the other children. To cause trouble, he would have had to have something to do with them, and for the most part he didn't. A few times they had drawn him into a game of chase, but after playing for only a few moments, he seemed to become frightened and withdrew.

Because he remembered running for his life on the night killers had invaded his home? Rinehart wondered.

"If anybody bothers you, don't be scared. Just get Miss Mercy. She'll take care of you. Or better yet, come and find me. I'll protect you. No one will ever hurt you while I'm around, Donald." He watched the boy closely as he spoke the name. He thought Caleb started a bit, but if he actually did, the reaction was so small that most eyes would have missed it. It took the keen gaze of a trained investigator to see.

Rinehart was more convinced than ever the silent and mysterious Caleb was really Donald Litchfield.

He might have tried to worm something else out of the youngster, but at that moment Mercy appeared in the open doorway. She laughed and said, "The two of you look so solemn. Are you having a serious conversation?"

"Well, I'm talking and Caleb's listening," said Rinehart. "I'm not sure how serious it is."

Mercy moved a step into the compartment. "Caleb, would you like to join the other children? They're playing a game—"

Before she could finish, the conductor came into the car and started along the aisle, calling in his deep voice, "Big Rock! Comin' in to Big Rock, Colorado!"

"I didn't know we were in Colorado yet," Mercy said to Rinehart. "We must have crossed over from Kansas during the night."

"I had a pretty good idea once I saw those mountains." He pointed out a window at some picturesque, snow-capped peaks rising not far away. "Nothing like that in Kansas, that's for sure. That's the flattest place I think I've ever seen."

The mountains weren't the only things covered with snow. The train passed fields a brilliant white. The snow was at least six inches deep, maybe more. Certainly more in places where it had drifted. There were giant waves of it pushed up by the wind. The landscape had a cold, eerie beauty about it.

"I wonder how long we'll be stopped in this Big Rock place." Mercy answered her own question. "Not long, I imagine. In most of these frontier settlements, there's no need for a long layover. A few passengers get on, a few passengers get off . . . some freight might be loaded or unloaded. Then we'll be moving on."

"That's right. You've seen places like this before, haven't you? On other trips west that you made."

"That's right. In fact, I'm fairly certain I've been through Big Rock, but I don't believe the train ever stopped before. Or maybe it did, but it was during the middle of the night and I wasn't aware of it."

Rinehart knew from previous stops that Mercy and the Gallaghers would keep the children in the train cars. That made sense. No telling what a kid might do, and they didn't want to have to search some squalid little frontier hamlet for a runaway or one who had simply wandered off.

Big Rock didn't appear to fit the description that had just gone through his mind as the train rolled up next to a large, red-brick depot building. In fact, while it wouldn't really qualify as a city, it looked like a fairly large and successful town with a good number of businesses and a lot of houses, all of which had snowy roofs. The trees were covered with snow, as well. The place looked like something out of a painting, wholesome and innocent and very appealing.

Certainly nothing like the filthy back alleys of the big city where his job usually took him.

The train shuddered to a halt. He stood up and extended his hand to Caleb. "Why don't we go out on the rear platform and look around?" he suggested. Glancing quickly at Mercy, he added in a half-whisper, "I hope that's all right."

"He won't do it," she said, shaking her head sadly.

"I'll bet he will, so he can look at the mountains. Come on, Caleb. I don't think you've ever seen anything quite like those peaks."

For a moment, Caleb didn't budge. Then, to Mercy's obvious surprise, he put his legs down and reached over to take Rinehart's hand.

"For Heaven's sake!" she whispered. "How on earth did you get through to him?"

"Kids like me," Rinehart said with a cocky grin—although there had never been any evidence of that in his life until that very moment.

He held Caleb's hand and led the boy out of the compartment and into the aisle. They turned toward the rear of the car as Mercy watched them with amazement in her beautiful eyes.

Before they could go out onto the rear platform, the door of the vestibule at the front of the car burst open and Peter Gallagher hurried in. He caught sight of the three of them and called, "Miss Halliday! Miss Halliday!" as he came toward them. "This is a disaster!"

"What's wrong?" Mercy asked.

Gallagher flicked a venomous glare toward Rinehart, then turned his attention back to the auburn-haired young woman. "I've just been talking to the conductor. He told me the bad news. Evidently there was an enormous snowstorm up in the mountains west of here last night, and the snow is so deep in the passes that the train can't get through. We're stuck here in Big Rock!"

CHAPTER 27

Far east of Big Rock

Out on the Great Plains, another train chugged westward. Laird Kingsley sat on one of the bench seats in a passenger car, puffing on a cigar and looking out the window at the flat, snow-covered landscape. He wasn't really seeing the view, however. His mind's eye was filled with the image of his wife Alice standing in the doorway of their Brooklyn brownstone with their child Harry in her arms, both of them smiling and waving good-bye as Kingsley left to set out on the job he had been hired to do.

That job was to murder a young boy only a few years older than his own son.

Of course, Alice didn't know that, and Harry was too young to understand much of anything other than that his papa was leaving.

Alice—young, beautiful Alice—was aware that her husband's job was something he never talked about at home, and she was intelligent enough she had to suspect that most, if not all, of it was illegal. She was also smart enough never to press him for details.

It was enough that they had a comfortable home and an adored child. That represented an island of peace and sanity in the sea of blood and violence through which Kingsley swam every day and many nights. Without his family, he would go mad.

They kept away the memories of all the people he had killed, the torture he had carried out, the misery he had delivered to countless others. That was a separate part of his life, the part that made all the good things possible.

"Laird, laddie, ye look like you're a million miles away."

Kingsley turned away from the window and looked over at the man sitting beside him. Big Steve Corrigan was his second in command, a brutal, ruthless Irishman, none too bright but smart enough to follow orders. Kingsley knew he could depend on Corrigan. It had been the Irishman's sausage-like fingers that had snapped the delicate neck of Claire Litchfield that night some six months earlier in the mansion on Riverside Drive in New York. Two others had beaten Grant Litchfield to death while Kingsley had gone for the boy, but the little brat had slipped away from him.

Kingsley had experienced a sick, hollow feeling in the pit of his stomach when they found the old abandoned tunnel with small, fresh footprints in the dust and he realized that Donald Litchfield was gone, vanished into the night.

He and his men had searched all over the city without turning up a sign of the missing boy. For several days after that, Kingsley had worried that the coppers would turn up at his house to arrest him, even though logically he knew that Donald wouldn't have been able to recognize him and his men. Still, the fear that one part of his life would intrude into the other was always there.

Gradually, that fear had faded. The kid had fallen into the river and drowned, Kingsley had told himself, or been run over by a wagon and a team of draft horses, or fallen victim to some other deadly fate. He couldn't still be alive after so long.

Then William Litchfield had sent word to Kingsley, and the fear started all over again. . . .

"There ye go, driftin' away before ye can even say anything to me," Corrigan went on. "What the devil's the matter, Laird?"

"You're an Irishman, Steve. You're bound to know the feeling of someone walking over your grave."

"Oh, aye!" Corrigan nodded his head slowly and solemnly. "It'll chill ye to the bone, even more than that weather out there. Ye have a bad feelin' about this job, do ye?"

"Wouldn't anybody?"

Corrigan's broad, thick shoulders rose and fell in a shrug. "I've found that enough money soothes most bad feelin's. The world is a hard, cruel place, and fellas like you and me, we're just the instruments of that fate, laddie."

"I suppose that's one way to look at it," Kingsley said with a humorless laugh.

A short time later, the train slowed as it neared a town. He didn't know the name of the place and didn't care. It would feel good to get out and stretch his legs on the platform, even though he knew it would be cold. He had never felt anything quite as chilly as the wind that blew out on the endless plains.

When the train shuddered to a halt at the depot, Kingsley and Corrigan stood up. Kingsley looked along the benches in the car. Several more of his men were scattered among the passengers. He had brought eight men total, plenty to do the job. Killing the boy wouldn't be difficult, of course, but to get to him they might have to get through that private detective, and there was no telling who else might try to interfere.

They climbed down from the car to the station platform, and just as Kingsley had expected, the icy wind cut like a knife. He pulled his hat down and raised the collar on his overcoat.

Passengers were getting off the train and others were getting on. As the two men from New York walked briskly back and forth, he noticed several individuals huddled together. One of them he recognized as the conductor. The other, judging by the clothes he wore, was the engineer. They were talking to two of the locals.

The conductor seemed to be upset about something. After a considerable amount of animated discussion, he turned and strode along the platform. Kingsley moved to intercept him and held out a hand to stop the blue-uniformed man.

"Excuse me, sir," the conductor said impatiently. He tried to step around Kingsley, but he found the formidable bulk of Big Steve Corrigan blocking his path and had to come to an abrupt stop.

"Is something wrong?" Kingsley asked.

For a second, the conductor looked like he wasn't going to answer, but then he shrugged and said, "The stationmaster got a wire from farther up the line. The division manager has ordered this train to stop here."

"To stop?" Kingsley repeated in surprise. That wasn't good news. "For how long?"

The conductor shrugged again. "We don't know. There was a big storm last night in the Rockies, and some of the passes have been closed by snow. In fact, the westbound that's in front of us didn't make it through."

"It crashed?" asked Kingsley as his eyes widened. A train wreck would make his job easier . . . and harder. The kid might have been killed in the catastrophe, but how was Kingsley going to determine that?

"No, no," the conductor replied with a wave of his hand. "It's just stuck, too, like we are, only a lot closer to the passes that are closed down. I think the wire from the division manager said it was stopped in a town called Big Rock."

"Well, what're we gonna do?" rumbled Corrigan. "We can't just sit here in this burg."

"No choice. Chances are the weather will break, and the pass will clear enough in a few days for trains to make it through again. They'll probably attach a snowplow to the locomotive that's stuck in Big Rock and send it on ahead to try to clear the tracks through the passes. Then it can go back and pick up the rest of the train. I hope you fellas didn't need to be anywhere by Christmas. It'll be after that, maybe even after New Year's, before we can get through."

Something occurred to Kingsley. "What if the

snow *doesn't* melt off any? Is there any chance the passes will stay closed for the rest of the winter?"

"I've never known that to happen this early"—the conductor spread his hands—"but who knows? Now, if you'll excuse me, I need to start letting the other passengers know that they either need to make arrangements to head back east if that's what they want, or else stay here until we can move on. There are a couple hotels in town, and they ought to be able to put up everybody. What are you two gentlemen going to do, turn back or wait here?"

"Neither," said Kingsley in a flat, hard voice. "We can't afford to wait."

"What—" the conductor began, but Kingsley jerked his head for Corrigan to follow him and strode off, leaving the puzzled railroad man behind.

"What are ye doin', Laird?" Corrigan asked. "If that other train's stuck, too, there ain't no reason we can't wait here. We're still the same distance behind it when we were startin' out."

"What if it gets through in a few days and then another storm comes along before our train reaches that Big Rock place? We might get stuck there while those damn orphans go on their merry way to California. What would we do then?"

Corrigan scratched his rock-like jaw and frowned in thought. "Yeah, I guess you're right," he said after a moment. "But what're we gonna do? This train's not goin' anywhere."

"A train's not the only way to travel out here. Gather up all the boys, get our things together, and meet me back here."

Corrigan looked completely puzzled, but he nodded. "You're the boss, laddie."

A short while later, Kingsley led the group of hard-faced men in overcoats away from the train station and along the main street of the frontier settlement. He had asked the stationmaster—one of the men who had been talking to the conductor and the engineer, the other being the telegrapher—where the nearest livery stable was, so he knew where he was going.

They soon reached the big, cavernous barn. The double doors on the front were closed, but Corrigan pulled one of them open and the men trooped inside. It was chilly in the livery barn, but not nearly as cold as outside. The air smelled of hay, manure, and horseflesh. Kingsley had been around enough carriage houses that the blend of smells was familiar to him.

An old man in overalls, a flannel jacket, and a shapeless old hat came out of a small office to the side. He looked surprised to see so many obvious easterners in his establishment. "Somethin' I can do for you gents?"

"We need to buy some horses," Kingsley said briskly.

"You mean saddle mounts? Or have you got a buggy or somethin' like that?"

"Saddle mounts."

The old-timer rubbed his jaw, which bristled with silvery stubble, and drawled, "Well, I usually rent out saddle mounts, instead of sellin' 'em. . . ."

"We probably won't be able to bring these back," snapped Kingsley. "That's why I'd rather buy them."

He would pass the expense along to William Litchfield, so he didn't really care.

Fleetingly, the thought crossed his mind that he and his men could just *steal* the horses they needed, but if they did that, they would probably have lawmen coming after them. Also, he seemed to remember hearing that in the West, they hanged horse thieves. He didn't need that sort of trouble.

"How many of you are there?" the liveryman asked.

"Nine." Kingsley tried to contain his impatience. Couldn't the old codger count?

"And you all need horses?"

"That's right."

"I ain't sure I got nine horses that I could sell. . . ." The old man's words came out of his mouth as slow as molasses.

Kingsley could tell that Corrigan was getting impatient. The big Irishman might lose his temper if the conversation kept up much longer, and Kingsley didn't want that. He took a roll of greenbacks out of an inside pocket in his coat.

At the sight of the money, the old-timer's eyes widened and he spoke a little faster than before. "I reckon I could come up with nine mounts. You'll need saddles and tack?"

"Yes, of course."

"I can figure you a price. Just lemme go back in the office . . ."

"How about a thousand dollars for everything?" Kingsley suggested.

The liveryman didn't have to think very long about that. His head bobbed up and down on his scrawny neck. "Yeah, I suppose that'd be all right."

"Get them saddled and ready to ride as quickly as you can. What about a pack animal?"

"Yeah, I reckon, but I might have to charge a little more. . . ."

"I think you're getting plenty." Kingsley's voice packed enough of a menacing tone to cut through the old man's greed.

The liveryman nodded in quick agreement. "I can throw in a pack hoss."

Kingsley turned to his men. "A couple of you find a store and buy some supplies. We'll be on the trail for a few days."

"Where you boys headed?" the old-timer asked.

"A place called Big Rock. You know it?"

"Heard of it, that's all. Ain't never been there." Recognition dawned on the liveryman's face. "I think that's where Smoke Jensen lives. Close by, anyway."

"Who's Smoke Jensen?" Kingsley asked in idle curiosity.

"You never heard o' Smoke Jensen? Why, mister, he's just about the fastest gun that ever did live."

Kingsley snorted. Some cowboy who fancied himself a gunman. That wasn't anything to worry about.

CHAPTER 28

Sugarloaf Ranch

When Smoke woke up the morning after Preacher and Eagle-Eye had patched up their differences, he went to the window in the second floor bedroom wearing only the bottom half of a pair of long underwear, and pushed back the curtains. He wasn't really surprised when he looked out on a world wearing a thick white mantle.

Preacher had said that the storm might be a big one, and sure enough, a couple feet of snow lay on the open areas. Drifts several times that deep could be seen in numerous places. The sky still had a lot of gray clouds in it, but no snow was falling and Smoke saw blue peeking between the clouds here and there.

The door behind him opened and he glanced back over his shoulder.

Sally was standing there, wrapped in a thick robe. She had a cup of coffee in her hand. Steam rose from it. "So you're awake at last," she said with a smile. "I was beginning to think you were going to sleep half the day."

"How long's the sun been up?" asked Smoke.

"Five minutes at least. Maybe ten."

His smile widened into a grin. "I guess you must've worn me out last night."

"Be careful or I'll throw this coffee at you instead of letting you drink it."

"I reckon it'd warm me up some, either way." As Sally came closer to him, he added, "Although I can think of even better ways to warm up."

"Go ahead and start on that while you get dressed," she said as she handed him the coffee. "Then come on down to breakfast. We're going into Big Rock this morning. Christmas Eve is the day after tomorrow. We still have a lot to do to get ready for the party, you know."

"I don't see how. You and the ladies in town have been planning it for more than a month."

Sally shook her head. "I wouldn't expect you to understand. You're a man, after all."

"Yeah, I am," Smoke agreed. He tried to slip his free arm around her, but she laughed and moved away before he could. He chuckled and sipped the hot coffee.

When he went downstairs a short time later, carrying the cup, he found Preacher, Eagle-Eye, and Ace and Chance sitting at the long table in the dining room, all of them eagerly putting away a big breakfast of ham, eggs, flapjacks, and fried potatoes. Sally set a similar platter of food in front of Smoke's chair at the head of the table.

Smoke was glad to see that all the hard feelings between Preacher and Eagle-Eye seemed to have evaporated. Between bites, the two old mountain men were reminiscing about events from the fur trapping era, some forty to fifty years earlier. Preacher's time in the mountains actually went back farther than that, although Eagle-Eye's didn't.

"Finally decided to crawl outta your soogans, did you?" Preacher jibed as Smoke sat down at the table.

"These young fellas wasn't never as eager to get up and get to work as we were back in our heyday, Preacher," Eagle-Eye said.

"I wouldn't want to say they was plumb lazy," drawled Preacher, "but I seen a young fella yawnin' once while he was tryin' to get outta the way of a buffalo stampede."

"I reckon he made it?"

"Yeah . . . and then he took a nap." Preacher shook his head. "Wonder whatever happened to ol' Breck Wallace. I ain't seen nor heard anythin' about him for a heap o' years."

Smoke had heard Preacher mention Breckinridge Wallace before, but he didn't know what had happened to the old frontiersman, either. Odds were, the man was dead.

Smoke looked over at Ace and Chance and asked, "How did you fellas sleep last night?"

"Best night's sleep I've had in a long time," Ace said.

"Me, too," Chance added. "You and Mrs. Jensen have a mighty nice spread here, Smoke."

From the kitchen, Sally said through the open doorway, "You're supposed to call me Sally, Chance. We're all friends and family here."

"Yes, ma'am. I'll try to remember that."

Smoke devoted himself to his food for a few minutes, as did the other men, then after washing down some ham and eggs with coffee, he said, "Sally and I are going into Big Rock this morning, if any of you boys want to come along."

"It looked like a nice town when we passed through it," Ace said. "Anything to do there?"

"There's a billy-ard parlor," said Preacher, "happen you like pokin' balls with a stick."

"And there's a theater and opera house," Smoke said, "but it's closed down for the winter. The fellow who runs it can't hardly abide the cold weather, all that snow and ice, so he usually heads south until spring. Mostly I sit around a saloon and restaurant called Longmont's and talk to the owner, who's an old friend of mine."

"Louis Longmont?" asked Ace, raising his eyebrows slightly. "I've heard of him. He used to be a gunman, didn't he?"

"Fast on the draw," Smoke confirmed. "Still is. That doesn't necessarily make a man a gunman, though. Louis is a gambler and a businessman, but more than anything else he's a gentleman." Smoke paused then added, "He plays an excellent game of chess, too."

Chance poked a thumb toward his brother. "That's Ace's game. Poker's more my speed. Maybe a little blackjack now and then."

"You'll find somebody at Longmont's to accommodate you," Smoke said.

"I wouldn't mind goin', too," Eagle-Eye said. "Been a while since I been in a big city."

Smoke smiled. "I'm not sure Big Rock qualifies as a big city."

"When you've spent most o' the past forty years in a tradin' post in the middle o' nowhere, it does!"

Smoke couldn't argue with that. Anyway, even though Preacher and Eagle-Eye appeared to have made peace, Smoke liked the idea of the two old-timers going to town with them so he could keep an eye on them.

After breakfast, he hitched up the buggy horse, then saddled his own mount while Ace, Chance, Preacher, and Eagle-Eye got their horses ready to ride. It was a formidable group that set out for Big Rock a short time later.

The snow on the trail slowed them down a little, but it wasn't anything the horses and the buggy couldn't make their way through. The rugged scenery with its covering of white was so pretty it looked like it ought to be on a calendar, thought Smoke.

Big Rock

As they approached the settlement and moved along Main Street, the Jensens, Preacher, and Eagle Eye could see numerous columns of smoke rising from various chimneys, which added to the picturesque quality of the scene. Despite the snow, the town was bustling.

Smoke noticed that a train was stopped at the depot. No smoke was puffing from the locomotive's diamond-shaped stack, which meant it didn't have any steam up. The fact that the westbound hadn't pulled out yet caused his curiosity to perk up. He pulled his horse alongside the buggy and leaned over slightly in the saddle. "I think I'll ride on down to the train station," he told Sally.

"Are you expecting something—or someone?" she asked.

"Nope, not at all. Just wondering why the westbound's still here."

"I reckon I can tell you that," said Preacher. "The snow's so deep in the passes up yonder that iron horse can't get through."

Smoke suspected that the old mountain man was right, but he still wanted to find out for sure. He didn't have any particular reason for doing so, but he was in the habit of indulging his curiosity whenever he could.

"You go ahead." Sally knew him well enough to know that once he got his mind set on something, he had to go through with it. "I'll see you later at Louis's. We can have lunch there."

That idea put a grin on Smoke's face. There wasn't a better place in Big Rock to eat, not even Delmonico's. He waved a farewell as Sally sent the buggy horse trotting on toward the church.

Preacher said to him, "Reckon we'll go on down to the depot with you. Might be somethin' interestin' goin' on, although I sorta doubt it."

"Only one way to find out," Chance put in with a smile.

The five men rode to the station, dismounted, and tied their horses at the hitch rails in front of the big, redbrick building. As they opened the doors and walked into the large, drafty, high-ceilinged waiting room, Smoke spotted Phil Clinton talking to the stationmaster, Sam Bailey. Clinton, the editor and publisher of the *Big Rock Journal*, was writing quickly on a pad of paper.

There must be some sort of story here after all, thought Smoke.

He noticed a large group of children, probably close to twenty in all, being herded through the lobby by a couple women and a man. The adults were dressed like Easterners, and all three had strained, worried expressions on their faces.

Smoke and his companions went up to the stationmaster and the newspaperman. He nodded in greeting. "Sam, Phil. What's going on?"

Bailey's prominent Adam's apple bobbed up and down as he said, "The snow is too deep in the passes for the trains to get through, so the line's shut down for the time being."

Preacher nodded, a satisfied look on his face because his prediction had proven accurate.

"The train's stuck here," Bailey went on. He lowered his voice. "And so are all those dang orphans."

"Orphans?" Smoke repeated.

Clinton told him, "This is one of those orphan trains. You've probably heard of them, Smoke."

Smoke shook his head. "Can't say as I have."

"I have," Ace said. "Some group back East brings orphans out West where they find new families and get adopted. I've read about it in the newspaper."

"You can read about it in the *Journal* in a few days, too," Clinton said. "I'll be doing a story about these particular orphans being stranded here." He eyed Eagle-Eye, Ace, and Chance. "I don't believe I'm acquainted with these gentlemen. . . ." As a newspaperman, he was always interested in newcomers to Big

Rock. You never could tell when a visitor to the settlement might be worth a few lines of type in the paper.

Smoke said, "You've met Preacher, of course. This is an old friend of his, Eagle-Eye Callahan."

"Eagle-Eye," said Clinton. "That's certainly a colorful nickname, Mr. Callahan."

"I got it 'cause I'm so sharp-eyed," Eagle-Eye said proudly.

Clinton nodded. "That's what I assumed."

"And these two young fellas are Ace and Chance Jensen," Smoke went on.

"Ah, relatives of yours?" Clinton asked.

"Not that we know of, but they're good friends anyway. We met down in Texas last year."

Clinton smiled at Ace and Chance. "As visitors, what are your impressions of Big Rock?"

"Seems like a mighty nice place," Ace said.

"It is," Smoke said. "You couldn't say the same thing about Fontana, the first settlement in this area. It was a mile or two from here, and it was full of outlaws and killers."

"What happened to it?" asked Chance.

Preacher chuckled. "Smoke happened to it. That's enough of an answer, right there."

"Oh," Ace said. He and Chance nodded as if they knew exactly what the old mountain man meant.

Smoke let that pass. He wasn't the sort to boast about any of his accomplishments—and he had plenty of them—especially considering the fact that he was still a relatively young man. To change the subject, he asked, "What's going to happen to those orphans?"

Sam Bailey shook his head. "I reckon we're going

to have to try to find a place for them to stay. It won't be easy. There are twenty of 'em, as well as the three folks who are taking care of 'em. I'm not sure the hotel can accommodate that many."

An idea popped into Smoke's head. He didn't know if it would work out—and he didn't know if Sally would go along with it—but he thought there was a good chance she would. She loved children and had mentioned more than once that someday she wanted to have a whole houseful of her own.

It might be good practice for that, thought Smoke, although he was sure she never had in mind having twenty children of her own!

"Sam, why don't you let me talk to the folks who are in charge of those kids? Maybe we could put them up out at the Sugarloaf. Some of them, anyway. I'm not sure we'd have room for all twenty. I'd have to talk to Sally about that."

"Shoot, if you could take half of them, that would be a big help, Smoke," Bailey replied. "The folks at the hotel might be able to find a place for the others. If you're sure you want to make such a generous offer, come along and I'll introduce you to the people in charge."

"Let's do that," Smoke said with a decisive nod.

As the men started toward the group of children that had gathered on the other side of the big waiting room, Preacher said quietly to Smoke, "You sure it's a good idea doin' this without talkin' to Sally first?"

"She'll be fine with it," Smoke said confidently. "Anyway, it's only for a few days, more than likely. How much trouble can a few kids be?"

CHAPTER 29

The sound of numerous footsteps approaching from behind her made Mercy Halliday turn around. She almost gasped at the sight of the men crossing the lobby toward her.

They looked so . . . She couldn't come up with the right description. *Threatening wasn't* the word since they all appeared friendly enough.

But they still seemed dangerous somehow. All of them were wearing guns except the stationmaster, whom she recognized. The man had talked to her and the Gallaghers earlier to explain the situation.

A ruggedly handsome ash-blond man with extraordinarily broad shoulders appeared to be the leader. Accompanying him were two older men wearing buckskins, and two younger men, one big and attractive in a rough-hewn way and the other slightly smaller and more conventionally handsome. Unlike the others, he wore a suit and had a more sophisticated air about him.

"Peter," Mercy said.

He turned toward her with a harassed expression on his face. "What—" He stopped short as he saw the men coming toward them. His eyes widened and Mercy thought he looked frightened. She could understand that. The Western men were rather daunting.

The leader's voice was quiet, controlled, and polite as he stopped in front of them and pinched the brim of his hat "Ma'am." He nodded to Grace and added another respectful, "Ma'am. I hear you folks have a considerable responsibility on your hands."

"You could certainly say that," Peter responded. "We have to look after all these children and find a place for them to stay because of this abominable weather."

"Mr. Jensen here thinks he can help you out with that," the stationmaster said. "By the way, this is Smoke Jensen, one of the valley's leading citizens."

Hearing that description seemed to make Peter a little more amenable. He nodded, only a little grudgingly. "It's a pleasure to meet you, Mr. Jensen. I'm Peter Gallagher. This is my wife Mrs. Gallagher and our associate Miss Halliday. We're with the Children's Aid Society of New York City."

"New York City," one of the older men said. "I was there once. Didn't care much for it. Like to broke my neck lookin' up at the buildin's. Some of 'em musta been three or four stories tall."

"Not like the mountains, eh, Preacher?" Smoke said with a smile. He turned back to Mercy and the Gallaghers. "This is my old friend Preacher and his friend Eagle-Eye Callahan."

"Very colorful nomenclature," muttered Peter.

"Norman who?" said Preacher.

Smoke ignored the exchange. "And those two young fellas are Ace and Chance Jensen."

Judging by the way they nodded as Smoke said their names, Mercy figured the bigger of the two was Ace, while the one in the brown suit was Chance. If that was right, he was the one who took his hat off and held it over his chest. "It sure is a pleasure to meet you folks."

The way he was looking at her when he said it made it seem that he was talking directly to her. She felt her face flush momentarily but didn't know if the reaction was from embarrassment or pleasure.

Peter asked, "What is it we can do for you gentlemen?"

"It's what we can do for you, I hope," Smoke said. "My wife and I have a ranch with a large ranch house several miles west of town. We've got plenty of room for some of you folks if you'd like to stay with us. I reckon we can take at least half of the youngsters."

Peter frowned. "That's a very generous offer, but I don't know if we should split up the group—"

"I don't see why not, Peter," his wife interrupted him. "Mr. Bailey already told us there might not be enough room at the hotel for all of them."

"Yes, but we haven't even checked with the hotel yet."

Mercy could tell he was irritated that Grace had spoken up.

He bristled. "I really ought to do that. I think it would be best to keep the children together if we can."

"Of course, dear. Whatever you say," Grace murmured.

"That's fine," Smoke said. "We'll be in town until sometime this afternoon. If you'd like to take me up on the offer, I'll be at Longmont's Saloon."

"A saloon?" Peter repeated, clearly not happy about the idea of venturing into such an establishment.

"It's a restaurant, too," Smoke explained. "Not as fancy as what you've got back in New York, I reckon, but plenty respectable, even for the ladies."

"I can vouch for that," the stationmaster said. "Longmont's is nothing like the Brown Dirt Cowboy."

Peter's lip curled as he said, "The Brown Dirt Cowboy?"

Mercy wished he wouldn't be quite so condescending. Mr. Jensen and his companions seemed like nice men, and there was no need to insult them. She watched their reactions and decided they didn't seem bothered by Peter's attitude.

Smoke touched a finger to his hat brim again. "See you folks later."

Chance added, "I surely do hope so."

Again, Mercy felt her face warming.

When the men had walked off, Peter said quietly, "It's out of the question that we'll let them take any of the children out to that ranch. Can you imagine? It just wouldn't be safe. There are all sorts of things that could happen to them, and they're our responsibility."

"I doubt if they would be in any more danger on a ranch than they were on the streets of New York, where they came from," Grace pointed out. "If anything, probably less so, since they'd have Mr. Jensen and his friends looking out for them. He's certainly quite an . . . impressive . . . individual."

"You really think so? He seemed like just another roughneck cowboy to me."

"Then you weren't paying enough attention, Peter."

He frowned at his wife's comment. "I'm going to the hotel to see about the situation there. You and Mercy stay here and keep an eye on the children." Without giving them a chance to agree or disagree, he strode off, leaving them behind.

Mercy wasn't sure how she hoped the situation would turn out. The idea of spending a few days out of town on a ranch was intriguing, but also a little frightening. Would there be outlaws? Savage Indians? She had made several Western trips, but she'd never ventured far away from the train stations. All she really knew about frontier life came from the illustrated newspapers, and they weren't noted for their restraint.

The children were restless, of course. They didn't like being told to sit on the benches in the waiting room and be still and quiet. That went against their nature. Mercy and Grace stood nearby, watching them to make sure no one wandered off, while they waited for Peter to come back from the hotel.

Mercy was taken a little by surprise when a deep voice asked from behind her, "Who were your new friends?"

She turned quickly to see Ed Rinehart standing there with a curious expression on his lean face.

He'd had mixed emotions about the idea of being

stuck in Big Rock for a few days. Although the delay could give him a chance to get to know the boy called Caleb better and maybe find out for sure if he was really Donald Litchfield, little towns made him nervous. He was accustomed to life in the big city. But there was nothing he could do about the snow-fall in the mountains, so he resolved himself to making the best of the situation. That might well involve spending more time with Mercy Halliday, and he couldn't complain about that.

He'd seen her and the Gallaghers talking to a bunch of cowboys, and for some reason that had bothered him. Maybe it had something to do with the way one of them kept smiling warmly at Mercy every time he said something. As soon as the men and Peter had departed, the detective had indulged his curiosity and strolled over to where the women were waiting with the children.

Mercy smiled. "Oh, Mr. Rinehart . . . I mean, Ed. I thought you'd left and gone to the hotel."

"No, I've just been waiting to see what was going to happen." Keeping an eye on her and the children was what he really meant, of course. "I saw you talking to those fellows. Seems like nearly everybody out here packs a gun."

"Yes, it's very different from New York, isn't it? I suppose the frontier is dangerous enough that most people feel the need to be armed."

"I suppose so," Rinehart agreed, not mentioning that he had a pistol in the pocket of his overcoat, a derringer in his vest pocket, a knife in a sheath strapped to his left forearm, and a sap and a pair of brass knuckles in another overcoat pocket.

Mercy said, "The gentleman I was talking to is named Smoke Jensen."

"Smoke. That's an odd name."

"I'm sure it's a nickname. At any rate, he's a rancher and has a large house not too far from town. He suggested that some of the children could stay with him and his wife if there's not room for them here in town."

Grace was listening unabashedly to their conversation. She put in her thoughts about it. "I think the children would really enjoy that. A chance to spend some time on a real ranch, I mean."

"Maybe so," Rinehart said, but he didn't much care for the idea. He needed to watch over Caleb and the other boys about the same age, at least until he determined which one was really Donald Litchfield. That would be more difficult to do if some or all of them were out at some ranch where anything might happen.

Of course, he had to admit that the men who had been talking to Mercy had certainly appeared capable of handling any trouble that might come up.

"Peter's opposed to the idea," Grace went on.

That right there was almost enough to be in favor of it, Rinehart thought wryly. He looked at Mercy and asked, "What do you think?"

"I'm not sure. As Grace says, the children might enjoy it. One of us would have to go with them, though. We couldn't send them out to Mr. Jensen's ranch without someone from the Society watching out for them."

Grace shook her head. "Peter would never do it.

He would consider such a thing 'roughing it', like in Mr. Twain's book."

"I suppose I could go. . . ." Mercy said.

Rinehart tried not to frown. He didn't want to let Caleb out of his sight, and he felt the same way about Mercy. He gave thought to some way to get himself invited to go along, if indeed things worked out that way.

A few minutes later, he saw Peter Gallagher striding back into the railroad station. Gallagher seemed upset, and that didn't bode well.

Didn't look promising, Rinehart thought.

"What did you find out, Peter?" Grace asked as her husband came up to them.

"That lout at the hotel said there was only room for eight of the children. It seems that the place is busier than usual because people are in town to visit relatives over the holidays or some such humbug. Also, the town puts on a big Christmas Eve celebration, and a lot of people have come in from outlying ranches and the like for that. What a terrible confluence of circumstances. I told the man we could put ten children in each room and let them sleep on the floor, but he wouldn't allow it."

"Well, then," said Grace, "I don't see what else we can do other than accept Mr. Jensen's kind offer."

"I won't hear of it. Perhaps we can appeal to the local churches and see if there are families in town that will take in a child or two apiece—"

"Oh, Peter, that's an excellent idea!" Mercy exclaimed.

"It is?" He looked more than a little surprised that

she would make such a comment about any of his suggestions.

Rinehart felt the same way.

"Yes, it is," Mercy went on. "The whole idea was to find good homes for the children and arrange for them to be adopted. We don't have to go all the way to Sacramento to do that. We can see if there are families right here in this town, or at least in the area, who would welcome a child with love."

"You mean . . . they could be adopted *here?*"

"Why not? And until we can arrange that, perhaps Mr. Jensen and his wife would be willing to take in all of them for the time being. They could spend Christmas on . . . what was it he called his ranch?"

CHAPTER 30

Standing in his usual place at the bar, Louis Longmont cocked an eyebrow when Smoke walked in with Preacher, Eagle-Eye, Ace, and Chance. As usual, the gambler looked elegant doing it. "Quite the entourage, Smoke."

"You mean these fellas?" Smoke asked with a grin. "Yeah, they started following me around, and I can't get rid of them."

Preacher said, "You go to callin' us an on-tour . . . on-tore . . . whatever fancy two-bit word it was you was a-flingin' around, and we'll just leave. Ain't that right, Eagle-Eye?"

"Not just yet," said Eagle-Eye. "I ain't never had a drink in no fancy French saloon."

"Then allow me to get you one, *mon ami*," Louis said. "That means *my friend*."

"I know that. I dealt with enough French-Canadian trappers to pick up a little of the lingo. They'd come over the border sometimes into Montana to pick up supplies at my tradin' post."

"This is Eagle-Eye Callahan, an old friend of Preacher's." Smoke didn't mention anything about how Eagle-Eye and Preacher had almost wound up as mortal enemies. That was over and done with . . . he hoped. "And these youngsters are Ace and Chance Jensen."

Louis gave him another of those quizzical looks. "Long-lost relatives?"

"Not that we know of," Ace said. "It's a pleasure to meet you, Mr. Longmont. We've heard a lot about you from Smoke."

"And some of it might even be true," Louis said with a twinkle in his eye. "It's not lunchtime yet, so I assume you don't want alcoholic drinks, but I have some fine Creole coffee in the pot. With chicory, molasses, and cream, it'll warm you up on a cold day like today."

"Sounds good to me," Smoke said.

"Johnny, Creole coffees all around," Louis said to the bartender. "We'll be at the rear table."

The six men took seats around the table, and Johnny soon had steaming cups of the rich, dark concoction in front of them.

Eagle-Eye sampled his and smacked his lips. "Dang, that *is* pretty good. Might be even better with a shot of whiskey in it. Reckon I can wait until later, though."

Preacher said, "Smoke, you best talk to Sally about takin' in all them orphans. She might not want to be crowded outta house and home that way."

"I don't think she'll mind. Anyway, I already made the offer, so it's too late to take it back now."

Louis turned to Ace and Chance. "Tell me about yourselves, gentlemen. What brings you to Big Rock?"

"We came here with Eagle-Eye," Ace explained. "The three of us sort of fell in together."

Eagle-Eye snorted. "This youngster's bein' too modest. Him and his brother run off a bunch of no-good scoundrels who were trying to rob me. Those owlhoots likely woulda killed me if it hadn't been for these two."

"Sounds like the sort of thing you would have done, Smoke," Louis pointed out.

"More than likely," Smoke agreed. "I never liked to see anybody being ganged up on."

Chance said, "When we found out Eagle-Eye was on his way to Smoke's ranch, it was one more reason to throw in with him. We all got acquainted last year down in Texas."

"I remember you telling me about that, Smoke," Louis said. "That was around Christmas time, too, wasn't it?"

Smoke grinned again. "Christmases are usually pretty eventful. I'm hoping this one won't be."

"Except for havin' a passel o' orphans runnin' around," said Preacher.

"Well, yeah, there's that."

The men sat and enjoyed their coffee for a while, mostly in silence. None of them tended toward meaningless chatter.

All six of them quickly came to their feet as Sally came into the saloon and looked around.

Her face lit up with a smile as she started across the room toward them, stopping at their table. "Such gallant gentlemen. Any woman would be glad to see such a group welcoming her."

Louis pulled a chair over from a nearby table. "Please join us. Would you care for Creole coffee?"

"That sounds wonderful. Thank you."

Louis signaled to Johnny McVey, who brought over another cup of the savory brew. Sally took a sip from the cup and sighed in satisfaction.

Smoke asked, "Did your meeting go all right?"

"Yes, it did. Everything is ready, or at least it will be by Christmas Eve. This should be one of the best celebrations ever." She paused, then added, "I hear that the train is stuck here because of deep snow in the passes, so there'll be even more people than usual on hand for it."

"Um, about that . . ." Smoke began.

Before he could go on, the door of the saloon opened and another shapely female figure entered the establishment. He recognized Miss Halliday from the Orphan Train. She saw the group at the rear table and started toward them just as Sally had done a few minutes earlier.

Seeing the attention of all six men diverted toward the doorway, Sally half-turned in her chair to see what was going on. The sight of the beautiful, auburn-haired young woman who was obviously headed their way made her look at Smoke and raise her eyebrows.

Chance was the first one on his feet. "Miss Halliday, it's so good to see you again."

"You, too, Mr. Jensen. And the other Misters Jensen and your friends."

"I'm Sally Jensen," Sally said. "Smoke's wife."

Miss Halliday extended a gloved hand. "It's such a

pleasure to meet you, Mrs. Jensen. I'm Mercy Halliday, from the Children's Aid Society."

"I've heard of your group. You do such good work, finding new homes for all those children." Sally paused as realization dawned on her face. "Do you mean to tell me that you have a group of orphans here in Big Rock right now?"

Mercy nodded. "That's right. We were on our way to Sacramento with twenty children, until the Lord intervened with that magnificent snowfall. At first, we thought we would just wait here until we could resume our journey on the railroad, but then my fellow Society members and I realized we could just do our work here."

"Find homes for the children, you mean?" Sally smiled. "That's a fine idea! There are a lot of wonderful families in this valley, and I'm sure some of them would welcome new additions with love and open arms."

Mercy nodded toward Smoke. "And of course, your husband's kind offer just made it that much easier to put our new plan into action."

"My husband's offer?" Sally glanced at Smoke. "I'm afraid I don't know what you're talking about, Miss Halliday."

Smoke said, "Well, that's what I was about to tell you."

"Mr. Jensen said that some of the children could stay at your ranch," Mercy explained. "Actually, we were hoping that all of them might be able to stay with you while we're arranging their adoptions."

"Twenty children?" Sally's friendly smile never budged, but Smoke saw concern flash in her eyes.

However, the reaction was fleeting. Her glance in his direction told him they would talk about it later, but her voice was sincere as she told Mercy, "I think that's a wonderful idea. We'll find the room for them. Some of the older boys might like to stay in the bunkhouse with our ranch hands. We don't have a full crew at this time of year, so there are empty bunks out there, as well as the guest rooms in the house."

"Really? Thank you so much, Mrs. Jensen." Mercy's smile was dazzling.

At least Chance seemed to think so.

Smoke noted the way the younger man was looking at her then asked, "Will the other two folks who are traveling with you be staying with us, as well?"

"Peter and Grace?" Mercy shook her head. "I'm afraid not. Peter insists that they stay here in town at the hotel. I'll be looking after the children by myself."

"Not by yourself," Sally corrected her. "You'll have me helping you, and a whole crew of cowboys, to boot." She laughed. "Don't worry. We'll see to it that they don't teach the children how to cuss and chew tobacco!"

Ray Morley lounged against the bar in the Brown Dirt Cowboy Saloon with a mug of beer in front of him. The lean, dark-faced outlaw looked around the room. Without pausing or giving any indication that he knew them, his eyes passed over the couple other members of Jim Bleeker's private army sitting at one of the tables and nursing drinks. Several more men from the group of killers had drifted into town over the past few hours, coming in individually or in pairs so they wouldn't attract any attention.

The rest of the men and Bleeker were still out at the ranch they had taken over. He didn't want to come into Big Rock because of the possibility that Monte Carson might spot him and recognize him before the gang was ready to strike. Morley was there to scout out the situation and get word back to Bleeker so they could plan their attack.

So far, the operation Bleeker had in mind looked like quite a challenge. Big Rock was full of people who had come in for the holidays, and many of them were ranchers and cowboys who were armed and knew how to use their guns.

There was a big difference, though, between hombres who used their guns primarily to shoot snakes, mountain lions, and other varmints, and professional killers accustomed to ending the lives of other men. In a gun battle, one member of Bleeker's gang was worth a dozen or more settlers.

Morley had heard considerable talk around town about the big party that was going to take place on Christmas Eve. It seemed to him that would be the perfect time to strike. Everybody would be gathered in one place, rather than scattered around town where opposition would be harder to root out. Not only that, but a lot of women and kids would be on hand, and their menfolk would be less likely to fight back if they knew that stray bullets would be flying around their loved ones. They would surrender in order to save their families.

Hell, they would probably turn Monte Carson over to Bleeker if it meant protecting the town!

Of course, in the long run that wouldn't do them much good, since Bleeker intended to loot Big Rock and burn it to the ground right in front of Carson's eyes before killing him.

Morley picked up his beer and drained the last of it. The bartender, a bald, bullet-headed man in a stained apron, asked him, "Want another, mister?"

"No," Morley replied with a shake of his head. "I think I've got everything I need for now. Thanks anyway."

The woman sitting in a corner of the train station waiting room wore a bonnet and had the collar of her overcoat turned up, so not much of her face was visible. The bonnet contained and concealed a thick mass of lustrous, raven curls, and the collar hid lovely features with a touch of the exotic about them.

A small carpetbag at her feet contained all her belongings, everything she had brought with her from New York. It had taken most of her remaining funds to purchase the ticket, so she hadn't been able to afford to eat much during the trip.

That didn't matter. She had her hate to sustain her.

She had been one of the first passengers off the train, once it was apparent that it wasn't going on but was stopping. She had found the out of the way corner and waited. Dark eyes alertly watched the comings and goings in the depot. She saw the group of children come in, shepherded by two women and a man.

A short time later, a man wearing an overcoat and a fedora walked in after them, and although he tried to be unobtrusive about it, the woman in the corner saw the way he was watching the children and their escorts. Something about them was of great interest to the man in the fedora.

The younger of the two women, perhaps? The prettier one, with auburn hair? If the man in the fedora was attracted to her, that was interesting. Very interesting indeed. The woman in the corner thought it might be something she could use against him. Something to make him realize what a bad mistake he had made when he'd humiliated her and forced her to flee.

For a detective, Ed Rinehart was a fool, thought Seraphine DuMille.

The woman who was going to kill him was twenty feet away . . . and he had no idea.

CHAPTER 31

Rounding up twenty orphans wasn't quite as big a job as putting together a herd of cattle for a trail drive, thought Smoke dryly a while later, but it had its challenges.

For one thing, there was the matter of transporting them out to the Sugarloaf. He solved that by renting a couple wagons at the local livery stable. He would tie his saddle horse on the back of one of the wagons and drive that one. Ace had volunteered to handle the team hitched to the other vehicle.

It took some work, just to get that many youngsters from one place to another without any of them running off. Not that they were bad kids or that any of them wanted to run away and not come back. They were just exuberant and full of energy. They were in a new place, surrounded by new things, and they wanted to take in all of it at once. Getting them out of the depot and into the wagons took some work.

Luckily, Smoke had plenty of help. Mercy Halliday was used to dealing with the children, of course, and Ace and Chance were young and had plenty of energy of their own. Chance, especially, was eager to pitch in, and Smoke had no doubt that was because he wanted to impress Mercy.

Sally proved to be good with the little ones—she had been a school teacher—despite not having any of her own yet. Even Preacher and Eagle-Eye lent a hand, although at their age they didn't have the patience to do much.

Peter Gallagher stood by with a dour expression on his face. When the orphans were all loaded onto the wagons, he said, "I'm still not sure this is a good idea. I don't like letting these young ones out of my sight."

"You're welcome to come along with us and stay out at the Sugarloaf," Smoke told him, being cheerful about it despite the fact that he didn't like Gallagher very much. "We'll sure find room for you, although it might have to be out in the bunkhouse."

A little shudder ran through Gallagher as he shook his head. "No, thanks. My wife and I will remain here in civilization." He looked around at Big Rock. "Or what passes for it."

"The ranch is only a few miles out of town," Smoke pointed out. "But you do what you think is best, Mr. Gallagher." Not having the sour-faced hombre around was sort of like dodging a bullet, he thought. He couldn't complain about that.

A few feet away, Grace Gallagher was saying to Mercy, "I wish I was coming along with you, dear. I feel terrible about saddling you with the responsibility of all of the children. But Peter insists that we're staying here at the hotel."

"That's all right," Mercy assured her. "I'll have lots of help. Mrs. Jensen promised me that their cowboys will be glad to look after the older boys. They can even teach the boys some of the things they'll need to know if they're going to live and work here in the West. This seems almost like a perfect arrangement to me. It was a real stroke of luck when Mr. Jensen made his generous offer."

Smoke was looking around to make sure all the youngsters were on the wagons when a voice asked from behind him, "What in blazes is all this?"

Smoke turned and smiled at Sheriff Monte Carson. "We're going to have some company for a while out at the Sugarloaf, Monte," he explained. "These children are orphans who are going to find new homes here in the valley. They'll be staying with us until all the arrangements are made."

"Yeah, I heard something about that from Sam Bailey a few minutes ago," Monte said. "Mighty nice of you taking them in like this, Smoke. I reckon it was Sally's idea?"

From the seat of the lead wagon, where she was already sitting, Sally said, "Not at all. Smoke came up with this all on his own, Monte. But I think it's an excellent idea."

"Well, good luck to you." The sheriff added under his breath to Smoke, "You're probably going to need it."

Ace was about to climb to the seat of the second wagon when his brother shouldered him aside.

"I'll take this one," Chance declared.

"I already said I'd drive," Ace objected.

"Yeah, but I decided I want to do it." Chance looked over Ace's shoulder as he spoke.

Ace looked around and saw Mercy Halliday coming toward them. Understanding dawned on his face. "Oh."

"Just go see to the horses, why don't you?" suggested Chance.

Ace chuckled and shook his head. "Fine by me, if you're interested in a gal who has twenty kids."

"They're not *her* kids."

"They are right now."

Chance frowned as Ace walked toward the back of the wagon. His brother might have a point there. But she was good-looking enough to make the risk worthwhile.

She hadn't yet reached the wagon when a tall, lean man strode up alongside her. Chance's frown deepened as she stopped and smiled at the stranger. The two of them started talking.

Ed Rinehart said, "So you're on your way out to Jensen's ranch, I see."

"That's right," Mercy replied.

Rinehart had been asking around town, and he'd heard all about how Smoke Jensen was a famous gunfighter who had taken on nineteen outlaws at once in an epic battle and killed all of them. And that was only one of his many exploits.

"I wonder if he might have room for one more," mused Rinehart.

Mercy smiled and cocked her head slightly to the side as she asked, "You need a place to stay, too?"

"With people being stuck here from the train, the

hotel has filled up," Rinehart explained. That wasn't completely true. He might have been able to share a room with another male traveler, but he didn't want to let the children that far out of his sight.

Not to mention, he didn't care much for the idea of letting Mercy go out there by herself, either.

"I don't know," she said, "but I can introduce you to Mr. Jensen and you can talk to him about it."

Rinehart nodded. "That would be fine. I appreciate it."

Before Smoke could climb up on the lead wagon, Mercy and a man he hadn't met approached. He recalled seeing the hombre in the train station earlier but hadn't been aware that he had any connection to her.

"Mr. Jensen, this is Mr. Rinehart," the young woman said. "He's from New York as well."

"Ed Rinehart," the man said as he stuck out his hand. "It's a pleasure to meet you, Mr. Jensen."

Smoke shook hands with him and nodded. "You're a friend of Miss Halliday?"

"Well, I hope so," Rinehart answered with a smile. "We got acquainted on the train on the way out here."

"Mr. Rinehart has been very helpful with the children," Mercy said.

"Mighty kind of you" Smoke nodded, wondering what it had to do with him.

She put an end to his wondering. "I was hoping you might be able to find room for him, too."

"You're not staying here in town, Mr. Rinehart?" Smoke asked.

The man shrugged. "I might be able to double up

with someone at the hotel, but I was hoping to avoid that."

"I'm not sure a crowded bunkhouse would be any better."

"It would be as far as I'm concerned." Rinehart smiled. "Besides, I have to admit I'm curious about what a real Western ranch is like. I've heard about them and read about them, but this is my first trip out here."

"I have to warn you," Smoke said, "it's not like what you've read in the dime novels, and those wild west shows like the one Bill Cody took back East aren't very realistic, either. Mostly ranch life is just a lot of hard work."

"I'd be glad to pitch in and do whatever I could to help earn my keep while I'm there," Rinehart said.

Smoke waved a hand and told him, "I don't reckon that's necessary, although we never turn down any help. If Miss Halliday vouches for you, we'd be glad to have you."

Mercy said, "You're putting a lot of stock in my opinion, Mr. Jensen, considering that you've only known me for a couple hours."

From the wagon, Sally said, "Smoke is a good judge of character, and I like to think I am, too. As long as you're a friend of Mercy's, you're welcome on the Sugarloaf, Mr. Rinehart."

"Thank you, ma'am," Rinehart said as he took off his fedora and nodded to her. "Very kind of you."

Smoke noticed that Sally and Mercy were on a first-name basis already. That was another mark in the young woman's favor.

"Do you have a horse, Mr. Rinehart?" Smoke asked.

"No, I thought I'd rent one at the livery stable, if I can."

Smoke shook his head. "No need for that. You can ride mine." He gestured toward the big gray stallion tied to the back of the wagon.

Rinehart looked a little leery of that idea. "I'm, uh, not really an experienced horseman."

"You'll do fine," Smoke assured him. In truth, the stallion did have a salty nature at times and required a firm hand on the reins, but Rinehart had an athletic look about him and Smoke figured the Easterner could handle the horse. It would be a good test of Rinehart's mettle, too.

"I'll get my bag from the depot and be right back," Rinehart said.

While he was gone, Mercy told Smoke, "Thank you, Mr. Jensen. I know when you left home this morning, you never dreamed you'd be coming back with so many guests!"

Sally laughed. "It's the time of year for guests."

Rinehart was back in a minute with his carpetbag and added it to the pile of bags in the second wagon.

Smoke noticed how Chance was frowning at the man from New York and thought, *A little jealousy at work there.* Chance liked Mercy, too, and he had seen how she smiled at Ed Rinehart. Smoke chuckled a little as he climbed to the wagon seat next to Sally.

She asked, "What's funny?"

"I'm just glad I'm not quite as young as I once was," he told her.

"You have a long way to go until you're old, Smoke Jensen."

"If I live that long." He slapped the reins against the horses' backs and got the team moving. The wagon rolled along the street with the other vehicle following. Ace had taken the reins of Sally's buggy, since Chance had taken his place on the second wagon. Preacher, Eagle-Eye, and Ed Rinehart followed on horseback.

The gray stallion was a little skittish at first, but Rinehart soon had it under control, Smoke noted as he glanced over his shoulder. As they passed Monte Carson on the boardwalk, Smoke grinned and nodded to the lawman, who returned a friendly wave.

Within minutes, the group had left Big Rock behind.

CHAPTER 32

On the way to Sugarloaf Ranch

The trip was loud. The children, most of whom had never been out of New York before, exclaimed in excitement as they saw the towering mountains on both sides of the valley and the tall, snow-mantled pines along the trail. They were full of questions, and they laughed happily at being in a new place despite the cold weather.

A cleaner, better place, as far as Smoke was concerned. He had seen some of the big eastern cities for himself, and he knew he never would have been able to be happy there. He was thankful, not for the first time, that Sally had adjusted so well to life in the West.

Other than all the talk and laughter, the journey to the ranch was uneventful.

Sugarloaf Ranch

Pearlie and Cal came out of the barn as the wagons rolled up in front of the ranch house.

The foreman exclaimed, "What in the he—" then caught himself at the sight of all the children.

Cal had a big grin on his face as he said, "Looks like you're already taking on new hands for the spring round-up, Smoke."

"Got to, since so many of the layabouts already riding for me don't know how to do a good day's work," Smoke replied with a grin of his own. "Boys, that's Miss Halliday back there on the other wagon next to Chance. She's from the Children's Aid Society in New York."

Pearlie and Cal nodded to Mercy and pinched the brims of their hats.

Cal, who had an eye for a pretty girl, said, "Mighty pleased to meet you, ma'am."

Smoke could have told him that if he had any thoughts about wooing Mercy, he would find himself already in competition with Chance and Rinehart. Cal would have to find that out on his own, however. Smoke wasn't going to get in the middle of that.

"These children are orphans looking for new homes here in the valley," Sally explained. "Smoke and I have agreed to let them stay here while all the arrangements are made."

"And it's very kind of you," Mercy said from the second wagon.

Smoke climbed down and turned back to help Sally. Chance was already on the ground and moved to give Mercy a hand, but Ed Rinehart was there ahead of him, reaching up to her. Chance glared but backed off, since there wasn't much of anything else he could do.

The children were already jumping down from the wagons.

Preacher and Eagle-Eye tried to keep them under control, leading Preacher to exclaim, "Dadgum it. They're runnin' around like a bunch o' chickens with their heads cut off!"

It took the two old-timers, Ace, Chance, Mercy, Rinehart, and Pearlie and Cal to keep the youngsters herded up reasonably close together.

Smoke said to Pearlie, "Some of the older boys are going to be staying in the bunkhouse with you fellas."

"Sounds like a good idea," said Pearlie. "I'll try to keep Cal from bein' too bad an influence on 'em while they're here."

"Me?" Cal said. "You're the one who was fixing to cuss in front of them!"

"You hush!" Pearlie said.

The next couple hours were hectic ones as Sally and Mercy figured out where each of the children was going to stay. As usual, the youngsters were excited. Because of their backgrounds, they were used to a lot of change in their lives, and all seemed to be looking forward to spending time on the Sugarloaf.

All except for one little boy, who stood watching intently and never said anything, even when someone spoke to him.

Everyone seemed fine at supper, which was an extremely crowded affair in the Jensens' dining room.

The long table was full, and Smoke and others had brought in tables and chairs from other rooms so that everyone had a place to sit and eat. The meal was controlled bedlam. It had taken a near-miraculous effort for Sally to throw together enough food for the entire group.

Before everyone finished eating, some of the younger children were getting drowsy. A few of them were practically asleep by the time Mercy started to carry them upstairs to put them down in their temporary rooms. Chance Jensen volunteered to help her, of course, so Rinehart had to pitch in, as well.

Caleb's eyelids were drooping, so Rinehart took hold of him under the arms and lifted him. "Are you tired, pal?"

Caleb didn't answer. That wasn't surprising, but the way his head drooped on Rinehart's shoulder and he snuggled against the detective's chest was a little unexpected.

The kid is warming up to me, thought Rinehart.

That was good . . . if he really was Donald Litchfield. And even if he wasn't, somehow it felt pretty good anyway.

After the little ones had been put to bed, the older children were still in the dining room along with all the adults when one of the girls asked Smoke, "Don't you have a Christmas tree, Mr. Jensen?"

"No, honey, we haven't gotten around to harvesting one this year," Smoke replied with a smile.

"But sometimes you have them, don't you? We had one in the orphanage one year."

"Just once?"

"Yes." The girl looked and sounded sad. "Someone donated that one. The orphanage couldn't afford to buy one, and nobody else ever did it again."

Smoke exchanged a glance with Sally, then said, "You know what? I'll bet we could go out tomorrow and cut one down. There are plenty of places on the Sugarloaf where we could find a good tree."

Sally said, "I think that's a wonderful idea. We'll decorate it and make it look like the most festive Christmas tree ever."

"I think that's a wonderful idea," Mercy said. "We can make the trip an outing for the children, if that's all right."

"Don't see why not," Smoke said.

"I'd be glad to come along and help," Chance volunteered.

Rinehart didn't hesitate. "I'll come, too. Sounds like a lot of fun." Actually, tramping around in the snow, wielding an ax and cutting down a tree, then dragging it back to the ranch house and carrying it inside didn't sound like fun at all, but if Caleb and the other little boys he was supposed to be protecting were out there, then he needed to be, too.

And if that slick Chance Jensen was going to be doing his best to impress Mercy, Rinehart wasn't going to let that pass unchallenged, either.

"It's settled, then," Smoke said with a nod. "We'll hitch up the wagons in the morning and go find us a Christmas tree. So all you youngsters better turn in and get yourselves a good night's rest."

That brought the usual complaints from some of the children, which Mercy promptly shushed. She and Sally ushered the ones who were staying in the house upstairs, while Pearlie, Cal, and Rinehart headed for the bunkhouse with the older boys.

His job had gotten him into a lot of odd circumstances, Rinehart mused as he walked through the cold air toward the bunkhouse, but that was maybe the strangest of them all. Living like a cowboy in the middle of nowhere, protecting some kids from a threat that might or might not exist, and trying to sort through his unexpectedly complicated feelings for Mercy Halliday.

It made chasing goons, yeggs, and hooligans through the back alleys of New York seem nice and simple.

"So you're goin' out to cut a Christmas tree in the mornin'," Preacher said from behind Smoke.

Smoke was standing on the porch, bundled in his sheepskin jacket, getting a last breath of fresh air before turning in. He turned his head to look at his oldest friend in the world and nodded. "That's right. You want to come along with us?"

"I reckon not. I've cut down trees to use for firewood, but I ain't never cut one down just to hang glittery gee-gaws from it."

"The kids like it."

"Well, I guess it won't do no harm. But you and the other fellas can handle the chore just fine without me and Eagle-Eye."

"He's going to be a curmudgeon, too?"

"I ain't sure what you mean by that," snapped Preacher, "but I'll bet a hat it ain't nothin' good. Fact of the matter is, we was thinkin' about leavin' tomorrow."

That took Smoke by surprise. "Not before Christmas?"

"We thought we might head on up into the high country, maybe visit some of our old stompin' grounds."

"Not at this time of the year," Smoke protested. "That sounds more like something you'd do in the spring or summer."

"Eagle-Eye says he knows where there's a friendly band o' Crow who still live up in the mountains instead o' goin' in to the agency durin' the winter. There ain't many like that left, Smoke. Just like there ain't many like me and ol' Eagle-Eye."

"You were one of the first mountain men, and you're just about the last, I reckon," Smoke admitted.

"No, not the last," said Preacher. "In your heart, you're the last o' the breed that got started so long ago. I knowed it not long after I first run into you and your pa. Oh, you've settled down some. You got this ranch and the best wife any man could ever want, but inside, the high lonesome is still alive in you. I'm bettin' it always will be."

"Maybe so"—Smoke rested a hand on his old friend's buckskin-clad shoulder—"but I still think it would be best if you and Eagle-Eye stayed here until after Christmas. Sally would be disappointed if you left now."

Preacher scratched his grizzled jaw. "Well, I sure would hate to disappoint that little gal o' yours."

"Besides, if you leave before Christmas Eve, you'll miss out on all the good food at the party. It's only a couple more days."

"You're right about that, too, I reckon." Preacher nodded decisively. "All right, I done made up my mind. We'll wait until after Christmas. But when it's come and gone, me and Eagle-Eye are headin' for the tall and uncut."

"It's a deal." Smoke looked out at the night and added, "Look. It's starting to snow again."

CHAPTER 33

Big Rock

It was a bitter cold, half-frozen, dispirited bunch that rode slowly into town late that night. The nine men were hunched forward in their saddles, gloved hands clasped around the horns to keep them from falling off as they moved along the deserted street.

He was so cold, Laird Kingsley thought that if he toppled off his mount, he would shatter like a chunk of ice when he hit the ground.

It had started snowing an hour earlier, and he had worried that if the drifts got too deep along the railroad tracks they were following, the horses wouldn't be able to get through. He'd briefly considered options. Spending the night out in the open would mean freezing to death, and leaving the tracks to find another way to Big Rock would likely result in becoming lost in the trackless wilderness.

Either way, an icy fate would await them.

Luck had been with them, however. The snow was falling harder all the time, but they had been able to stay with the railroad and make it through. They'd reached the settlement that was their destination. Yellow light spilling through window glass drew the men with its promise of warmth.

"Lord have mercy, I th-think I'll never b-be warm again," Big Steve Corrigan said through chattering teeth. "Saints preserve us, are we really here at last?"

"We are," Kingsley said. Enough light came through the windows of the building in front of which they reined in for him to read the sign on the awning above the boardwalk—BROWN DIRT COWBOY SALOON. "A fire and some whiskey will warm us up soon enough. First, though, somebody has to take care of these horses."

He looked around and spotted what appeared to be a livery barn on the other side of the street in the next block. He pointed at the place and went on. "Paulson, Davis, take them down there to that place and make arrangements for them."

"Hell, Laird, why us?" objected one of the men he had named. "We're as cold and tired as anybody else."

"That's right, you're as cold and tired as the rest of us, but you're also the ones I gave the job to," Kingsley said, his voice hard. "Do you feel like arguing?"

"No, no, that's not what I meant," the man replied hastily. He turned to the other man Kingsley had picked. "Come on. Let's get this done. Sooner we're finished, the sooner we can get inside."

The men all dismounted, and the two charged with taking care of the horses took the reins and led the animals along the street. The other men, with Kingsley in the lead, went into the saloon.

Kingsley didn't know if the Brown Dirt Cowboy

ever closed, but it was doing a good business on that snowy evening. A number of roughly dressed men he took to be cowboys were standing at the bar, and most of the tables were full. Several poker games were going on. Three saloon girls, all wearing skimpy dresses revealing pale flesh covered with goose bumps, moved among the customers delivering drinks and trying to summon up the enthusiasm to flirt a little.

The clothes might be different, but a saloon was a saloon was a saloon. Kingsley felt almost as much at ease as he would have in a similar establishment in Hell's Kitchen or the Bowery.

The bartender was certainly a familiar type, a plug-ugly in a dirty apron. The man's sleeves were rolled up to reveal brawny forearms. He smiled at Kingsley, revealing a missing tooth. "What can I do for you gents?"

"We're frozen," said Kingsley. "We need something to warm us up."

"I got just the tonic for you, mister." The bartender set empty glasses on the bar and reached for a bottle on the back shelf.

Kingsley shook his head. "Not that. The good stuff." He took a ten dollar gold piece from his pocket and slid it across the hardwood.

The bartender's eyes widened and he nodded. "Sure thing, mister." He reached under the bar, brought out a bottle, and poured several drinks.

Corrigan snatched up one of the drinks, downed it like water, and sighed. "Ah, 'tis like the Good Lord has breathed the breath of life back into me."

"Where'd you fellas come from?" the bartender asked curiously. "I don't recall seein' you around Big

Rock before, and no offense, but it don't look like you're from these parts."

Kingsley threw back his drink as well and felt it kindle a very welcome warmth in his belly. "Right now, we're just some cold, weary pilgrims. Is there any place in town to get rooms for the night?" He pushed the empty glass across the bar.

The bartender obligingly splashed more whiskey into it and shook his head. "The hotels are full up, I've heard. The boss, Emmett Brown, rents out some of the rooms upstairs, but they're taken as well."

"By who?"

"Well, I don't know as that's any of your—" the bartender began.

Corrigan reached across the bar and put a hand on the man's shoulder. He didn't seem to squeeze, but the bartender suddenly winced in pain.

"The boss asked ye a question, lad," Corrigan said quietly. "Ye'd be well advised to answer."

"Well, I-I know that those fellas there at that table rented a couple." The bartender nodded toward a table where four men were playing poker.

"See, now, that wasn't so hard, was it?" said Corrigan.

Kingsley went over to the table where the poker players ignored him for a moment before one of them glanced up and asked in a surly voice, "Yeah? Whatta you want, mister?"

"You gentlemen are going to find somewhere else to stay tonight so we can have your rooms," Kingsley said bluntly.

"Is that right? Well, the hell with you, mist—"

Corrigan closed his hand on the back of the cowboy's neck and leaned down. "I know a trick, lad, where I can put me hands on either side of a man's head and twist it right off his shoulders. D' ye want to see?" He put his hands on the man's head, resting them lightly but firmly on either side.

One of the other men at the table said, "Hey, you can't come in here and—"

"Shut up, Al!" said the first man.

The rest of Kingsley's men surrounded the table, not making any threatening moves but definitely intimidating the men sitting there.

"Actually," Kingsley said, "we're going to rent those rooms from you. That's only fair." He took his wallet from an inside pocket of his coat and removed a twenty dollar bill. He dropped the greenback on the table, then looked around the room and went on in a louder voice, "We need two or three more rooms, and we're willing to pay for them."

Corrigan said, "Ah, boss, ye don't have to do that. Let me twist off a few heads. It's been a while."

"No, Steve, we're not looking to cause trouble." Kingsley smiled. "This is a business deal, pure and simple."

Corrigan sighed and nodded. "All right. But the other way woulda been more entertainin'."

Five minutes later, Kingsley and all his men had rooms upstairs in the Brown Dirt Cowboy.

Instead of turning in, though, Kingsley sat at one of the tables with Corrigan and a couple others to warm up more. The Irishman had brought the bottle from the bar, and Kingsley soon had a pleasant glow about him that almost made him forget about how cold he had been earlier.

The saloon had settled down after the few moments of tension. Men were talking at the other tables, and he suddenly sat up straighter as the word *orphans* cut through the whiskey fuzz in his brain. He looked around, figured out which table the voice had come from, and told Corrigan, "Bring those men over here."

Corrigan nodded, stood up, and lumbered over to the other table. A moment later, he prodded the two townsmen up to Kingsley's table like a couple serfs being brought to an audience with their liege lord.

"You men said something about orphans," Kingsley said without preamble. "What about them?"

The two looked nervous. They were probably stable hands, store clerks, something like that.

One of them swallowed and said, "You haven't heard about the orphans from the train, mister?"

"The train that's stuck here because of the blizzard in the mountains, you mean?"

"That's right. There was a passel of orphans from New York on it. You, uh, you fellas are from back East somewhere, aren't you?"

Kingsley ignored the question and asked another of his own. "Where are the orphans now?"

"Smoke took 'em."

"Smoke?" Kingsley repeated, then he remembered what the liveryman had said when he'd bought the horses. "You mean Smoke Jensen?"

"Yes, sir. The folks who brought the orphans from New York decided to adopt 'em out to folks in Big Rock and around here. Until they do, the kids are staying out at the Sugarloaf. Smoke and Mrs. Jensen offered to put 'em up for the time being."

"Very generous of them," said Kingsley. "Where is this Sugarloaf Ranch?"

"West of here, about seven or eight miles."

Kingsley nodded. "All right. Thank you."

"We can, uh, go back to our table?"

Kingsley waved a hand in dismissal.

Corrigan sat down again. "I figured them orphans were gonna be here in town somewhere, not out in the country. This is gonna make it harder to get to 'em."

"Maybe, but on the other hand, there won't be any law around when we do find them." Kingsley remembered something else the old liveryman had said. "This Smoke Jensen is supposed to be quite a gunman."

Corrigan blew out a contemptuous breath. "He wouldn't last ten minutes in the neighborhood we come from, laddie."

"You're probably right," Kingsley said with a smile. "Anyway, it doesn't matter. We still have a job to do. Tomorrow, Steve, we're going to take a ride out to this Sugarloaf and figure out the easiest way for us to kill everyone on it."

CHAPTER 34

Sugarloaf Ranch

Breakfast the next morning was as loud and hectic an affair as supper had been the night before. At least Sally had more warning and time to prepare. She was up well before dawn getting ready, so the long table in the dining room was heaped with food when Mercy, Rinehart, Ace, and Chance brought the children in to eat.

They hadn't forgotten about the discussion of a Christmas tree. The girl who had brought it up said, "Are we still going to cut down a tree today, Mr. Jensen?"

"We sure are," Smoke said. "You little ones eat your breakfast, and then we'll see about getting ready. You'll have to bundle up good, though. It's mighty cold out there." The storm that had blown through during the night had brought even more snow, but he figured the wagons could get through it all right. The draft horses were powerful, and the wagons were sturdily built.

The sky was still overcast, with the potential for more snow later on, but for the moment none was falling.

All the children wanted to go on the outing, so both wagons would be needed. He asked Pearlie and Cal to see to hitching up the teams, then asked the other adults, "Who's coming with us today?"

"I need to go wherever the children go," Mercy said. "With Mr. and Mrs. Gallagher back in town, I'm responsible for them."

Not surprising, considering Mercy's response, Chance immediately said, "I figured Ace and I would come along."

"I wouldn't mind," Rinehart said, which was also what Smoke expected.

"That's fine," he told them. "I'll drive one wagon. Ace, how about you handle the other one?"

Chance began, "I can—"

Smoke held up a hand to stop him. "You and Mr. Rinehart are going to be our outriders." His firm tone left no room for argument.

Preacher said, "I reckon me and Eagle-Eye are gonna spend the day sittin' by the fire."

"These old bones of ours take some warmin' up," Eagle-Eye added.

"That's fine," Smoke said again. He smiled at the orphans, all of whom watched him with eager faces . . . except the solemn little one called Caleb. "I think we're going to have plenty of help."

A short time later, the children donned their coats, left the house, and climbed into the wagons. Sally provided a number of blankets and quilts so they could bundle up even better once they were sitting in the wagon beds.

Ace helped Mercy climb onto the seat of one vehicle.

That was a pretty good compromise, thought Smoke. Ace didn't seem to have any romantic interest in the auburn-haired young woman, so Chance and Rinehart were on equal footing, both looking on with jealous scowls as Ace settled himself beside her and made some low-voiced comment to her that made her smile and laugh.

Smoke put a long crosscut saw and a Winchester on the floorboard of the driver's box, then took the reins and got the big, sturdy horses moving. The wagons rolled out, their wheels cutting ruts in the deep snow as they left the ranch headquarters and headed into the foothills of the neighboring mountains.

It was a good thing he was familiar with every foot of the Sugarloaf. The thick coating of snow would have made it difficult for him to know where to drive otherwise. As it was, he was able to follow a familiar trail into the pine-dotted hills.

As he drove, he cast several glances toward the slopes looming above them. The two nights of heavy snowfall had filled many of the gullies and crevices and piled up thick drifts on the mountainsides. He didn't expect that to cause a problem, but still, it would be a good idea to keep an eye on the situation. More than once, he had seen avalanches come thundering down those slopes, but always from a safe distance.

They needed to find a good tree, cut it down, and get back to the ranch.

* * *

Laird Kingsley and Big Steve Corrigan knelt behind the thick trunk of a fallen tree and watched the wagons crawl forward several hundred yards below them. Kingsley had a small spyglass that he pressed to his eye. Through the lens, he studied the people on the wagons. He didn't recognize any of them, but he was able to make a head count of the children and knew that all twenty of the orphans were there.

Somewhere among them was the little boy they were to kill.

Kingsley lowered the spyglass and said, "Sometimes an opportunity presents itself, Steve, and a smart man knows when to seize it."

"I never claimed to be smart," said Corrigan. "That's why I always leave the thinkin' to you, laddie."

Kingsley turned his head and looked at a clump of large boulders a few yards to their right. Lower on the slope were several huge snowdrifts. If something were to dislodge one of those drifts, like some falling rocks, and started it sliding down the snow-packed gully . . .

A smile drew his lips back, but the expression was a cold, deadly one.

He hadn't expected the scouting expedition to provide him with the means to carry out his job, but like he had told Corrigan, a man had to know when to strike. When they had ridden out from Big Rock, he hadn't planned on doing anything except getting the lay of the land. They had located the ranch headquarters, spied on it from a distance, and then moved up to higher ground to keep an eye on the wagons when the group left the ranch house. They were right in his sights, figuratively speaking.

"Look at those boulders over there, Steve," he said to Corrigan. "Do you think you could push one of them down so it would get the others rolling?"

A smile equally as menacing as Kingsley's appeared on Corrigan's big, brutal face. "Aye, that I could! Ye might have to help me a bit. I don't know, but I think 'tis a splendid idea, lad."

"Let's give it a try, then."

Smoke heard a cracking sound and muttered, "Blast it!" as his wagon lurched sharply. As hard as he had tried to avoid all the obstacles hidden under the snow, the odds had been against him. He just hoped the wagon wasn't damaged too much.

He hauled on the reins and pulled the team to the side. Waving Ace ahead with the other wagon, Smoke called to the brothers and Rinehart, "Got a little trouble here. I'll see how bad it is and then catch up if I can."

"What about the kids in that wagon?" Ace asked as he pulled the second vehicle alongside.

"There's not room for everybody in one wagon, so they'll stay with me."

That brought a chorus of objections from the children in Smoke's wagon.

He waved them down. "You'll still be able to help with the tree later, even if the others find the one we'll be cutting down."

He took the saw from the floorboard and handed

it to Ace,who placed the saw at his feet then slapped
the reins against the backs of the horses and got his
team moving again. The wagon rolled on, heading
up a gentle slope toward a large stand of trees. Just
beyond the trees, the snow-covered mountainside
reared up sharply.

Smoke jumped down from the box and bent over
to look under the wagon. Sure enough, he saw a
crack in the front axle. That was what he had heard.
The damage wasn't too bad, he decided. The axle
was just cracked, not broken. In fact, he thought it
might hold together well enough for him to get the
wagon back to the ranch house. Once there, he could
do some repairs before returning it to Big Rock.

The deep snow made it hard to walk, but Corrigan
went first and broke a good trail with his elephant-
like legs. He and Kingsley used the trees for cover as
they made their way across the slope. It took them
several minutes to reach the boulders, even though
the actual distance they covered wasn't all that far.

Kingsley studied the arrangement of the rocks,
picked out the one he thought was the best for their
purposes, and rested a gloved hand on the boulder.
"This one."

"Outta me way." Corrigan moved into position behind the boulder and crouched down, then leaned
forward and placed his shoulder against the curving
surface of the rock. He shifted his feet around in the
snow, searching for the best place to brace them.

When he was satisfied that he was where he needed
to be, he started to push. A low-pitched grunt came

from his throat as he shoved against the boulder. It didn't budge. He grunted again and pushed harder.

Kingsley looked down the slope and stiffened as he saw that the two wagons had veered apart. One of them was sitting off to the side while the other was still coming on. That was annoying, but it couldn't be helped.

Well, he told himself, *if the avalanche is big enough, it will still crush both vehicles and all those troublesome orphans under tons of snow and rock.*

Mercy pointed to one of the trees they were approaching. "How about that one? It's perfectly shaped."

"It sure is," Chance said from horseback as he rode alongside the wagon on the left side.

"I'd be glad to help cut it down," Rinehart offered from his mount on the right side.

"I don't know," said Ace as he brought the wagon to a stop. "It's not very big. On the other hand, it *is* pretty, and I reckon it'd be a lot easier to get into the house than some of these other trees."

"It's settled, then," Mercy said with a smile.

Chance swung down hurriedly from his saddle and held out a hand to Ace. "Give me that saw."

Rinehart had already dismounted, too. He offered, "I can take it."

"I've got it," Chance snapped.

"Here," Ace said as he handed the saw to his brother. "It needs a man on both ends, so you can both use it."

Chance and Rinehart took hold of the saw and positioned the blade against the tree trunk, kicking some of the snow away first so they could make their cut fairly low to the ground. Ace wrapped the reins around the wagon's brake lever and leaped to the ground. He moved over to the tree and reached between the branches to grasp the trunk higher up and steady it. The saw's teeth made a rasping sound as they bit into the rough bark.

With both Chance and Rinehart putting their best efforts into it in order to impress Mercy, it didn't take them long to saw through the tree. From the back of the wagon, the children called encouragement to them.

"Lend a hand here, will ye, Laird?" The big man sounded slightly breathless from his exertions.

"Of course," Kingsley said as he moved over beside Corrigan. Both of them leaned down and put their shoulders against the boulder. They braced themselves and started to shove.

The rock continued to resist their efforts.

Both men grunted and panted and pushed . . .

And then, with a faint grating sound, the boulder shifted. Quickly, so as not to lose what they had gained, they renewed their efforts and the boulder moved a little more. It was tipping forward.

One more good shove would do it.

In the clear, crisp air, even though he was a couple hundred yards away, Smoke had no trouble hearing the shouts from the excited youngsters. He smiled, glad that they were enjoying themselves.

He glanced idly up the mountainside beyond the trees, and something caught his eye. Rising from behind one of the boulders up there was what looked like puffs of smoke.

No, it wasn't smoke, he realized. It was steam. Somebody was up there breathing hard . . . puffing away like an engine, in fact. Their breath was fogging up in the cold air. What could they be doing to make themselves breathe so hard, he wondered?

The answer that came to him a split second later sent horror stabbing into him.

He jerked his gaze back to the other wagon. Rinehart and the Jensen boys had just lifted the tree they had cut down into the back of the wagon, setting it up in the middle of the excited children.

Smoke cupped his hands around his mouth and bellowed at the top of his lungs, "Ace! Chance! Get the hell out of there!"

This was no time to worry about cursing in front of the orphans. Smoke wanted his young friends to understand how important it was for them to *move*. He saw their heads whip around toward him, and he pointed up the slope.

With a low rumble, the boulder he had noticed a minute earlier began to move, rolling slowly and ponderously toward the other rocks below it.

CHAPTER 35

Ace's eyes widened as he saw the boulder start to move, but that split second of reaction was all he allowed himself then he was leaping onto the wagon as he called to Chance and Rinehart, "Get out of here! *Move!*"

Raised in the West, both Jensen brothers knew about the devastating power of avalanches, and Rinehart realized from the way they were acting that something was terribly wrong. He grabbed his horse and practically vaulted into the saddle like Chance did.

Ace grabbed the reins and hauled the team of horses around. Rinehart brought his mount up next to the wagon seat and leaned over to slide an arm around Mercy Halliday.

"Oh!" she cried. "Ed, what are you doing?"

"Good idea, Rinehart!" Ace said as he slapped the lines against the backs of the team. "Take her out of here!"

Rinehart lifted the startled young woman off the seat and perched her in front of him on the horse. She started to slip, but Chance was there to reach out and steady her until Rinehart got a better grip on her. Romantic rivalry was totally forgotten for the moment, in the face of the threat.

"Ed, no!" Mercy said as Rinehart kicked his horse into a run. She reached a hand back toward the wagon, a futile gesture since the mount was already galloping away. "The children—!"

The orphans were shouting and crying in fear. Most of them didn't understand what was going on, but they could tell by the way the adults were acting that something was very wrong. They were jolted around as the wagon lurched into motion.

Smoke's keen eyes spotted movement where the boulder had been a second earlier. He saw two men up there and knew they had pushed the big rock until it toppled over and started to roll. Snatching the rifle from the floorboard, he brought it smoothly to his shoulder and fired several shots as fast as he could work the Winchester's lever.

That was all he had time for. He threw the rifle back on the floorboard, leaped to the seat, and grabbed the reins. He thought the avalanche that was bound to result from the actions of the two men might not reach the wagon, but with the lives of ten children at stake, he couldn't afford to take that risk. The wagon's damaged axle would just have to hold together for a while.

He pulled the team around, yelled at them, and slashed their rumps with the reins. The horses lunged forward in their harness.

As the wagon bounced roughly over the snow-covered ground, Smoke called to the children, "Hang on, kids!"

The rumble from the slope grew louder. He glanced over his shoulder and saw that several of the boulders were rolling, knocked off balance by collisions with the first one. They struck the huge drift of snow at the head of the gully, and suddenly the rumble was a roar as tons of snow shifted and slid, picking up more and more of the white stuff.

Ace heard that ominous, thunder-like sound and looked back to see the avalanche bearing down on them. He whipped the horses, but they could only go so fast in the deep snow.

The deadly mass of snow and rock raced after the fleeing wagon, which seemed incredibly puny in the face of such onrushing devastation. A cloud of swirling snow had risen from the avalanche and blocked Smoke's view of the mountain. He couldn't see the two men on the slope anymore.

He would deal with them later, he thought grimly. At the moment, his only concern was getting the kids to safety.

Ahead of the wagon with Ace at the reins, Chance slowed his mount and then wheeled it around, waving Rinehart and Mercy on ahead. "Keep going!" he shouted over the growing racket from the avalanche. "Get Miss Halliday to safety!"

Chance looked back at his brother at the reins. It seemed like the leading edge of the avalanche was mere feet behind the wagon, but he knew that wasn't right. He also knew the wagon couldn't outrun the falling snow and rock.

He heeled his horse into a gallop again and pounded back the way he had come. Waving his arm, he signaled for Ace to swing the wagon to the left. Ace understood and the wagon suddenly veered in that direction.

The vehicle bounced crazily from the rough terrain under the snow. It had to hold together. If a wheel came off or an axle broke, everyone on the wagon was doomed.

Suddenly, the wagon hit a big enough bump that the rear wheels left the ground. Several of the children flew in the air above the wagon bed, screaming in terror. All of them came back down inside the vehicle as Ace struggled to control it . . . except one.

One of the little boys tumbled out and landed in the snow. That cushioned his fall and quite possibly saved his life, but he was in even more danger from the avalanche.

Seeing his brother looking around and afraid that Ace would stop the wagon and try to save the little boy, Chance shouted, "I've got him!" and sent his horse lunging toward the youngster, who was floundering back to his feet. The snow-covered landscape flashed past Chance as he got every ounce of speed he could out of his horse.

Not surprisingly, the boy seemed disoriented. He staggered around in circles, fighting the deep snow. Chance was close enough to recognize the boy as the one who never talked, according to what Mercy had told him and Ace. He struggled to recall the lad's name, then as it came to him he shouted, "Caleb! Over here!"

Caleb stopped running aimlessly and turned toward him. To the little boy it must have looked like Chance's horse was about to trample him. But Chance sent the racing mount closely past Caleb as he leaned down from the saddle and hooked an arm around his body. That desperate grab jerked Caleb off his feet and Chance swung the boy up in front of him, wheeled the horse, and galloped after the wagon.

The leading edge of the avalanche was less than fifty yards behind them, barreling toward them like a runaway freight train.

Chance looked around, saw that Rinehart and Mercy were well ahead and had in fact caught up with the wagon Smoke was driving. They were going to escape, Chance was sure of it.

He could have, too, if he had kept going, but he hadn't been able to abandon Caleb to his fate. Nor was he going to leave Ace. The Jensen boys were going to live or die together as they always had.

Chance held Caleb tightly against him and hunched his shoulders as small rocks and chunks of snow began to pelt his back. He drove his heels into the horse's flanks, urging the animal on. The air around them was full of flying snow.

They broke out of it abruptly. The rampaging engine of destruction that was the avalanche swept past behind them, missing them by a matter of feet. When Chance's vision cleared, he saw the wagon ahead of them with Ace at the reins, still pushing the team hard to get well clear.

On the wagon seat, Ace twisted his head to look behind him, and at first his heart sank when he didn't see Chance.

Then horse and riders emerged out of the swirling

cloud of snow and Ace's heart took a leap. Chance galloped on, putting more distance between the avalanche and himself and the little boy he had saved.

Ace kept the wagon moving for another hundred yards before he hauled back on the reins and slowed the team. Chance caught up, drawing alongside the wagon and reining in. They all came to a halt.

Turning around on the seat, Ace asked, "Is everybody all right back there? Anybody hurt?"

"We nearly lost the tree!" one of the girls said.

"We're all right, I think," a boy answered Ace's question. "What about Caleb?"

Chance moved his horse closer to the wagon. "He's probably pretty shaken up."

Ace stood up on the driver's box, reached over, and took Caleb from Chance. He set the little boy over the seat into the wagon bed, looked him over, and didn't see any injuries. Caleb still hadn't said anything, but his eyes were open wider than usual, as if he were still in a state of shock.

Hearing a horse coming, Ace turned to look and saw Rinehart riding toward them with Mercy in front of him. There was still a low rumble in the air as snow and rock shifted, but the main body of the avalanche had reached the bottom of the slope and spent its force. The danger appeared to be over.

Mercy didn't wait until Rinehart reached the wagon. She slipped down from the saddle and ran toward them, clambering awkwardly through the snow. It would have been faster for her to stay mounted, but her obvious anxiety made her too impatient.

"The children!" she gasped as she came up to the wagon. "Are the children all right?"

"They seem to be," Ace assured her. "We barely made it out of the way in time, but close doesn't count."

"I thought I saw one of them fall out of the wagon. . . ."

"That would be Caleb," said Ace. "But he's fine, thanks to my brother."

Chance had dismounted, and Mercy turned to him and threw her arms around him in a grateful embrace. "Thank you for saving him. I . . . I can't thank you enough. Either of you. You saved all the children."

Ed Rinehart frowned. Not only was Mercy hugging Chance, but she was also thanking the Jensen brothers without mentioning his role in getting her clear of the avalanche.

Chance clearly didn't mind the hug, but Mercy's effusive praise seemed to be making him a little uncomfortable. He looked over her shoulder as she embraced him again. "Here comes Smoke and the other kids."

Smoke drove up and brought the other wagon to a halt. His face was set in grim, hard lines, but it relaxed a bit as he asked, "Anybody hurt over here?"

"No, we all came through it all right, seems like," said Ace. "I'd call that pretty much of a miracle. What in the world started that avalanche?"

Smoke's rugged features hardened again. "Not what. *Who.* I spotted a couple fellas up on that slope right after they started the first boulder rolling."

Ace's eyes widened as he said, "You mean—"

"I mean they tried to kill us all," Smoke said. "And when I find them, I intend to ask them why."

CHAPTER 36

The first order of business was to get the kids and Mercy back to the ranch house. Smoke took it easy with the wagon by not putting too much strain on the damaged axle now that the danger had passed. It held together as both groups slowly made their way back to the ranch house.

Knowing that someone had tried to kill them, he was even more watchful than usual, just in case the two men he had spotted tried some sort of ambush. His Winchester was on the seat beside him, in case he needed it in a hurry.

Chance rode with his rifle across his saddle, too, and he and Ace never stopped looking around as they headed toward the Sugarloaf headquarters.

Thankfully, the return trip was uneventful. Sally was watching for them and stepped out onto the porch to greet them as the two wagons rolled up and stopped in front of the house.

She knew Smoke as well as anyone on earth, including Preacher, and realized from the look on his face that something was wrong. Quickly, she went down the steps and moved to the side of the wagon Smoke was driving. "What is it?" she asked as she reached up and put a hand on his knee while he was setting the vehicle's brake.

"We nearly got caught in an avalanche."

"Oh, my God! I thought I heard something earlier. Is everyone all right?"

"We're fine, but the two fellas who started it aren't going to be when I catch up to them."

Sally stared up at him for a second before she found her voice again. "You mean someone tried to kill these . . . these *children?*"

He had thought about that on the way back and couldn't see any reason in the world why somebody would want to kill a bunch of orphans. On the other hand, he had made plenty of enemies over the years, although damn few of them had been left alive. Some of them were bound to have brothers, fathers, and sons who might like to even the score, though. That seemed a more likely explanation of what had happened.

But they could try to figure that out later. "Let's get these youngsters inside." He forced a smile onto his face. "And we've got a tree to set up and decorate, too."

Pearlie and Cal had emerged from the bunkhouse and came up in time to hear that last statement.

Pearlie said, "We'll give you a hand with that, Smoke. We'll be glad to help out, won't we, Cal?"

"Yeah," said the young cowboy. "Maybe in return for some bear sign."

"Bear sign?" a little girl piped up in one of the wagons. "What's that?"

"Oh, honey," said Pearlie with a grin, "you got a world o' good eatin' in front of you, just waitin' for you to discover it."

"We almost got buried by a bunch of snow," another girl said, causing Pearlie and Cal to frown in puzzlement.

"You did?" Cal asked.

"We'll tell you all about it later," Smoke said.

The children had been terrified during their narrow escape, but with the resiliency of youth, they had put that behind them and were concerned primarily with decorating the Christmas tree. Pearlie and Cal carried the pine inside and set it up in a bucket of dirt they had prepared earlier while the others were gone. Once the children were inside and had taken off their coats, Sally gathered them around the tree and started taking suggestions about how they ought to decorate it.

Smoke caught the attention of Preacher and Eagle-Eye, who were sitting by the fire in the big living room as they had planned, and inclined his head to indicate that they should join him outside. Preacher knew Smoke well enough to realize that something had happened.

A short time later, the large group of grim-faced men stood on the front porch, their breath fogging in front of their faces as they discussed the near-tragedy.

"Who in blazes 'd do such a thing and endanger all them younguns?" Preacher demanded angrily.

"Those varmints ought to be strung up and horse-whipped, and that's just for starters!" added Eagle-Eye.

"I figure it had to be some old enemies of mine," said Smoke. "I'm heading back up there to pick up their trail. Preacher, I thought maybe you and Eagle-Eye could come with me."

"Durned right we will! I want a shot at those rapscallions."

"Ace and I are coming, too," Chance declared.

Smoke shook his head. "No, I want you boys to stay here. It's possible that whoever's responsible for this might try to strike here at the ranch, and I want plenty of good men on hand to protect the place and everybody on it." He was thinking mostly of Sally when he said that, but there were Mercy Halliday and the children to consider, too. They would also be in danger if the Sugarloaf came under attack.

"Chance and I were thinking we'd go with you . . ." Ace's voice trailed off as he saw the resolute expression on Smoke's face. Although they hadn't been around him all that much, he and Chance already knew it was a waste of time arguing with him once his mind was made up.

"How about us, Smoke?" asked Pearlie.

"You'll stay here, too."

"You're liable to need help if you track those fellas down. I know you only saw two of 'em, but there's liable to be more where those came from."

"If I need a hand, I'll send for you," Smoke promised. He looked at Preacher and Eagle-Eye. "In the meantime, let's get ready to ride."

* * *

Nobody had asked him what he intended to do, thought Rinehart as the group dispersed. Smoke certainly hadn't asked him to go along.

And why would he? As far as Smoke and everyone else on the Sugarloaf knew, he was just a tenderfoot from back East, a man whose business they didn't even know who had attached himself to the group of orphans. They weren't going to depend on him for anything.

In the back of his mind lurked the suspicion that he was the only one who knew the real reason for everything that had happened. William Litchfield had been afraid that his brother's murderers might go after the missing boy. They might have finally tracked Donald to the orphanage and figured out that he was among the bunch of children. If that was true, the easiest way for the killers to dispose of Donald would be to wipe out *all* the children. That would be a ruthless, heinous crime, but it would serve their ends.

The question was, should he tell Smoke about his theory? The whole situation with the murders back in New York and the missing boy was so complicated it might be too much for him to grasp. On the other hand, he seemed pretty shrewd. And he might be headed into more trouble than he knew, if the men he was going to try to track down were really professional killers from back east.

"Mr. Jensen?" Rinehart said as Smoke started back inside. "If I could talk to you in private for a moment . . . ?"

Smoke swung around to face him, and Rinehart

instantly saw a spark of suspicion in the other man's keen gray eyes.

Quietly, Smoke said, "You sound like a man with something on his mind, Ed."

"I may . . . know something about what happened today."

"In that case, it'd probably be a good idea for you to tell me about it."

A hard undertone in Smoke's voice told Rinehart that he didn't have much choice in the matter. For the next few minutes, the detective laid out the situation as concisely and clearly as he could.

Smoke asked a question now and then and finally nodded. "You could be right. It'd take a pretty sorry hombre to try to kill a bunch of kids like that, but I reckon we already knew that."

"I can come along with you if you'd like, when you try to track them down."

Smoke shook his head. "No, I think you might be of more use here, in case they circle around and try to hit at the ranch. I assume you're armed?"

"I am."

"Good. There are plenty of other guns in the house, too, if you need to use any of them. You should probably get one of the Winchesters, make sure it's loaded, and keep it close by."

"All right. I can do that," said Rinehart.

Smoke nodded. "I'm glad you told me about this, Ed. I had a hunch there was more to you than met the eye. Good to know what it is."

Rinehart had instinctively liked Smoke from the start and realized that he was glad to have the man's approval and respect. "Just be careful. If those men are hired killers from New York—"

"Don't worry, Ed." A faint smile appeared on Smoke's face. "I've run up against plenty of gun-wolves in my time."

Rinehart suddenly had a feeling that was quite an understatement.

On the road to Big Rock

A feeling of deep disgust soured Laird Kingsley's stomach as the horse beneath him plodded on toward the town. Fate had presented him with a perfect opportunity to complete his job, he and Corrigan had seized that opportunity . . . and yet those damn orphans were still alive.

Kingsley and Corrigan hadn't waited around for long once that driver started taking potshots at them. The range was long, but a lucky shot—or an unlucky one, depending on your point of view—was always possible. They had stayed in the area long enough to see the aftermath of the avalanche, though, and Kingsley had been disgusted to realize that all of their intended targets had escaped alive.

From the horse beside him, Corrigan asked, "What're we gonna do now, laddie? Get the rest of the boys and pay a visit to that ranch, like we figured startin' out?"

Kingsley considered for a moment and then shook his head. "No, there are too many men there, too well-armed, and the place is too fortified. It might take an army to get to those blasted kids."

"What're we gonna do, then?" Corrigan asked again.

"We'll have to let them come to us," Kingsley said slowly as he frowned in thought. "You heard the talk in town. There's going to be a big Christmas Eve party in Big Rock tomorrow night. The orphans will be there. That fellow who came out here with them plans to announce that they're looking for new homes. There'll be a big crowd, and surely in all that commotion, we'll have a chance to get close to the Litchfield kid."

"Will ye know him when ye see him?"

"I'll know him," Kingsley said confidently. "And I'll be the last thing *he* ever sees."

Sugarloaf Ranch

Smoke and Preacher had tracked plenty of bad men over the years. Even though Eagle-Eye had lived a settled life for decades, he hadn't lost much of his own skill when it came to reading sign.

Anyway, even somebody from back East like Ed Rinehart would have been able to follow the trail left by the two men who had started the avalanche. Their tracks where the deep snow had been disturbed were obvious.

The trail led to a spot in some trees where a couple horses had been waiting. From there, Smoke and the two old mountain men backtracked and found that the would-be killers had followed them from the ranch headquarters. Anger burned inside Smoke at the knowledge of such evil lurking so close to his home.

After the avalanche, the two men had circled wide around the ranch until they'd come back to the road that ran through the valley. The snow was pounded down from all the travelers on the road and the trail disappeared in a welter of tracks.

"Well, that's the end of it, I reckon," Preacher said as the three men sat on their horses looking at the road. "Ain't no way to track 'em over that. But at least it looks like they ain't headed back to the ranch."

"Smoke, is there any way what happened could've been an accident?" asked Eagle-Eye.

"I don't see how," Smoke replied with a shake of his head. "It took a lot of effort to start that boulder rolling. It wasn't just because somebody leaned against it."

"Then they were sure tryin' to kill you, all right," said Preacher. "And when somebody does somethin' like that and fails . . ."

Smoke nodded grimly. "Chances are they're going to try again."

CHAPTER 37

All the grown-ups on the Sugarloaf maintained an air of watchfulness the rest of that day and on into the evening. Sally, Mercy, and the children decorated the Christmas tree in the living room, festooning its branches with ribbons and strands of colorful berries that Sally strung together. Smoke was still angry about the avalanche when he, Preacher, and Eagle-Eye returned to the ranch headquarters after losing the trail, but his mood improved when he saw the festive tree.

That evening, he felt positively mellow as he sat near the fire and listened to the children sing Christmas carols.

That didn't make him any less alert for trouble, however.

He had talked to Pearlie about setting up shifts of guards from among the crew, so he was confident that someone would be watching over the place all night. If those mysterious strangers tried to cause any more mischief, they would find a hot lead welcome waiting for them.

Nothing else happened, and the night passed quietly.

In the morning, the children were more excited than ever. At last it was Christmas Eve and they would be going into Big Rock for the celebration. Sally, Mercy, and the older girls would spend the morning in the kitchen, getting all the food ready to take into town.

The sky was still partially overcast, but the sun was shining, too, and it appeared there wouldn't be any more snowstorms.

That was good, thought Smoke. They had had enough snow for a while, and as long as new storms held off, the weather wouldn't interfere with the Christmas Eve party in Big Rock.

In fact, everything seemed to be pretty much perfect.

Somehow, that worried Smoke even more than if it hadn't been.

Crockett Ranch

Ray Morley rode up to the ranch east of town and dismounted. To one of Jim Bleeker's men who was lounging on the porch, smoking a quirly, he asked, "Jim inside?"

"Yeah," the outlaw replied. "You want me to unsaddle your hoss and put it away, Ray?"

"That's right. I won't be heading back to town until later." Morley handed over the reins and went into the house to report to Bleeker.

He found the big man sitting at the table with a cup of coffee in front of him. Over at the stove, the late rancher's wife was stirring a pot of stew. Her shoulders drooped in despair, and her head was down. She didn't even look at Morley when he came in.

He didn't see the two girls. They were probably in the bedrooms, furnishing sport for the men. Something to pass the time while they waited to loot and destroy Big Rock.

"Hello, Ray," Bleeker greeted Morley. "Everything still on schedule?"

"Yeah, they're still having that big Christmas Eve party this evening, but it's even more than that now. They've got a bunch of orphans in town. They came in on the train that's stuck there. The folks in charge are hoping they'll find some suckers to adopt the kids tonight."

"Well," Bleeker said with a smile, "that's not going to work out very well for them, is it?" He sat forward in his chair and grew more serious. "This afternoon, we'll all ride into town, one or two at a time the way the boys who are already there did. There's enough of a crowd that they won't be noticed, isn't there?"

"Yeah, there are a lot of people around," Morley agreed. "It shouldn't be any problem getting the whole bunch into position, spread around town."

"What about Carson? Have you seen him?"

"Oh, yeah. I was able to ask around about him, you know, nothing suspicious, but he's in town, all right. I've laid eyes on him several times."

"Happy being a lawman, is he?"

"Seems like it. Folks around town are proud of

their gun-fighting sheriff. He's left his past behind him, Jim."

"He thought he did, anyway." Bleeker's big hands tightened around his coffee cup. "But it's going to catch up to him before the sun rises on Christmas morning."

Big Rock

One of the soiled doves who worked in the Brown Dirt Cowboy Saloon, clad in a stained silk robe, carried a cup of coffee into Laird Kingsley's room. Her hair was disarrayed from the night she had spent tussling with him on the bed. He had taken out some of his anger over what had happened out at Jensen's ranch on the girl, but she hadn't seemed to mind his rough lovemaking.

He was sated and feeling a little guilty about cheating on his wife. Bedding a saloon girl wasn't *really* cheating since it didn't mean anything. Anyway, like his work, it was a part of his life separate from his family.

"Merry Christmas," the girl said as she handed the coffee to him. She tried to summon up a bright smile and was partially successful.

"Not until tomorrow," he said as he sat up and took the coffee from her. "This is just Christmas Eve."

"Yeah, well, but you know what they say . . . 'tis the season."

Kingsley grunted. If things had worked out differently, he would be home with Alice and Harry, spending the holiday with his wife and child. The job for William Litchfield had been too pressing to wait, though.

The girl sat down beside him on the bed and asked, "You want to have another go at it?"

Kingsley shook his head. The idea was vaguely repulsive. "You can go. In fact, knock on Big Steve's door and send him over here."

"You fellas have plans to make?"

"If we did, I certainly wouldn't share them with the likes of you," snapped Kingsley. He saw the quick look of hurt that appeared in the girl's eyes but ignored it. He didn't care about a saloon girl's feelings.

She stood up and flounced out of the room.

A few minutes later, Corrigan came in without knocking. The big Irishman wore trousers with the suspenders pulled up over his long underwear. "Mornin', laddybuck," he greeted Kingsley. "I'll bet ye brooded all night about missin' those brats yesterday."

"Didn't you?"

Corrigan shook his head. "No, like I told ye, I leave the thinkin' to you, and that includes worryin' about what didn't happen that should have. Anyway, ye said we would be makin' another try for the Litchfield boy tonight."

"We have to do more than make a try. He has to die. I want the men spread out through the crowd at that celebration. When I've spotted the boy, I'll signal you, and you pass the order for the others to start raising hell. During all the uproar, I'll get close to the kid and take care of him—quietly."

"Plan to cut his throat, do ye?"

"Whatever I have to do to make sure he's dead."

Sugarloaf Ranch

Mid-afternoon, Sally began supervising the job of loading up everything for the trip to Big Rock. The back of the buggy she usually used was soon filled with the pies and cakes she had been baking over the past few days, along with a couple baskets full of bear sign, Pearlie and Cal's favorite. A basket of fried chicken and a tub of potato salad were also there. Many other people attending the celebration would provide food, as well. There would be enough good things to eat in Big Rock that evening to satisfy a small army.

When it came time for everyone—mostly the or-phans—to board the wagons, Smoke pointed to the first one and told Ace and Chance, "You boys take that one."

"I figured we'd each drive a wagon," Chance objected.

Smoke knew good and well that the young man intended to be at the reins of whichever vehicle Mercy Halliday chose. But Smoke had his own ideas about that and waved Rinehart over. "Ed, can you handle a team of horses?"

"Sure," Rinehart replied. "I've driven buggies and carriages in my time. Never a ranch wagon like this, but I'm not worried about it."

"Good," Smoke said with a nod. "You and Miss Halliday can ride on the second wagon, then."

It was the one the little boy called Caleb had climbed into. If Rinehart's theory about the boy was correct, Caleb was the key to a murder investigation back in New York and the probable target of the men who had tried to wipe out all of them the day before. Since it was Rinehart's job to protect the youngster, Smoke wanted him to stay close to Caleb.

Besides, it was a little amusing to frustrate Chance's romantic notions. Smoke knew the young man wasn't serious about Mercy. Both of the Jensen boys were too fiddle-footed to settle down any time soon. Eventually, though, Rinehart and Mercy would be returning to New York. If Ed was serious about the auburn-haired beauty, he could pursue her there.

When all the children were in the wagons, bundled up again in blankets and quilts because the temperature was still quite cold, Smoke mounted up, as did Preacher, Eagle-Eye, Pearlie, Cal, and the rest of the Sugarloaf crew except for a few unlucky punchers who had been chosen to stay behind and keep an eye on the ranch. The cowboys had chosen lots to see who would have that job. Cal had heaved a sigh of relief when he wasn't among them. Missing out on the party—and the bear sign—would have been almost more than he could stand.

Smoke moved his stallion alongside Sally's buggy. He thought she looked beautiful in a fur hat and a thick coat with a fur collar. As she smiled up at him, he asked, "Are you ready?"

"Of course," she replied. "It's Christmas Eve. I've been looking forward to this for a long time."

Smoke grinned. "All right." He moved out in front of the vehicles and the men on horseback and raised a hand over his head, sweeping it forward in the same sort of signal he would have used to launch a cattle drive. The stallion pranced along in a sprightly manner as he took the lead in the procession bound for Big Rock.

Near Big Rock

At the same time, two men rode toward the town from different directions—one from the north, one from the east. Each sat tall in the saddle and had a grim demeanor.

Each hoped and planned to reach the settlement by evening.

CHAPTER 38

Big Rock

The streets were crowded when the group from the Sugarloaf reached the town. Many of the people waved and called out greetings to Smoke and Sally, who were well-known and well-liked in those parts. She headed the buggy toward the Episcopal Church, where all the food was being collected, while he spotted Monte Carson and Louis Longmont on the boardwalk near Louis's saloon.

He reined his mount over to them. "Merry Christmas, fellas. Or Merry Christmas Eve, anyway."

"Christmas soon enough," said Louis. "Less than twelve hours from now."

Smoke nodded and looked around. "It looks like the town is busting at the seams, Monte."

"Yeah, it sure is," the sheriff agreed. "I'm glad the holiday season's got everybody in a peaceful mood. If anybody was bent on starting trouble, my deputies and I might have our hands full."

"Speaking of that . . ."

Monte's eyes widened as he said, "Uh-oh. I don't like the sound of that. Don't tell me all hell's about to break loose, Smoke. Not today, of all days."

"Well, I hope not. But something happened yesterday I reckon you ought to know about." He dismounted, looped the stallion's reins around the hitch rail, and stepped up onto the boardwalk to explain in a quiet voice about the avalanche that had almost proved fatal . . . not only to him and his friends but also to the group of orphans.

Monte and Louis listened intently as Smoke's account caused solemn expressions to settle onto their faces.

"So you don't know who was the real target, you or those kids," Monte said.

"That's right. Ed Rinehart's convinced those varmints were after one of the kids in particular, but there's no guarantee he's right."

The lawman grunted. "Rinehart could've let me know he's a detective when he got off the train the other day. Fella like that ought to notify the local authorities when he comes into a town."

"I reckon he's so used to operating in secret, it never even occurred to him."

"Like Old Sleuth in the dime novels," commented Louis. He took a cigar from a vest pocket and clamped it unlit between his teeth. "It seems we need to keep our eyes open. Whatever their motivation, those two miscreants might make another attempt on the life of whoever it is they want to kill."

"Yeah," said Monte. "You wouldn't recognize them, Smoke?"

He shook his head. "I never got a good look at

them. They were too far away. Just a couple fellas dressed in dark clothes, that's all I know."

"Could be just about anybody, then."

"Rinehart, Ace, and Chance will be watching the children all day and this evening. I made sure of that, although the boys don't know what's behind it unless Ed chooses to tell them."

"You trust this fella Rinehart?" Monte asked.

"Yeah, I do," Smoke said. "He may be from New York, but he seems like a pretty decent sort."

"We're liable to find out," Monte said gloomily. "Well, this isn't going to be as merry a Christmas as it seemed a few minutes ago."

"We don't know that," Smoke pointed out. "It could be that nothing will happen except folks will have a good time."

"Do you really believe that?" asked Louis.

"I will . . . when I see it."

People began lining up outside the church to file in and sample all the delicious food heaped on long tables that had been carried in and set up for the occasion. Sally and the other women in charge of the meal stood behind the tables and piled all sorts of appealing dishes on the plates of the people who moved past them.

The orphans were so excited about being in town for the celebration, as well as the possibility that some of them might even find new families, that it was difficult keeping up with them. Mercy and the Gallaghers had their hands full, even with the help of Ace, Chance, Cal, and some of the other young punchers from the Sugarloaf.

Caleb sat on a bench just inside the church doors, watching everything that went on, and Ed Rinehart made sure he never got too far from the boy. He knew he was gambling that Caleb really was Donald Litchfield, but every instinct he had developed in his years as a detective told him that was true.

If there was one thing he had learned, it was to follow his hunches.

Smoke trusted his hunches as well, so he'd stayed on the move as the afternoon passed, circulating around the settlement. To all appearances, he was just visiting with friends, smiling, laughing, shaking hands, and slapping backs, but in reality he was eyeing every stranger he saw, especially the ones who looked like they might be from back East.

He paid less attention to those who appeared more at home in the West.

Preacher and Eagle-Eye Callahan had been tasked with the same mission. Smoke had warned them not to be too obvious about what they were doing, but it wasn't easy for the two old mountain men to be subtle. It just wasn't their nature in anything. Preacher tried not to glare at those he found suspicious, though, and Eagle-Eye did likewise.

Louis Longmont and Monte Carson were also part of the effort. That was nothing new for Monte, who was always on the lookout for trouble where the safety of his town was concerned. The people of Big Rock had given him the opportunity to put his less than savory past behind him, and he would always be grateful to them for that. He wasn't sure he could ever repay that favor.

With so many people in town, it was impossible to keep track of all of them.

As dusk settled down over Big Rock and people began drifting from the church toward the center of town where the celebration would take place, Smoke's taut nerves told him that trouble was still quite possible. If anything, the danger was worse—several hundred people were going to be crowded into the street in front of the bandstand that had been set up. The local musicians who played patriotic music every Fourth of July were setting up to entertain the throng with a medley of Christmas music. They had been practicing for more than a month.

He noticed a bunch of kids near the bandstand and recognized Peter Gallagher rounding them up. Gallagher's wife was there, too, along with Mercy and Rinehart. Mercy had explained that Gallagher was going to get up at some time in the evening, introduce the children, and announce that they were looking for homes. Smoke thought it was a good idea overall and was sure the effort would draw some worthwhile responses . . . but it would also draw attention to the youngsters and expose them to more threats.

Spotting Ace and Chance in the crowd, he worked his way over to them. Nodding to the Jensen boys, he raised his voice to be heard over the hubbub. "You fellas keep your eyes open and your guns handy, but don't burn any powder unless you absolutely have to. If guns start going off in a mob of folks like this, it's liable to cause a riot."

"Chance and I were just talking about the same thing," said Ace. "Don't worry, Smoke, we'll be careful."

"I know you will." He moved on and found Preacher and Eagle-Eye in the crowd.

The old-timers looked uncomfortable. They weren't used to being around so many people. There was a good reason men such as them preferred the high lonesome. They were happy with their own company, or that of a few good friends, and only occasionally enjoyed being around crowds.

"I ain't never seen so much hoopla over a holiday," said Preacher.

"It's not just a holiday," Smoke pointed out. "For a lot of folks, Christmas is one of the holiest days of the year, along with Easter."

"Maybe so, but most of these yay-hoos ain't got religion on their minds tonight. This here is just an excuse to have a big ol' party."

Smoke shrugged. "You're probably right. But at some point in the evening, some of them will stop and think about the true reason we celebrate Christmas. That's not a bad thing."

"Reckon not," Preacher admitted grudgingly.

"You haven't seen anybody lurking around who looks like he's about to start trouble, have you?"

"No . . . but if you was fixin' to raise a ruckus, you wouldn't go and shout it from the rooftops, now would you?"

The old mountain man had a point there.

Elsewhere in the crowd, Smoke located Pearlie and Cal. Each was holding one of Sally's bear sign and taking a bite now and then.

Smoke walked over to them and grinned. "How many of those have you boys eaten?"

"I've kinda lost track," Cal said sheepishly. "Enough that I'm starting to feel a mite light-headed, though."

Pearlie snorted disgustedly. "That's the only thing light about you, boy. You keep eatin' the way you have been since you hit town, you'll wake up on Christmas mornin' weighin' three hunnerd pounds!"

"You're a fine one to talk," said Cal. "You've put away a heap of those bear sign yourself, and that was after wolfing down three or four plates of food down at the church!"

"I don't care how much you eat," Smoke told them. "Just don't let it keep you from being alert."

"Don't worry about that," Pearlie assured him. "Our eyes is wide open."

"Speak for yourself," muttered Cal. "I'm thinking I could use a nap right about now."

Smoke laughed and moved on. Despite what Cal had said, he knew he could count on the young puncher.

A few minutes later, he was standing near the edge of the crowd when someone came up beside him and linked an arm with his left arm. He looked over to see Sally smiling up at him.

"Are you through feeding the multitude?" he asked.

She laughed. "It was Jesus who did that, not me. Anyway, there are enough ladies still working down at the church that I won't be missed, and I want to hear the music."

"You're just in time, then," Smoke told her. "I think they're just about to strike up the band."

CHAPTER 39

Jim Bleeker stood in the shadows of an alley, watching Monte Carson on the boardwalk across the street. The sheriff wore a sheepskin jacket against the chill in the air, but his hat was thumbed back on his thinning hair. Bleeker could see his face clearly. It was the first good look he'd had at the man in more than eight years, and he was glad to find that the hatred he felt hadn't subsided in the slightest.

It would have been a damn shame to go all that way, kill all the people he had killed, and make all the plans he'd made, only to discover that he no longer cared enough to go through with his revenge.

Well, that wasn't going to happen, thought Bleeker as a cruel smile tugged at his lips. He wanted to see Monte Carson suffer just as much as he had during those long days and nights behind the walls of the penitentiary.

The lawman had found himself a good home. He had put his hired gun and outlaw past behind him and was a respectable citizen, a defender of law and order. If anything, seeing the way the people of Big Rock smiled at him and shook his hand stoked the fires of Bleeker's loathing.

Bleeker was really going to enjoy making the town suffer—and making Monte Carson watch.

A footstep made Bleeker turn his head.

Ray Morley said quietly, "It's just me, Jim."

"Everybody in position?" Bleeker asked.

"Yeah. There are men all around that crowd gathering in the street. Just about everybody in town is going down there to listen to the music. You want us to open fire on them when the musicians start to play?"

Bleeker considered, then said, "No, not then. They've got a bunch of orphans they're going to parade up there after a while, don't they?"

"That's the talk around town," said Morley. "They're looking for homes for the brats. Around twenty of them, I think."

Bleeker nodded slowly in the shadows. "When the orphans get up there and whoever's in charge of them starts to talk, you, me, and half a dozen other men are going to join them. If we've got them covered, Carson and everybody else in town will have to do what we tell them." The boss outlaw chuckled. "Nobody wants to be responsible for a bunch of orphans getting slaughtered. They've already had enough bad luck in their lives."

"Yeah," Morley agreed. "Just like the bunch out at that ranch."

All the members of the Crockett family were dead when Bleeker and his men rode away from there earlier. Bleeker had wanted to burn the place down, as he had Doolittle's farm outside Huntsville, but he'd decided not to risk it. Somebody was bound to see the column of smoke and investigate. Folks would know there were two-legged predators on the loose.

They would know that before Christmas Eve was over, anyway, but not until Jim Bleeker was good and ready.

"When we throw down on those orphans, the rest of the men need to fan out and cover the crowd. Kill anybody who looks like he's going to put up a fight. I don't expect there'll be many of them. We ought to be able to buffalo them pretty quickly. Then it'll just be a matter of having them throw their guns in a pile, if they don't want the blood of those brats on their hands. Then"—his breath came out of him in a long, satisfied sigh—"we can start stripping Big Rock clean and making Monte Carson suffer the whole time."

The Brown Dirt Cowboy Saloon was practically deserted. Most of the hombres normally soaking up Emmett Brown's liquor and cavorting with the saloon girls were on their best behavior for one night of the year, acting like decent fellows for a change.

Laird Kingsley stood at the bar with Big Steve Corrigan. He had a glass of Brown's best whiskey in his hand. The rest of his men were waiting out on the boardwalk, but Kingsley had lingered for one final drink before setting out to complete the job that had brought him there.

He solemnly regarded the amber liquid in the glass, then tossed back the drink. As he set the empty glass on the bar, he said to Corrigan, "The talk is, they're going to have those orphans up on the bandstand in a little while. I'll be able to take a good look at them then, just to make sure which one is the Litchfield kid. We'll make our move after that."

"Aye," Corrigan said, nodding ponderously. "'Tis a good plan. That way, we'll get to listen to the music as well. 'Twill bring back memories of me childhood, it will."

Kingsley smiled. "Are you getting sentimental, Steve?"

"'Tis an Irishman I am, lad. I was born sentimental!"

"Just don't let it make you hesitate when the time comes."

Corrigan shook his head. "Not a chance in hell of that."

The local musicians in Big Rock weren't the most talented in the world, but what they lacked in skill they tried to make up with enthusiasm. They played sprightly Christmas carols and solemn hymns with the same fervor. The big crowd gathered in the street in front of the bandstand and sang along with many of the tunes. Smoke wasn't much of a singer, but as he stood there with his left arm around Sally's shoulder, even he felt moved to join in.

As the concert continued, the crowd grew. Night had fallen, and the people who had been left at the church drifted down to join the others. Everyone was full of good food and pleasantly warm, despite the December chill in the air.

At the eastern edge of Big Rock, a lone rider walked his horse slowly up to the livery stable. The big double doors were closed, but a light was on inside, visible through the narrow gap between the doors. A crudely lettered sign was tacked to one of the doors. The newcomer moved close enough to read it. GONE TO CRISMUSS PARTY—PUT HOSSES IN CORRAL.

The rider followed those instructions, opening one of the barn doors, leading his mount inside, unsaddling it, and then opening the gate into the attached corral where a number of horses milled around, their breath fogging in the cold air. When he was confident that his horse would be all right for a while, he left the livery stable and started walking slowly and carefully toward the center of town, where there was a big crowd and a lot of light, noise, and music.

As he passed a window, light from inside the building fell across his face for a second. The glow revealed features drawn tight with pain and determination. It was obvious he had gone through a lot to get there—and he wasn't going to let anything stop him from reaching his goal.

The band concluded its concert by playing "Silent Night." Again, the crowd sang along, but quietly, as befitted the beautiful, poignant carol. Sally rested her head on Smoke's shoulder, and he enjoyed the moment of tranquility even as a small voice in his brain warned him to remain alert.

The twenty orphans had climbed onto the back of the bandstand during the song. As the musicians low-

ered their instruments and stepped back, the youngsters moved forward. Peter and Grace Gallagher
were with them, along with Mercy Halliday. Smoke
spotted Ed Rinehart at the rear of the stage, keeping
an eye on them.

Gallagher stepped to the front of the stage, raised
his hands, and called, "If I might have your attention,
please? Your attention?"

The crowd had gotten noisier when the music
concluded, but folks settled down again to listen to
him.

He smiled as he looked around and said in a loud
voice, "I'd like to introduce myself. My name is Peter
Gallagher. I'm from the Children's Aid Society of
New York, and many of you already know why I'm
here."

He didn't mention his wife or Mercy, which didn't
surprise Smoke. Right from the start, he had pegged
Gallagher as the sort who would do as little of the actual work and take as much of the credit as he possibly could.

Gallagher swept a hand toward the children and
continued. "You see here twenty poor orphans from
the slums of the city, lost and abandoned, tossed by
the storms of fate, in desperate need of families who
will take them in and give them loving homes. The
Society has cared for these children, fed them, clothed
them, made sure that they're healthy. They're fine
workers. It is my fervent hope that some of you will
find it in your hearts to welcome them into the
bosom of your families."

Smoke wondered how long the speech was going

to last. He had a feeling the man was just getting wound up, even though Gallagher had already said everything that really needed to be said.

Just about everyone in the crowd was standing still, with heads tipped back as they looked up to the bandstand, watching and listening to Gallagher. Smoke caught movement from the corner of his eye and turned his head. Monte Carson was standing on the boardwalk to the left of the bandstand, watching Gallagher like everybody else.

And coming up behind him with a grim, resolute look on his face was a tall stranger with a gun on his hip.

"Monte."

Big Rock's sheriff heard the voice rasp his name behind him. Something was vaguely familiar about it. He felt like he had heard it before, but maybe not for years.

He had made enough enemies in his life that natural caution made him rest his hand on the butt of his revolver as he turned to see who had spoken to him. Shock went through him as he recognized the man's rugged features. Time had changed them some, and the face had a certain gauntness to it, as if the man had been ill, but Monte knew him, all right. There was no doubt about that.

"Frank Morgan!" said Monte. "By God, it really is you!"

"Yeah, it is," the gunfighter known as The Drifter said as he moved closer to Monte.

"I didn't know if you were still alive."

"It was a pretty close thing," Frank said, "but that doesn't matter now. Monte, there's trouble coming to your town, bad trouble. In fact, I'm surprised it's not already—"

At that moment, someone up on the bandstand screamed.

CHAPTER 40

Smoke saw rapid movement on the four steps leading up to the back of the bandstand and his instincts immediately told him something was wrong. He had his gun out by the time a lean, dark-faced man charged across the platform, looped an arm around Peter Gallagher's neck, and pressed the barrel of a revolver to his head. Gallagher's wife clapped her hands to her cheeks and screamed as she saw her husband threatened.

"Nobody move!" the gunman shouted. Behind him, other men had leaped onto the bandstand and leveled guns at the children, as well as Mercy, Grace, and Ed Rinehart.

Shots blasted at the edge of the crowd. More shouts and screams filled the air.

Sally clutched Smoke's left arm and exclaimed, "Smoke, what—"

He lowered the Colt in his right hand. If a full-scale gun battle broke out in the street, a lot of innocent people would die from the bullets flying around wildly.

A big man dressed in black from head to foot strode to the front of the bandstand and fired a gun into the air. Shocked silence fell over the crowd.

It was broken by an angry exclamation from Sheriff Monte Carson. "Jim Bleeker!"

The man in black swung toward the lawman. His lip curled in a sneer as he said, "That's right, Carson. The man you betrayed all those years ago."

"You're loco!" Monte said. "I never betrayed you. I just rode away. I figured out you were a mad dog and I didn't want to have anything to do with you!"

"You're a damn liar," Bleeker grated as he thrust his gun toward the sheriff. Then he frowned. "Wait a minute. Who the hell's that with you? *Frank Morgan?* You're supposed to be dead!"

"Not hardly," said the tall man standing next to Monte. "That's just the story a friend of mine put out so you'd think you'd gotten rid of me, Bleeker."

An ugly grin stretched across Bleeker's face. "But you didn't get here in time to warn Carson, did you? You're too late, Morgan! It's too late for all of you!"

Smoke had heard of Frank Morgan, but he had never crossed trails with the famous gunfighter. At the moment, he didn't look particularly dangerous. In fact, he looked like he was recovering from a bad illness. Either that, or a bullet wound, which was actually more likely, Smoke realized.

He wasn't sure what was going on, but it was obvious the man called Bleeker had some sort of grudge against Monte Carson that he wanted to settle. The shooting a few moments earlier told Smoke that

Bleeker had men posted all around the crowd to keep the townspeople under control. That threat, along with the men who were menacing the orphans with their guns, insured that nobody would do anything foolish.

It couldn't be allowed to continue. Smoke knew that sooner or later he would have to make a move.

He glanced around, spotted Ace and Chance a few yards away in the crowd, and knew from their tense attitude that the young Jensens were anxious to spring into action, too. Smoke looked the other way, saw Preacher and Eagle-Eye, and could tell that the old mountain men felt the same way. Louis Longmont was on the boardwalk opposite from Monte and Frank Morgan. The gambler was a deadly shot, but for the moment, he was holding himself on a tight rein.

A quick count in his head told Smoke he had eight allies he could count on. He didn't know how many men Bleeker had, but with Preacher, Eagle-Eye, Ace, Chance, Rinehart, Monte, Louis, and Frank Morgan siding him, Smoke would have been willing to take on almost any odds . . . except for the fact that there were a couple hundred innocent people in harm's way.

As those thoughts were flashing through Smoke's brain, Bleeker continued. "Big Rock is *my* town now, Carson, mine to do with whatever I want. And there's not a damn thing you can do to stop me!"

"Your fight is with me, Bleeker," the sheriff responded. "Leave those kids alone. Let everybody get out of the way, and then you and me can settle things between us, just you and me."

Bleeker grinned as he shook his head. "That's not the way it's going to be. I'm going to loot this town and then burn it to the ground, and anybody who tries to stop me gets a bullet! You're gonna watch the whole thing, too. I'm going to destroy everything you care about, you damn traitor, and then—only then— am I going to kill you!"

"I'm telling you again, I never betrayed you. I didn't go to the law about that bank job you were planning in San Antonio, if that's what you think happened. You're wrong, Bleeker. You've gotten so twisted up from hate that you don't know what you're doing."

"Oh, I know, all right. I know good and well what I'm doing." He turned his head and nodded to the man who was holding Peter Gallagher. Smoke realized what was about to happen, but even he wasn't fast enough to prevent it.

Gallagher had just enough time to force a terri- fied squeak past the arm pressed across his throat be- fore his captor pulled the trigger. The gun boomed and blew a bullet right through Gallagher's brain. The other side of his skull exploded.

Bleeker roared with laughter and shouted, "That's just the start! You're all going to die, and it's Monte Carson's fault!"

The sheriff cried out a horrific sound as his hand stabbed toward the gun on his hip.

In the crowd not far from the bandstand, Big Steve Corrigan said quietly to Laird Kingsley, "What're we gonna do *now*, laddie?"

Kingsley had already spotted the dark-haired,

solemn-faced Litchfield boy up on the platform. "We'll let those owlhoots do our work for us, if they will. And if they don't—we'll finish it."

Frank Morgan's hand closed around Monte's wrist before the sheriff could finish his draw. "Not yet," Frank warned him. "Too many folks are gonna get hurt."

"They're going to get hurt anyway," Monte snapped. "Bleeker's crazy!"

On the bandstand, the outlaw boss pointed to the street right in front of the platform and ordered, "Everybody who's armed, pile your guns up right here, and do it now! If you don't, my men will go ahead and open fire."

Despite that threat, no one moved to comply. Western folks, even those who lived in the settlement, didn't cotton to being threatened and pushed around. The whole situation was a powder keg waiting to go off, and Smoke realized bleakly that no matter what he did, he probably couldn't prevent that explosion from happening.

Bleeker's face darkened with rage when no one obeyed his order. He bellowed, "All right! Ray, let's give these fools another example of what it means to defy me!" He flung a hand toward Grace Gallagher.

The man who had killed her husband turned from the bloody corpse crumpled at his feet and stepped toward Grace, who screamed again as the man's gun rose toward her.

Before the weapon could come level, a rifle shot cracked somewhere along the street, and the gunman's head jerked. He stood there for a heartbeat with blood welling from the hole that had appeared suddenly in his forehead, then his knees folded up and he collapsed.

By the time he hit the platform, two more shots had rung out, and a pair of Bleeker's men spun off their feet, drilled cleanly.

The fuse had been lit—and it was a mighty short one.

Christmas Eve or not, hell erupted in Big Rock.

Ed Rinehart had no idea who had shot the three men, but there were still more outlaws on the bandstand menacing Mercy and the children. He shouted, "Mercy, get down!" as he yanked his pistol from his pocket and fired at one of the gunmen.

The bullet struck the man's shoulder and shattered it. He fell, blood spraying from a severed artery, and Rinehart knew he would probably bleed to death in a matter of moments.

All the kids were screaming and crying. Mercy and Grace hovered over them, forcing them down and shielding as many as they could.

Bleeker roared in insane fury and turned his gun toward them, but before he could fire, Monte Carson leaped onto the bandstand and tackled him. Both men toppled off the front of the platform and crashed to the street.

It was chaos. People were pushing and shoving and trying to get out of the line of fire as more guns went off.

Smoke told Sally, "Get as many folks out of here as you can!" He hated to leave her side, but he knew that the rest of Bleeker's men had to be dealt with.

Almost magically, a path seemed to clear as the citizens scrambled out of the way. He found himself striding forward, gun in hand, with Ace and Chance moving in from his right to join him and Preacher and Eagle-Eye angling in from the left. With clear shots at Bleeker's men, flame spouted from the muzzles of their revolvers.

Frank Morgan joined the battle from one flank, Louis Longmont from the other. Their shots were swift and deadly accurate. An outlaw fell every time one of the gunfighters squeezed off a round.

Over all the chaos, the mysterious rifleman continued to pick his targets, drilling several more of Bleeker's men. Smoke spotted a muzzle flash from the roof of the hotel and realized the unknown marksman was up there. Smoke didn't know who he was, but clearly he was on the right side of this fracas.

On the ground in front of the bandstand, Bleeker and Monte battled desperately, hand-to-hand. Bleeker had managed to hang on to his gun, but as he tried to bring the weapon to bear, Monte grabbed his wrist and held it off. At the same time, he closed his right hand around Bleeker's throat.

Bleeker pounded at the lawman with his left fist, but Monte hunched his shoulders, ducked his head, and endured the punishment. He threw all his strength into the dual effort to keep Bleeker from shooting him and to choke the life out of the man.

Bleeker landed a punch solidly, knocking him to the side. As he rolled in the street, Bleeker rolled with him, tearing loose from the grip on his throat. He planted a knee in Monte's belly to pin him to the ground with his greater weight.

Using both hands, the sheriff grabbed the wrist of Bleeker's gun hand and shoved the outlaw's arm up, jabbing the revolver's barrel into Bleeker's throat. His eyes barely had time to widen in alarm before Monte slid his hand along the weapon and got a finger inside the trigger guard, on top of Bleeker's finger. It didn't take much pressure to make the gun go off with Bleeker's own finger still on the trigger.

The gun roared and sent a slug blasting up into Bleeker's hate-filled brain. The exploding gases made his head practically fly apart in grisly pieces. Blood and gray matter showered down on Monte before he could shove the dead man aside. He grimaced as he clambered free of the corpse.

The battle continued in the street, but not for long. Smoke and his allies were just too fast and accurate for their enemies, despite the fact that Bleeker's men were all hardened killers. They fell with Jensen lead in them.

An eerie, echoing silence settled over Big Rock, broken only by the sobs and whimpers of the wounded. The earlier celebration was forgotten in the aftermath of battle.

Ed Rinehart scrambled across the platform to kneel beside Mercy.

She had her body draped across those of several of the orphans, including Caleb. Rinehart didn't see any blood on any of them, but he clutched at Mercy anyway and lifted her. "Are you all right? Please, be all right!"

She turned her head to look at him. Her beautiful green eyes were wide with shock, but he didn't see any pain in them. She gasped, "I-I'm fine, Ed. But the children—"

She broke off as a child's voice shouted, "It's him! The man who killed my mother and father!"

Rinehart and Mercy were startled to realize that it was Caleb who had spoken. They saw him pointing toward the steps at the back of the platform.

A man stood there with a snarl on his face as he pointed a gun at Caleb. His finger tightened on the trigger.

CHAPTER 41

Rinehart's left arm shot out and swept Mercy and Caleb down onto the platform as he lunged in front of them. He felt a hammer blow against his left shoulder as the stranger's gun blasted. The bullet's impact slewed Rinehart halfway around and knocked him to his knees.

Before the would-be killer could fire again, the short-barreled pistol in Rinehart's right hand blasted. The man on the steps jerked back and would have fallen if he hadn't been caught by a huge man coming up behind him.

The second man bellowed, "Laddie!" as he looked down at the wounded man in his arms. Blood welled from the bullet hole in the man's chest as his mouth opened and closed without any sounds coming out.

The big man lowered him to the steps, then roared like a bull and charged Rinehart like one of those maddened, horned beasts.

Rinehart emptied the other rounds in the little

pistol's cylinder into the behemoth's body, but they seemed to have about as much effect as insect bites would have had. The man shrugged off the bullets, swatted Rinehart's empty gun aside, and reached down to grab the front of the detective's coat and shirt. He hauled Rinehart into the air and shook him like a dog shaking a rat.

The shots had drawn Smoke's attention. He looked up at the platform and saw Rinehart being shaken around like a rag doll, holstered his gun, put a hand on the bandstand, and vaulted up onto it.

The monstrous individual who had hold of Rinehart was several inches taller than Smoke and probably outweighed him by seventy or eighty pounds, but he didn't hesitate. He grabbed the man's shoulder with his left hand, hauled him around, and slammed a punch to the slab-like jaw.

Smoke was incredibly strong, even more so than the tremendous breadth of his shoulders would indicate. The blow knocked the big man back a couple steps and made him drop Rinehart.

Smoke saw blood on the detective's left shoulder but didn't have time to notice any more than that because the big man caught his balance and charged him, swinging ham-like fists at the ends of arms as thick as the trunks of young trees. Smoke blocked the first punch, but the second one got through and clipped him on the side of the head. Even though it was only a glancing blow, it packed enough power to spin him halfway around and knock him off balance.

He ducked a sweeping blow that would have taken his head off his shoulders if it had connected and stepped in to hook a fast left and right into his opponent's midsection. It was like punching a wall. Smoke darted back as the big man tried to wrap him up in a bear hug that would have splintered his ribs.

Smoke could have drawn his gun and put a bullet through the man's head, but as far as he could see, the man was unarmed. It occurred to him suddenly that the massive hombre was big enough to have dislodged that boulder from its resting place and started the avalanche. Smoke was almost certain that was what had happened.

Was he one of Bleeker's army of hired killers? Something about that idea didn't seem right. The brute wore a suit and looked more like an Easterner than the Western gun-wolves Bleeker had recruited.

He might be one of the killers from New York that Rinehart had mentioned. As soon as Smoke realized that, the whole thing made sense. He'd figured out two groups of murderers were in Big Rock, ruining the town's Christmas Eve celebration.

The big man charged again. Smoke went low, diving at his knees and cutting his legs out from under him. The man's weight and momentum carried him forward off the edge of the platform. Smoke rolled over, came up smoothly on one knee, and palmed out his Colt. He wasn't going to shoot an unarmed man, but he didn't mind walloping one over the head with a gun butt if he had to.

That wasn't necessary. The big man was lying in the street with his head cocked at an unnatural angle and his eyes turning glassy. He had broken his neck when he landed. The behemoth's own weight had done him in.

Gun still in hand, Smoke rose to his feet and looked around. The battle appeared to be over. A lot of bodies were sprawled in the street, but thankfully, only a few of them appeared to be those of people from Big Rock and the surrounding area. Nearly all of the slain were outlaws from Bleeker's bunch or hard-faced men in dark suits, the rest of the gang that had been after Caleb.

Thinking about the boy made Smoke swing around quickly. He saw Rinehart sitting up with Mercy kneeling beside him, an arm around his shoulders to support him. Caleb stood on Rinehart's other side. From the way Mercy was looking at the detective, Smoke knew that Chance might as well give up if he'd had any thought of courting the young woman. She had given her heart to the detective.

Caleb seemed like he was trying to make up for his lengthy silence. He was babbling away.

Rinehart's face was pale from loss of blood, but his eyes were sharp and alert as he held up a hand to get the boy to slow down. "Wait a minute, Caleb. Wait a minute," he urged. "You're saying that you're Donald Litchfield, right?"

"Yes, that's my name, but I-I didn't want to be Donald anymore. I like being Caleb. Nobody tries to hurt me when I'm Caleb. I'm afraid."

"You don't have to be afraid, Caleb," Mercy told him. "Those men are dead now. They can't hurt you anymore."

"But Uncle William's not."

Rinehart stared at the youngster. "You mean William Litchfield?"

Caleb bobbed his head up and down. His face was solemn as he said, "I heard them talking that night in the house, while I was hiding. That man"—he pointed at the one Rinehart had shot—"told that great big man—" he pointed to where Corrigan lay on the street—"Uncle William would be unhappy if they couldn't find me. He said the job wouldn't be done if they didn't find me."

"Good Lord," Rinehart muttered. He'd seen a lot of sordid things in his career as an investigator, but it looked like what Caleb was saying was almost too much for him to grasp.

Smoke had learned enough about the case to figure out what the little boy meant. It had been Caleb's own uncle who had hired killers to get rid of Caleb—well, Donald Litchfield—and his folks. Hard to believe, sure, but some folks would do anything for money.

"Smoke, are you all right?" Sally asked urgently from the street in front of the bandstand where she had returned after shepherding some of the people at the celebration to safety.

Smoke turned and smiled at her. She was surrounded by Ace and Chance, Preacher and Eagle-Eye, Louis and Monte, and the tall gunfighter Frank Morgan. Even in the midst of the carnage, she was about as safe at that moment as anybody could ever be.

"I'm fine," Smoke told her. "Looks like the rest of you are, too, thank goodness."

He caught another movement from the corner of his eye and turned to see a man walking along the boardwalk toward them, carrying a Winchester with the barrel canted back over his shoulder. Tall, rangy, dressed in dark clothes, he had a thin moustache that curled up slightly at the ends and a rugged face that looked like it had been hacked out of mahogany.

"Luke!" Smoke exclaimed.

"Hello, little brother," Luke Jensen drawled. He frowned slightly as he looked over at Ace and Chance. "You two, again? You make a habit of showing up right around Christmas, just in time to land in trouble?"

"Looks like we could say the same about you, Luke," Ace replied. "I seem to recall you did the same thing last year."

Smoke said, "That was you on the roof of the hotel with the rifle, picking off those varmints, wasn't it?"

"Yeah. I had just gotten to town when the trouble started, so I decided I'd find some high ground and figure out what was going on. It didn't take all that long to determine who needed to be shot and who didn't."

Monte Carson said, "You were on Jim Bleeker's trail, Luke?"

"It didn't start out that way," Luke answered with a shrug. "I was tracking down some other fellas who planned on throwing in with Bleeker. They wound up dead. Bleeker's wanted down in Texas on suspicion of murdering a prison guard and his family. There's a sizable reward for him, I discovered, and I'm sure most of the men with him have bounties on their heads, as well. Trying to find them seemed like it might be worthwhile." The corner of his mouth quirked. "But it seems that you'll get to collect the bounty on Bleeker, Sheriff. You earned it."

"Don't want it," Monte said curtly. "Texas can have it." He glanced around at the settlement. "I got everything I need right here in Big Rock."

Mercy said, "Would you men quit jabbering and go fetch the doctor? Ed's hurt!"

"I'll be fine," Rinehart said. "This is just a scratch."

"Maybe a little more than a scratch," Smoke said with a smile as he finally pouched his iron. "Looks like you lost quite a bit of blood. One of the town's docs is bound to be around here somewhere. Let's get you on your feet."

Smoke got on one side of Rinehart and took most of his weight while Mercy stood close by on the other side and steadied him. They walked down the steps to the boardwalk, moving around the body of the man Rinehart had killed.

With a flicker of movement, someone stepped out of the shadows at the mouth of a nearby alley and lunged toward the detective. Smoke saw light shine on a knife blade. So did Mercy, who threw herself forward to get in the way of the unexpected attacker. She cried out and staggered back as the knife went in and out of her side. She lifted a hand and pressed it to the wound. Blood seeped between her fingers.

The woman with the knife screamed curses as she darted toward Rinehart again. The detective's hand dipped in his pocket and came up clutching a derringer, which popped as he lifted it and fired. The beautiful dark-haired woman stumbled and dropped the knife. It clattered on the boardwalk at her feet.

"Seraphine DuMille!" Rinehart exclaimed.

"I . . . curse you!" the woman gasped as blood trickled down her chin from the corner of her mouth. "I curse you . . . and all your descendants . . ." She collapsed and didn't move again.

"Mercy!" Rinehart cried as the young woman began to sag. He pulled loose from Smoke's grip and caught hold of her, and both of them sank slowly to the boardwalk. Cradling Mercy against him, he tipped her head back and pressed his lips to hers, then said urgently, "Hang on. You're going to be all right."

She held on to Rinehart with one arm, reached out with the other hand, and clasped the hand of Caleb, who stood next to them. "I know," she said in a whisper. "I know."

CHAPTER 42

Sugarloaf Ranch

Snow was falling again on Christmas morning, but unlike the near-blizzards that had raced through the area a few days earlier, it was light and gentle, beautiful in its tranquility.

Standing on the porch, Smoke hoped things were as peaceful in Big Rock, although he knew that for some, Christmas Day was a time of sorrow. Seven citizens had been killed in the fighting, another eighteen injured. It was a miracle that those casualties weren't worse.

Ed Rinehart and Mercy Halliday were among the wounded, but Dr. Colton Spalding had assured Smoke that both of them would recover from their injuries. Mercy's stab wound suffered at the hands of the vengeful woman named Seraphine DuMille was only superficial and looked much worse than it really was. The bullet that struck Rinehart hadn't broken any bones, so while he would be stiff and sore for a while, in time he would be fine.

None of the orphans had been injured, even with all the bloody chaos swirling around them. Sally claimed that was a sign God had been watching over them, and Smoke couldn't disagree with her.

Grace Gallagher would be returning to New York with her husband's body as soon as possible. She had offered to take the children with her, but numerous people had already come forward to inquire about adopting them, so Sally had stepped in and offered to take care of them until all the arrangements could be made. Mercy would soon be in good enough shape to help her.

Frank Morgan was staying in Big Rock with Monte Carson. They were old friends and trail partners and had plenty to catch up on.

There had been a moment, the night before, when Smoke and Frank had traded an intense look, sizing each other up. Some people said Smoke Jensen was the fastest man with a gun in the entire West, while others claimed Frank Morgan was. Both knew that, and it was only natural for them to wonder which of those was true.

Neither man had any real interest in finding out, as they had proven when Smoke stuck out his hand and Frank had grinned and clasped it in friendship. Rivals they might be, but not enemies. Never enemies, when one good man shook the hand of another.

The ranch house was crowded on that Christmas morning, what with twenty orphans on the place, plus Ace and Chance, Preacher and Eagle-Eye, and Luke Jensen. Preacher and Eagle-Eye still planned to go off and visit their Indian friends for the rest of the winter, but Ace and Chance would probably stay around for a while. Chance wanted to make sure Mercy was all right, and Ace had promised to help Sally keep up with the kids.

The two old mountain men were sitting in the living room, spinning yarns for the youngsters gathered around the Christmas tree.

Smoke hoped they wouldn't come up with any stories that were too bloody or outrageous. He was enjoying the snowfall, belly full with a good breakfast and a cup of coffee in his hand when a footstep made him look around.

His older brother stepped out onto the porch, also with a cup of coffee. Luke took a cigar from his pocket and angled it into his mouth but didn't light it. "So. Christmas."

Smoke nodded. "Yep. That it is."

"I don't recall us having any big Christmas celebrations when we were kids, back on the farm in Missouri."

"That's because we didn't. There was always too much work to be done on that hardscrabble place. Pa never really was cut out to be a farmer."

"No, he wasn't," Luke agreed. "I can't say I ever really missed that stretch of rocks and dirt." He paused. "I just missed the people I left on it."

Smoke nodded slowly. "We missed you, too."

"Life works out the way it does," said Luke with a shrug. "Sometimes you can wrestle it around the way you want it for a little while, but such victories are small and rare."

"You're mighty gloomy for a holiday."

"Sorry. I was just thinking about how I would have

liked to spend more Christmases with my family . . . and with Lettie."

Smoke frowned. "Lettie Margrabe? The schoolteacher back home?"

"That's right." Luke chuckled. "You didn't know about Lettie and me? Just before the war started?"

Smoke let out a surprised grunt. "I never heard anything about it until now."

"Well, now you know. Whatever happened to her, anyway? She marry some storekeeper and wind up with a bunch of kids?"

"I don't have any idea," Smoke said. "She left town not long after you went off to the war."

"How about that?" Luke shook his head. "Maybe she was broken-hearted over losing me."

"I doubt that." Smoke added with a grin, "You weren't much of a catch, even back in those days, and you're sure not now, just a broken-down old bounty hunter!"

"That's me," Luke agreed.

Later that day, Ace found his brother in the barn where Chance was tending to their horses. "I heard something funny this morning."

"Oh?" Chance seemed only idly curious. "What's that?"

"I heard Smoke and Luke talking out on the porch after breakfast."

"You mean you were eavesdropping on them."

Ace shook his head. "No, not really. It was just an accident, but I heard Luke mention a woman he used to know before the war, back where they came from in Missouri. A woman named Lettie."

Chance looked baffled. "I expect Luke's known a lot of women in his life. What's special about this one?"

"That name. Is there something about it that's familiar to you?"

"Lettie?" Chance frowned in thought, then shook his head. "Can't say as there is. It's not that common a name, I suppose, but there are bound to be a lot of women called Lettie."

"I think I remember Doc saying it once, when he'd been drinking."

Chance stared at his brother for a moment, then demanded, "What the hell are you getting at, Ace? Luke knew a woman named Lettie, and maybe Doc did, too. I hate to break it to you, but Doc knew a *lot* of women."

"Yeah, I know. It just seems odd to me, that's all."

"You know what, brother?" Chance clapped a hand on Ace's shoulder. "You think too much. Sally's gonna have lunch ready soon, and I know good and well there's some leftover pie, if we can beat that cowboy Cal to it. *That's* what I'm thinking about, and you should be, too."

"Yeah, you're probably right," Ace agreed. "Anyway, the past is . . . the past, isn't it?"

"It sure is," said Chance. "And I'm looking to the future. And pie."

The Jensen boys headed for the ranch house and didn't look back.

EPILOGUE

Colorado, December 1926

"That's a crazy story!" the sour-faced man exclaimed as the older gent who had been spinning the yarn sat back and sipped his coffee. "You couldn't know all that stuff that happened . . . if it really did."

"Oh, it all happened," the old-timer said. "Like I told you, I was there for some of it, and some of it I heard about later, after I became good friends with everyone else who was involved." He shrugged. "A little of it is guesswork, I reckon, but not much."

The red-faced man who was the leader of the trio of strangers leaned forward. "You're one of the guys you've been telling us about, is that it?"

"That's right." The older man extended his hand. "Edward Rinehart. Glad to meet you."

The red-faced man didn't take his hand. "Rinehart was from back East. You look and sound like a cowboy."

"Well, I've been here for forty years," Rinehart

said with a slight shrug. "You pick up some of the habits of the place where you live."

"You never went back to New York?"

Rinehart shook his head. "Not permanently. I went back and saw to it that William Litchfield got what was coming to him for having his brother and sister-in-law murdered. He went to prison. One of the other convicts wound up killing him. His wife . . . well, that's a sad thing. After she lost everything, she took poison and killed herself. Terrible tragedy.

"Something good came out of it, though. My wife and I adopted the little boy. Changed his name legally to Caleb." Rinehart sipped his coffee. "He's a vice-president of the railroad now. There's talk about him running for senator."

"So you married that girl Mercy."

Rinehart nodded solemnly. "Best thing I ever did."

"So you came out of the whole thing smelling like a rose," the red-faced man said. "All you had to do was kill a guy named Laird Kingsley."

Rinehart's voice hardened a little as he said, "He gave me no choice. Anyway, the man was a murderer, a hired killer. He was willing to kill all those innocent children." Rinehart shook his head. "No, sir, I never lost any sleep over shooting him."

"Maybe you should have."

Rinehart's gaze sharpened. "Why? What's he to you, mister?"

"My grandfather," the red-faced man snapped, "and you might say I've gone into the family business." He bolted up out of his seat, and so did the two men who'd come into the diner with him. All of them reached under their coats and brought out heavy automatic pistols.

"Now I'm finally gonna settle the score—"

Before the red-faced man could go on, the older man who had been sitting nearby in one of the booths made his move, striking like a whirlwind. He flew out of the booth, wrapped his left arm around the neck of the closest man, who happened to be the sour-faced gangster, and reached around to pluck the Colt 1911-A1 from his hand.

The gun was a far cry from an old-fashioned revolver, but he handled it like it was an extension of his arm. He thrust it toward the other two killers as he barked, "Get down, Ed!"

Rinehart hit the floor. Behind the counter, Al had already dived out of sight.

The leader of the trio and the other man opened fire, but their slugs thudded into the body of the sour-faced gangster. The gun in the old-timer's hand roared and bucked as the slide moved smoothly back and forth. Those killers from back East knew how to take care of their weapons, anyway.

But they didn't know who they faced, and they died without knowing as bullets ripped through them, picked them up, and threw them backwards to land in crumpled heaps on the floor. The tang of burned powder filled the air in the diner, mixing with the scent of coffee.

The old-timer let go of the sour-faced man, who collapsed like his late companions. The gun battle had taken only a handful of heartbeats. The old man laid the gun on the table and extended a hand to Rinehart. "Let me help you up, Ed."

"Thanks," Rinehart said as he climbed to his feet. "And thanks for taking care of those fellows."

Smoke Jensen grinned. "Shooting a few varmints is the least I can do for an old friend. By the way, Merry Christmas."

Come, All Ye Faithful, for an Exciting Preview

SMOKE JENSEN. MATT JENSEN. FALCON AND
DUFF MACCALLISTER—TOGETHER
FOR THE FIRST TIME!

**They just wanted to get home for Christmas . . . but
fate had other plans.**

The year is 1890. A Texas rancher named Big Jim
Conyers has a deal with the Scottish-born Wyoming
cattleman named Duff MacCallister. Along with
Smoke and Matt Jensen, the party bears down on
Dodge, Kansas, to make a cattle drive back to
Fort Worth. But before they can get out of Dodge,
guns go off and a rich man's son is killed.

Soon the drive turns into a deadly pursuit, then a
staggering series of clashes with bloodthirsty Indians
and trigger-happy rustlers. And the worst is yet to
come—the party rides into a devastating blizzard, a
storm so fierce that their very survival is at stake.

From America's greatest western author, here is an
epic tale of the unforgiving American frontier and
how, amid fierce storms of man and nature, miracles
can still happen.

NATIONAL BESTSELLING AUTHORS
WILLIAM W. JOHNSTONE
with J. A. Johnstone

A LONE STAR CHRISTMAS

*Available December 2016, wherever
Pinnacle Books are sold.*

CHAPTER 1

Marshall, Texas, March 12, 1890

It was cold outside, but in the depot waiting room, a wood-burning, pot-bellied stove roared and popped and glowed red as it pumped out enough heat to make the waiting room comfortable, if one chose the right place to sit. Too close and it was too hot, too far away and it was too cold.

There were about nine people in the waiting room at the moment, though Rebecca knew that only four of them, including herself, were passengers. Two weeks earlier, Benjamin Conyers, better known as Big Ben, had taken his 21-year-old daughter into Fort Worth to catch the train. Now, after a two-week visit with Big Ben's sister in Marshall, Texas, it was time for Rebecca to return home. Her Aunt Mildred had come to the depot with her to see her off on the evening train.

Everyone agreed that Rebecca Conyers was a beautiful young woman. She had delicate facial bones and a full mouth; she was slender, with long, rich, glowing auburn hair, green eyes, and a slim waist. She was sitting on a bench, the wood polished smooth by the many passengers who had sat in this same place over the last several years. Just outside the depot window, she could see the green glowing lamp of the electric railroad signal.

"Rebecca, I have so enjoyed your visit," Mildred said. "You simply must come again sometime soon."

"I would love to," Rebecca replied. "I enjoyed the visit as well."

"I wish Ben would come with you sometime. But I know he is busy."

"Yes," Rebecca said. "Pa always seems to be busy."

"Well, he is an important man," Mildred said. "And important men always seem to be busy." She laughed. "I don't know if he is busy because he is important, or he is important because he is busy. I imagine it is a little of both."

"Yes, I would think so as well," Rebecca said. "Aunt Mildred, did you know my mother?"

"Julia? Of course I knew her, dear. Why would you ask such a thing?"

"I don't mean Julia," Rebecca said. "I mean my real mother. I think her name is Janie."

Mildred was quiet for a long moment. "Heavens, child, why would you ask such a thing now? The only mother you have ever known is Julia."

"I know, and she is my mother in every way," Rebecca said. "But I know too, that she wasn't my birth mother, and I would like to know something more about her."

Mildred sighed. "Well, I guess that is understandable," she said.

"Did you know her? Do you remember her?"

"I do remember her, yes," Rebecca's Aunt Mildred said. "I know that when Ben learned that she was pregnant, he brought her out to the house. You were born right there, on the ranch."

"Pa is my real father though, isn't he? I mean he is the one who got my real mother pregnant."

"Oh yes, there was never any question about that," Mildred replied.

"And yet he never married my mother," Rebecca said.

"Honey, don't blame Ben for that. He planned to marry her, but shortly after you were born Janie ran off."

"Janie was my birth mother?"

"Yes."

"What was her last name?"

"Garner, I believe it was. Yes, her name was Janie Garner. But, like I said, she ran off and left you behind. That's when Ben wrote me and asked me to come take care of you until he could find someone else to do it."

"That's when Mama, that is Julia, the woman I call Mama, came to live with us?"

"She did. You were only two months old when Julia came. She and Ben had known each other before, and everyone was sure they were going to get married. But after the war, Ben seemed—I don't know, restless, I guess you would say. Anyway, it took him a while to settle down, and by that time he had already met your real mother. I'll tell you true, she broke his heart when she left."

"Why did my real mother leave? Did she run away with another man?"

"Nobody knows for sure. All we know is that she left a note saying she wasn't good enough for you," Mildred said. "For heaven's sake, child, why are you asking so many questions about her now? Hasn't Julia been a good mother to you?"

"She has been a wonderful mother to me," Rebecca said. "I couldn't ask for anyone better, and I love her dearly. I've just been a little curious, that's all."

"You know what they say, honey. Curiosity killed the cat," Aunt Mildred said.

Hearing the whistle of the approaching train, they stood up and walked out onto the depot platform. It was six o'clock, and the sun was just going down in the west, spreading the clouds with long, glowing streaks of gold and red. To the east they could see the headlamp of the arriving train. It roared into the station, spewing steam and dropping glowing embers from the firebox. The train was so massive and heavy that it made Rebecca's stomach shake as it passed by, first the engine with its huge driver wheels, then the cars with the long lines of lighted windows on each one disclosing the passengers inside, some looking out in curiosity, others reading in jaded indifference to the Marshall depot which represented but one more stop on their trip.

"What time will you get to Fort Worth?" Aunt Mildred asked.

"The schedule says eleven o'clock tonight."

"Oh, heavens, will Ben have someone there to meet you?"

"No, I'll be staying at a hotel. Papa already has a room booked for me. He'll send someone for me tomorrow."

"Board!" the conductor called, and Rebecca and her aunt shared a long goodbye hug before she hurried to get on the train.

Inside the first car behind the express car, Tom Whitman studied the passengers who would be boarding. He didn't know what town he was in. In fact, he wasn't even sure what state he was in. It wasn't too long ago that they'd left Shreveport. He knew that Shreveport was in Louisiana, and he knew it wasn't too far from Texas, so he wouldn't be surprised if they were in Texas now.

"We are on the threshold of the twentieth century, Tom," a friend had told him a couple of months ago. "Do you have any idea what a marvelous time this is? Think of all those people who went by wagon train to California. Their trip was arduous, dangerous, and months long. Today one can go by train, enjoying the luxury of a railroad car that protects them from rain, snow, beating sun, or bitter cold. They can dine sumptuously on meals served in a dining salon that rivals the world's finest restaurants. They can view the passing scenery while relaxing in an easy chair, and they can pass the nights in a comfortable bed with clean sheets."

At the time of that conversation, Tom had no idea that within a short time he would actually be taking that cross-country trip. Now he was in one more town of an almost countless number of towns he had been in over the last six days and ten states.

This town wasn't that large, and although there

were at least ten people standing out on the platform, there were only four people boarding, as far as he could determine. One of those boarding was a very pretty young, auburn-haired woman, and he watched her share a goodbye hug with an older woman, who Tom took to be her mother.

One of the passengers who had just boarded was putting his coat in the overhead rack, just in front of Tom.

"Excuse me," Tom said to him. "What is the name of this town?"

"Marshall," the passenger answered.

"Louisiana, or Texas?"

"Texas, Mister. The great state of Texas," the man replied with inordinate pride.

"Thank you," Tom said.

"Been traveling long?" the man asked.

"Yes, this is my sixth day."

"Where are you headed?"

"I don't have any particular destination in mind."

"Ha, that's funny. I don't know as I've ever met anyone who was travelin' and didn't even know where they was goin'."

"When I find a place that fits my fancy, I'll stop," Tom said.

"Well, Mister, I'll tell you true, you ain't goin' to find any place better than Texas. And any place in Texas you decide to stop is better than any place else."

"Thank you," Tom said. "I'll keep that in mind."

In the week since he had left Boston, Tom had shared the train with hundreds of others, none of whom had continued their journey with him. He had managed to strike up a conversation with some of them, but in every case, they were only brief acquaintances, then they moved on. He thought of the passage from Longfellow.

> *Ships that pass in the night, and speak each other in*
>   *passing,*
> *Only a signal shown and a distant voice in the dark-*
>   *ness;*
> *So on the ocean of life we pass and speak one another,*
> *Only a look and a voice, then darkness again and a*
>   *silence.*

With a series of jerks as the train took up the slack between the cars, it pulled away from the station, eventually smoothing out and picking up speed. Once the train settled in to its gentle rocking and rhythmic clacking forward progress, Tom leaned his head against the seat back and went to sleep.

Once Rebecca boarded, found her seat, and the train got underway, she reached into her purse to take out the letter. She had picked the letter up at the post office shortly before she left Fort Worth to come visit her Aunt Mildred. The letter, which was addressed to her and not to her father, had come as a complete surprise. Her father knew nothing about it, nor did she show it to her Aunt Mildred. The letter was from her real mother, and it was the first time in Rebecca's life that she had ever heard from her.

Her first instinct had been to tear it up and throw it away, unread. After all, if her mother cared so little about her that she could abandon her when Rebecca was still a baby, why should Rebecca care what she had to say now?

But curiosity got the best of her, so she read the letter. Now, sitting in the train going back home, Rebecca read the letter again.

> *Dear Becca,*
>
> *This letter is going to come as a shock to you, but I am your real mother. I am very sorry that I left you when you were a baby, and I am even more sorry that I have never attempted to contact you. I want you to know, however, that my not contacting you is not because you mean nothing to me. I have kept up with your life as best I can, and I know that you have grown to be a very beautiful and very wonderful young woman.*
>
> *That is exactly what I expected to happen when I left you with your father. I did that, and I have stayed out of your life because I thought that best. Certainly there was no way I could have given you the kind of life your father has been able to provide for you. But it would fulfill a lifetime desire if I could see you just once. If you can find it in your heart to forgive me, and to grant this wish, you will find me in Dodge City, Kansas. I am married to the owner of the Lucky Chance Saloon.*
>
> *Your mother,*
> *Janie Davenport*

Rebecca knew about her mother; she had been told a long time ago that Julia was her stepmother.

But she didn't know anything about her real mother, and on the few times she had asked, she had always been given the same answer.

"Your mother was a troubled soul, and things didn't work out for her. I'm sure that she believed, when she left you, that she was doing the right thing," Big Ben had said.

"Have you ever heard from her again?" Rebecca wanted to know.

"No, I haven't, and I don't expect that I will. To tell you the truth, darlin', I'm not even sure she is still alive."

That had satisfied Rebecca, and she had asked no more questions until, unexpectedly, she had received this letter.

From the moment Rebecca had received the letter, she had been debating with herself as to whether or not she should go to Dodge. And if so, should she ask her father for permission to go? Or should she just go? She was twenty-one years old, certainly old enough to make her own decision.

She just didn't know what that decision should be.

She read the letter one more time, then folded it, put it back in her reticule, and settled in for the three and one-half hour train trip.

Fort Worth, Texas

The train had arrived in the middle of the night, and when Tom Whitman got off, he wondered if he should stay here or get back on the train and keep going. Six and one-half days earlier he had boarded a train in Boston with no particular destination in mind. His only goal at the time was to be somewhere other than Boston.

Now, as he stood alongside the train, he became aware of a disturbance at the other end of the platform. A young woman was being bothered by two men. Looking in her direction, Tom saw that it was the same young woman he had seen board the train back in Marshall.

"Please," she was saying to the two men. "Leave me alone."

"Here now, you pretty little thing, you know you don't mean that," one of the two men said. "Why, you wouldn't be standin' out here all alone in the middle of the night, if you wasn't lookin' for a little fun, would you now? And me 'n Pete here are just the men to show you how to have some fun. Right, Pete?"

"You got that right," Pete said.

"What do you say, honey? Do you want to have a little fun with us?"

"No! Please, go away!" the young woman said.

"I know what it is, Dutch," Pete said. "We ain't offered her no money yet."

"Is that it?" Dutch asked. "You're waitin' for us to offer you some money? How about two dollars? A dollar from me and one from Pete. Of course, that means you are going to have to be nice to both of us."

"I asked you to go away. If you don't, I will scream."

Pete took off his bandana and wadded it into a ball. "It's goin' to be hard for you to scream with this bandana in your mouth," he said.

Tom walked down to the scene of the ruckus. "Excuse me, gentlemen, but I do believe I heard the lady ask you to leave her alone," he said.

Tom was six feet two inches tall, with broad shoulders and narrow hips. Ordinarily his size alone would be intimidating, but the way he was dressed made him appear almost foppish. He was wearing a brown tweed suit, complete with vest, tie, and collar. He was also wearing a bowler hat, and he was obviously unarmed. He could not have advertised himself as more of a stranger to the West if he had a sign hanging around his neck proclaiming the same.

The two men, itinerant cowboys, were wearing denim trousers and stained shirts. Both were wearing Stetson hats, and both had pistols hanging at their sides. When they saw Tom, they laughed.

"Well now, tell me, Dutch, have you ever seen a prettier boy than this *Eastern* dude?" Pete asked. He slurred the word "Eastern."

"Don't believe I have," Dutch replied. Then to Tom he said, "Go away, pretty boy, unless you want to get hurt."

"Let's hurt him anyway," Pete said, smiling. "Let's hurt him real bad for stickin' his nose in where it don't belong."

"Please, sir," the young woman said to Tom. "Go and summon a policeman. I don't want you to get hurt, and I don't think they will do anything if they know a police officer is coming."

"I think it may be too late for that," Tom replied. "These gentlemen seem rather insistent. I'm afraid I'm going to have to take care of this myself."

"Ha!" Pete shouted. "Take care of this!"

Pete swung hard, but Tom reached up and caught his fist in his open hand. That surprised Pete, but it didn't surprise him as much as what happened next. Tom began to squeeze down on Pete's fist, putting vise-like pressure against it, feeling two of Pete's fingers snap under the squeeze.

"Ahhh!" Pete yelled. "Dutch! Get him off me! Get him off me!"

Dutch swung as well, and Tom caught his fist in his left hand. He repeated the procedure of squeezing down on the fist, and within a moment he had both men on their knees, writhing in pain.

"Let go, let go!" Pete screamed in agony.

Tom let go of both of them, and stepped back as the two men regained their feet.

"Please go away now," Tom said with no more tension in his voice than if he were asking for a cup of coffee.

"You son of a . . ." Pete swore as he started to draw his pistol. But because two of his fingers were broken, he was unable to get a grip on his pistol and it fell from his hand. The young woman grabbed it quickly, then pointed it at both of them.

"This gentleman may be an Eastern dude, but I am not," she said. "I'm a Western girl and I can shoot. I would like nothing better than to put a bullet into both of you, and if the two of you don't start running, right now, I will do just that."

"No, no, don't shoot! Don't shoot!" Pete cried out. "We're goin'! We're goin'!"

The two men ran, and the young woman laughed. To Tom, her laughter sounded like wind chimes. She turned to him with a broad smile spread across her face.

"I want to thank you, sir," she said. She thrust her hand toward him, but when he shied away she looked down and saw that she was still holding the pistol. With another laugh, she tossed the gun away, then again stuck out her hand.

"I'm Rebecca Conyers," she said.

"I'm Tom . . . ," Tom hesitated for a moment before he said, "Whitman."

"You aren't from here, are you, Mr. Whitman?"

Tom chuckled. "How can you tell?"

Rebecca laughed as well.

"What are you doing in Fort Worth?"

"This is where the train stopped," Tom replied.

Rebecca laughed again. "That's reason enough, I suppose. Are you looking for work?"

"Well, yes, I guess I am."

"Meet me in the lobby of the Clark Hotel tomorrow morning," she said. "Someone will be coming to fetch me from my father's ranch. He is always looking for good men. I'm sure he would hire you if you are interested."

"Hire me to do what?"

"Why, to cowboy, of course."

"Oh. Do you think it would matter if I told him that I have never been a cowboy?"

Rebecca smiled. "Telling him you have never been a cowboy would be like telling him that you have blond hair and blue eyes."

"Oh, yes. I see what you mean," he said.

"It's easy to learn to be a cowboy. Once he hears

what you did for me tonight, you won't have any trouble getting on. That is, if you want to."

"Yes," Tom said. "I believe I would want to."

As Rebecca lay in bed in her room at the Clark Hotel half an hour later, she wondered what had possessed her to offer a job to Tom Whitman. She had no authority to offer him a job; her father did the hiring and the firing, and he was very particular about it.

On the other hand, before she left to go to Marshall last week, she heard him tell Clay Ramsey that he might hire someone to replace Tony Peters, a young cowboy who had left for Nevada to try his hand at finding gold or silver. Rebecca had a sudden thought. What if he has already hired someone to replace Peters?

No, she was sure he had not. Her father tended to be much more methodical than to hire someone that quickly. But that same tendency of his to be methodical might also work against her, for he would not be that anxious to hire someone he knew nothing about.

Well, Rebecca would just have to talk him into it, that's all. And surely when her father heard what Tom Whitman had done for her, he would be more than willing.

Rebecca wondered why she was so intent on getting Mr. Whitman hired. Was it because he had been her knight in shining armor, just when she needed such a hero? Or was it because with his muscular build, his blond hair and blue eyes, that he might be one of the most handsome men she had ever seen? In addition to that, though, there was something else about him, something that she sensed more than she saw. He had a sense of poise and self-assuredness that she found most intriguing.

Because it had been unseasonably warm, and because Tom liked to sleep with fresh air, he had raised the window when he went to bed last night. He had taken a room in the same hotel as Rebecca because she had suggested the hotel to him. He was awakened this morning by a combination of things, the sun streaming in through his open window, and the sounds of commerce coming from the street below.

He could hear the sound of the clash of eras, the whir of an electric streetcar, along with the rattle and clatter of a freight wagon. From somewhere he could hear the buzz and squeal of a power saw, and the ring of steel on steel as a blacksmith worked his trade. Newspaper boys were out on the street, hawking their product.

"Paper, get the paper here! Wyoming to be admitted as state! Get your paper here!"

Tom got out of bed, shaved, then got dressed. Catching a glimpse of himself in the mirror, he frowned. He was wearing a three-piece suit, adequate dress if he wanted to apply for a job with a bank. But he was going to apply for a job as a cowboy, and this would never do.

Stepping over to the window, he looked up and down Houston Street and saw, on the opposite side, the Fort Worth Mercantile Store. Leaving his suitcase in his room, he hurried downstairs and then across the street. A tall, thin man with a neatly trimmed moustache and garters around his sleeves stepped up to him.

"Yes, sir, may I help you?"

"I intend to apply for employment at a neighboring ranch," Tom said. "And I will need clothes that are suitable for the position."

"When you say that you are going to apply for employment, do you mean as an accountant, or business manager?" the clerk asked.

"No. As a cowboy."

The expression on the clerk's face registered his surprise. "I beg your pardon, sir. Did you say as a cowboy?"

"Yes," Tom said. "Why, is there a problem?"

"No, sir," the clerk said quickly. "No problem. It is just that, well, sir, you will forgive me, but you don't look like a cowboy."

"Yeah," Tom said. "That's why I'm here. I want you to make me look like a cowboy."

"I can sell you the appropriate attire, sir," the clerk said. "But, in truth, you still won't look like a cowboy."

"Try," Tom said.

"Yes, sir."

It took Tom no more than fifteen minutes to buy three outfits, to include boots and a hat. Paying for his purchases, he returned to the hotel, packed his suit and the two extra jeans and shirts into his suitcase, then went downstairs, checked out, and took a seat in the lobby to wait for the young woman he had met last night.

As he waited for her, he recalled the conversation he had had with his father, just before he left.

"You are making a big mistake by running away," his father had told him. *"You will not be able to escape your own devils."*

"I can try," Tom said.

"Nobody is holding it against you, Tom. You did what you thought was right."

"I did what I thought was right? I can't even justify what I did to myself by saying that I did what I thought was right. My wife and my child are dead, and I killed them."

"It isn't as if you murdered them."

"It isn't? How is it different? Martha and the child are still dead."

"So you are going to run away. Is that your answer?"

"Yes, that is my answer. I need some time to sort things out. Please try to understand that."

His father changed tactics, from challenging to being persuasive. *"Tom, all I am asking is that you think this through. You have more potential than any student I ever taught, and I'm not saying that just because you are my son. I am saying it because it is true. Do you have any idea of the good that someone like you—a person with your skills, your talent, your education, can do?"*

"I've seen the evil I can do when I confuse skill, talent, and education with Godlike attributes."

Tom's father sighed in resignation. *"What time does your train leave?"*

"At nine o'clock tonight."

Tom's father walked over to the bar and poured a glass of Scotch. He held it out toward Tom and, catching a beam of light from the electric chandelier, the amber fluid emitted a

burst of gold as if the glass had captured the sun itself.
"Then at least have this last, parting drink with me."

Tom waited until his father had poured his own glass,
then the two men drank to each other.

"Will you write to let me know where you are and how
you are doing?"

"Not for a while," Tom said. "I just need to be away from
everything that could remind me of what happened. And
that means even my family."

Surprisingly, Tom's father smiled. "In a way, I not only
don't blame you, I envy you. I almost ran off myself, once. I
was going to sail the seven seas. But my father got wind of
it, and talked me out of it. I guess I wasn't as strong as you
are."

"Nonsense, you are as strong," Tom said. "You just
never had the same devils chasing you that I do."

Tom glanced over at the big clock. It showed fifteen minutes of nine. Shouldn't she be here by now?
Had she changed her mind and already checked
out? He walked over to the desk.

"Yes, sir, Mr. Whitman, may I help you?" the hotel
desk clerk asked.

"Rebecca Conyers," Tom said. "Has she checked
out yet?"

The clerk checked his book. "No, sir. She is still in
the hotel. Would you like me to summon her?"

"No, that won't be necessary," Tom said. "I'll just
wait here in the lobby for her."

"Very good, sir."

Huh, Tom thought. And here it was my belief that
Westerners went to bed and rose with the sun.

As soon he thought that, though, he realized that

she had gone to bed quite late, having arrived on the train in the middle of the night. At least his initial fear that she had left without meeting him was alleviated.

When Rebecca awakened that morning she was already having second thoughts about what she had done. Had she actually told a perfect stranger that she could talk her father into hiring him? And, even if she could, should she? She had arisen much later than she normally did, and now, as she dressed, she found herself hoping that he had grown tired of waiting for her and left, without accepting her offer.

However, when she went downstairs she saw him sitting in a chair in the lobby. His suitcase was on the floor beside him, but he wasn't wearing the suit he had been wearing the night before. Instead, he was wearing denims and a blue cotton shirt. If anything, she found him even more attractive, for the denims and cotton shirt took some of the polish off and gave him a more rugged appearance.

Although Tom had gotten an idea last night that the young woman was pretty, it had been too dark to get a really good look at her. In the full light of morning though, he saw her for what she was: tall and willowy, with long, auburn hair and green eyes shaded by long, dark eyelashes. She was wearing a dress that showed off her gentle curves to perfection.

"Mr. Whitman," she said. "How wonderful it is to see you this morning. I see you have decided to take me up on my offer."

"Yes, I have. You were serious about it, weren't

you?" Tom asked. "I mean, you weren't just making small talk?"

Rebecca paused for a moment before responding. If she wanted to back out of her offer, now was the time to do it.

"I was very serious," she heard herself saying, as if purposely speaking before she could change her mind.

"Do we have time? If so, I would like to take you to breakfast," Tom said.

Rebecca glanced over at the clock. "Yes, I think so," she said. "And I would be glad to have breakfast with you. But you must let me pay for my own."

"Only if it makes you feel more comfortable," Tom said.

"Let's sit by the window," Rebecca suggested when they stepped into the hotel restaurant. "That way we will be able to see when Mo comes for me."

"Mo?"

"He is one of my father's cowboys," Rebecca said. "He is quite young."

Rebecca had a poached egg, toast, and coffee for breakfast. Tom had two waffles, four fried eggs, a rather substantial slab of ham, and more biscuits than Rebecca could count.

"My, you must have been hungry," Rebecca said after Tom pushed away a clean plate. "When is the last time you ate?"

"Not since supper last night," Tom said, as if that explained his prodigious appetite. "Oh, I hope I haven't embarrassed you."

"Not at all," Rebecca said. "Tell me about yourself, Mr. Whitman. Where are you from? What were you doing before you decided to come West?"

"Not much to tell. I'm from Boston," Tom said. "I'm more interested in you telling me about the ranch."

"Oh, there's Mo," Rebecca said. "I won't have to tell you about the ranch, we'll be there in less than an hour."

Tom picked up both his suitcase and Rebecca's, then followed her out to the buckboard.

"Hello, Mo," Rebecca greeted.

Mo was a slender five feet nine, with brown eyes and dark hair which he wore long and straight.

"Hello, Miss Rebecca," Mo said with a broad smile. "It's good to see you back home again. Ever'one at the ranch missed you. Did you have a good visit?"

"Oh, I did indeed," Rebecca answered.

Seeing Tom standing there with the two suitcases, Mo indicated the back of the buckboard. "You can just put them there," he said. Then to Rebecca. "Uh, Miss Rebecca you got a coin? I come into town with no money at all."

"A coin?"

Mo nodded toward Tom. "Yes ma'am, a nickel or a dime or somethin' on account of him carrying your luggage and all."

"Oh, we don't need to tip him, Mo. His name is Tom, and he's with me. He'll be comin' out to the ranch with us."

"He's with you? Good Lord, Miss Rebecca, you didn't go to Marshall and get yourself married up or somethin', did you?" Mo asked.

Rebecca laughed out loud. "No, it's nothing like that," she said.

"Sorry I didn't bring the trap," Mo said to Tom. "This here buckboard only has one seat. That means you'll have to ride in the back."

"That's not a problem," Tom said. "I'll be fine."

"I hope so. It's not all that comfortable back there and we're half an hour from the ranch."

Tom set the luggage down in the back of the buckboard, then put his hand on the side and vaulted over.

"Damn," Mo said. "I haven't ever seen anybody do that. You must be a pretty strong fella."

"You don't know the half of it," Rebecca said.

CHAPTER 2

Live Oaks Ranch

Live Oaks Ranch lay just north of Fort Worth. The 120,000 acres of gently rolling grassland and scores of year-round streams and creeks made it ideal for cattle ranching. There were two dozen cowboys who were part-time employees, and another two dozen who were full-time employees. The part-time and full-time employees who weren't married lived in a couple of long, low, bunkhouses, white with red roofs. In addition, there were at least ten permanent employees who were married, and they lived in small houses, all of them painted green, with red roofs. These were adjacent to the bunkhouses. There was also a cookhouse that was large enough to feed all the single men, a barn, a machine shed, a granary, and a large stable. The most dominating feature of the ranch was what the cowboys called "The Big House." The Big House was a stucco-sided example of Spanish Colonial Revival, with an arcaded portico on the southeast corner, stained-glass windows, and an elaborate arched entryway.

Inside the parlor of the Big House, the owner of Live Oaks, Rebecca's father, Benjamin "Big Ben" Conyers, was standing by the fireplace. Big Ben was aptly named, for he was six feet seven inches tall and weighed 330 pounds. Rebecca had just introduced Tom to him, explaining how he had come to her aid last night when she had been accosted by two cowboys.

"I thank you very much for that, Mr. Whitman," Big Ben said, shaking Tom's hand. "There are many who would have just turned away."

"I'm glad I happened to be there at that time," Tom replied.

"Mr. Whitman is looking for a job, Papa," Rebecca said. "I know that Tony Peters left a couple of weeks ago, and when Mo picked me up this morning, he told me that you hadn't replaced him."

"I don't know, honey. Tony was an experienced cowboy," Big Ben said.

"Nobody is experienced when they first start," Rebecca said, and Big Ben laughed.

"I can't deny that," he said. "Where are you from, Mr. Whitman?"

"I'm from Boston, sir."

"Boston, is it? Can you ride a horse?"

For several years Tom had belonged to a fox-hunting club. And unlike the quarter horses, bred for speed in short stretches that were commonly seen out West, fox-hunting thoroughbreds were often crossed with heavier breeds for endurance and solidity. They were taller and more muscular, and were trained to run long distances, since most hunts lasted for an entire day. They were also bred to jump a variety of fences and ditches. Tom was, in fact, a champion when it came to "riding to the hounds."

But he also knew that the sport had mixed reactions, from those who felt sorry for the fox, to those who thought it was a foolish indulgence, to those who did not understand the skill and stamina such an endeavor required.

"Yes, sir, I can ride a horse," he said.

"You don't mind if I give you a little test just to see how well you can ride, do you?" Big Ben asked.

"Papa, that's not fair," Rebecca said. "You know that our horses aren't like the ones he is used to riding. At least give him a few days to get used to it."

"I don't have a few days, Rebecca. I have two hundred square miles of ranch to run, and a herd of cattle to manage. I need someone who can go to work immediately. Now, maybe you're right, everyone has to get experience somewhere, so I'm willing to give him time to learn his way around the ranch. But if he can't even ride a horse, I mean a Western horse, then it's going to take more time than I can spare."

"I'm sorry, Mr. Whitman," Rebecca said. "If you don't want to take Papa's test, you don't have to. We'll all understand."

"I'd like to take the test," Tom said.

"Good for you," Big Ben said. "Come on outside, let me see what you can do."

A tall, gangly young man with ash blond hair and a spray of freckles came up to them then.

"Hello, Sis. I heard you were back."

"Did you stay out of trouble while I was gone?" Rebecca asked. Then she introduced the boy. "Mr. Whitman, this is my brother, Dalton."

"Are you going to work for Pa?" Dalton asked.

"I hope to."

"Then I won't be calling you Mr. Whitman. What's your first name?"

"Dalton!" Rebecca said.

"I don't mean nothin' by it," Dalton said. "I'm just friends with all the cowboys, that's all."

"My name is Tom. And I would be happy to be your friend."

"Yes, well, don't the two of you get to be best friends too fast," Big Ben said. "First I have to know if you can ride well enough to be a cowboy. Clay!" Big Ben called.

A man stepped out of the machine shed. "Yes, sir, Mr. Conyers?"

"Get over here, Clay, I've someone I want you to meet." Then to Tom, Big Ben added, "Clay is the ranch foreman. And I'll leave the final word as to whether or not I hire you up to him."

"Good enough," Tom said.

Clay was Clay Ramsey, who Big Ben introduced as the ranch foreman. Clay was thirty-three years old, with brown hair, a well-trimmed moustache, and blue eyes. About five feet ten, he was wiry and, according to one of the cowboys who worked for him, as tough as a piece of rawhide.

"Saddle Thunder for him," Big Ben said, after he explained what he wanted to do.

"Papa, no!" Rebecca protested vehemently.

"Honey, I'm not just being a horse's rear end. If he can ride Thunder, he can ride any horse on the ranch. There wouldn't be any question about my hiring him."

"I can ride a horse, Mr. Conyers," Tom said. "But I confess that I have never tried to ride a bucking horse. If that is what is required, then I thank you for your time, and I'll be going on."

"He's not a bucking horse," Clay said. "But he is a very strong horse who loves to run and jump. If you ride him, you can't be timid about it; you have to let him know, right away, that you are in control."

"Thank you, Mr. Ramsey. In that case, I will ride him."

"Ha!" Dusty McNally, one of the other cowboys said. "I like it that you said you *will* ride him, rather than you will *try* to ride him. That's the right attitude to have."

Thunder was a big, muscular, black horse who stood eighteen hands at the withers. Although he allowed himself to be saddled, he kept moving his head and lifting first one hoof and then another. He looked like a ball of potential energy.

"Here you are, Mr. Whitman," Clay said, handing the reins to Tom.

"Thank you," Tom said, mounting. He pointed toward an open area on the other side of a fence. "Would it be all right to ride in that field there?"

"Sure, there's nothing there but rangeland," Clay said. "The gate is down there," he pointed.

"Thank you, I won't need a gate," Tom said. He slapped his legs against the side of the horse and it started forward at a gallop. As he approached the fence, he lifted himself slightly from the saddle and leaned forward.

"Come on, Thunder," he said encouragingly. "Let's go see if we can find us a fox."

Thunder galloped toward the fence, then sailed over it as gracefully as a leaping deer. Coming down on the other side Tom saw a ditch about twenty yards beyond the fence, and Thunder took that as well. Horse and rider went through their paces, jumping, making sudden turns, running at a full gallop, then stopping on a dime. After a few minutes he brought Thunder back, returning the same way he left, over the ditch, then over the fence. He slowed him down to a trot once he was back inside the compound, and the horse was at a walk by the time he rode up to dismount in front of a shocked Big Ben, Clay, and Dusty. Rebecca was smiling broadly.

Tom patted Thunder on his neck, then dismounted and handed the reins back to Clay. "He is a very fine horse," Tom said. "Whoever rides him is quite lucky."

"He's yours to ride any time you want him," Big Ben said. "That is, provided you are willing to come work for me."

"I would be very proud to work for you, Mr. Conyers."

"Come with me, Tom, is it?" Clay invited. "I'll get you set up in the bunkhouse and introduce you to the others."

"Tom?" Rebecca called out to him.

Tom looked back toward her.

"I'm glad you are here."

"Thank you, Miss Conyers. I'm glad to be here."

* * *

Tom ate his first supper in the cookhouse that evening. Mo introduced him to all the others.

"Where is Mr. Ramsey?" Tom asked. "Does he eat somewhere else?"

"Mr. Ramsey?" Mo asked. Then he smiled. "Oh, you mean Clay. Clay is the foreman of the ranch, but there don't any of us call him Mr. Ramsey. We just call him Clay 'cause that's what he wants us to call him."

"Clay is married," one of the other cowboys said. "He lives in that first cabin you see over there, the only one with a front porch."

"He married a Mexican girl," another said.

"Don't talk about her like that," Mo said. "Maria is as American as you are. Emanuel Bustamante fought with Sam Houston at San Jacinto."

"I didn't mean nothin' by it," the cowboy said. "I think Senor Bustamante is as fine a man as I've ever met, and Mrs. Ramsey is a very good woman. I was just sayin' that she is Mexican is all."

"I assume that none of you are married," Tom said. "Otherwise you wouldn't be eating here in the dining hall."

"Ha! The dining hall. That's sure a fancy name for the cookhouse."

"I don't mean any disrespect for Clay," Mo said. "But it don't make a whole lot of sense for a cowboy to be married. First of all, there don't none of us make enough money to support a family. And second, when we make the long cattle drives, we're gone for near three months at a time."

"And Dodge City is too fun of a town to be in if

you are married, if you get my meanin'," one of the other cowboys said, and the others shared a ribald laugh.

A couple of cowboys decided to razz the tenderfoot that first night. Tom had been given a chest for his belongings, and while Tom and the rest of the cowboys were having supper, Dalton and one of the cowboys slipped back into the bunkhouse and nailed the lid shut on his chest.

When Tom and the others returned, Tom tried to open the lid to his footlocker, but he was unable to get it open.

"What's the matter there, Tom? Can't get your chest open?" Dalton asked.

By now Dalton had told the others what he did, and all gathered around to see how Tom was going to react. Would he get angry, and start cursing everyone? Or would he be meek about it?

Tom looked more closely at the lid then, and saw that it had been nailed shut by six nails, two in front and two on either side.

"That's odd," he said. "It seems to have been nailed shut."

The others laughed out loud.

"Nailed shut, is it? Well, I wonder who did that?" Dalton asked.

"Oh, I expect it was a mistake of some sort," Tom said. "I don't really think that anyone would nail the lid shut on my chest as a matter of intent."

"Whoo, do you think that?" Dalton asked, and again, everyone laughed at the joke they were playing on the tenderfoot.

"All right, fellas, you've had your fun," Mo said.

"Wait a minute, Tom, I'll get a claw hammer and pull the nails for you so you can get the lid open."

"Thank you, Mo," Tom said. "I don't need the claw hammer to get the lid open."

"What are you talking about? Of course you do. How else are you going to open the lid if you don't pull the nails out first?"

"Oh, it won't be difficult. I'll just open it like this," Tom said. Reaching down with both hands, he used one hand to steady the bottom of the chest and the other to grab the front of the lid. He pulled up on the lid then and, with a terrible screeching noise as the nails lost their purchase, the lid came up. Reaching into the footlocker, Tom removed a pair of socks.

"Ahh," he said. "That's what I was looking for."

"Good God in heaven," someone said, reverently. "Did you see that?"

"Dalton, I don't think you ought to be messin' any more with this one. He's as strong as an ox."

Sugarloaf Ranch, Big Rock, Colorado, May 1

"Did you get a count?" Smoke asked Pearlie.

Pearlie held up the string and counted the knots. There were fourteen knots.

"I make it fourteen hundred in the south pasture," he said.

"I've got another eleven hundred," Cal added.

"And I've got just over fifteen hundred," Smoke said.

"Wow, that's better than four thousand head," Pearlie said. "We've got almost as many back as we had before the big freeze and die-out."

The big die-out Pearlie was talking about happened three years earlier when there had been a huge 72-hour blizzard. After the blizzard, the sun melted the top few inches of snow into slush, which the following day was frozen into solid ice by minus thirty-degree temperatures. Throughout the West, tens of thousands of cattle were found huddled against fences, many frozen to death, partly through and hanging on the wires. The legs of many of the cows that survived were so badly frozen that, when they moved, the skin cracked open and their hoofs dropped off. Hundreds of young steers were wandering aimlessly around on bloody stumps, while their tails froze as if they were icicles to be easily broken off.

Humans died that year too, men who froze to death while searching for cattle, women and children in houses where there was no wood to burn and not enough blankets to hold back the sub-zero temperatures. The only creatures to survive, and not only survive but thrive that winter, were the wolves who feasted upon the carcasses of tens of thousands of dead cattle.

Sugarloaf Ranch had survived, but nearly all the cattle on the ranch had died. Then Smoke heard from his friend, Falcon MacCallister. Falcon's cousin, Duff MacCallister, recently arrived from Scotland, was running a new breed of cattle.

Duff MacCallister had been spared the great die-out disaster because his ranch was located in the Chugwater Valley of Wyoming, shielded against the worst of winter's blast by mesas and mountain ranges. Also his ranch, Sky Meadow, had no fences to prevent the cattle from moving to the shelter of

these natural barriers, and the breed of cattle Duff
MacCallister was raising, Black Angus, were better
equipped to withstand the cold weather than were
the Longhorns.

Smoke went to Sky Meadow to meet with Duff,
and after his visit, agreed to buy one thousand head
of Black Angus cattle. That one thousand head had
grown into a herd of nearly four thousand in the last
four years, and it had been a very good move for
Smoke. Whereas the market price for Longhorn had
fallen so low that Smoke's neighbors, who were still
raising that breed, were doing well to break even on
their investment, the market price for Black Angus,
which produced a most superior grade of beef, was
very high.

"You men take care of things here," Smoke said.
"Sally is coming back today, and I'm going to meet
her at the train station."

"I'll go get her," Cal volunteered.

Pearlie chuckled. "I'm sure you would, Cal. We've
got calves to brand and you'll do anything to get out
of a little work."

"It's not that," Cal said. "I was just volunteering, is
all."

"Thanks anyway," Smoke said. "But she's been
back East for almost a month and I'm sort of anxious
to see her again."

When Smoke reached the train depot in Big Rock,
he checked the arrival and departure blackboard to
see if the train was on time. There was no arrival time
listed, so he went inside to talk to the ticket agent.

The ticket agent was huddled in a nervous conversation with Sheriff Monte Carson.

"Hello, Monte, good evening, Hodge," Smoke said, greeting the two men. "How are you doing?"

"Smoke, I'm glad you are here," Sheriff Carson said. "We've got a problem with the train."

"What kind of problem?" Smoke asked. "Sally is on that train."

"Yes, I know she is. We think the train is being robbed."

"Being robbed, or has been robbed?" Smoke replied, confused by the remark.

"Being robbed," Sheriff Carson said. "At least, we think that is what it is. The train is stopped about five miles west of here. There is an obstruction on the track so that it can't go forward, and another on the track to keep it from going back."

"How do you know this?"

"Ollie Cook is the switch operator just this side where the train is. When the train didn't come through his switch on time, he walked down the track to find out why, and that's when he saw the train barricaded like that. He hurried back to his switch shack and called the depot."

"And I called Sheriff Carson," Hodge said.

"I'm about to get a posse together to ride out there and see what it's all about," Sheriff Carson said.

"No need for a posse. Deputize me," Smoke suggested. "Like I said, Sally is on that train."

"You are already a deputy, Smoke, you know that," Sheriff Carson said.

"Yes, I know," Smoke said. "But I don't want people thinking I've gone off on my own just because

Sally is on the train. I need you to authorize this, in front of a witness."

"All right," Sheriff Carson said. "Hodge you are witness to this. Smoke, you are deputized to find out what is happening with that train, and to deal with it as you see best."

"Thanks," Smoke said.

Hurrying back outside, Smoke jumped into the buckboard he had come to town in, and slapping the reins against the back of the team, took the road that ran parallel with the railroad. He left town doing a brisk trot, but once he was out of town, he urged the team into a gallop. Less than fifteen minutes later, he saw the train standing on the railroad. Not wanting to get any closer with the team and buckboard, he stopped, tied the team off to a juniper tree, then, bending to keep a low profile, ran alongside the berm until he reached the front of the train. Hiding in some bushes he looked into the engine cab and saw three men, the fireman and engineer, who he could identify by the pin-stripe coveralls they were wearing, and a third man. The third man had a gun in his hand, and he waved it around every now and then, as if demonstrating his authority over the train crew.

Smoke moved up onto the track, but since he was in the very front of the locomotive, he knew that he couldn't be seen. He climbed up the cow catcher, then up onto the boiler itself, still unseen. He walked along the top of the boiler, then onto the roof of the cab. Lying down on his stomach, he peeked in from the window on the left side of the locomotive.

The man holding the gun had his back to that

window so he couldn't see Smoke, but the engineer and the fireman could, and Smoke saw their eyes widen in surprise. He hoped that the gunman didn't notice it.

"You two fellas are doin' just fine," the gunman said. "As soon as we collect our money from all your passengers, why we'll move the stuff off the track and let you go on."

Smoke leaned down far enough to make certain that the cab crew could see him, then he put his finger across his lips as a signal to be quiet.

"You got no right to be collecting money from our passengers," one of the two cab crew said.

"Well, the Denver and Rio Grande collects its fees, and we collect ours," the man said with a cackling laugh.

In mid-cackle, Smoke reached down into the engine cab, grabbed the man by his shirt, pulled him through the window, then let him fall, headfirst, to the ground.

"Hey, what . . ." was as far as the man got, before contact with the ground interrupted his protest. Looking down at him, Smoke could tell by the way the man's head was twisted that his neck was broken, and he was dead.

Smoke swung himself into the engine cab.

"Who are you?" one of the men asked.

"Smoke Jensen, I'm a deputy sheriff," Smoke said. "How many more are there?"

"Four more," one of the men said.

"Five," the other corrected. "I saw five."

"Where are they now?"

"Well, sir, after they found out we wasn't carryin'

any money in the express car, they decided to see what they could get from the passengers, and that's what they are doing now."

"How about the two of you going down to move the body of the one who was in here with you? I don't want any of the others to happen to look up this way and see him lying there."

"Yeah, good idea. Come on, Cephus, let's get him moved."

As the two train crewmen climbed down to take care of their job, Smoke crawled across the coal pile on the tender, then up onto the top of the express car. He ran the length of that car, then leaped across to the baggage car and ran its length as well. Climbing down from the back of the baggage car, he let himself into the first passenger car.

"One of your men has already been here," an irate passenger said. "We gave you everything we have."

"Shhh," Smoke said. "I'm on your side. I'm a deputy sheriff. Where are they?"

"There was only one in here, and he went into the next car."

"Thanks," Smoke said. Holding his pistol down by his side, he hurried through the first car and into the second one. He saw a gunman at the other end of the car, holding a pistol in his right hand and an open sack in the other. The passengers were dropping their valuables into the open sack.

"What are you doing in here? You get back in the other car and stay there like you were told!" the gunman said belligerently.

"I don't think so," Smoke said. He raised his pistol. "Drop your gun."

"The hell I will!"

Instead of dropping his gun, the train robber swung the pistol around and fired at Smoke. His shot went wide and the bullet smashed through the window of the door behind him. Smoke returned fire, and the gunman dropped his pistol and staggered back, his hands to his throat. Blood spilled through his fingers as he hit the front wall of the car, then slid down to the floor in a seated position. His head fell to one side as he died.

During the gunfire women screamed and men shouted. As the car filled with the gun smoke of two discharges, Smoke ran through the car, across the vestibule, and into the next car.

The gunman in the next car, having heard the shot, was looking toward the door as Smoke ran in.

"Red! McDill! Slim, get in here quick!" the gunman called.

Smoke and this gunman exchanged fire as well, with the same result. The gunman went down and Smoke was still standing. When he ran into the next car, he saw the robber dashing out through the back door. He chased him down as well, but he didn't have to shoot him. When the gunman went into the next car, he was brought down by a club wielded by the porter. "Good job," Smoke said.

"The other two has done jumped off the train," the porter said.

Smoke jumped down from the train as well, then he moved away from it to try and get a bead on the two who were running. Smoke snapped off a long shot, but missed. He didn't get a second shot because the outlaws were on horseback and galloping away.

Smoke stood there for a moment, still holding his smoking pistol as he watched the two robbers flee.

"You need to develop a better sense of timing," someone said, and turning, Smoke saw Sally standing there on the ground behind him. He embraced and kissed her, then he pulled his head back.

"What do you mean, a better sense of timing?" he asked.

"If you had been five minutes earlier, the robbers wouldn't have gotten my reticule."

"Sorry. How much did they get?" Smoke asked.

"Just my purse," Sally said with a little laugh. "I had already taken everything out of it."

By now, several others had come down from the train and they were all thanking Smoke for coming to their rescue.

"Look here!" someone shouted. "The two that got away dropped their sacks!"

"The ones inside never even made it off the train with their sacks," another said. "Ha! Ever'thing they took is still here!"

"Cephus, how long will it take you to get the steam back up?" the conductor asked.

"Fifteen minutes," Cephus said. "Maybe half an hour."

"Do you want to wait until they get the steam back up? Or do you want to come with me now?" Smoke asked. "I left a buckboard just up the track a short distance."

"My luggage is on the train," Sally said.

"Miss, after what your man just did, if you want your luggage, I'll personally open the baggage car and get it," the conductor said.

Mitchell "Red" Coleman and Deekus McDill were the two robbers who got away. They got away from Smoke's avenging guns, but they did not get away with any money.

"Nothin'!" McDill said. "We didn't get a damn thing!"

"Maybe the day ain't goin' to be a total loss," Red said.

"What do you mean, it ain't a total loss?"

"Look over there," Red said.

"What, a store? What good is a store goin' to do us? We ain't got no money to buy nothin'."

"Who said we were goin' to buy anything?" Red said.

McDill understood what he was talking about then, and he smiled and nodded.

Fifteen minutes later Red and McDill rode away from Doogan's store. Jake Doogan and his wife both lay dead on the floor in the store behind them. Their total take for the robbery was seventy-eight dollars and thirty-five cents.